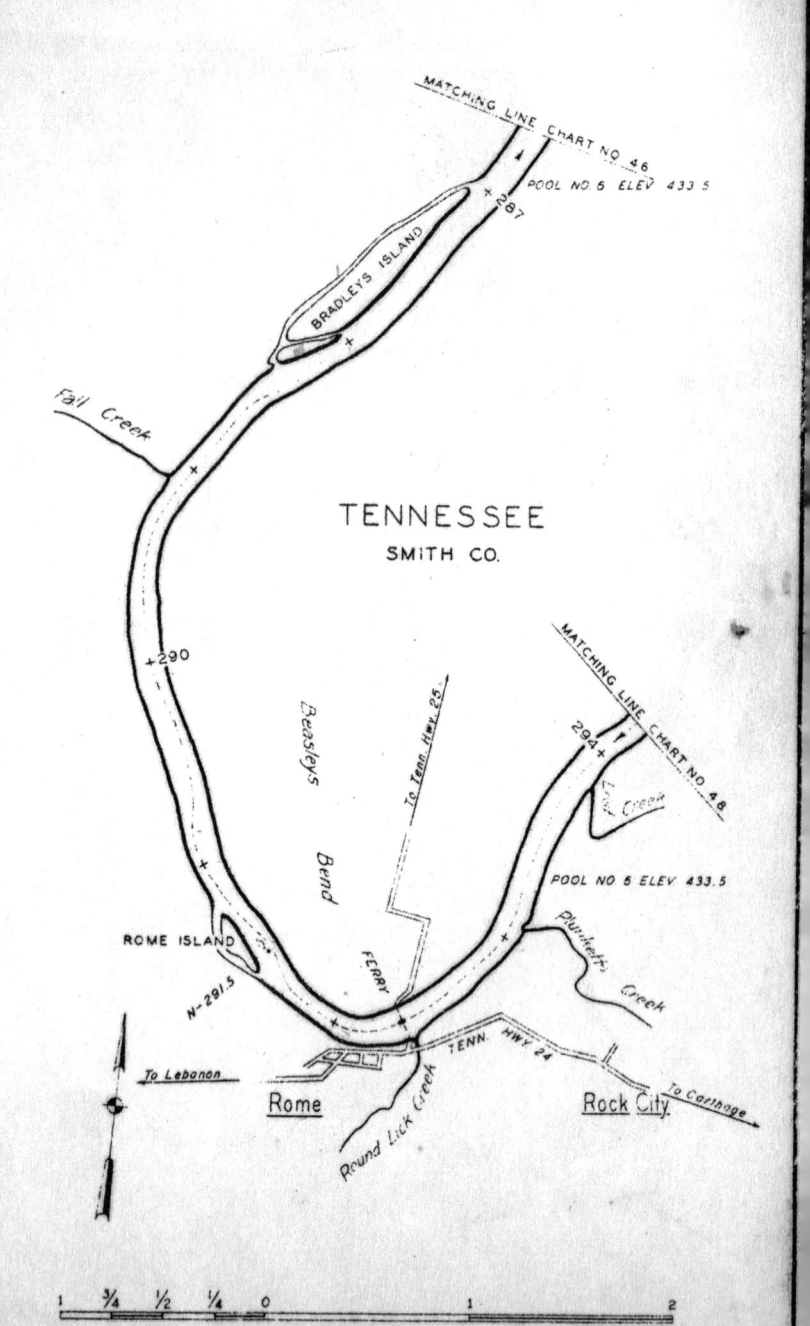

CUMBERLAND RIVER
CHART NO. 47

MATCHING LINE CHART NO. 46
POOL NO. 5 ELEV. 433.5
+287
BRADLEYS ISLAND
Fall Creek
TENNESSEE
SMITH CO.
+290
Beasleys Bend
MATCHING LINE CHART NO. 48
294+
POOL NO. 5 ELEV. 433.5
To Tenn. Hwy. 25
Plunketts Creek
ROME ISLAND
N-291.5
FERRY
To Lebanon
Rome
Round Lick Creek
TENN. HWY. 24
Rock City
To Carthage

Scale of Miles
1" = 0.6 Mile

SMITH CO.
MILE 286.6 TO MILE 294.2

LEE CLAY JOHNSON

BLOODLINE

PANAMERICA

Copyright © 2025 by Lee Clay Johnson
All rights reserved under International
and Pan-American Copyright Conventions
Published in the United States by Panamerica,
a division of County Highway LLC, First Edition 2025
Printed in Hudson, New Hampshire, by Kase Printing

Design by François-Xavier Delarue
Cover Photograph by Jack Spencer
Typography by Ksenya Samarskaya & Céline Hurka

ISBN: 979-8-9991467-0-0
@panamericabooks / @countyhwy

Manufactured in the United States of America

In memory of Evan David Johnson
my twin bro
1983–2024

BLOODLINE

ONE

The headwaters of this river come from forks leaking westward out of the Appalachians. They join in the foothills like estranged brothers and are then fed by countless and nameless tributaries dribbling from porous slabs of Kentucky limestone to form the Cumberland, which widens and deepens and continues snaking westward, twisting and falling through the rolling region and finally dropping down into Tennessee, where it spills through the concrete walls of the Cordell Hull Dam, the tailwaters bending around and meeting up with the Caney Fork, a cold, north-flowing river, in the town of Carthage, the county seat of Smith County, near where the father now waits for what's his.

"Ain't much opportunity in this world for boys like you," he says. His youngest son is lying on the passenger-side bucket seat beside him, wearing a grocery bag for a diaper, listening.

They all slept here in the van last night beneath a line of hackberry trees. Now it's near dawn and the sky has the color of a bruise. Some kind of sticky insect shit lacquers the windshield.

The side door's slid open to the woods and the father can see his wife standing out there half-vanished in the morning mist, showing the older brother where to take a piss. "Careful," she says. "Not on the cattle fence, honey."

"We don't need no electric lemonade," the father calls.

"He's doing fine," she says.

When the baby crunches up his face for a cry, the father says, "You got your momma's sense of humor. You know that?"

Everything they own is packed into the van and bumper stickers cover the rear windows to keep folks from spying in. The father's shirt bears an image of the old battle flag, peeking from his low-buttoned flannel. He turns the ignition to battery mode and the digital clock blinks 7AM. The gas gauge marks low, but that could be the incline they're parked at. He jogs the radio for some talk he can relate to, but this close to Nashville it's all happy shit that isn't telling the truth. Everybody's singing zip-a-dee-doo-dah, oblivious to what surrounds them.

The sawmill hasn't hired him yet. That's because he didn't have time to apply. He was selling used cars up in Lexington, where he was born and hardly raised, at an auction lot called Mega Motors, when one afternoon—was it just yesterday?—his boss accused him of having memory problems. Like leaving keys in car ignitions, not calling customers back. Stuff like that.

The father explained that his condition had an official medical term, thank you very much. It was called *far-memoried*, kind of like far-sighted, but pertaining to memory. And one of the symptoms was that historical events, especially those of the heroic and violent variety, were constantly bumping up against his present day, so much so that it was difficult for him to hold onto the more recent things that didn't matter much anyway. This job, for example.

"The hell are you talking about?" his boss said.

"Wait right there and I'll show you." The father walked back into the cinderblock office, punched a code into the little safety deposit box, which opened on oiled hinges, and grabbed a zipped-up bank-bag full of cash. He came out the front, waving it at his boss, and got into his van. Daring the fucker to even think about getting the law involved. Every damn car in that lot was illegal to some degree—fake titles, manipulated odometers—and the father knew this because he'd done much of the rigging himself, on his boss's orders.

While driving home he counted the bills between his legs, with the windows rolled up so the money wouldn't fly away. Didn't amount to much, but it was enough for leaving.

When he got back to their place, a small unit on the county line with a dirt-circle around a tree in the front yard from where the dog used to be tied up, he found his wife on the couch staring at a muted TV. He could smell she was stoned. The boys were sleeping on the floor. "Pack our shit," he said.

He called around about who might be hiring and made some plans. That evening they abandoned their rental, drove west and hit 65 South. A hook-moon reeled in the night, as they followed the taillights down into Tennessee. They got off the interstate, followed some back roads and he began listing his reasons for leaving, though she hadn't asked.

He told her what his boss had told him, offered his thoughts on all that and said his memory problem wasn't really a problem at all. "Don't you think?"

She didn't answer because she didn't know where she stood on that. Sometimes it seemed his memory was slipping, and other times he recalled events from long before he was even born, so vividly that it seemed like he'd been right there to see them. The truth was, though, that facts weren't of much concern to him. If they didn't align with his mythical reality, they simply didn't exist. She knew the stories he told were ones he chose to justify his purpose and place in this steaming red corner of the country. So she kept quiet and let him ramble.

"My far-memory's a natural gift from God," he said. "That's what it is. I can see the past and it's right here right now. God hath done made it so."

She looked back to make sure the boys were still asleep.

"Plus I like the idea of livin' along the Cumberland," he said. "Near Beasley's Bend. That was my family's escape route."

His mother had told him the same story when he was little, though when he taught himself to read and did a little research, he discovered that his only traceable ancestral past on his father's side stretched in the opposite direction, not down into Dixie but up north on the border of New York and Canada, where those old people trapped beavers for pelts.

But even that wasn't the whole truth. According to his mother, his father was hardly his father, just a man who'd come down to Kentucky to paint barn exteriors, and once the work dried up found himself stuck. One evening while getting supper at the gas station, he met a woman who needed a ride. When he asked where she was going she said, "Anywhere." So he took her back to his shack and that's where she gave birth to Winston—on the pull-out sofa—only five months later. The father ignored the math, pretending the baby was his, but the mother liked to remind little Winston of the mystery: he had a daddy someplace else whose past was glorious.

Growing up, he had no bathroom, not even an outhouse, just piles of empty paint cans everywhere, which the family used to take their crap out of the house and down into the creek. Once he got old enough to understand this wasn't what paint cans were made for, he asked his father about it, and when the old man didn't answer, his mother told him that his line ran deeper than beaver trappers and paint cans, that he was of valorously noble blood, that his real father was somewhere else entirely, that if history had turned out differently nobody would be shitting in paint cans and they'd be living the good life right where they belonged, back on the land his real daddy's people had escaped from.

His mother took him to read about their history on a plaque at the base of an equestrian statue on the courthouse lawn of Cheapside Park in historic downtown Lexington, where he ran a forefinger over the stamped bronze letters, and above those words the old colonel, John Hunt Morgan, straight-backed, arms at his sides, was mounted atop his horse, Black Bess, from a legendary line of bluegrass saddle stock. "That's who we're from," she told him.

They often returned to visit the monument, and he was just old enough, nine or ten, for these trips to shape his romantic sense of history and heroism and who he was.

Later, his autodidactic research provided no hint of his mother's claim to this lineage, but he needed it to be true so badly, felt it in his bones so deeply, that he decided it couldn't be false, had to be correct, and just like that he began believing he really did have blood in the game. After visiting that statue, in bed he could hear the hooves pounding down the street like the tapping fingers of some impatient god. Still can.

Last night during the ride in, his wife stared out her window at the moon while he told her yet again of that one Civil War battle, more alive in his mind than their wedding day—it was one of his jukebox numbers. But when she realized what was actually happening right now, she turned to him and said they couldn't do this, that they had to turn around and get back home to Kentucky. But he kept driving, slowly so as not to waste gas, straight down into the town of Lebanon, Tennessee. As the family rolled past the college and through the little town square with the monument of General Hatton and left the village limits and followed Carthage Highway to Old Rome Pike, he pointed out the places where blood had been shed and land had been stolen. The road dipped and swerved along the Cumberland River. And when he finally pulled them into an empty lot with a chainlink gate, somewhere in a derelict hamlet called Rome, he cut the engine and told his wife to quit worrying. "Breathe in that good air," he said. "We're home."

That was last night. Now it's morning and he's just waiting around in the van, ready to talk to somebody about working for the mill here. He can't see the river from where he parked, but he can't miss its warm, vegetal scent. It's right down there past the sawmill, its banks with soil so rich you could grow just about anything in it. Gentle rolling land, open for the taking.

The birds are hushing and the fog's clearing. The gate to the sawmill's entrance is chained shut with a sign hanging from it, NO WALK-IN APPLICATIONS & NO UNSOLICITED EMPLOYMENT. But he'll stick around and give them a chance to clarify themselves. Once they talk to him, they won't be able to say no. Nobody ever did. Too much damn charm.

The baby's gumming his fingers like little root vegetables, and the father says, "I got a story for you. May 5th, 1862. Rainin', early mornin'."

"Oh, God," the mother says. "This again?" She helps the brother back into the van and covers his ears. "I don't want them hearing about it." She opens the styrofoam cooler, slushes ice around and hands the brother a juice barrel. "Plus May 5th's my birthday, remember?"

"And a fake holiday to boot," the father says. "Cinco de somethin'."

"I want lemon cake with buttercream frosting," she tells him. "Blue cursive letters spelling my name. Not my age, just my name."

"On the real one I'm talkin' about, the Kentucky Cavalry was holed up over in Lebanon under the orders of John Hunt Morgan."

"*There's* a name for you. Almost a whole sentence of its own, isn't it?" She turns to the older brother. "Like I've been teaching you: subject, verb, object."

"He's too young for that school crap," the father says.

"But old enough for your fucked-up stories?"

"It's called heritage," he says. "Anyhow, he's gonna be

a hands-on kinda guy. Like his daddy is. Ain't that right?"

The brother nods, drinking his juice. He knows words but doesn't use them much, not since they got him on the hyperactivity medicine.

The father's eyes go gray as he traces an invisible map in front of him and starts telling how pickets were set along the roads going into town, the very roads they drove last night, and how eight hundred men were camped on the grounds of Cumberland College and all over the public square. Meanwhile, the Union general, Ebenezer Dumont, was leading his troops along Murfreesboro Pike, where waiting for them was a schoolboy, keeping dry beneath a cedar, and when he saw the column of Union cavalry coming up the road, he jumped on his horse and got out in front of them and started shouting about the Yankees coming. "And then," the father says, turning to the baby, "they shot him dead as bacon."

He gets so lost in describing the ensuing battle that he doesn't notice a woman has just unlocked the gate and is coming across the gravel toward their van.

She takes her time approaching. Her hair's pulled into a loose braid with strands around her ears the color of fishing line. She taps on his door.

"Who the hell?" the father says.

"My name's Miss Becka. Can I help you?"

"I don't know," he says. "Can you?"

She takes a metal case from her shirt pocket, pulls out a hand-rolled cigarette and lights it with a wooden match. "Now who're y'all?"

"Winston Alcorn," he says.

"And?"

"And back there's Mandy," he says. "With little James in her arms. And that's Dustin next to her."

"I heard y'all pulling in here round midnight," she says. "You get any sleep?"

"More than we could handle," Winston says. "You live nearby or somethin'?"

"Closer than Kentucky."

"How'd she know that?" Mandy asks him.

"Plates," Miss Becka says.

"She's a sharp one," Winston says.

"What brought you down here?" she says.

"Work."

Miss Becka takes a drag and speaks through the smoke. "You'll need to drive into Nashville for any of that."

"I called around," Winston says. "Heard this sawmill was hirin'."

"You try the nuclear plant over in Hartsville?"

"They ain't open yet."

"Don't they need help building it or something?"

"I've worked sawmills before," he says. "And I heard this one offers good insurance stuff. Family plans?"

"Somebody did his homework," she says. "Where in Kentucky y'all coming from?"

"Home of the colonel who lost his horse here," he says.

"That story?" Miss Becka says. "*Please.*"

But Winston's already off, telling how the battle led to where she's standing right now, and when the troops got to the river the old Rome Ferry, anchored in the mud on their side, the southern side, was right there waiting for them, with Comer the blind mule posted up on the treadmill gearbox, ready to get it cranking with one lash of the whip, but Morgan had to leave his horse behind. "Black Bess," he says, opening his hands as if the legend were inscribed there. "I grew up near the statue of it. From the road you could see his balls."

Miss Becka squints to take his measure. "That horse was a *mare*," she says. "Listen to the name. A filly with testes? I don't think so." She shakes her head. "But that ferry's still down there, except it's been dragged up on the bank and left to rot."

"Why'd they go do that?"

"Cost too much," she says. "When the state quit funding it, I lost half my customers at the mill. Nobody wants to do all that driving."

"You run this mill," Winston says.

"That's what I do."

Winston takes his comb from the cup holder, runs it through his hair, buttons his flannel up and gets out of the van. "You should've told me," he says. "It's very fine to meet you, ma'am."

He starts telling her about what his boys have been through, and she begins leaning in and looking at his family back there. He can see her attitude toward him shifting, which is what he hoped for in people when he wanted to sell them a car: find that tender spot, could be anything, and just keep pressing on it. That spot for her seems to be his boys. "You got any little ones of your own?" he says.

"Okay, look," she says. "How are you with a mill saw? Horizontal band-blade."

"My specialty."

She studies him. "The one you'll be on holds the log stationary. Which means the blade's moving along the wood."

"I know. I'm cool with that. Perfect."

"Fine then," she says. "I've got some gloves and chaps you can borrow today."

"That's what I'm talkin' about," Winston says.

She lights another cigarette and blows smoke at the fence. This isn't the first time she's bent the rules, but this'll be fine. "And the rest of y'all can come wait in my office," she tells Mandy.

"Nah, they're good," Winston says. "Tell her y'all're good."

. . . .

For Mandy, it's all backward and forward and sideways at once. She doesn't know what Winston's up to, but he's up to something, that's for sure. She watches Miss Becka lead him through the gate, around the corner and out of sight.

She figures she'll probably have to wait here all day, so might as well get comfortable. She kicks back, takes a hit of daytime weed from her little bowl and watches the mill's tin roof through the trees.

Then Dustin says something. He hasn't really talked since they left.

"What was that?" she says.

But he ignores her and goes back into his solitary place where nobody can reach him.

She nurses James from a bottle, then tries to fall asleep by thinking of the horse farm they used to live near. There were always horses out in those fields. She loves horses but she's never had one. She grew up outside Lexington, watching them and wishing. She's only going to relax if she can forget where she is for a few seconds.

But here in this van with these needy little men, that's impossible. Even the weed isn't helping.

More vehicles keep pulling in. People with jobs and lives. A pair of guys come walking down off the highway. One is tall and silent, the other short and wide and jabbering. Passing the van, they look in at Mandy in synchronized speculation. The boys finally conk out, then she must have too because a flash of violence wakes her up, racing through her like a current of electricity. She cracks the door for a breeze and can hear the sucking sound of the river down there. Eventually some dogs start howling in the distance, and the sound of a siren twists and wails up along the river road.

She knows what this means. She'd felt it in her dream.

An ambulance tears into the gravel lot, flashing and honking, and a crowd of workers is coming up the drive with Winston in the middle. On either side of him are the two guys who glanced in at her, leading him and holding his arm in the air with a belt tied below what used to be his hand—now just a bouquet of blood and bone.

All Mandy can do is watch. This must be the beginning of what Winston had in mind. She never knew what it would look like, and maybe he didn't either, but here it is, a wide-open emergency.

Winston glances up toward the van, his face as thin and white as a whittled stick. He nods at Mandy, right at her, sending something into her, a promise, a message, an affirmation that he knows what he's doing. She's just got to trust him.

A couple medics climb out the back of the ambulance and lift Winston onto a stretcher, load him in and peel out of the lot.

Things go quiet.

Some of the millhands are left standing around looking at her van. The short guy's shirtless and pointing up at her so she ducks down. Then here comes Miss Becka shaking her head, saying something. But Mandy can't hear anything right now.

Miss Becka leans in through the front window. "What in the *hell* is your husband up to?" she says. "What does he want?"

Even if Mandy knew the answer, she wouldn't tell.

TWO

The guy's pushing him down a hallway and he's trying to count the paneled lights passing above him, flat on his back, but his vision keeps smoldering on the edges like some burning photograph and he can't keep up. "Slow down," he says.

The man's got a blue surgical mask over his orange beard. "We're almost there," he says. "Hold tight."

"Let me up, Doc," Winston says.

"I'm a nurse," the man says, "and I can't do that."

"Kinda place is this shit?" he says. "I know where I'm going. I can walk there. Get me off this."

"That's just your adrenaline talking, sir. You'll be all right soon." The nurse parks him in a windowless room, straps his fucked-up arm onto a table and rolls over a coatrack-looking thing with two little white curtains hanging from it. He pulls the curtains closed at his elbow so Winston can't see what's happening on the other side.

More nurses swarm. Needle pricks and beeps. Finally they hook him up to the good stuff and warm honey fills every little cell of his body. "How's that feel?" the nurse says.

"Hit me again," Winston says.

Two clean-shaven doctors show up, uninterested in any aspect of Winston except for what's on their side of the curtain. They sit on stools and hunker over his wound, eyeglasses aglow in the surgical light just above the coatrack curtain.

Though Winston can feel the pressure of pulling and hear the sounds of scissors snipping, it's all at a soft distance. The morphine is moving inside him and taking him to that place he's been to before. Yup, here it comes, kicking up dust down the old dirt road, carrying him home from the battle that belongs to no one but himself. And maybe a few lonely others, his boys and such.

The guy-nurse brings him back into the room. "Where you think you're going? Stay right here with us now."

"Good luck with that," Winston says. He kind of likes this game of hide and seek, disappear out into the blackness and see if they can find him. He could tell them about where he just went, what he just saw, but who'd believe him? And with the drugs loosening his tongue, he's got to be careful not to give too much away. Keep it his little secret.

"I been here before," he finally says. "Y'all remember me? I do."

"We've got no record of your name," the nurse says. "That's just *one* of the problems."

"It was a long, long time ago," Winston says. "When nurses was ladies and doctors was men—and soldier men, too."

"Just keep talking," the guy says. "That's good." He puts an IV line into Winston's left arm and hooks up a bag of fresh blood. "On a one-to-ten scale," he says, "where's your pain level at?"

"Zero," Winston says. "Negative."

The surgeons are over there talking. One says, "We need to get him into the OR."

More hallways lead to a room with an operating bed that has a single armboard sticking off the side. "That must be for Win-win," he says. Then they hook the heavy-duty stuff into his IV, all the lights swirl and dim as he's cast backward into his own dark interiors. He can make out a faded scene, almost quaint in its old-time sepia. When he enters the vision he's on a lopsided hospital mattress, the sheets soaked with sweat and the whole room reeking of human fluids. Next to his bed, there's a surgeon wiping that bonesaw across his boot sole. He only does it once, but it happens again and again, on replay, echoing in Winston's eyes, over and over. Then a greenbottle fly breaks the loop by buzzing in through the open window and landing on Winston's mangled nub. He can't brush it off or blow it away, he's tied down and cannot move at all. He watches the fly lay a mess of larvae into his open wound, little white squiggling things. When the fly takes off, Winston goes with it out into a tulip poplar tree, up into the branches where the bark smells floral and spicy beneath the hot sun. His consciousness is no longer attached to him but somewhere between everything, riding the back of this greenbottle fly. Across the floodplain, a locomotive's chugging along the river, a cloud of coal smoke bending backward from its smokestack. The landscape wavers in the noon heat.

Slowly he emerges back into the present century as subtle tremors run throughout his body. It isn't from fear. Nope. It's just how beautiful it all was back there.

Today must be a different time of day, or a different day, or a different time of a different day. The lights are off and the building has that ghostly feeling of everybody sleeping, all souls elsewhere. The dark floors refract the glow of monitor screens. His arm's wrapped tight in a cocoon and strapped onto a stainless-steel tray bolted into the side of the bed.

He tries retracing every step that brought him here, but the only thing he can remember is stepping into Miss Becka's sawmill all suited up in the kevlar gear she'd loaned him. The noise of the grinding, singing saws filled the big room, all the way from the concrete floors up to the high exposed rafters, and once he heard those harsh harmonies he'd known exactly what he had to do. It was time.

He was helping guide the beltsaw down the top length of a red cedar when the man he was working with looked away for a second, and Winston did it: shook off his glove and put his hand right in line with the beltsaw driving steadily down the trunk. He felt the humming in the wood before it hit him—and brother, did it hit him! It was like gunpowder.

His own hot blood misted the side of his face. Past and recent-past melding. He kept his eyes closed and let the saw shake him all to hell and back.

A couple hundred years or a split second. His partners shut the thing down and backed the belt off, pulling loose some mangled knuckles, flesh and bone. Winston was ruined past the wrist, and he believed his shoulder was dislocated, too. His blood ran and dripped off the tree trunk and mixed with sawdust into a strange kind of purple mud beneath his shoes that smelled of backwater.

The man took off his own shirt and belt and tied it above Winston's elbow to stop the bleeding. "Name's JR," he said. "I just helped you. Don't forget that."

The rest of the work crew were shouting out contradictory advice. Lay him down! Keep him standing! Give him water! Don't let him open his mouth! Then Miss Becka came in and told them to back off and shut up. "Help's on the way. Get your shit together. And don't slip in the blood."

The screaming ambulance took him on a ride to die for along US 70, wailing through Lebanon's square—around old General Hatton himself, with Winston's arm suspended in a weird salute—and zipping on through Hermitage past Andrew Jackson's plantation and following the highway to Donelson Hospital, where the ER staff checked his vitals and sent the ambulance straight into Nashville.

Shaking and shivering, Winston kept lecturing any medics around him about the history of the path they were following, describing the running battles and burning mills and makeshift cemeteries—a few of the details accurate, most exaggerated.

One medic somewhere, a black woman, worked on him and listened to his delirious, desperate histories. "You are where you are right now," she told him. "Stay that way."

"Ain't got no choice," he told her. "My time ain't come yet."

And then there was that nurse guy last night or whenever it was. What did Winston say to him? Did he talk too much? Give his plan away? Speaking of which, where's his wife and his boys at? That's the real question.

He tries moving but they've tied him down like in those dreams, time repeating history again. Under the heavy blanket of the sleepy gas, his brain keeps folding back over on itself. He can't even holler for help—just a no-mouth shout every time he tries. Just hold yourself together. Don't go back there in your mind just yet, and don't say nothing about it to nobody, not even to Mandy. You got this, just hang in there a little longer. It'll be worth it in the end. You're a new man now. You've been cleansed by blood and so has the land. You don't win a little. You Wins-a-ton.

Say it with yourself now.

. . . .

Things are picking up outside his door, and a nurse comes in holding a clipboard with some sort of form on it. "Can you sign this for us?"

"I can," Winston says. "Question is, am I going to?"

"We just need your signature, sir. In case something happens."

"Like it didn't already?"

"While you're here in recovery," she says.

"Oh, so that's where I am." He looks around, trying to get his bearings. "Looks like my signing hand's AWOL."

"How about with your left?" she says. "We just need an intentional mark."

Another nurse arrives. "Just sign it," she says. "With the hand that's left."

Winston can't tell if that's supposed to be funny.

"One quick thing with the pen across the line," the new nurse says, "and we'll be ready to move forward with fixing you up."

Left-handed and low-blooded, Winston takes the pen, scrawls his name in big wrong-handed letters along the line—adding one extra letter, an *a* in the middle—and just like that his transformation into the man he always should've been is complete.

"That your real name?" she says. "Wins-*a*-ton?"

"Sure is." He nods, pleased by the sound of it. "And you Lose-a-ton."

"This isn't what your license says."

"But that's what it is," he tells her.

. . . .

Another morning brings clean bright floors and a bunch of rolling walls dividing up the space. Nurses are going around calling out "Winsy" and he guesses they think he's cute. He'd flirt back, but they're still feeding his arm liquid lottery tickets and his tongue isn't following his orders. Drool's slugging down the sides of his mouth, and another new nurse—a woman, again, as they should be—washes his cheeks with a warm cloth. He watches her moving above him, slower and slower, until it's another goodbye.

This time it's the baby's breath that wakes him up. Sweet pumpkin and spoiled milk. He knows who that is. Mandy holds little James up to his face and dances him around in a striped onesie that says Lion Tamer on the front. There's something in his little face that makes Winston have a feeling akin to pain but minus the pain. What is it? This baby thinks his daddy's worthwhile. He loves him and just can't help it. Despite what Daddy's put him through—and what he's been denied, food and sleep and diapers and everything else—James believes in his pure beating heart that this man lying right here in front of him, Daddy Winsaton, is a good man. It surprises the hell out of Winston to see it all so clearly in his little face, even the natural propensity to believe a flat-out lie.

"I'll make it up to you," he tells James. "There wasn't no way around their bullshit but this one. You'll get it someday." He glances over at Dustin, who's in the corner with a plastic bottle of apple juice. "Big brother too."

"What do they have you on?" Mandy says.

"Pain killers to kill the pain."

"They ought to give everybody a little bit of that," she says.

His wrapped-up hand-area's giving him the sensation of a helium-filled balloon about to burst. "Where'd James get that little striped uniform from?" he says.

"They gave it to us."

"Who's they?"

"The folks that're putting us up," she says. "The McDonald's House people."

From his cocooned arm, a tube curls out the end like a fun straw, draining pink fluids into a bag. He straightens himself up and says, "We don't need no handouts."

"It's just for food and shelter," she says.

"Right," he says. "Sure."

"They're trying to figure out what's going on." She

bounces James on her knee, watches Dustin in the corner and then speaks in a side-mouthed whisper. "They're talking about what happened to you and wanting to know whose fault it was."

"They got any answers yet?" he says. "Cause I'd sure like to know."

"I mean, I thought—"

He grabs her necklace with his good hand and pulls her in close. "You go ahead and keep every little thought of yours to your little self. Dokie?"

"Okay," she says, and fixes her chain.

"That's my Dandy Mandy." He rests back down. "Good girl."

After a while she says, "Remember that lady? Miss Becka?"

"Yeah?" His eyes become dark slits.

"They're saying she better have the right insurance for what happened."

"They who?"

"You know," she says. "Just some people. I saw this billboard, had a lawyer's phone number on it. They specialize in personal injuries. Especially work-related."

"All they do is take your money."

"The consultation was free."

"So you're talking to a lawyer."

"This guy's different than most of them," she says.

"I bet he is."

"He wants to help us win. Says he can get a *settlement*." Mandy rubs money-fingers at Winston. "We might be sitting pretty. Might could sue her for everything she's got. That's what he's talking about."

"And how's he gonna make that happen?"

"Figure out her standing, then go at her on a personal level."

"Exactly what I'll do."

"Y'all might be more alike than you think," she says. "He's working on a claim."

"What kind?"

"The kind I haven't paid a cent for yet."

"Good," he says. "So don't."

"Oh, we won't," she says. "The research he's done already shows Miss Becka's either got the wrong kind of coverage or let it lapse. Which could be a jackpot."

"You been busy doing stuff, ain't you?"

She winks at him. "Your plan's my plan, baby."

"Partners in crime," he says, and they bump fists—his left, her right.

Little James reaches for her shirt and starts whining and revving up for a cry. She swats his hand away as Dustin goes into the bathroom and flushes his juice bottle down the toilet. "These critters aren't real helpful."

"They's just adjustin'," Winston says. "They'll get used to it."

"How's your hand feeling?" she says.

"Like it's gone," he says. "Is it?"

"They ain't told you?"

"I didn't ask," he says. "That or don't remember."

"Psh. Oh yeah. Real gone."

"Fine then," he says.

. . . .

He was older than Mandy by about a decade—maybe even two if you were counting experience, which he was.

He scared her, and that made her want to be closer. He'd fought in some war—Vietnam, he'd said—though he'd never confirm any details, even when she asked again and again, and because of his steadfast refusal to confirm basic facts about who he was and what he'd done, he could talk to her about various things in the world with an authority she didn't know how to question. There was something oddly reassuring about his ridiculous confidence: she'd never seen much of that. His fearlessness was frightening yet magnetic, and the closer she got the harder it was to pull away.

One of the first things he promised her was a horse, which she's still waiting on. And now here in the hospital room, he brings it up again. "We're gonna get you a chestnut strutter."

"I thought you'd forgot."

"I don't never forget," he says. "But even if I did I'm remembering now, ain't I?"

"Yeah," she says. "Just don't fuck me over."

How she's looking at him right now makes him feel like he's almost back to being a man again—able to take care of his family. Been too long. He sacrificed his body to get them everything they deserve. His land and his history. Her horse. Went to battle and back, really. She believes in him, and all it took was a lawyer stepping in. Ain't that some shit. "This might sound crazy," he says. "But I can almost see our future."

He describes their trucks and houses and pools, their flags flying from big proud crosses. He can almost feel the breeze off the river. But he doesn't want to deal with insurance claims. Too many strings, too much time. He wants a good old-fashioned out-of-court settlement. He wants money, yes, but even more than that, he wants land, Miss Becka's land, his old family's rightful area. He wants everything of Miss Becka's that he saw down there.

It isn't just the sawmill he wants, but that old two-story colonial-looking thing next to it, too, what he guesses is her own little haunted mansion, and all that waterfront acreage that he bets comes along with it. Also that old ferry. Because when Winston wins, he doesn't just win a little. Say it with him: he Winsa*ton*.

Mandy shakes him awake. "You were sleep-talking."

He's breathing hard and feeling hopeful from whatever dream that was. Over his lap is a tray of lunch, most of it uneaten. Dustin's slumped in the corner, playing with an empty urine container. James sits on the big chair, sucking at a bottle. "What was I saying?" he says.

"Couldn't tell. But James was making some sense of it. Weren't you, bubby?" She lifts him up and flies him over Winston while making prop-plane sounds with her mouth.

. . . .

After a week of X-rays and meetings and more X-rays, Winston finds himself sitting in his room with Mandy, the boys and a surgeon who says in a week they'll need to put pins in his arm to help stabilize the broken bones. "And after that, you'll be free to go join your family."

"No rush," Winston says.

"Sooner the better," Mandy says, bouncing the two little guys on her knees.

"And if y'all can't fix my hand back up to what it was like," Winston says, "I won't hold it against you."

"That's cause you won't be able to," Mandy says. "He can explain that to you."

The surgeon takes off his reading glasses and looks at Winston. "Your right hand, sir, is not coming back. Even if we had it, we wouldn't be able to reattach it. Down there? It's like the frayed end of a rope."

Winston nods like he's trying to understand. But in truth, he knew what he'd lost right when it happened, and this is what he'd been preparing himself for. "You telling me it's gonna effect my ability to work?" he says. "To earn a honest paycheck?"

"This whole process will take some time," the surgeon says.

"I ain't scared of that," Winston says. "We go hand in hand, me and time."

"Remind me." The surgeon inspects the fluid in the drain tube. "This was your dominant hand, correct?"

"That's right," Winston says. "I just want to get back to work."

With the boys starting to pull at her shirt, Mandy closes her eyes and nods in theatrical understanding.

"I can't tell you how all that's going to turn out," the surgeon says. "But I'm afraid full recovery's still far away."

"We can live with that," Mandy says. "We're still waitin' on some other developments anyway."

. . . .

A couple days before Winston gets his pins in, Mandy calls his room to tell him about Dustin. "Something just snapped inside him," she says. "This kid, he doesn't even listen. The medicine isn't working."

Winston tells her to put him on the phone, and when she does he hears a boy-roar and then gets hung up on. He waits, but nobody calls back, so he doesn't try either. He'll be out of here soon enough. Then he'll have all the time in the world to straighten out that little son of a bitch. He doesn't know about Mandy, but he isn't gonna put up with unruly shit like that. Gotta keep your soldiers in line. Even old Robbie Lee during battle had his son in the trenches. Yes, sir, he did.

The morning he's scheduled to go in for the surgery, his fever has gone down. Getting pushed in a wheelchair and wearing a nightie, he listens to the nurses saying his name the way he likes it said.

When he comes out of the anesthetic, he finds himself sitting in a reclined hospital bed with sutures going up and down his arm like railroad ties. Three metal pins emerge from his hot swollen skin and the whole thing feels on fire. It's the first time he's really seen what's been going on down there. This's significant. He follows the tracks to the end of the damage, where a rubber hand has been attached, fake as a cartoon, even the fingernails Silly Putty pink. It's larger than his old real one, which he's cool with. Bigger the better, old daddy always said. He brings it up in front of his face and holds it out in greeting to no one. "Nice to meet you," he says.

. . . .

When the hospital valet service drops him off, Mandy's round face is right there in the window of their new first-floor apartment deal. His arm's wrapped up and slung from his shoulder. The pain meds they sent him back with get him floating up the stoop and through the front door. Mandy sits him down in the recliner in the main room and can't help but stare at his prosthesis. "So that hand?" she says. "Painted like that so your mind doesn't get confused about what it is?"

"Smells like a fresh drywall job in here." Winston looks around the room. "There's dust in every corner and they ain't even painted the walls."

"I told them not to," she says.

"Oh, you *told* 'em not to."

"I like the natural look."

"Like fuckin' sheetrock?"

"Because that's what it is," she says. "It's honest. The boys are missin' you." Mandy sees he's got his eyes closed. "Chair's nice, ain't it. How's your new hand feeling?"

He opens his eyes and studies Dustin over in the corner throwing a toy truck against the wall. "He been acting up all this time?"

"I just don't know what to do with him," she says. "I kinda gave up."

"All right." Winston whistles at him. "Dust-bin!"

The boy doesn't respond. Just stays in the corner and continues his small project of destruction.

"Dust-bowl," Winston says. "Look here."

"Mind your daddy," Mandy says. "Go on."

Dustin spins around, chucks the toy and nails Winston's swollen arm, sending his father into a tight-faced place of elevated pain.

"Get to your damn room," Mandy says. "Now!"

"He's got a hell of an aim, doesn't he?" Winston's eyes are locked on what he can't believe is his offspring. "Natural born pitcher."

"Or something," Mandy says.

"Something or nothing. That'll be his choice."

"He's too young to start thinking like that just yet."

Winston gives her a backhanded wave. "Boy knows exactly what he's doing."

"He didn't mean to hit you, though," she says. "I don't think."

"No, just accidentally nailed me perfect where it counts." Winston gets himself up out of the chair, unslings his arm, goes and crouches next to Dustin and lays his new pink oversized hand on the boy's shoulder. When he turns to see, Winston brushes his cheek with the rubber and Dustin runs headlong into the bathroom with the door slamming shut behind him. Winston steps quietly down the hard-carpeted hallway and checks the knob.

"It'll open if you push hard enough on it," Mandy says. "Don't matter if he locked it."

Winston shoulders into the bathroom and opens the cupboard door to reveal his son folded up among value packs of Clorox wipes and Lysol spray. "Come on out here. You gonna learn to show some respect."

Dustin nods with his eyes somewhere else.

"Say it then," Winston says.

"What?"

"Say *Daddy Wins-a-ton*." And when the boy finally mumbles it, Winston goes back out into the hallway. "Just remember that the next time you think about not listening to nobody."

"So's this how it's gonna be?" Mandy says.

"You should've seen his face." Winston re-slings his arm, sits back in his chair and begins shaking in a silent fit of laughter. "Worth five bucks."

. . . .

Without any definite end to their time in this temporary abode, their lives start to feel slow and fast all at once, the same day every day, again and again. Which Winston's cool with. And Mandy too. His oxies have been giving all the crying and fighting a soft haze that's helping them both.

Night and day come and go, and even that's hard to tell since Winston hung his Army Surplus wool blanket over the only window. Now it's just TV shows that orient them. When the lawyer first visits, Mandy brings him into the living room and introduces him to Winston, who's sitting in his chair and staring at the bright colors of morning news television.

"This here's Robert Allen," she says. "My lawyer. Ours."

"I didn't hire no lawyer."

"I know," Mandy says. "I did."

Winston mutes the TV. "So," he says.

"Happy Monday," the lawyer says.

"How much is your percentage, Mister Robert Lawyer Allen?" Winston says.

"You can just call me Rob."

"Why should I?"

"Winsy, honey," Mandy says. "He's got some good news for us. Okay? So just listen?"

Winston keeps looking at the muted TV. "All ears," he says.

"Firstly," the lawyer says, "you're more than eligible for disability compensation due to the obvious damages. So I hope that's on your radar."

"They already got a case manager here working on that," Winston says.

"Perfect," Robert Allen says. "So that should keep a basic paycheck coming in. And I'm happy to help assist in that, if need be. But there's something more, too. Something bigger. This case has been a bit peculiar."

"That'll happen on these big jobs," Winston says.

"Exactly right," Robert Allen says. "But I do believe we have it under control. This was job related, yes?"

"Hundred percent."

"And you were there as an officially hired employee, yes?"

"My first day of work," Winston says. "Boss lady couldn't get me in there quick enough, rushing me through the paperwork to get me in there on the saws."

Allen smooths his short-trimmed beard. "But she neglected one thing. She let her insurance lapse."

"Lapse," Mandy says.

"So how's she gonna pay for all this?"

"That was our question," Allen says. "We asked her that very thing."

"We told her we were gonna sue her," Mandy says.

"Bingo," Winston says.

"But she can't be sued because of the lapse," Robert Allen says. "I mean, she *can* be sued, technically, but she wouldn't be able to afford it on her own." He motions for Mandy to continue.

"We showed her the potential costs to scare her," Mandy says, "which was obviously more than she'd ever be able to pay. And when she admitted that, Mister Allen told her there was another option."

"Always is," Winston says.

"It was your wife's idea," Allen tells him.

"Winston's, really," she says. "But I perfected it. Mister Allen told her we'd drop all charges, settle up out of court. If she'd give us her land."

Winston leans forward on the edge of his recliner. "Plus everything on it."

"The buildings, the business, the land," Mandy says. "It's all lapsed out."

"She actually laughed," Allen says. "Said she hadn't been breaking even on the place for years. Happy to pay with it. Said she's got her own little spot down on the Caney Fork."

"Ain't that special," Winston says.

"It's something the government gave her father when he was a ferry captain," Allen says. "It's legitimate."

"Captain," Winston says. "The old Rome Ferry."

"That's what she told me," Allen says. "She has a lot of history there, old family stuff, but she just can't keep it all together anymore. She said it's simply worn her out and she's ready to downsize. And I can tell she knows she was in the wrong."

"She's responsible for *this*." Winston holds up his hand. "Directly."

"That's right," Allen says. "Even if you were at fault, it wouldn't matter because of her insurance."

"Lapsed," Winston says.

"Uh huh," Mandy says.

"Now you're getting it," Robert Allen says. "I told her that you're interested in taking the property and the buildings as payment for what her insurance can't cover. It's a rundown swampy stretch, and the appraisal comes in short of what she'd probably have to pay you in cash, but cash is what she doesn't have. And this would be immediate compensation. *And* your family would have a place to go."

"That's what I'm talking about," Mandy says.

"If I may," Allen says, then sits on the couch. Down the hallway James is starting to cry. "This person, Becka," Allen says, "she's an unmarried lady and isn't getting any younger. She's hoping this will start a new chapter for her. Only thing is: this is where the claim ends if you accept her offer. You can't come back with more demands. No further legal action."

"Done and done," Winston says. "You telling me that spot's mine? Where's the deed?"

The lawyer knits his fingers together. "Mandy was able to use your savings to cover the recording fees and transfer taxes, which allowed her to sign the deed."

"You signed it already?" Winston says.

"Went ahead and did the hard work for you," Mandy says.

"Hope you spelled my name right."

Like an awkward magician, Mandy brings a piece of paper out from her back pocket and flaps it in the air. "Voila." But won't let Winston hold it.

"So I got my land?" he says. "That's what's going on?"

"*We*," Mandy says. "*We* got it."

"Amen, hell yes." Winston falls back in his recliner and clicks the mute off. The sound comes in fuzzy and loud, so he gets up. "Watch this," he says. He puts one of his arm-pins against the antenna and the signal clears. "Believe that shit?" he says. "They ought to advertise the benefits of this."

After the lawyer's gone and everybody's eaten a late lunch of boloney and ketchup sandwiches, Mandy lays a sheet out on the carpet. She takes two of Winston's oxy pill bottles from her purse, taps out the immediate release for herself and the slow release for him. They pop their dosages and shoot them down with Kool-Aid.

Mandy crawls onto the sheet with the boys, and before long they're all conked out and snoring at Winston's feet, their layered breathing lapping around him in and out like the rhythm of river waves, murmuring *Winsaton, Winsaton* in and out and conjuring up the slick banks of the Cumberland. It is raining and he knows about rain: John Hunt Morgan rides through it atop Black Bess and leads his soldiers down to that old water's edge where the old Rome Ferry's anchored and Comer the blind mule stands on his circular treadmill gearbox. "I'm gonna get you a horsey," Winston whispers into the room. "Promise."

. . . .

At first Mandy asks like it's a joke: *Are we home yet?* They were ready to move into their newly won river spread, but the process of Miss Becka moving out was taking longer than anyone expected. Then she won't quit saying it, not quite *asking* it anymore, just repeating it from down in that sleepy place she gets to with Winston's pilly-pills, saying it over and over, *Are we home yet, are we home yet...* Until one morning James is sitting at Winston's feet and puts together the words his mommy's been teaching him. "Home yet," he says. "Home yet."

Even back in the bedroom Dustin pauses from whatever evil-boy demolition he's working on, and says, "Y'all hear that?"

"Hush your mouths," Winston says. "We'll be home yet soon."

Mandy hushes while James keeps on repeating the refrain, having no idea what it means, not yet, but enjoying the comfort and fun of saying it. And now that he's caught hold of these words—*home yet, home yet*—and won't let go of them, Winston decides this is a battle that isn't worth fighting, since it's one he could never win, so without announcing the rule to anyone else because it is already in effect, he retreats back into himself and takes on a vow of silence. Like any good general, he'll lead by example. Everybody shut the fuck up, please. Including you, he thinks, which is him.

. . . .

By the day his pins come out he still hasn't said a word. Not even to the doctors. And then a few days later, when Miss Becka has fully cleared out and they finally can *go home yet*, Mandy gets their stuff packed up by a moving company. Winston isn't much help, but he's already done everything a man needs to do: sacrifice quietly and alone and secretly hold it against everyone around him. Now it's his job to sit back and enjoy watching these guys sweat like hogs under the weight of his accomplishments.

The movers prop the apartment door open and the heat coming off the Nashville streets rolls in. Apparently

Winston missed winter entirely and summer's here early. He adjusts himself in his jeans and leans back in his chair with his feet up on a box fan, while the young bucks and their sinewy straps carry all this heavy shit. He'd love to throw them some instructions—keep goin', don't drop nothin'—but keeps his mouth shut and just mutters to himself, counting out the boxes in rhythm as if he were auctioning them off, mimicking the monotonous patter of his old boss at Mega Motors and now understanding the attraction: the headlong incessant unstoppable chatter, talking about nothing until it becomes something: money hopefully, money eventually. *One boxy one boxy, two boxy two boxy, three boxy three boxy, four boxy four boxy, five...* Pretending he's making cash off all his family's useless junk feels good, and maybe that's a possibility for his future. Or is that just the pills talking? He reclines with the electric fan blowing a breeze up his pants, and keeps counting in a silent galloping rhythm only he can hear.

. . . .

Bible folks will tell you they don't know where Jesus went off to before he came back as a living fulfillment of the prophecy. But Winston's got a pretty good idea about that. Check this out. Jesus started as a carpenter, right? Then he disappeared, right? Where'd he go to? Now think about it. He was probably negotiating an out-of-court settlement against his old boss. Like any hardworking man with half a mind will do.

On a steaming weekend in early June, they finally get to Miss Becka's old house where their boxes are stacked on the hardwood floor in the living room. It's dark and damp in here and the whole place smells of cigarettes and mildew. Winston closes his eyes and inhales the historical odors. Mandy props a couple windows open with pieces of cordwood from the shed out back and begins unpacking.

In the ad section in the *Carthage Courier*, which he grabbed from a gas station on the drive here, Winston finds a little area to fill out and advertise his own kind of sale: an auction at the old sawmill, a couple Sundays away, all equipment must go. He fills out the form with the stub of a pencil, tears it from the page, digs around and finds an envelope and stamp, then walks his new business proposal to the mailbox. Then he drives to Walmart and buys a battery-powered fifty-watt bullhorn. Red and white with a rubber pistol grip and a siren button on the side in case of emergencies. He drops it in his sitting chair and will make it wait a little while.

The house is coming along slowly, and Mandy doesn't know about Winston's planned event until a week later when he points the ad out to her in the paper. "Why Sunday?" she says. "That's the Lord's day, when people worship."

"Worship my ass," Winston says. "That's my day now."

"How do you plan to sell all that old junk?" she says. "You don't know what any of it's worth. And even if you did, you wouldn't be able to *communicate* it," she says, "because you don't talk." She puppet-mouths with her hand.

He walks over to his chair and takes up the bullhorn. "Oh no," she says.

He hits the side button and releases a wailing

screeching siren distorted by its own feedback. He clicks it off and holds it up to his face. "I been thinkin'," he announces.

"Jesus God, that's loud," she says.

"They're gonna do the bidding themselves and decide on the price of things."

"What if we lose money?" She's got her fingers in her ears.

"That ain't possible," he says. "It's all gain."

"I mean, what if our stuff's worth more than they give?" She's walking into the kitchen now.

"It ain't a loss if it's an investment," he calls through the bullhorn. "Which then makes it a gain."

She huffs at his logic. "And how you plan on a junk auction being an investment?"

"Gonna make it a weekly thing." He hits the siren for a second. "Use my auctioneerin' skills."

Mandy touches her temples to short-circuit a headache.

A galloping drone gathers and comes stampeding in rhythm out of the bullhorn: "One dolla one dolla, two dolla two dolla, three dolla three dolla..."

"You mean to tell me *that's* what you been working on in your head all this time without me?"

"Four dolla four dolla, five," he says. "That's how we gonna stay alive." He hits the siren again.

. . . .

Winston's been working so hard preparing for the auction that he forgets to shave. Sunday morning he lathers around his mouth and scrapes it clean with a plastic razor, clearing open a landing pad for the bullhorn, ready to do some shouting.

At noon, about half the county shows up. They park in the top lot and along the highway: black folks and white folks fresh from their separate churches, all here looking for a deal. Crushed stones snap beneath the soles of their dress shoes. Oldtimers in overalls talk about the last time they were here, how things used to be. Young parents push strollers, flanked by kids on bikes. Folks walk down the gravel drive in their own groups, each of them curious to meet this new neighbor of theirs, to see inside the mill and get a chance to own a little piece of history. At the building's entrance, Winston stands with his bullhorn hanging from his shoulder by a guitar strap, greets his customers with a tight-lipped "Hidy" and waves them on in with his rubber hand.

A short guy walks in, talking and pointing around. "Remember me?" he says. "JR. I used to work this mill. How's your hand doing?"

"Come on in," Winston says. "I'll give you a special deal."

"I'm just here looking for a job."

"Well, we'll see about that."

Inside the mill, Mandy sits at a table with a money-box in front of her. Dustin and James peer out from behind her, little wild animals shy of strangers. JR waddles around with his hands behind his back in solemn reverence for used tools that only country folks possess. His friend, the tall man, follows quietly and obediently behind him. Winston raises the bullhorn and the crowd begins trying to haggle, but he shakes his head at every lowball proposition and tells them that another customer plans to outbid them by five bucks and they should prepare to spend a little more than they planned. "Everything in here has history with it," he says through his horn. "It comes with a story. Know what I'm sayin'? Besides, you gotta wait for the auction to start. You gotta play by the rules. Like everybody else." He hits the siren.

They glance around, shocked by the noise and suspicious of which neighbor might already be in competition with them. Winston knows that the tightest bonds can be sliced in half with a single dollar bill. After some chatting and lying and assessing how much they're willing to spend on each piece of equipment, big and small, no penny too dirty, Winston brings the bullhorn up to his lips, his gray chops bristling out, and makes an announcement to the growing crowd. "Gather round, gather round," he says. "When the price goes up, the deal goes down."

The bidding begins with the lesser stuff—chairs and tables and scraps of lumber and bundles of boards—but as Winston gets comfortable with the bullhorn and settles into his own rhythm, he moves along to one of the main prizes, the portable planer with a horizontal band blade. Below it on the concrete floor is a twisting dark stain like a dammed-up river. Winston's voice takes on a galloping pace now, alive with the monotone insistence that there's more money out there, more crumpled cash to be made, all the folks leaning in around him, hypnotized by his toneless patter: "Hundred at the top, and we don't stop," he says. "Can I get a light with a hunda-biddy hunda-biddy one..."

"Here!"

"Hunda-biddy hunda-biddy two…"

"Ho!"

"Hunda-biddy hunda-biddy three."

"Here right here!"

"Snake in the grass's made of cash," Winston says. "Hunda-biddy hunda-biddy four, four! Hunda-biddy hunda-biddy-five, five!"

Folks are calling out and flashing wallets as quick as Winston can name the next price. Mandy watches it all, taking note of every winning bid, keeping track of the bidders and how much they're spending on what. She keeps this list in the back of her mind. All of it will be of use one day.

"Now we movin' on up past one man's hand," Winston says, "and I wanna know how much sawin' can you stand?" He pats the machine behind him and winks back at the audience in cartoonish villainy. "Cause I can promise you folks one thing more: she sure does cut, and I'm a-keepin' score."

He holds up his rubber hand and everybody laughs except Mandy, who knows this joke isn't funny at all, not even a joke. This is business. Her business. She studies him while he talks, making sure he keeps on track. Don't mess it up now, she tells herself.

"Can I get a six biddy six with a hunda-biddy quick…"

"Yeah, here!" somebody calls.

People in the crowd are cheering and gawking. Some are checking their wallets and calling out with their own bids higher and higher.

"Seven fifty," one says.

"Eight biddy eight?" Winston says.

"Nine nine nine," an old boy calls.

"One thousand here," another says. And that gets folks quieted down. Near the door stands a black man in a clean dress shirt and a John Deere cap. "One thousand," he says, "clean and green."

"One K's okay, fine by me," Winston says. "Any more up cause we can't go down."

Nobody responds. All just mumbling.

"Sold and sold," Winston says. "Done and done. Come back next week for a little more fun."

"But hey now, ain't you got more to sell?" somebody says. "We can see it piled up all over."

"That's right," a woman says. "We come here for a fair chance to win."

Winston takes the bullhorn from his mouth and blows on it as if it were smoking from a gunfight. More people are talking at him now, and he just stands there, contemplating what he's created. "We done," he says. "Anybody got a qualm, come on down and show me who's wrong."

Mandy picks up her money box and goes around collecting payments. Everybody else starts getting their things together and heading out as Winston makes one final announcement: "If you wanna bet it, don't forget it. One week start from today. If you wanna play, you gotta pay."

. . . .

After the place has emptied, and after Mandy has counted and organized the bills, Winston folds some dollars into an envelope. The next morning, he mails it off to that same newspaper, with an ad about the newest and biggest flea market happening in the oldest building this side of the Cumberland.

His Sundays get bigger. More money pushing the prices up on everything. More folks coming and then telling more folks about it. More Sundays pass, then more and more, and now Winston is making bank. Not only has he sold all the mill's old junk, he's also renting his services out to folks with their own shit to sell, which is really where each buck starts adding up, and he rents out space for them to set up their own little stands. The only part of the building that isn't for lease is the section stained by his blood. That's his.

Week by week, month by month, year by year, and the customers are still returning. He's built a congregation to rival any of the churches this side of Nashville. Mandy isn't sure if Winston even realizes what progress they've made, but she sure does. His disability payments finally come through, after a couple years of applying and Mandy working with lawyers, and while he's making more and more money, he seems to need still more auctions, still more money, still more auction-stuff to get more stuff.

By the time Dustin's in school at Carthage Elementary, James is learning, as Mandy says, to use his words. But Winston's teaching him that it isn't just the words that are important but also the volume. Sometimes he speaks to his boy inside with the bullhorn, especially when the little twerp won't listen. "Can you hear me *now*?" he yells though it, directly into James's face. Mandy keeps telling him to shut up, but Winston keeps the family fed and the mill building packed to the limit at the top of every week.

They begin buying more stuff that Winston always wanted but nobody really needed. At one auction, he's selling a riding lawnmower with a bent deck that nobody wants except for one customer who says he can fix it but can't quite afford it. "What else you got to pay for it with?" Winston says.

"I got a pool," the guy says. "Above ground. All yours if you move it."

"Does it hold water?"

"Sure it holds water," he says. "It's a pool ain't it?"

"It doesn't hold water, I want the mower back."

"I'll drive it back fixed if it don't."

"Done deal then," Winston says.

He hires a crew of boys to drain it, move it, install it and fill it up in his yard. That night he goes out to it with a drill, puts a quarter-inch hole in the bottom and lets it piss. Next morning he calls the guy. "That pool's got a leak like you said it didn't."

"Naw," he says. "That ain't right."

"I'll tell you what's right," Winston says. "You drive me back my mower."

"But I already put new belts and blades on it. Straightened out the deck."

"Good," Winston says. "That was the deal. Now drive it back over."

The guy comes riding the mower down the shoulder of the highway and turns into Winston's yard. He parks it and leaves it running right next to the pool. He bends down to inspect the little hole that let all the water out. Plastic shavings from a drill are curled in the grass.

Winston watches him inspecting it. "Told you so," he says through the bullhorn.

The man says something but can't be heard over the noise of the mower. And he doesn't want to turn it off because he wants to show Winston that he made good on his side of the deal. Finally he walks back off down the highway, shaking his head. Winston patches the hole and begins charging neighborhood kids admission to his pool.

He continues expanding the auction operation to support his new buying habits. Space runs out inside the mill building, and vendors begin setting up along the driveway and out along the riverbank. Folks in motorboats come cruising by just to check out whatever's being sold onshore. Mandy charges every vendor on their property for use of the land—plus they have to hand over every piece of merchandise that isn't sold at the end of the day. That's the deal here.

When a piece of junk won't sell—an old doll house, a cat crate—Winston tells Mandy to "put something with it." She'll scavenge through whatever pile they're sifting through and pull another piece of junk that might compliment the unwanted object. She pairs a set of redundant walkie-talkies with an old oil lamp, a block set of kitchen knives with a bean bag.

And the leftovers that won't sell in any possible combination? Winston ropes off a patch of woods where it all gets dumped behind a sign that reads Cash & Smash. In there, he charges folks, mostly males, to demolish stuff that defined their battered pasts: rusted and gutted automobiles, TVs, mirrors, boats, windows, bottles, lawnmowers, aquariums, kennels and beds, all the way up to a female mannequin who was dotted with cigarette burns and had a pentagram carved into her crotch—all of it once worth something, then worth nothing, now worth the price of men's rage, which is, by Winston's estimate, one buck per minute.

And his bedrock is the fast-growing market for items that *always* sell: pistols and assault rifles without serial numbers. Winston wears the guns in holsters around his waist and slung over his shoulders while walking around and talking through the bullhorn about what might be coming soon and how these guns are the only thing between you and your stuff and everybody who wants your stuff.

Today he's selling a modified AK-47. "We got a semi-automatic with a bump-stock lock," he says. "Shoot 'em up, shoot 'em up, shoot 'em up good—kids'll thank you later for a safe neighborhood. Can I get a starting bid, bid, biddy bid bid?"

"Got first dibs," a bearded man says.

"Biddy biddy here, biddy biddy how, who's payin' most for some peace of mind now?"

During these auctions, James and Dustin keep close together on the edge of the action. When things get loud and crazy, James starts crying. And with Mandy busy keeping track of the money, Dustin's the only one tending to him. To stop the crying, he shows his little brother how to color his skin yellow with dandelions. They sit out in the field and away from the noise, rubbing flowers against their skin. This will remain the earliest memory James has of his brother.

In eighth grade, Dustin gets kicked out of school for bringing a pistol to class. They find it in his backpack after some kids report seeing it. He claims he didn't know it was in there. Winston picks him up from school, takes him back home without saying a word, and walks him down, still wearing his backpack, to a catalpa tree on the bank.

A young man now accustomed to how his father does things, Dustin expects a man-to-man smackdown, all narrated aloud through the bullhorn. He keeps his gaze on the ground while picking at the rash of pimples across his throat, waiting to hear the amplified voice and then feel the dull smack of his father's rubber hand across his face. But nothing happens.

"Where'd you get it?" Winston says.

"One of the stands."

"Whose stand?"

"Mr. Richards."

"Richards," Winston says. "That the guy?"

"Yeah."

Mr. Richards is a black man who Winston was reluctant to rent a stall to at first, just following his instincts. Then he saw all the homemade weapons Richards was hawking—from Indian war clubs made from root balls to garage-project pistols to military-grade assault rifles with no ID or identifying features. Impossible to tell how old or new any of it was. Winston figured he'd bring in some money with those things, so he let the guy start selling. Since he'd done Richards a favor, Winston tells Dustin: "I think he'll be okay. Probably won't notice one little missing thing."

"Hasn't yet," Dustin says.

"So what happened to it?"

Dustin takes off his backpack and opens it to show Winston the pistol there at the bottom.

"They didn't take it?"

"I think they forgot to, they was so pissed, just told me to get out. So I grabbed up my bag and left."

"Shows they don't know how to deal with what they're dealing with," Winston says. "That gun's yours now. Keep it safe."

"I got a box for it," Dustin says. "But now I can't keep playing baseball."

"That ain't got nothing to do with school, does it? You're too good of a pitcher. Coach won't let you quit."

"They said I couldn't play no more."

"They still need a closer, don't they? You got a service they need. Every Alcorn does. You hear me?"

"Yessir."

"You don't need no school to throw a ball where it's supposed to go."

"But what am I supposed to do meantime?"

"Anything you want."

"But I don't know what I want."

"But, but, but—nothing. All right, look here." He picks a green worm off one of the heart-shaped catalpa leaves above them. "This right here's perfect catfish bait," he says. "And you know who'll pay top buck for it?"

"No."

"Guess," Winston says. "Who's paying for fishing bait?"

"Fishermen?"

"There you go," Winston says. "Daddy didn't raise a complete fuckup. You got some money-making to do. You got that sixth sense, don't you?"

"Who needs school," Dustin says.

"That's what I'm talking about," Winston says. "And you know what else you got that's akin to me?"

Dustin's scared to look at his father, who sounds wild and far away. "No, sir."

"What you got is a intuition sense of *what* belongs to *who*."

"Okay," he says.

"And not just that, neither. You're willing to take what you want and fight for it." Winston motions up to their land. "Nothing in this world is acquired otherwise."

"Okay," Dustin says.

"You get it," Winston says, "just don't know it yet. Now go sell them worms."

. . . .

During the warm mornings, Dustin sells plastic cups full of the wriggling worms from a little table near the river—and at Winston's direction he hires James to help him sell them. "Family business," Winston tells them.

Mandy, not so concerned with her boys' actual education as she is with having her little dropouts reported to the state, hooks him into the Heritage Homeschool organization and begins sending in their passing grades: Selling worms? Math and Biology. Talking to customers? English and Social Studies. Meanwhile, Winston takes a nickel a day from the earnings, just to avoid hypocrisy and keep them in line with his rules for rental spaces.

Then he begins to go after what he really wants: an air-conditioned box of his own to put alongside the main house for him and Mandy to live in. After all, the boys are getting old enough to need their own place and that old ruin should be enough for them.

So Winston saves up his disability checks, along with cash from the auctions, and makes a down payment on a brand-new doublewide. Heavenly Homes trucks it in, inching the oversized load backwards down the crooked, narrow washboard drive, snapping branches off all along. They drop it alongside the old farmhouse, hook it into the existing well and septic, and when Winston and Mandy move in, they leave the boys alone together in the leaning two-story wooden structure, which at one time may or may not have been either a plantation house or the servants' house for a plantation house that could've got burned during a raid—all depending on who you asked, and where you were when you asked them. Winston has stories that change with his mood, and so does every vendor and bidder who attends his auctions.

. . . .

The summers are green and unbearably hot everywhere except for the water, so that's where the boys mostly stay, working and swimming and fishing. But fall brings on clear skies and cool nights, and one late November morning the house throws a shadow across the yard, and within that shadow the grass is white with frost. Everything outside the shadow in the sunlight is thawed and warming and steaming. James watches this from his bedroom window.

The boys are big enough now to split their own wood and heat the house themselves. Home Economics: A-plus. With more time on his hands, now that he and Mandy have their own place, Winston moves on to fixing up the old half-submerged ferry, the last of the projects on the list he'd made in his mind more than a decade ago.

He tells Mandy he plans to sell it, though he might actually keep it, depending on whether or not it floats good and could take him into Nashville. He might need it one day. Daddy's own little getaway. A portable, floatable auction house. Or something else.

He sends his boys back and forth on errands and teaches them the wisdom of stepping back when you don't know how to fix something and paying for some cheap labor. He posts a Help Wanted ad in the local paper, and the first call he gets is from a man who claims to have worked at the mill years ago and knows more about it than most people. "Remember me?" he says.

"So why you wanna come work here?" Winston says. "And why should *I* hire you?"

"Cause me and my bud need something steady. And I'm the one who tied up your arm to quit the bleeding to start with."

"I don't remember that."

"Well I do. And I'm still missing my belt and my shirt because of it."

And so he hires this handyman-mechanic from Rawls Creek Road, a short, talkative guy named JR Hix, who brings along his helper, a tall mute with a crooked face named Willy. For their first big job, they winch the ferry onto the bank, jack it up off the ground and put it on blocks. They weld the bottom and rebuild the sides, replace the old engine with an inline eight-cylinder diesel rig that funnels great clouds of blackness into the sky. JR puts on a new chain belt that runs to the paddleboard, where Willy's attached new wooden planks he made from pieces of cedar in the scrap pile.

One evening Winston and the boys are standing on the ferry deck and examining the tin roofing over the pilot's cabin, which JR and Willy just finished fastening down. Winston turns to look up the bank to his yard, his property, all of it. His. The old house, leaning in the low slanting light, and casting its shadow over the new mobile home and the pool. Over to the right is the sawmill where the flea-market and the auctions happen. All his little lawn jockeys are lined up along the entrance. And just over the hill you hear people in Cash & Smash hammering away at shit, and their laughter isn't really laughter.

He's accomplished everything he set out to do many years back. So what does a man do with himself now? He has everything, so why doesn't it feel like enough?

He turns to his boys. James with fuzz on his upper lip, Dustin with razor burn across his throat acne—both with the same lazy attitude. They get it from their mother. He picks up his bullhorn and aims it up the slope at the help: "I hope y'all're happy."

A voice comes floating down from the yard. "Aw, we happy," JR says. He and Willy are sitting on a stump, eating donuts out of a paper Key Stop bag. "We always happy working for you, Mr. Winsaton."

He sets the bullhorn between his feet, strokes his rubber hand in thought, picks the horn back up and announces, "Goddamn glad somebody is."

THREE

At school, the students and even the teachers are always talking about how James wears the same clothes every day: toe-busted tennis shoes, knee-patched jeans, a threadbare t-shirt under a nylon Tasmanian Devil jacket. All of it used to be Dustin's.

James is getting called into the office today because at a school somewhere else, some boys walked in with guns and shot the place up. Given what they did over there, his school here implemented a dress code that Winston Alcorn refuses to participate in, telling the principal that his family doesn't have enough money for a new wardrobe. In fact they *do* have the money, plenty of it, but he just has different ideas about how it gets spent.

After two warnings, the vice principal calls James in and puts him down in a ladderback chair in her office. "So, mister," she says. "This is what is called your exit interview."

"Cool," he says.

"Do you have anything to say for yourself?"

"Nah," he says. "I'm good."

"We had to kick your brother out too," she says. "For behavior I can see you moving toward."

"I ain't like him," James says.

"Aren't you worried about *becoming* like him?"
"I don't know. Not really."
"Why not?"
"Because he's different."
"Look at me," she says.

If their eyes meet, he'll dive across this desk and tear her sour pinched face apart and prove her right, that there *is* something in him that wants to cause chaos inside these painted cinderblock walls, just like Dustin almost did, that to him there is something enviably evil in the boys with enough guts to make principals and teachers go running for their lives, that the only thing keeping anybody in control is the threat of violence. That's the only explanation that can make her understand where he's coming from. But he's too scared to say anything like that, and even *he* doesn't even know exactly where he's coming from. All of *that's* more Dustin's style. James just sits here, staring at his feet.

"You'll never amount to anything," she says. "Your future is *flat*." She reaches across her desk and passes a hand under his motionless eyes. "Can you hear me?" she says. "Do you understand me?"

"Whatever," he says.

"Flat," she says.

"Can I go now?"

"Fine." She claps her hands for him. "We're done here. This is useless."

"I agree with that," he says. "I know it is."

"And what else do you know, mister?" she says. "Now that you're talking, I'd like to know what it is that you know."

"Nothing."

"That's right," she says. "You know nothing."

He stands up, keeping his eyes down. "I don't know nothing."

And it's true. This is the one thing he's known since before he can remember. So he accepts his expulsion as he has all the punishments in life so far and walks out of school this day, never to return, unsurprised, as though this has already happened to him before. He already saw his brother go through it so he knows the deal.

He walks the highway back home with his head down, not out of shame but out of habit, along the river, always down there somewhere, steaming the leafy green drapery of kudzu. Back home a free young man, he finds Dustin on the back porch cleaning the homemade pistol that set *him* free.

"How goes it, dude?" Dustin says.

"They kicked me out. For wearing your clothes."

"Shit." Dustin sets the gun down. "Clothes ain't even mine. Used to be. But now they ain't. That's because they're yours."

James isn't about to smile, no matter how hard Dustin tries getting him to. "So what do I do?"

"Come on," Dustin says, "follow me."

He walks his little bro down to their riverbank, under that catalpa tree, the same one that Winston took him down to a few years back, and right there just like that he passes along the family business, brother to brother. "I'm old enough now to have bigger concerns than these fuckin' worms," Dustin says. "How about it? You wanna take over?"

. . . .

So begins the first real job of James's life—mostly hanging out on the water under that budding tree and selling freshly emerged worms to fishermen. He sells them alive in plastic cups or frozen in bags, men in the boats swear by both.

The few vague friends he might've had evaporated when he left school, so now he's mostly alone with the water and the woods. He puts a trolling motor on the back of his canoe, runs trotlines in the mornings and checks them in the evenings. Sometimes he'll snag a catfish and bring it home to fry, if he feels like skinning and cooking, but usually, if the cat's still alive, he'll just release it back down into its muddy home.

If he makes it back to the house with nothing in hand, he eats dry ramen noodles for supper, the noodles crushed and shaken in the bag with the flavor mix. He crunches and munches in bed and waits for Dustin to return from wherever he is.

One morning, after running his trotlines from tree roots on the bank, he comes back up and finds Dustin getting dressed in the high school baseball uniform.

"The hell're you doing?" James says.

"Team asked me to pitch one last game," Dustin tells him. "They need a closer."

Dustin always said he hates playing on teams of any kind, but standing here in that uniform he looks happier than James has seen him in a while.

"When's the game?"

"Today."

"Well, duh," James says. "Like *when*?"

"Pretty soon here."

"Is Winston going?"

"I didn't tell him," Dustin says. "Anyway, you know they won't let him watch."

Winston made him play ball back in the day because of his arm, and even went to some of the games. He'd always call for Dustin to throw pitches high and fast and inside, and naturally a batter soon would get hit, the benches would clear and Winston would run out there to mix it up with the teenagers. That's why he got banished.

"Can I come along?" James says. "I'd like to see you pitch."

"I don't care. But you can't ride with me. I'm taking my friends because this is their last game. They're graduating, like I would've been."

After Dustin leaves, James rides his bike up the highway and over to the school's fields in a low stretch of floodplain in south Carthage. He sits at the end of the bottom bleacher and watches the whole game. Dustin doesn't get off the bench until the ninth inning, when the game's tied with the bases loaded. He comes trotting out, taller than most of the boys, and standing there on the mound he looks like a weird statue of himself.

He throws two fastballs for strikes that clap in the catcher's mitt with a nice tight pop. The batter says something and Dustin steps off the rubber and stares at him. Even if Winston isn't here, his attitude sure is. Dustin steps back onto the rubber, winds up, and burns one right into the kid's ribs.

This pushes the winning run in and the game's over—lost by this delinquent they let play out of what, kindness and concern? Well, Dustin always fucks himself up by getting pissed off.

He leaves the field with a few friends and James wonders where they're going. Probably to the Bomb Shelter, the bar in Carthage that lets high school seniors drink beer as long as they order fries. He's heard Dustin brag about it before. And he also knows he isn't invited to that. So he rides his bike home along the shoulder of the highway, pedaling fast to get back before dark. But the house is so quiet it spooks him into going down to check on the trotlines he'd run that morning. The dam's been releasing all day, though, and all the roots are below the surface. He stays there until pink brushed clouds reflect in the water. At least he can do some shore casting. It's about time for the bass to start biting.

He walks up and down the bank, casting his little striped Rapala crank bait and making it dive and dart, a decent imitation of a scared or injured shad. It's well into dark and not a single hit. He's winding up for one last cast when he hears a vehicle turning in off the highway, and then the voices of Dustin and his friends. He reels his line in and runs up to the house. In his bedroom, he can smell beer and sweat and cigarettes, and Dustin's standing over there in the dark corner.

"What would you say if I told you something?" he says.

"Depends on what, I guess."

Dustin steadies himself against the wall with his forehead. "What if I told you I made a decision?"

"I'd ask what, I guess."

"Quit guessing," he says, "and just ask."

"So what kind of decision did you make?"

"Like the kind that says I'm leaving." He headbutts the wall.

"Quit," James says. "Where you going?"

He pushes off the wall and steps toward James. "The army don't really tell you that at first. Just gotta wait and see."

"You serious?" James says. "I don't believe you."

But Dustin doesn't answer him. His friends are outside yelling for him. "Come on, Shelly's already there."

"Shelly's waiting for it, man."

"Shelly wants to run with the big dogs tonight."

"You'll understand soon enough," Dustin says.

"You're too drunk to drive."

"But not to ride," he says, then punches James's shoulder and takes off.

James gets to the window in time to see him jumping into the back of his little truck, the bed packed full of guys holding beer cans and hollering as they bump over the potholes and turn onto the highway.

James sits down on his bed. It's dark outside and the sounds of evening birds and bugs are thinning. And here in this room it's getting even darker and quieter. He takes his shoes off and lies down. He knows he needs to make a decision, too. But what about? He doesn't know, and that's the problem. Was Dustin even serious? He's always talking shit. James spreads out on top of the sheets and his eyes begin shutting. Once, then again, he catches himself slipping down into a murky sleep and tries to stay awake but can't keep from sinking.

Late in the night, his eyes open when something crashes in the kitchen. Then he hears Dustin cussing and saying some crazy shit he can't quite make sense of. Something about a dog? When Dustin staggers into his room—"I found me a hound, brought that bitch back home"—James pretends to be asleep and Dustin leaves for his own room. After a while he hears his brother snoring next door and knows he'll never get back to sleep now. He should go wake him up, tell him to roll over, but he doesn't dare. Never disturb your big bro when he's sleeping off a night at the Bomb Shelter.

James wishes he could take himself for a drive, cross the highway bridges and watch the dark water rolling below him, but he doesn't have any wheels yet. And is Dustin really leaving for the army? James will just have to wait around for the truth to reveal itself slowly, like he's been doing his whole life.

Dustin's always been allowed to do anything he wants, and that plus the snoring pisses James the hell off. He rolls onto his side to face the wall and flips his cell phone open but it's run out of charge. Who would he call anyway?

A strong wind's stirring the trees up.

The bedroom window's open and a strip of duct tape covers a tear in the screen. Dustin had got pissed off about something and put his fist right through it. Later that day a roll of duct tape sitting on the stoop. No note, but they knew it was a reminder from their father that even though they lived in this separate house, they still shared a common plot of land, and with that plot came responsibility and respect. How did they ever get this house, this land? Winston's never said a word. But there are rumors.

He'd cleared out a big spot near the water for JR and Willy to keep working on the rotting old ferry. Even dozed a path down through the trees, from the highway to the river, so work trucks could deliver tools and parts to that iron tub of a wreck. Winston's told him and Dustin, in bits and pieces, that the ferry will be a venue for interests that their mother won't acknowledge, but that the locals, he believes, are salivating for. In short, a floating auction market and radio station that will, when he's not holding auctions, speak the truth about the condition of silenced men such as himself, this place he calls home and all the history contained within it. He'll preach his truths on the river and be able to broadcast his thoughts to a more appreciative audience than his ungrateful boys and his sneaky wife. Now the ferry's getting closer to running. That's probably why Dustin's getting the hell out. Or says he is. He's always talked shit about leaving, always bragging about what he'd be doing if he stayed. "Tittie and ass contests," Dustin said once. "That's what I'd get popping on that bad boy's deck. Float on down to Nashvegas and show 'em how it's done."

Looking out the window, down toward the water through the trees, James stares at the ferry propped up there on the bank. It's been getting tinkered with for years. Will it ever actually *float*? Maybe that isn't the point.

A tugboat's coming down the river, he can hear it chugging. Sounds like it's wrangling a barge. As it passes, he unplugs his phone from the charger in the wall. Mandy refuses to give her boys any internet because, as she says, "The first thing you'll be doing is callin' phone-sex lines. Then you'll get your own email accounts. Then next thing you know you're locked up in somebody's basement. It's a gateway to hell."

But there's still not enough power in the phone's battery. Why wasn't it charging? Shit, the electricity's gone out again. Either that or Winston's pinching pennies. In a couple of years James'll be eighteen and able to do anything he damn well pleases.

But he'll never be older than his brother. Of course not. But maybe he'll do better than whatever shit Dustin gets up to.

. . . .

The electricity coming back on wakes him up in the dark: the refrigerator rattling back to life out in the kitchen, the floor fan back to whirring, the clock ticking again. So James gets up to look around.

Dustin's bed's unmade and empty. Didn't he ever come home? Was he still out drinking?

Through the windows the sky's beginning to brighten. He hears an outboard motor down on the water—an early morning angler cruising through the mist. Fish'll be feeding soon, clouds catching the colors of dawn. But James is still sleepy and he gets back in bed. The tape on his window screen's so thin you can almost see through it.

Then he hears an odd sound outside, right below his window, sniffing and puffing and scratching, a couple whimpers. James gets up, goes over and looks out to see a hound tied to the spigot. It's a young bluetick female with the number 13 spray-painted on her side. Must've got lost from a hunting pack, either that or just left behind. Happens all the time, a dog getting dumped for being lousy at its job. And Dustin went and found it. For once he'd actually told the truth.

FOUR

Up where the bank flattens into fescue and limestone, Miss Becka stands at a wooden shelf nailed into the trunk of a shedding cedar. She tosses a string of fish guts and it breaks the grid of light flashing over the water, turns inside a cloud of shiners darting and nibbling and sinks to the quilted bottom. She tosses the cleaned largemouth into a cooler, and from the galvanized washtub at her feet pulls another one out and presses its tail onto the slip-spike at the end of the board. The gills flare red. "Didn't think *you* were still alive," she says. She flips the filet knife around, holds it by the blade flatwise and knocks the fish over the head with the handle. The body shivers. She flips the knife again, slips the blade tip into the vent, slices up to where the gills meet, fingers into the opening and rips everything out in one smooth pull. The heart hangs beating in the sunlight. The stomach sac is a tight pallid oval, and while she's inspecting it a voice from the water speaks her current thought so exactly that she wonders for a second if it isn't simply her mind come aloud: "What they been eatin'?"

A lanky young man is sitting in a canoe pointed downstream, with a trolling motor on the back. He's wearing a trucker cap, sunglasses with mirrored lenses the color of gasoline on water, and some racy t-shirt of the Big Johnson variety, which she chooses not to read.

He's up against the bank, holding a bunch of scrub brush for an anchor. Over the side, he's pulling out the guts she just tossed and dropping them into a red plastic Folger's container between his feet.

"Didn't hear you coming," she says.

"Maybe you just wasn't paying attention."

"Excuse me?" She squints. Is this who she thinks it is? The young man glances upriver and she sets her knife down. "Are you Dustin?"

"When's the dam start spilling?" he says.

"Not till later. I'm Miss Becka."

"I know."

"And you live over at the old mill."

"I know that too."

"Saw you last night at the Bomb Shelter," she says. "I was working. I served you. How're you feeling today?"

"You know." He adjusts his sunglasses. "Living the dream."

"And how's your little brother?"

"Gettin' all grown up."

"What's his name again?"

"James," Dustin says.

"That's right," she says. "Y'all are Winston's boys."

"I ain't nobody's boy no more."

"Whose are you then?"

"Nobody's, I said. If you had so many questions, whyn't you ask them last night?"

"You were..." she says. "How shall I put it? So you don't belong to nobody at all anymore? Not even that young woman you were with last night. You were following her around pretty close."

"She's from the college." He hocks a loogie into the water. "Anyways, I asked you what they been eatin'."

"Here." She flings the sac at him. "You figure it out."

Dustin catches the slimy string of organs one-handed, rinses it in the water, brings the pallid pouch up to his mouth and tears it open with his teeth. "Crawdaddies," he says, and pushes one out.

"Figures," she says. "How digested is it?"

"Half."

"Probably fed around sunup," Miss Becka says.

"Well, duh. That's when they're hungry."

Miss Becka takes a kitchen fork from her back pocket and runs it up the fish's body from tail to head, sending scales down onto her rubber boots. She flips it, scales the other side, and tosses it into the cooler. "What do you want?" she says.

"You got more innards up there?"

She wipes her hands on her pants, coloring her lap with fish blood. "That was the last of them."

How long before this young man shows up at her door asking for more than fishing bait? Folks around here used to think she had money. Some still do. But now Winston has more than she does. And it's all because of what used to be hers. But that was years ago. Mistakes were made. This boy here is getting older, and he'll want to know about it someday. She wonders if she'll be the one to tell him. Wouldn't that be something.

For all this time, from a distance, she's watched Winston spend money and make money and spend it again, all on his flea market madness: thirty-foot-tall crosses, Confederate cannons, battle flags and any brokedown junker that can be wheeled into his lot. He believes they'll all get fixed one day and make him a millionaire. Shoot, maybe it's already happened. Down near the river, in the trees and among the crosses, holding outdoor auctions—she watches them from the water sometimes—with people coming from all over, ready to believe his lies and pay for some piece of rigged-up trash. He's got a strange rapport with them.

"Your daddy still holding those auctions?" she says.

"Course he is."

"How's the ferry coming along?"

"Near done."

"Is he planning to sell it?"

"If the price is right."

"You know my family used to run that ferry?"

"No shit," Dustin says. "So you gonna be there to see it off?"

"He selling it at the auction?"

"Think so."

But she can't tell what he's thinking behind those mirrored lenses. Can only see two tiny reflections of herself. "I doubt I can afford it," Miss Becka says. "But I'd like to see it."

"Come on by," Dustin says.

"Tell Winston I might show up for it," she says. "No bad blood."

"Why would there be?"

So he definitely doesn't know. Miss Becka picks the knife up again. "My father and my father's father worked that ferry."

"You just said that," Dustin says. "Winston wants to get it running again so he can start his own business with it."

"Is he planning to use it to take folks across?" she says. "That'd be nice. The bridges are too far away."

"I don't think the return on that would satisfy him."

"It wasn't enough for my folks," she says. "I thought he was gonna sell it."

"He wants to sell it but still keep it," Dustin says. "That's the kinda deal he's looking for."

"Well." Miss Becka pinches a scale from the board and rubs it between her fingers. "That makes perfect sense."

"Thanks for the guts." Dustin pushes off the bank with his paddle and the current catches the canoe.

Miss Becka figures he'll float down to the Cumberland, then make a left and continue downstream to her family's old place. His family's. It's a long trip, but not so hard from this direction. What was he doing this far up the Caney without a fishing pole? Then it hits her.

"Don't go running trotlines around here," she calls.

But she just gave him those guts for bait. Goddamn it.

FIVE

On the back porch facing the highway, James is screwing around with a tangled Zebco reel when Mandy slides open the side window of the doublewide. "I'm heading over to Cooksey's Market," she says. "You wanna come with me?"

"Not really," he says, but he knows she isn't asking.

"I got to talk to you. Come on."

A spring pops loose under the drag-control knob and sends an eight-pound coil down around his bare feet. "Can't you just tell me now?"

"Put some shoes on," she says.

On the bench seat in the cab, they roll west past a lone derelict farmhouse with a historical marker out front, nothing about the war, as Winston would have it, but an old musician named DeFord Bailey, a harp-playing black man who escaped what he was born into by making his instrument sound like a train. He wound up at the Grand Ole Opry, then was forgotten. Mandy had told James about him during a homeschool lesson, when she was still trying to impart some sort of education, in defiance of Winston's orders to teach military history. James could use a train of his own right now.

He knows that whatever his mom's wanting to talk about must be something serious when she holds right off Lebanon Highway onto Old Rome Pike—the long cut. James presses his forehead to the window and watches Spring Creek glittering alongside before sliding off into a cow pasture, its shallow banks held together out there by old stone walls. Probably some good baitfish in there: shiners under the mossy overhangs.

"So," Mandy says. "I wanted to talk to you—"

"Let me guess." He presses the electric window button and lets it drag down his face, smearing an oily mark along the glass. "About Dustin?"

"How'd you know?"

"What else does anybody talk about?"

"Look at me." She pats his leg. "You're important too."

"Mom! You're not supposed to take your eyes off the road. Even I know that."

"You'll have your license soon."

"Not soon enough." He keeps clicking the window button but it's all the way down.

She slows and stops there in the road. "Wanna give it a spin?"

"You serious?"

"I mean," she says, "long as you don't *actually spin* it." She puts it in neutral, gets out and goes around the front. He scoots over on the bench and takes the warm spot where she was sitting.

She gets in and asks if he needs to move the seat up any, but if anything the seat needs to go back. Her little boy, no longer little nor a boy. "Hold the brake and clutch to put it in gear," she says. "Then ease off the clutch as you give it gas."

"I know."

"All right. Just checking."

The truck stalls. She doesn't say anything, just lets him figure it out. Soon enough, after a lurch and a jump, they're moving, cool spring wind coming through the windows.

"You know that girl Dustin's been seeing?" Mandy says.

"Never met her."

"Neither have I," she says.

"But I know what you're gonna say, though."

"He tell you all this already?"

"Kinda."

"How's it make you feel?" she says.

James picks at a loose thread in the seat between his knees. "Ain't a big deal," he says.

"Him leaving?" she says. "That isn't a big deal to you?"

"Shit happens." But he can feel the heat behind his eyes. He wasn't planning on talking to her or to anybody about how he's been feeling. Maybe when he's older he'll be able to hold it in, won't even feel it anymore. Like Dustin. "I wish he wasn't leaving. I wish he was staying."

"Did he tell you why he's leaving?"

"Not really. Just said he was joining the Army. Wants to go infantry. I bet Winston's psyched."

"Your father would go *with* him if he could."

"I wish he would," James says.

"He served when he was younger. Before we met."

"Sure he did."

Now it's Mandy who's looking out the window. "That's what he says."

"He's been wanting somebody to join ever since I can remember. So Dustin finally did it."

"True," she says. "But do you know why he joined?"

"Come on," James says. "Just look around." He brakes at a four-way stop and stalls out. "I just hope it isn't too far away. Like will I get to visit him? You got any idea where he's going?"

"I believe it's Georgia."

"It's all the same shit anyway." He opens the driver's-side door.

"What's that supposed to mean?" she says.

"He can't wait to leave," James says. "Doesn't care where he goes, long as he's gone. And I can't blame him."

Mandy nods.

"Every night he's been going to the Bomb Shelter," he says. "And I mean *every* night."

"Which is where he met this girl, I think. You know that, right?"

"I heard about her."

"I have too," Mandy says. "But not enough. Does she work there?"

"Doesn't need to," he says. "She goes to Cumberland. Just drinks there. Probably comes from money."

"Dustin needed a job," Mandy says.

"Well, he found one."

"And he needed direction."

"And he found that too. You sound like Winston now."

"Winston," Mandy says. "He's your father, you know."

"That's what I heard."

"Then call him such."

"So *this* is what you wanted to talk to me about?" he says. "Manners?"

"And now you sound like your brother."

"I sound like me."

"Listen," Mandy says. "I know you don't want him to go. I don't either."

"Y'all don't even live in the same house with us," James says. "So, like, why would you care? How you even know he actually signed up? I wouldn't be surprised if he was lying. Just like Winston."

"That house is like just another room," she says. "Only separate." She looks around the cab like it's mic'd. "Besides, would *you* want to live with him?"

"Nope," James says. "But you do."

"I got plans," she says. "It isn't just your father running the show here. I hope you know that. Don't you feel hopeless, okay?"

James gets out and goes around, and Mandy slides over to the driver's side. She starts the truck and clunks it into first gear, then second. The limit on this road is 35 and James doubts she's even doing that. He looks out his window again for Spring Creek, but it must've veered farther off somewhere back there. Now they're turning onto Highway 70, toward where Mandy said they were going in the first place. He sticks his arm out the window and the wind lifts his hand like it's a plane taking off.

Soon Dustin will finally be leaving like that, going from here to wherever they're sending him. A place where everything's dirty. Least that's what James thinks. It's all of what he's seen of it on TV. He'll never have the guts to go somewhere like that, a place where everybody wants to kill you. And for good reason, probably. He's never even been into Nashville, except for back when he was a baby, which he can't remember so it doesn't count. Dustin says he can remember being there, but all he saw was the apartment the hospital gave them while Winston was losing his hand. Least that's something—more memories than James's zero.

Mandy steers across the two-lane highway and pulls into the front lot of Cooksey's. "Look who's here," she says. Next to the entrance, on a bench made out of trunk-lengths and a rough-cut two-by-eight, sit JR Hix and Willy.

"They're always here. It'd only be interesting if they wasn't."

"Weren't," she says. "Me and you gotta work on your grammar."

JR has a yellow nylon rope tied around Willy's waist, leashing him to the awning's front support beam. Maybe for real, probably for show. This pair has been Winston's go-to for cheap labor since the early days, and they move around the mill building and the property with familiarity and ease. He mostly hires them to do work his sons won't touch, which is most work these days: clearing trees, organizing junk into piles, welding cracks in the ferry's steel bottom, endlessly tinkering with its diesel engine.

A couple years ago, Mandy told James that she remembered the two men staring into the van at her when they'd first arrived, a lifetime ago, and that she was going to keep a close eye on them.

James and Mandy get out of the truck and step up into the shade of the porch. JR quits talking for once, just watches them standing there.

"How're y'all?" Mandy asks.

"Where's Mister Winsaton?" JR says.

"We don't need any help right now," she tells him.

"But we need work."

"He isn't hiring," she says.

"He isn't hiring because we work for him. And y'all are having a big auction real soon. The signs are even up on the pinboard here."

"That's probably an old one," she says.

"It ain't old. Go on and look. Got the ferry for sale."

"I didn't know anything about that," she says.

"You're welcome, then."

James keeps quiet behind his mother, checking his phone for a signal.

"Who you trying to call on that thing?" JR says.

James shakes his head.

"Your big brother?" JR grins. "Trying to see where bubby went off to this time?"

Willy's head bobs and a string of spit drips from his mouth to the concrete. When he looks up, then wipes the back of his hand across his lips, his eyes are like two marbles pressed into his round hairless face. He focuses on James, the only other person who hasn't said anything.

James shuts his phone and slips it into his pocket. "My brother's a hero," he says.

"Heroes come home in boxes," JR says.

"You." Mandy points at him. "Hush."

"You don't know what you're talking about," James says.

"Let's wait till he gets back," JR says. "Then we'll see."

"Y'all quit," Mandy says.

She takes James by the arm and leads him to the door, but he pulls away and turns to face JR. "You don't know my brother," he says. "You don't know shit."

"Oh." JR taps his temple. "Sure I do, son."

"Come on now," Mandy says.

James used to think JR took Willy on because he felt sorry for him, but as he got older he understood that it was only for the donations he was given, clean dollar bills mostly from church folks and college kids from Cumberland. Dustin's girl's probably one of them. Why else would she be with him? A do-gooder's the only kind that's attracted to *his* kind.

Inside the market, he follows his mom down the narrow aisle. He's taller than her and brushes his hair to the side over his face so people who know him won't recognize him and people who don't will think he's cool.

When Mandy stops in the aisle, he almost runs into her. She points up at a family pack of paper towels on the top shelf. "You get that down for me?"

"No," he says. But he can, and he does.

. . . .

JR first heard that Dustin was leaving when Winston came by the store and told everybody. When JR asked if this meant there'd be some more work to do around the compound, Winston combed his dusty rubber fingers over his mutton chops and said, "Yeah—but shh, don't tell."

Bless Dustin's big dumb heart, JR thought, then rubbed his hands together and waited for what he knew was bound to be coming to him. And he was right. Winston finally pulled a five-dollar bill out of his wallet, and before he could even offer it JR snatched it, folded it once and tapped it into his shirt pocket. That fiver hasn't left his pocket since, because as long as he hangs on to it he'll have money to his name and he'll never be broke.

He takes it out now to show it to Willy, who's starting to get restless from the bad attitude Mandy and James left lingering out here on the porch. JR pops the bill to get his attention. "Takes money to make money," he says. "And making money is what it's all about. You remember that."

Willy's fingers lock into a contorted shape, which he turns like a kaleidoscope in front of his face.

"Good," JR says. "Glad we agree."

Willy puts his hands back down between his legs.

"But when I get me a date," JR says, "I don't want you going and messing with her. You just let us be."

But JR knows these educated girls don't fancy him. All they care about is Willy. They want to know stuff like *Is he okay?* Never a word about poor old lonesome JR. He'll need to convince them someday to redirect their compassion, because Willy's happy only if JR's happy. Can't they see that? JR's a real human being too, isn't he? When these girls come by, they gotta go through him first if they want to help Willy anymore. That's how it's gonna be from now on.

He puts the lucky money back in his pocket and rubs his hands together.

. . . .

James is at the counter bagging their groceries, but he keeps glancing out the window where he can see JR talking to Willy.

Everybody here in town, especially the college folks, knows what ratty shit JR's capable of. They sent out bulletins about him lurking around the Chinese restaurant, along trails in the woods, inside porta-potties at construction sites. Just a matter of time before they catch him and lock him up. But they won't catch him because he's never actually done anything. Least nothing James knows about. But what the hell is he saying to Willy out there?

He and Mandy carry the groceries out to the porch, where JR has Willy standing and blocking the stairs. "Excuse us," Mandy says.

Willy steps forward but JR yanks the rope back and tells him to sit down on the bench. "Don't worry," he says. "He's just anxious to get to work."

"Speaking of the devil," Mandy says.

They all turn to see a 3500 Dodge Ram Dually Mega Cab pull up and park in front of the market, temporary tags taped up in the back window. Winston sits behind the wheel, wearing a cap advertising a war he did not fight in. Or maybe did. He fought in one of them, damn it. What Winston believes is that he was somewhere once doing something important while human bodies came apart all around him. He couldn't tell if the mist was the sun setting or just blood in the air. The South dies every day. That's the world he lives in.

Winston comes down out of the rig and leaves the engine running. Willy makes a noise, a kind of impatient sound.

"What's he saying?" James says.

JR pulls the bill from his breast pocket. "I wrote you a poem, Mr. Winsaton. And it's right on the money." He slaps his knees in a hee-haw sort of way.

Winston motions for him to proceed.

JR clears his throat and pretends to read: "The troops float over the hills on bone dead horses. Their gray uniforms are gray in the heat and light. Which is gray too. And the guns are gray and the smoke is gray. Their eyes are gray. And their hair—it's gray."

"Title?" Winston asks.

JR pauses, waiting for an epiphany. "Gray?"

"That's good. I like that one."

Willy snorts, then puts his fingers in his mouth and begins pulling something out of it.

"Lordy," JR says. "He done found it."

Willy's gagging as he pulls out an actual string, held taught and dripping at arm's length. But he can't pull it any farther, since whatever's lodged in his throat seems stuck.

Beneath the porch roof here, everything's cool shade with a downward breeze from the fan hanging from the rafters, and beyond it the dusty crushed-gravel parking lot glows white and hazy. James looks out there, as if this bizarre emergency is slowing the moment down so he can remember it. Willy's mouth is wide open, as if some spirit's about to fly out of it. What if Willy'd told that poem to JR? What's this strange feeling? Is he already forgetting it?

"Stay back," Mandy tells James.

Willy wraps the string around his other fist, gives it a hard tug, and out pops a green object that bounces and flicks spit across the concrete.

"There it *is*!" JR says. "My yo-yo." He shakes his head. "I didn't think it'd ever show up again."

Willy seems calm now, back to his interior rhythms.

JR pulls the yo-yo off the ground, wipes it on his pant leg and winds it up, then strides back and forth in front of Willy, throwing the yo-yo down and letting it float back up to his fingertips.

Mandy leads James off the porch and Winston says he'll meet them back home.

"Will we see y'all at the auction?" JR says. "Gonna be a good time."

James could knock the smile off that face. "The auction's for Dustin."

"And for sellin' stuff," JR says. "That ol' ferry in particular. We're also gonna be fryin' some fish provided by yours truly."

"It's a going-away party. Because he joined the army."

"Boxes," JR says. "Remember?"

"Hush now," Mandy says. "Let's go."

James lays the groceries in the bed against the cab and gets in on his side. Winston climbs back into his rig but waits for them to pull out first. He doesn't like being followed.

"You shouldn't let them get to you," Mandy says. "Why do you talk to them at all?"

"I told JR so he knows the party isn't for him," James says.

"I think Winston already told him about it."

"That's the thing," James says. "He likes them two better than he likes me and Dustin. I wish I was going somewhere too."

"Hush for a minute." Mandy shifts into reverse and glances back. "I got a better plan for you than that."

SIX

The distant siren goes off at dawn, a warning that the turbines are starting and the water will soon be rising.

Miss Becka sits on her porch drinking instant coffee, an open journal in her lap containing notes of bird sightings. All the usual suspects this morning. Even the hummingbirds are zipping around. Then a surprise visitor, a little songbird the color of the sky, landing on a branch of the shadbush and picking off a larva. When Miss Becka lifts her mug, the bird shoots straight up into the canopy. A cerulean warbler. It traveled over three thousand miles just to be right here.

Today's Monday. She keeps these morning hours for herself before going in to work. She's been maintaining part-time hustles for so long that this provides a normal weekly rhythm that keeps her mind off the obvious and inevitable.

Weekdays, she goes to Carthage to the post office and sorts mail along with other part-time government employees. Snail mail's down, with the usual Republican shitheads cutting full-time positions, and because she's willing to work for close to minimum wage she fits into their desired demographic: a responsible older person with time on her hands.

Landing that gig was more than fifteen years ago, god help her, soon after she lost the mill—or gave it up, rather—and since we're doing math she might as well admit that she's sixty-seven years old. And sorting mail. Maybe all this real work in the real world has been good for her, though. Therapeutic, as the kids today might say. And she also gets to keep an eye on what's happening around the village. She's never opened anybody's mail, but she doesn't need to. Traffic court here, divorce lawyer there—she gets the obvious essentials.

After years of these mornings, she realized her evenings were beginning a little too early, with that chilled jug of Rossi making its appearance around three in the afternoon. So she talked with the lady who was running a tavern down behind the post office and asked if she could pick up a few evening shifts behind the bar. She'd poured a beer or two in her time.

When that lady asked if she was good with people, and she lied and said yes, she was given Thursday, Friday and Saturday and ever since has been covering those nights as well as most of the others. It's fun, usually just babysitting grown men while pulling them pints to suckle, but sometimes she gets some college kids or professors who venture east from Lebanon instead of west into Nashville, and she's gotten pretty good at talking with them. They like her because she once went to CU herself, and also knows a lot about the rivers and the land and all the history around here. She has roots in anti-Confed shit and used to protest Klan rallies with her dad, stuff their college is interested in now that they're finally starting to reckon with their past. Back when she was a student, they couldn't care less about any of that, but she did. She's been talking about removing those monuments for a long time.

There's this one young lady—what's her name?—who's been hanging out with Dustin, or rather getting followed around by him. She calls Miss Becka the Forest Warden, and Miss Becka kind of likes that. She might have taken up Green Studies, one of the college's new progressive majors, if they'd had it back then. Forest Warden: she'll take that. So long as folks don't start seeing her as a crazy old local. She's got these part-time gigs to keep from becoming one.

The owner of the lower building is a polite old racist belle named Madison Gentry, who wears bright colors, carries a big purse and paws at you like a cat while she talks. She hired Miss Becka because she agreed to work only for tips, no hourly wages, no taxes, none of that, if you please. Just the plastic piggy on the counter with the slot in its back for change. And it really isn't that much work.

Also, she likes being around booze and not drinking. She *could* drink while she's behind the bar, and sometimes she does, sometimes, but she prefers to wait until after her shift. A few more sober hours during the day will probably keep her kicking a few years longer. When she first started working the weekend evening shifts, she saw pretty fast that her eyes were clearer, her face was less bloated. And with the place literally down the stairs from the P.O., in this weird old basement-area that was built as a bomb shelter—that's how the tavern got its name—well, who'd say no to the prospect of adding a few more lonely years onto your lonely life?

But she's not thinking about any of that for the next two hours. Now is *her* time. She'll sink into her morning here on her river, drink her coffee, log bird sightings. After leaving the P.O. she'll do some fishing, then settle in with a pint glass of Rossi on ice. It's Monday, after all, no work at the bar tonight. For dinner she'll fry up one of those bass filets. Refill the pint glass. Talk to herself a little bit. Wander around with her hair hanging down like a witch. Go out into the water and weep at the stars. Then tomorrow morning wake up with a headache and remember why Tuesdays are the toughest.

Come back, cerulean warbler.

But it doesn't.

Low ghostly fog comes rolling down the river. Through the trees she can see eddies deepening, boulders disappearing. That's the cold water being released from the dam. She finishes the last of her coffee, walks down to the slick grassy edge and slips a foot in. That'll wake an old girl up. She feels the silky mud coming up between her toes. When the water's risen past her knees, she figures it's about time for work.

Her cabin's at the end of a rutted dirt trail. She drove down it a few times back when she was moving her stuff in but she didn't have four-wheel drive, and after one rainy summer it was useless, so she just let it grow back up. To get to her car, she hikes the trail through the tall fern and nettle up to the county road, where she parks in a gravel pulloff. Anglers used to use the area for access, but she put an end to that with some private property signs. From here, it's just a ten-minute drive into town. She steps over the new guardrail they put in despite her protests and gets in her old Camry. The shocks are gone so she takes bumps slow.

A little historical marker in front of the post office says it's one of the few buildings that survived the war. The reason the Union didn't burn it down—though the plaque doesn't say so—is because many of the workers were Union sympathizers who passed along intel about rebel positions. Miss Becka likes to think that those were her ancestors, but honestly doesn't know. She's never done the research and doesn't really want to. She parks in the lower lot down near the Bomb Shelter, climbs the outdoor wooden stairs and unlocks the second-story backdoor. Inside, she turns the alarm off and opens the side garage gate for the morning mail delivery.

There's magic in this building after it's been empty all night. Empty, but not unoccupied. She believes there's a spirit here who reads the letters in the personal boxes. Sometimes she'll find a letter's been misplaced, a mistake she'd never make. And sometimes a letter will be torn neatly at the top. When a customer complains, she tells them it was like that when it arrived. If she told the truth, they wouldn't believe her. "Good morning," she says into the room. The air is dry and warm in here. No activity. She flips the overhead lights on.

Her mother worked as a cook at the inn down the street while her father ran the sawmill. She passed along to Becka her recipe for fish-fry batter—eggs, flour, corn crumbs and root beer—and sometimes while cooking in the evenings, Becka spots her reflection in the little window above the sink. With her hands covered in flour, she looks like her mother's ghost. Her father had always wanted a son to take over the mill. "Only a man can work with wood," he used to say, so she spent many years proving him wrong, until the day the Alcorns came along. Winston said he was looking for work, and she took pity on him and his children and his wife. What did she have to lose? So much, so much. She didn't realize what he was up to. He was such a good liar—like he believed it all himself. Would she have been able to tell what he was up to if she'd been the son her father wanted? Well, she wasn't, and when she's being truthful she'll admit that a bittersweet freedom came with walking away. But there's still something wrong.

She's never told her father what happened. He's still alive, if you can call it that, over in the Second Wind nursing home. What would be the point in letting him know that his daughter turned out to be a girl after all. Sometimes she brings him a tin of sawdust to sniff. It keeps him thinking the saws are still running. It's the same can every time.

She unlocks the front door of the post office at 8:59 and she's in the back sorting through priority packages when she hears someone ring the bell at the counter. She comes out front carrying a roll of tape and sees a young woman standing there, waiting. She doesn't have anything in her hands, nothing to mail. "What can I do for you?" Miss Becka says.

"I've seen you at the Shelter, right?" she says.

"You go to Cumberland. I recognize your face. What's your name?"

"Shelly," she says. "Can I ask you something?"

Miss Becka puts the tape down and reminds herself who this young lady's been doing. Dustin Alcorn. Be careful now.

"I'm taking this class?" Shelly says. "And they want me to, like, interview a local?"

"Where're *you* from?"

"Murfreesboro."

"That's local." Miss Becka picks the tape back up. "Interview yourself."

"They want, you know, a *real* local, and you're sort of a legend."

"Oh, please."

"Oh, yeah," Shelly says. "Everybody thinks you're basically the Bell Witch. So I was wondering if you'd take me fishing?"

"You can do that on your own."

"Please, Forest Warden."

"I've got to get back to work."

"You could teach me about the land and the river and your family and stuff? Y'all are from here, right?"

"I do come from a long line," Miss Becka says.

"That's what I'm talking about," Shelly says. "Most people aren't rooted like that."

Miss Becka can tell there's something here besides a school project. "I guess I could take you on the river. You ever fished for trout?"

"Never," she says. "That would be so cool. My paper's due in a couple weeks."

"But promise you won't go showing Dustin Alcorn any of my spots, or his little brother. I know you're close with them. You gotta promise."

"Cross my heart," she says. "Dustin's leaving soon anyway."

"That so?"

She nods, takes the pen chained to the counter, asks for a piece of paper and writes down her cell number. "Let me know when I can come over," she says. "Just text me. This is going to be awesome."

"How about next Sunday? That's the only day I'm free."

"I'll be there."

"You know where I live?"

"Course," Shelly says. "Everybody does."

When she's gone, Miss Becka shakes her head. Hard to believe that girl's tied up with the Alcorns. That's the only reason she's even considering taking her fishing. Get to know her. Get her to trust her. And then, if it's not too late, help her.

She's never taught anybody to fish before. River secrets are precious things, and so far she's kept hers close. Folks will show up and ruin a hole. That's just what happens. First it's cigarette butts, empty cans and a fire pit, then you've got panties in the sand and a bunch of spooked trout. The kids start out partying at night, then hang around all day with a dozen rods stuck in the mud, treble hooks and chicken livers for bait. All this while what they need to be doing is anything else. And worse, they don't keep what they catch, just take pictures of their girlfriends screaming with the fish in their arms. Then they tear out the hooks or sometimes just cut the line and let them go. That's when you find catfish belly up.

This water needs her as much as she needs it.

The Caney Fork was a warm water river up until about 1948. Then the TVA built the dam, a nearly three-hundred-foot-tall wall of concrete and earth holding back a biblical flood of water. The river rushes out from the bottom, cold and clean, and Miss Becka helps keep her section stocked with trout—rainbows, browns, even brookies—right from her backyard breeding pond, a little spring-fed pool lined with mossy old river rocks.

A small grove of hemlocks surrounds the spring and works as a kind of filtration system. The water moves fast enough from there to carry leaves away, and it's covered by a net to keep out hawks and raccoons. Every evening after work she throws out a handful of feed and watches her little baby trout swarm and splash. Would Shelly maybe like to see that? She could help her write a killer paper about it. Somebody should.

Browns have held their own in the Caney since the dam was built, which makes them an enduring species, though still younger than Miss Becka's family in this area. She tells the state that browns and rainbows are all she's breeding, but lately she's been focusing on brookies, too. They're mysterious and ecologically fragile. Her hemlocks keep them alive. They're the most beautiful thing to pull out of the water, nearly black with topographical maps on their backs and spots on their sides. Last fall she got a seven-incher from the leeside of a boulder out on the main river. It was bigger than any of the others she'd released that year, which is how she knows they're surviving on their own.

Wild-born fish are smarter, which means fewer folks catch them, which means that soon enough Miss Becka won't need to stock the trout anymore because they'll be untouchable, except by her. And maybe by Shelly, if she listens. It'll be a fine day when she fishes her stretch without any of these clown-hatches in Orvis gear whipping brand new stiff-tip fly rods.

When folks around here get wind of a recent release of stocked trout, you start seeing empty cans of sweet corn or cups of night crawlers all over the shore, and it's obvious what's been going on. Sure, it bothers her, all the bobbers, but mostly because of what it might turn into. She tolerates that trashy kind of tackle because that's how people start. These Orvis guys, though, they don't know why they're throwing dry flies. Because some *sales* associate told them to? It's okay to start in the mud, then move up to clear water. Just depends on how you're raised.

Miss Becka would never kill a trout. Not even for Fishy Frydays at the Bomb Shelter. On those days she'll bring in a cooler of bass filets and batter and help Charlie the cook whip it up back in the kitchen. Fresh Native Catch. Nothing's more native than bass and cats. Even bluegills and pumpkinseeds are good eating. When she fishes hard, she hauls in enough to make herself some decent money on Frydays.

This cabin she lives in was built by her grandfather in 1907. It's been years since she had any visitors—which is kind of embarrassing. The place is a postcard from a time long gone. A chiseled boulder serves as a natural stairway up to the porch made from cedar planks sawed at the mill. The rest of the house goes back into the hillside, like a cave, which keeps the temperature stable. People's minds back then were ahead of their time. She runs electricity off a meter for a freezer and a little window unit she sometimes uses in the summer—mostly to fight humidity and mold—but that's it. She's never needed heat other than her woodstove, a double-door Grandpa Bear made of quarter-inch cast iron. With the firebricks, the thing weighs six hundred pounds. The mouth will take twenty-inch logs sideways, up to thirty inches if they go in at an angle. Get it roaring, then shut the eyes, and it'll stay hot all night long and kick back up in the morning. She likes burning white oak, but she'll settle for sycamore or beech or cottonwood when she has to. Cedar when someone comes over, which is never, but she keeps a stack out back just in case. It looks as beautiful when split as it smells while burning. Purple heartwood. If it's cool, she'll burn some for Shelly, with the doors open. Truth is, though, she burns mostly driftwood, which gets deposited directly in her front yard.

Her grandfather put the cabin where it is because it was land that the state gave to him. He delivered his son, Becka's father, in the cabin, right in the corner opposite from where Becka keeps her bed, and he watched his wife die while giving that birth. They kept to themselves, so nobody saw what happened, but folks in town have told and retold their own versions of this story so many times that nobody wants to hear it anymore. There's even a self-published version of it that's been sitting on the bookshelf at the Goodwill for years. The flour sack hanging on the wall was used as her father's birthing cloth. It looks like somebody spilled black tea on it. That's the kind of story she herself's interested in.

During a flood last year, some stuff got swept away, including her boat, her front door and her desk. The river gives a lot—stories, fish, peace of mind—but it also keeps a tab and comes collecting when it sees fit. And you never know when. One day at the P.O. Miss Becka listened to a professor from Cumberland tell her that the dam should be taken down to honor nature and the breeding habits of fish. Now, it's true: undammed rivers are more hospitable to a diversity of species. No argument there. Look at the Duck River. But ask that professor—and this is where Miss Becka is at fault, because she didn't—if he's ever lived on a river. Ever made money off of a river, other than talking about it in a classroom. Undammed rivers are wild and flood all the time. That one last year reminded her of what her family used to go through every spring. She'll take a dam and a pissed off college professor any day. And there's another lesson for Shelly. Maybe she's studying with this guy. Shoot, maybe that paper's for him.

The Caney Fork is a medium-sized snaker that never stops flowing, not ever, so the water filling the reservoir back there builds and gets released, again and again. Build, release, build. All the water behind that wall, silently and continuously pushing. When Becka goes, that's how she wants to: in a dam break, a sudden white rush with all her trout swimming and swirling around her. They'll float every curving mile down to the Cumberland and get lost in the depths.

The thought of death by water has never bothered her, but she does worry about some of the youngsters, even that river rat, Dustin Alcorn, who was obviously running trotlines, and whose father snatched away a good part of her life. That boy and his little brother just run loose. Becka knows their kind. Lost souls. She should quit worrying about them. But she can't help it.

A county cruiser drives past the front window and brings her back from wherever she just went. Both her hands are on the counter, pressing so hard the fingertips are white. What just got hold of her? Oh, she knows. It might be good to have Shelly come over on Sunday. Somebody to talk to. Maybe it'll be cool enough to burn some cedar. That's how she'd like to tell her stories. Over flaming purple heartwood.

SEVEN

The pork chops from Cooksey's are thawing on the grill. Dustin and James stand around flipping them over the grate and waving the smoke and ashes off. James asks Dustin where he was this past week.

"Went to MEPS and took the ASVAB."

"What's that even mean?"

"Means I passed. Infantry, baby. Then I went back and they gave us a serious presentation on UCMJ, which I really don't care about. But whatever. Now I'm a new person."

"What are you even saying?"

"For me to know and you to never find out," Dustin says. "Civilians don't get it."

James slaps the spatula at him. "You think the coals are hot enough?"

Dustin checks his phone for the time, then squeezes a stream of lighter fluid onto the smoldering situation and shuts the lid. "See how they like that."

"Just gonna make them angry," James says.

"You're a thinker and I'm a doer." He thumbs his chest. "That's the difference between us, little bro. Civilian and soldier. That's all."

"All you do is talk," James says. "I ain't your little nothing."

"On every level—yeah, you are." Dustin flicks James in the pecker and they fall back and start laughing.

"They're still gonna be frozen in the middle," James says.

"Where there's smoke," Dustin says in a false accent of wisdom, "there's cooked meat."

"Just throw a match in there," James says. "Come on, man."

Dustin lights up the matchbook that says Bomb Shelter Tavern and tosses it in. A small concussion rattles the grill as flames escape out the vent. "Now we're cookin'," he says.

Once the pork's thoroughly charred, James loads the pieces onto a cookie sheet and follows Dustin inside to where Mandy has the table set with a big plastic container of chow-chow and potato salad in the middle. They're eating at the boys' house tonight because Winston's down at the river working on the ferry, and whenever he gets done he'll want to clean up in his own home in peace and quiet. He can't stand to listen to chewing and talking and chewing after he's been working so hard to get that boat river-ready.

When they pull their chairs up to the table, Mandy says a quick prayer—"Lord Jesus, help everybody, and let us stay true to your plan, amen"—and they dig in. James keeps quiet the whole meal about what he and Mandy discussed in the truck. He just chews and watches his brother hunched over across from him, munching and swallowing and already ready for seconds. He's eyeing the last pork chop left on the tray. "You think Winston's coming?" he says. "Or can I?"

"Well, I haven't touched mine yet," Mandy says. "You take it. I've got flutters."

Dustin stabs the chop from her plate. "Don't mind if I do." He holds the whole blackened thing up on the prongs of his fork, winks at James, then sinks his big crooked teeth into it.

"I thought we were all gonna sit down and listen to what Dustin has to say," James says. "Don't you got something to say?"

Dustin pauses with a chipmunk cheek full of meat. Goes back and forth with cartoony eyes. Swallows. "What do you think I got to say?"

"Oh, right," James says. "We're waiting for Winston. Okay, fine, we can wait."

Mandy takes her phone from her purse. She reads it silently, her face lit white in that secret kind of light, then puts it down. She taps a pill from the prescription bottle and chases it with diet coke. "Your father will be here soon."

"Like next week soon, or now soon?" Dustin says.

"I said soon," she says. "Your party's tomorrow. He's getting things ready."

"It's just another auction to him," Dustin says. "It isn't even about me."

"You don't know that," she says. "He's just gotta put some clean clothes on, then he'll be over."

She gathers the dishes up, balances them on one arm—a skill she acquired back when she was waiting tables at a pizza joint—and carries them to the kitchen. According to what she's told James, that was back when she had a life of her own, before she met Winston. So why does she stay with him? He doesn't know the answer, but he believes there is one: it's got something to do with her promise that there's a bigger plan and he just has to trust it. Well, he doesn't, not quite yet. She takes the sheet cake from the refrigerator, shuts the door with her foot and sets it on the table for her boys to look at. But James knows it's all for show. Her spirits aren't as high as she's acting. It's just what she does when she's feeling down. He knows that about her. Which isn't a lot. But it's something.

They're waiting around the table with paper plates and plastic forks. The blue and white cake has Dustin's name across the top in red frosting. Little sugar stars sprinkled over it.

The kitchen door squeaks. No knocking. No announcement. The wind could've nudged it open. Then the familiar deliberate steps of his polished Dan Post cowboy boots on the splintered hardwood floor. In a slow, malicious waltz, Winston moves into the room in his black polyester slacks and pearl-snap party shirt, like some vintage television country singer famous for his fraudulent displays of emotion. The bullhorn hangs from his right shoulder, and he's holding a little square microphone connected with a winding cable to the speaker. He pauses to chew on some unpleasant thought concerning this family in front of him. Is it his? Must be. He steps up to the table and clicks the mic on, with an electric hiss.

"James," Mandy says. "Would you like to help clear the table?"

"You already did that," Dustin says. Her pills must be working.

"How about the cake?" she says.

"What about it?" Dustin says.

"We can go get that now."

"We already did, Mom," James says.

"Oh good," she says. "That's called thinking ahead."

"Takes a head to think ahead," Winston says out the bullhorn. The volume's so loud that everybody ducks. Winston pats her hair with his rubber hand.

"He doesn't want cake," Dustin says. "He wants supper. Daddy's hungry. Go get him what y'all just put away."

James goes into the kitchen, brings out a plate of their leftovers and sets it in front of Winston. Mandy shakes herself into awareness, gets up and pulls out a chair. "Sit here," she says. "And quit scarin' everybody."

The air around Winston seems to darken. James can focus only on him, nothing else. Even the crickets and cicadas seem to be holding their breath.

"I am," Winston says, his words blaring, "a great father." He hits the table with a hammer fist and sends his dish into the air. It clatters and scatters some potato salad and relish onto the table.

"I'm gonna miss you too, Dad," Dustin says.

Winston puts his fist in the palm of his rubber hand and looks around at everybody sitting down. "We're a happy family, ain't we?"

"Yes," Mandy says.

"Happy fucking family," he says.

"Please," she says. "It's his last evening with us."

"Responsibility and respect," Winston says. "That's what I'm about."

"You need to sit down," Mandy says.

"You don't know what I need."

"I'll get you a cold drink."

"That ain't it either."

"Please," she says.

"Nobility and honor," Winston says. "That's our heritage. Where we come from. That's what's worth fightin' for."

"I don't want to fight," James says.

"Course you don't," Winston says. "But Dustin does."

"Doer," Dustin says to James.

Mandy goes into the kitchen and comes back with a can of Diet Coke for Winston.

"When y'all won't listen to me, there's only one way to get through the noise of your tiny busy little brains and make them listen to me." He strikes the table again and spills his drink. Then he grips the bullhorn and speaks into it. "Are my words reaching y'all yet?"

"Yessir," Dustin says.

"There's one," Winston says, leaning closer to everyone over the table.

Mandy shuts her eyes and puts her fingers in her ears and nods.

"Let me ask a question," he says. "Why do I pay people to do shit my sons should be doing? You wanna know why?"

"No," Dustin says.

"Who the fuck asked you, son?" Winston turns on the siren and the speaker squeals. He plunges a rubber finger in his potatoes and says, "Fuck it, fuck it, fuck it."

James can't follow Winston's logic right now, but he knows he'll soon be in the path of his father's rage.

"So." Winston turns off the siren. "Back to my train

of fuckin' thought." He sucks his rubber finger clean. "I *pay* them to do the work my sons refuse to do."

"Sounds like a fair deal to me," Dustin says.

"It wasn't always like this." Winston walks around the room, projecting his voice at the walls. "I need me a crew who's happy to work for *free*. *Thankful* for the direction I give them. That's how it used to be. Content with what the Lord and me done provideth. Does *that* make sense to you, Dusty?"

"Yeah," Dustin says. "Sir."

"Maybe you'll learn a few good lessons while you're over there popping towelheads for us. And when you get back, you can continue the practice if you have to." He hangs the bullhorn back over his shoulder. "Life skills."

Mandy gets up. "Come on, James."

"Sit down," Winston says. "You know what I been putting up with? Workers who think they know everything. Demanding full pay for part work. That sound fair to you?"

"Looks to me like JR knows what he's doing out there," Mandy says.

"If it wasn't for me they wouldn't have anything to do out there," Winston says.

Dustin and Mandy are nodding down at the table and seem convinced of something. But James is still standing, ready to bolt.

"I haven't ate supper yet," Winston says. "I'm hungry." He slaps his belly. "Right in there," he says. "My happy, happy family," he says. "I'll just keep JR and Willy around. They ain't bad at workin'. And I can figure out how to quit payin' them."

"You're good at *that*," Mandy says.

"I'll just house them," Winston says. "Right here in this old house. Problem solved."

"But we live here," James says.

"We?" Winston says. "*You.*"

"Good luck, little brother," Dustin says. "I can't wait to get outta here."

Winston begins picking at the plate in front of him and James can't take his eyes off his father's face, showing no reaction at all. Winston just goes on eating, methodically, without hurry or pause.

"Makes me too worried to eat," Mandy says. "Dusty, promise you'll be safe over there."

"You ain't proud of our hero?" Winston puts his fork down. "What do *you* think, Jebby? You think a mother's fears ought to halt all plans of future and country and loyalty? There's a war out there."

"No?" James says. "I don't know."

"You wouldn't."

"Quit talking to him like that," Mandy says.

"Sit," Winston tells James. "Might make thinking easier for you."

"Y'all don't know what I'm doing or where I'm going," Dustin says. "So just hush."

"They better give you the good stuff," Winston says. "Else why go?"

"You gonna learn their language?" James says.

"I don't know," Dustin says. "We'll see."

"But what if something happens?" Mandy says.

"It's God's plan," Winston says. "You doubting *Him* now too?"

"I don't think He cares much about any of this," James says.

"There ya go. That's the attitude," Winston says. "Our resident cheerleader."

"Y'all keep talking," Dustin says. "I'll be right back after this commercial break." He goes into the kitchen and out the door. They hear his truck start up.

He must've left the kitchen door open because the dog he found comes slinking in and sniffing at the table with her mud-crusted muzzle. You can see tick bumps under her fur and along her rib lines. She's a disgrace in every way, a pure disgrace, and she comes right up to James.

"The hell is that?" Winston waves his knife, and the dog slinks off into a corner.

"Dustin found her," James says. "She's hungry."

"What's her name?" Winston says.

"Ain't got one yet."

She tests the air and lets out a wheezy old moan.

"I think her name's Flat," Winston says. "Cause that's how she sings." He gets up and reaches for the dog, but she scuttles around him, untrimmed nails scratching across the wooden floor, and goes cowering down the hall.

"See what you did?" Mandy says. "Everybody's scared of you."

"It's called respect."

James follows Flat down the hallway and hears Winston and Mandy starting to get into it. He takes Flat by the collar and leads her into his room and under the bed. He's too old and too big to be hiding under here, but he doesn't know where else to go with the dog. He stays there with her, listening to the fight out there. Flat's shaking with fear now, and James decides this minute that he will no longer call that man Dad or Father or any other word implying blood connection. The family line must be broken.

Dustin will be gone soon. James is on his own now. Better get used to that.

The fighting lasts into the night, so loud it sounds like it's coming from inside these cracked plaster walls insulated only by mouse nests. He's spent his whole boring life listening to mice scratching around in there. He can smell them from where he's lying. When he punches the wall and knocks a chunk of plaster off, he can see the little nests they've weaved with their tiny paws. There's even some green wool from Winston's old army blanket.

James can hear Mandy loud and clear. "Why'd you go and run our son off like this? Why'd you drag us here in the first place?"

"She never finished college like she wanted to," he tells Flat. "Never done anything she wanted to. Now hush up."

"A father's supposed to make the world safe for his boys to grow up in." Winston's got the bullhorn going. "That's what I've been doing. Look at all this. Everything I give to everybody. And I get nothin' in return? Nothin'? I'm bound for somethin' bigger and I know it in my bones."

"You ain't given me a thing."

"Maybe I might should."

"Don't touch me," she says.

"I do what I do to make this world safe for my boys. You can't be weak. Gotta be strong. Gotta *fight*. That's how this works."

"You ain't a fighter," she says. "Just an old liar. Now move."

"There's only two ways outta here," Winston says. "One is through me. And so's the other."

Some shuffling, then the thick smacking of fist against flesh. Now he's saying something else but James can't keep track of the words. Then dark thuds through the crumbling old walls. The shaking wooden floor. The bodies that made James dropping down and getting up and crawling toward each other, almost in forgiveness. Now it's getting dark and they're making apologies and saying they love each other and all they've got is each other. Winston has found his bullhorn and James hears him announce: "I love you. Kids just throw a wrench in it sometimes. Let's retreat back to the fort. Just me and you."

The old man starts complaining, and Mandy tells him to let her help him up.

Then they're finally gone, and James bets he knows where Dustin went to. Yeah, the Bomb Shelter. He'll come back home stinking of it. Tomorrow's the going-away auction, to celebrate his future, or at least his departure toward it. Whatever it actually is.

He snuggles up against Flat in the dusty, cobwebbed space. He pets her ears back against her skull. She's still shaking. "Straighten it up, pup," he says. "If you don't love it, leave it." All things he's heard Winston say. When James thinks of his brother going off to fight far away where everything's dirty, and being gone before he's even left, James takes a good long look at Flat and grabs her muzzle. She whines and tries to worm away, but James tells her to look him in the eyes. "You stay here," he says. "I'll take you with me when I go. Okay?"

He holds her paw and they shake. Her ears come up a little, and James takes that as an affirmation of her commitment to him. She's all he has, and he's all she has. They finally fall asleep.

. . . .

Dustin calls out, "Where you at, J-Bone?"

James is still under the bed, with Flat wagging her tail at the sound of Dustin's voice, and as he wakes up he can smell the booze and cigs. Dustin went and got rip-faced, rat-trapped, shelter-bombed. He starts talking quiet and then whispering a song, and his boots step in front of James's face. Then there's another voice, a girl's. James can feel Flat beginning to growl, but he puts two fingers in front of the dog's lips and she holds it in.

"Nah, he ain't in his damn room." Dustin stomps his feet. "But since we are, you thing, come on over here."

"What if he's watching us from somewhere?"

"Boy's gotta get taught somehow."

"Well, I guess we better give a good lesson then." Her feet come into view next to Dustin's. She's wearing heels and her toenails are painted. Nothing this clean and shiny has ever been inside this house. But she can hardly keep upright.

Dustin drops onto the bed and shakes loose a shower of sand and dirt. James is too scared to even wipe it from his face. The tall rubber heels of Dustin's logging boots, the ones mom bought him for Christmas, are caked with river muck and worn inward from his slanted walking.

Dustin's boots scoot away from each other and she's tripping around as she steps in between them.

"Wow," she says. "Well." She gets on her knees with both hands on the floor. The fingernails are painted too. Dustin's pants drop like he's taking a dump, and it sounds like he might've been.

All at once, James figures out this has to be the Shelly that his brother's friends, after the baseball game, claimed was waiting for him.

Horror stories come to life above him. Shelly's hands lift off the floor and she leans into what Dustin's pants no longer contain. James gags from the sounds of the hoggish sucking. All he can see is her knees on the wood, and above them her glittering skirt. Tingling spreads over his body, a little like it did the first time he saw the picture of a naked woman in a strange position on his phone's screen. Her skirt's a mess of sparkling orange light, and he realizes it's because the sun's peeking through the window. Dustin gets to his feet with his pants down and says, "Get up on that bed, thingy."

They start bouncing and the bed starts squeaking while bits of foam padding fall down on James, and he wonders if there'll be any of his mattress left to sleep on when they're finished. He can't tell if they're happy or hurting. Flat, who's still got her muzzle shut, is starting to whine, and when Shelly starts moaning really hard she goes deep down inside her old foxhound ancestry for a low, open cry. They're banging around up there and now Shelly's howling along with Flat. "That's it," she cries, "that's it, right there." But then everything slows down and it's quiet—except for Flat who's singing for the moon.

"What in the fuckin' fuck?" Dustin says, then jumps off the bed, looks underneath and is pulling Flat out, when his eyes lock down on James, who's too scared to move. "I'll be goddamned."

"What is it?" The bed creaks when Shelly sits up. "The *hell*?"

Dustin winks at James. His eyes are dull and crazy, and then with a drunken smile on his face, he looks like he's in a place that's both pleasurable and reasonable. All James wants is to get the hell out of here but he can't move.

"Just the goddamn dog," Dustin snorts, then grabs Flat and picks her up off the floor. James still doesn't dare move. He watches his brother's feet walking across the room, then hears him push Flat right out the window along with the duct-taped screen. She lands hard and yips.

Shelly's feet drop into view and she's pulling on her panties, pushing down her skirt. "That how you gonna treat our little girl?"

"Girl?" Dustin says. "For your info, it's a boy."

"You don't know shit."

"Listen," he says. "This is science we're talking. Science says babies take on the more dominant traits."

"*Dominant?*" she says. "Whoa."

"What would you call what we was just doing up there?"

"Okay, I'm out of here." She reaches down and brushes at her leg. "Fleas jumping all over me anyway."

"Talk about my home place just one more time and—"

"It speaks for itself," she says.

"There's a lot it keeps hid, too."

James stays fetal as Dustin reaches under and drags him out onto the floor.

"Oh, shit," she says.

"Consider the lesson complete," Dustin says. "James, meet Shelly. Shelly, meet James."

James can't run like he knows he should, and can't quit looking at Shelly. "I didn't see nothing," he says. "I promise."

She covers her mouth and points at James's lap. "You too? God almighty."

"That ain't nothing," he says.

Dustin pulls his pants all the way back up. "What you think?" he asks James. "You wanna test drive this ride? She's warm and ready."

Her skirt's caught in the panties on one side, and a line of muscle runs down her thigh. James shakes his head but can't look away.

She grabs her purse off the floor and whacks Dustin with it. "Good luck wherever *you're* going," she says. "Just don't die, okay?" She turns to James "Sorry," she says, "but your brother's an asshole."

James stands up. "No he ain't."

"I thought it was cool at first," she says. "Then I thought I could help. But what was I thinking?"

"Get the fuck outta here, Shelly," Dustin says, "before you wake up Winston. And before I let this animal loose." He pats James's chest.

"You're the one that's gonna die," James says to Shelly. "He ain't the one that's going to. You are."

They listen to her lurching down the hallway and tripping through the living room. Flat starts growling and barking at the front door.

"I can't even fucking leave!" she yells. "The fucking dog's got me trapped."

"The hound's getting in on it, too?" Dustin whistles out the back window, then leans out and pulls Flat back in by the collar. She goes jumping and crashing around the room, skidding sideways against the head of the bed, then jumps up into the blankets and does a quick spin. Wet with morning dew, she's nothing but fur and fun and teeth, which gets both brothers laughing and showing theirs.

Dustin catches Flat by the collar and holds her still. "Shh, baby, shh." They listen to Shelly's car go up the driveway. "I'm drunk," he says. "You want a drink?"

"I don't know," James says. "I'm not allowed to."

"Bullshit." Dustin leaves the room and comes back with a square bottle of Jack Daniel's, shaking it around to show what's left. "Today's my last day. So I give you permission."

James feels good when Dustin talks to him like this. "Okay," he says. "You first."

"Let's go hit the tree house," Dustin says. "Get all sappy about everything we're gonna miss out on in each other's lives and shit."

The fact that they have separate futures feels too big for James's mind. He knows he can't do anything about it, and he's like a little boy needing to throw a tantrum. But he holds it in. He needs to be done with all that.

Dustin stops in the kitchen and grabs a can of beer from the fridge. "Come on," he says. The screen door slaps, and he steps out onto the wet lawn.

"Hey, be quiet," James says. "They been at it since you left. You don't need to start waking them up now."

"Don't you ever turn out like him," Dustin says. "You got that?"

"Got it. But what about you?"

"Too late for me."

"Just be quiet," James says. "I don't want him coming out."

"He'll wake up soon as the hate leaves his system," Dustin says. "It's just like with booze." He holds up the bottle and peers through it at the rising piece of sun.

"We gonna drink it or just stare at it all day?"

"Hell yeah," Dustin says. "That's the little baby bro I know and love and am now gonna chug the rest of this damn whiskey with."

Dustin kicks at James and they chase each other across the ragged unmown field and down through the junkyard past the sawmill. James turns around and sees the lights in the trailer are still on from last night. Just look how the light bulbs blend into the daylight, still there but soon gone. His life won't ever be the same after his brother leaves, even after right now. Once he turns back around to Dustin it'll all be different.

Dustin stops to take a swig, then starts hollering. James catches up and pulls on his arm. "Hush now or they'll hear you. Come on. Why you drinkin' that already?"

"Because I'm leaving, ya clown. No more dumb questions. Let's move. Go go go. Advance forward."

The sun's coming up fast over the hills, sparkling the field and steaming the rich floodplains. Miles and miles of nothing but John Deere green. James turns and looks back at the compound, the above-ground pool beside the doublewide. The old house that he and Dustin live in stands beaten and stubborn. Most of the other buildings burned to the ground a long time ago.

How did this one survive? Somebody probably knows, but James sure doesn't. Doesn't really care, either. He just knows that the entire house, the big empty rooms and high ceilings and wooden floors, will be his when Dustin leaves. What will he do here by himself? The only thing worse would be if JR and Willy moved in.

The old sawmill where the auctions take place is surrounded by razor-topped wire fencing. Winston and Mandy won't be getting up for another hour or so. Maybe even later, considering last night. Still, he and Dustin should probably get to finishing that bottle. Flat comes bounding toward them, excited to join their adventure, and out here she's too fast to catch up to, zipping by and circling the boys, coming in close before faking and dodging away.

The long yard slants into trees that hold the riverbank together. Beyond that it gets sandy and muddy and rocky. The brothers find their path and walk the slope side-footed. Dustin slides down the steep wet part to the water's edge. "Chirp fucking chirp fucking chirp," he says. "How many times y'all birds seen it?"

James lands behind him while Dustin brings the bottle up to his mouth again. The birds are going and the sun is climbing and James feels suspended in this moment, like he could float around in it. He's free, least ways about to be, which isn't an ending but a beginning. It's nice to share this water and these birds with somebody. But what if you didn't need anybody to share it with? He's angry for not knowing how to feel, or for feeling so many things at once and not knowing what to do about any of it.

"What makes birds sing?" James asks.

"Oh, you know," Dustin says, "they're just naggin'. It's the lady birds that always makes that racket, squawking and screaming. Science proved it."

"You sure?"

"You got a lot to learn, bub," Dustin says.

They walk downstream along the shaded south bank on a flat-packed mud path. A Cheetos bag comes floating along and keeps up with their pace, showing them the enormous cottonwood leaning over the river. They stop beneath the glowing lime-green leafy underside of the canopy, in the cool shadow of it. The bag twirls in place, then takes on water and goes under.

They climb the trunk on nailed-in two-by-fours and up to a platform made of driftwood they gathered from the flowside of Reynolds Island. On top, Dustin points his beer can at some minnows scattering across the surface, looking like a miniature cloudburst near the bank. "You see that, bro?" he says. "Probly a smallmouth hunting them down there."

They crawl out to the edge of the platform and watch. Down on the other side of the river, a blue heron, still as a painting, stands in the shallows of Beasley's Bend. "This is a view I might miss," Dustin says. He lies back, cracks the can, rests it on his belly and closes his eyes. James keeps looking out at the bank on the north side. Farther downstream is a bluff two hundred feet high that the river bends into. This was a lookout in the Civil War, James forgets which side. Maybe both.

"Can I see that bottle?" he says.

"Aw, shit yeah." Dustin twists the cap off and flicks it over the side. "You know why they make these bottles square?"

"Give it to me."

"So it doesn't roll around while you're driving." Dustin takes an invisible steering wheel and goes back and forth, rocking the platform. "That'd be dangerous."

James holds the boards and waits for the swaying to stop. "Quit doing that," he says.

"Doing what?" Dustin rocks the platform again. "This?"

All James can do is move closer to him. It feels safer to be closer to what's causing the danger. He lifts the heavy bottle up to his mouth with both hands and takes a sip. He feels his face flush and wants to spit out the burn, but doesn't want to piss Dustin off. "God*damn*." He coughs and spits. "How can you drink that?"

Dustin hands him the can of beer. "With the assistance of Mr. Busch here."

James grabs it, takes a swing and burps. "You ain't gotta go, you know."

"I just need to keep low for a little while. You'll be older when I come back. And maybe then you'll get what I'm going through. Okay?"

"What if you come back different and don't like it?" James chugs and burps again.

"Once you start doing stuff it'll start to make sense."

"I do stuff."

"No you don't," Dustin says. "Jobs, I mean. Real ones."

"I got jobs out my ass with Winston. And the worm business."

"I give that a year. At most. You're gonna need to find something else to do." Dustin thumbs back toward land. "That man's greedy as shit. You think he'll keep feeding you forever?"

James inspects the can, looking for an answer. "I guess not."

"Damn straight he ain't."

"Maybe that place you go drinking would hire me."

"It's only part-time work at a place like that."

"Perfect."

"Anyway." Dustin rubs his eyes with his fists. "Listen, man. Winston ain't about to let you go work for *her*."

"Who?"

"Lady who tends the bar. Miss Becka. You know her. And she ain't ever gonna hire none of our asses. She knows too much about all this. About us."

"Like what?"

"Shit you don't even want to know. You need to get out of here if you want to work for anybody. Go to Nashville."

"I don't wanna go."

"I don't wanna go," Dustin repeats in a baby's voice. "What? So you can sit around the rest of your life here doing the same shit?"

"There's other places," James says. "Carthage. Or Lebanon. When're you coming back?"

"When they let me," Dustin says.

"You're an asshole." James gets up and flexes at him. "I could take you right here right now. Come on, get up. Let's see who hits the water first."

"Sit your dumb ass down before you fall off. Just get a job, okay? And if Shelly tries getting in touch while I'm gone—"

"I ain't giving *her* nothing."

"What if she comes asking, though? She likes us cause we're different. Thinks we're the real thing. She's one of those weirdos. But look, just get a fuckin' job."

"Why not the Bomb Shelter?" James says. "They cook stuff and I could wash dishes. You positive that Becka lady wouldn't hire me?"

"I already told you. Besides, that's where Shelly drinks."

"And you'd get pissed off if I started serving her?"

Dustin takes a drink, thinks, then another drink. "No. Not at all. I mean, course not. I guess that could be okay, you keeping an eye on her. She's in some kinda deep shit. That's why I gotta go off someplace. So I don't have to hear about it."

"So what am I supposed to do? You said we was never gonna leave each other." He hands the can back to Dustin.

"You remember a lot of the bullshit parts from this boring-ass movie we been making, don't you?"

"It was promises."

Dustin pretends to play the bottle like a fiddle while he drinks from it. "You'll have time enough to figure out how good a promise really is. And then I'll be back. Before you even know it, dude."

The river flows steadily below the branches of this tree. Off to the left are limestone bluffs with caves that crawl beneath the whole county. Some folks got lost in there once and came out near Bowling Green with foot-long beards. And to the right, the river rolls around Reynolds Island, the far tip of which catches a lot of driftwood. A serious log jam up there. And directly across from that is a line of sycamores and cottonwoods and beeches and one weeping willow. Beyond them you can see a farmer's rolling field starting to bake. Sometimes the cows wade into the shallows to suck down the water, and on hot days they stand there until dark, whipping flies with their tails and throwing broken lines of droplets in arcs over their backs. This place where they live. This place they love. This place they'll leave.

"What's on your mind?" Dustin says. "Makin' me nervous over there."

"Just wondering stuff," James says.

"Like what?"

"I don't know."

"Come on, man. I'm just asking."

James laughs. "I can't believe I caught y'all doing it."

"It's all natural, man. And God made nature, so I'm good." Dustin puts his hands up like he's innocent. "It was a holy act. Anyway, somebody had to teach you something at some point." He swishes the last of the beer in his mouth, twists and crushes the can, stands up and takes a pitcher's pose. "Think I can knock the leaf tip off that branch out there?"

"Either way that can's gonna land in the water."

He winds up, throws the can like a fastball and snaps the leaf clean off. The can spins and arcs and falls down into the water with the green leaf spiraling after it. Was it that last ballgame, the humiliation, that convinced Dustin his only hope was joining the army? He wasn't any good at school, then he wasn't good enough at baseball. Now what does he have? And what's wrong with Shelly? If James could come up with one other option for his brother, he would. But he can't even think up one for himself.

"How's your hand?" James says. "You just cut it?"

"Something did." Dustin inspects a loose flap of skin on his thumb. A line of blood's running down his forearm. "Don't start in on me. I'll be fine. Look at me. Do I look like somebody that's gonna be fine? Yes." The wind carries a whiff of smoke, and Dustin tests the air with his nose. "Almost forgot," he says. "The old man said he was fryin' some fish today, didn't he?"

"All for you," James says. "The whole county's coming. Plus the auction."

"Right. Sellin' all his junk to celebrate me going off. He ain't proud of *me*. He's proud of himself."

"Actually says he's finally selling the old ferry today."

"Like hell he is. He wants to start up some kind of fuckin' business with it." Dustin shakes his head and slugs the last of the bottle. "You're gonna have to leave too some day. By your own choice or somebody else's. Probably a girl's."

"Bring it," James says.

Dustin looks solid drunk now, staring at the mouth of the bottle and humming. "Will you miss me when I'm gone?"

"Course not. Let's talk about something else."

"That fish fry?" Dustin says. "It isn't starting for another buncha hours. We got time to go catch some of our own."

"I heard JR was bringing a whole load. Supplying all the fish for everybody."

"That sounds like some bible shit." The thought seems to sober Dustin up.

The smoke in the air's thicker now. "You smell that?"

"Goddamn," Dustin says. "I think he's finally burning the apple tree."

EIGHT

Miss Becka can't tell whether she's in a bad mood or not. But she's going around talking to herself. Okay, bad mood.

She closes the reception window at noon and Shana comes in with a couple of styrofoam boxes of Mexican like she always does. Miss Becka's told her time and again she prefers not to use styrofoam. That's why she likes Acapulco Grill over El Rey Azteca. They're both on Dixon Springs Highway, right across from each other, but around here people have their loyalties. And who's Miss Becka to judge? Or refuse a free lunch? She pulls the rolling gate down at the front counter and they huddle up at the break table.

"How's it been going today?" Shana says.

"Mrs. Edna came in twice asking about a package. I told her both times she'd picked it up last week, and both times she just said, 'Isn't that sweet of you, honey. I'll come back and check on it.'"

"I'm sure she will."

"No doubt."

"Father Time's a bitch," Shana says.

"I wonder when it'll be my turn."

"Don't think too hard on that," Shana says. "No use in it."

She's right: better to ignore those thoughts for now, focus on the simple things in front of you, like this pair of Santa salt and pepper shakers on the table, though it's early summer and nowhere near Christmas. Miss Becka opens her box of lunch and the steam curls out like a spirit.

"Nothing else new?" Shana asks.

"Just the usual."

"You sure?" she says. "You can talk to me."

"I know that."

"Then why don't you? Just tell me if something's wrong, all right?"

Miss Becka nods and pours some salsa onto her rice and beans, stirs it all together and takes a bite. Then she shuts the lid and pushes it away. "I think I need to go home."

Shana hasn't even opened her lunch yet. "Do what you need to. I'll shut the rest down."

"I appreciate it."

"You just need a nap," Shana says. "A shower and a nap. Doctor's orders."

Miss Becka taps the table with her plastic fork. "You might be right," she says. "So..."

"Uh huh?"

"This girl came in earlier in the week."

"Right."

"College student from Cumberland. Sweet girl, obviously smart. But she's mixed up with the Alcorns."

"Ain't that smart then."

"We all make mistakes, right? Living proof, right here."

"Don't," Shana says.

"But so this girl wants me to take her fishing. Teach her things. River-rat stuff. Says she's in an environmental class and wants to write about me. A research paper kind of thing."

"You worried it's for something else though?"

"It's just got me thinking about things."

"Listen," Shana says. "What old Winston Alcorn did to you and your family is *not* your fault. Everybody knows that."

"I shouldn't have been so *stupid*," she says. "I let him take it."

"You had no other choice. You were cornered."

"I never told my dad what I did."

"You need to get a satisfied mind," Shana says. "That's what this is about."

"I just wonder if I should tell him."

"Why would you? He wouldn't even understand."

"I guess it'd be for me. Like you say, I need my mind to be satisfied. But maybe he understands more than we know."

"Guilt," Shana says. "Let it go, honey."

"How?"

"I ain't here to help you with that. But." She takes out her pen. "What I *can* do is give you a prescription." On a notepad she writes—*Shower & Nap!*—and hands it to her. "Works for me every time."

Why is she embarrassed to tell Shana she doesn't have a shower, just an old claw foot tub? She shouldn't be.

. . . .

Out in the sun, Miss Becka feels better. Maybe it's

because she told Shana, and maybe it's the earthy sweetness in the air. River water, limestone, cedar, flowers. The promise of so many warm days to come. It gives her a bounce as she walks to her car. A good day to shuffle your feet on the surface of this planet, right here in this little town. Where everything's alive.

As she walks around back to her Camry, she notices the rear driver's-side tire's low, so she pops the trunk and gets the bicycle pump out. It's sort of embarrassing, but not as bad as paying for air from the Shell. That's what's wrong with this world: people paying for *air*.

. . . .

The volunteer fire department on the county line's giving a spaghetti supper tonight. She passes their station and gives a wave. Won't be able to make that one. But the auction's gonna be a doozy and she kind of wants to be there. She won't join the crowd, just get in her boat and see if she can catch any of it from the water. Toward the end of things, her family's ferry is supposed to come up for sale. She doesn't want to witness the bidding but is curious to see the work Winston's done on it.

And if she's going to be on the water, she might as well be fishing. And if she's fishing, she might as well be showing Shelly the ropes, like they talked about.

She plugs her phone into the cigarette lighter and clicks through her contacts. But wait a second. Shelly's probably spending Dustin's last day with him. She'll get in touch later and see how she's doing with her boyfriend gone. Ask if she can help at all.

The New Southern Baptist beyond the county line's power-washing their steeple, so she slows down to watch. With service over, they've brought out a hydraulic lifter and there's a man she might recognize high up in the nest spraying at the tiptop cross. When she turns into the lot, the guy stops spraying and pulls down the bandana from around his face. Yep.

"JR," Miss Becka says. "What they got you up there doing? Pastor catch you stealing money from the offering plate again?"

JR powers the motor off and lights a cigarette against the clear blue sky. "Pretty much."

"You don't have Willy up there with you, do you?"

"Does it look like it?" he says. "This thing can barely hold my fat ass."

"Where's he at?"

"In the van singin' to the radio. I'll be down soon."

She gets out of her car and goes over to the minivan. The bumper stickers are all faded, the paint job peeling and the side door removed completely. Willy's sleeping back there on the floor in a fetal position. At least it's in the shade of the church building.

"He's good," JR calls.

"I can see that," Miss Becka says. "Just wanted to check."

"Now you've checked."

"Don't get smart with me," she says.

"Don't make me come down there," JR says. "What're you doin' here anyway?"

"I'm off work," Miss Becka says. "That's what I'm doing." She lights a cig of her own and waits there smoking like it's a standoff.

"Auction tonight," JR says. "Winston says it's gonna be something wild. With Dustin leavin' and all."

"I heard," Miss Becka says. "Will you be working it?"

"Yes, ma'am," JR says. "He hired me and Willy as security."

"What's he afraid of?"

"You."

"Please."

"And I'm also supposed to be bringin' all the fish for them to fry up. They're having a fry, you know."

"Winston making you do that too?" she says.

"Ain't any more work than you used to have us doing."

"Aw shucks, the good ol' days," Miss Becka says. "Where's the fish coming from?"

"Don't you worry about that," JR says. "You should probably keep focused on one thing at a time. You're just interested in seein' who the ferry goes to, ain't you? You like torturin' yourself."

"You don't know me."

"I used to."

Miss Becka checks the tip of her cig. Rolled it too tight. Instead of lighting it back up, she slips it back in the flat tin case. "Maybe I just want to make sure Winston isn't up to anything that'll hurt anybody else."

JR pulls the handkerchief back around his face, hits the switch, ascends back into the sky, but then pauses it. "Miss Becka. You ain't tryin' to mess anything up are you? I can't stand to lose a job."

"Quit worrying."

JR shakes his head, starts up the air compressor. She can't believe it. JR washing a goddamn steeple.

Out on the highway, she keeps to the speed limit exactly. It's what she does when her nerves are going. Gets all precise and fussy. She parks in her turnaround and follows the trail down to her cabin. A long wall of stacked firewood four feet high lines the final stretch, with a brown tarp over it and stones and unsplittable knots holding it down. Glad she only has to hike this twice a day. Out of shape and getting old—it makes you wonder about things. You consider making plans. Well, you had a plan and you gave it away. Tomorrow you'll make a plan for tomorrow. That's the best we can do.

On the porch she squints through the trees at the river. The jon boat down there is tied to a trunk. The water is high, been rising all day, and seeing the boat being lifted and rocked between its holding-posts calms her down. She can feel her blood pressure dropping. Inside the cool darkness of her room, she sits down on the cot, unties her work shoes, sips water from the jar on the nightstand and lies down. Let's take a break before the rest of this continues.

NINE

Trucks and cars are parked along the shoulder in front of the Alcorn compound. A bunch of older folks are hanging out in the top lot, standing around and chewing and waiting for the auction to start. A wooden door ripped from its hinges leans against the open gate, spray-painted to read: BIGGEST AUCTION OF YEAR, COME SAY BYE DUSTY! BID ON FERRY, MORE.

JR pulls in the minivan, bumping off the highway and bouncing strutless through the gate.

"There goes security," says an old-timer.

"You think he'll stop?" says a woman wheeling an oxygen tank.

"If he's got brakes to," the man suggests.

Down on the lawn in front of the old mill, the wheels lock up and the van slides across the grass and skids through the crowd on the mud as neighbors scatter out of its path. Some youngsters jog alongside, laughing and kicking at the tires. Then the ground levels out and the van comes to a stop where the bonfire's smoking and crackling, the last of the apple tree up in flames, along with ancient scraps of cedar and pieces of unsellable furniture.

The missing side door reveals what's inside. All the seats have been taken out except for the front buckets, and in the back of the van is a church table with its legs folded under and pounds of fish filets wrapped in newspaper on top. James is crouched in the grass at the far end of the side yard and can see it all.

"Well well, Mr. Winsaton," JR says. "Where's the patriot soldier?"

"Hung the hell over." Winston thumbs sideways at the boys' house, and James drops into the tall grass. He doesn't need to see them, long as he can hear them. "He's in bed like a bitch," Winston says. "Nobody can get him up. Even tried a bucket of water."

JR climbs out of the van, goes around and unlocks Willy's door. "You try the bullhorn on him?"

"First thing I did. Fired off the siren. Nothing."

James hears some lady saying, "Ironic—that's the word." He recognizes the voice and looks up out of the grass to see Shelly standing there. And can't believe she's showing her face.

Winston takes the bullhorn up from between his feet. "Roost right up when the sun goes down, last one to cluck gets the whole round." He pulls it away from his lips and slings some spittle into the air. "Gimme some cash and I'll drop the stash. Sold as seen, not a refund to glean, if you know what I mean. Show it to me, show it to me, show it to me—hot—I like a purse full of cash or whatever you got."

The growing crowd gathers, anticipating further instructions from this lurid merchant.

"Biddy biddy one, biddy biddy two. Howdy do, howdy do. Start right here in a minute or two."

Scattered applause. The milling and talking resumes.

James crawls closer to Winston and JR.

"I been wondering about the ferry," JR says. "All that work we did on it?"

"Good hard work," Winston says. "Y'all worked hard and good."

"Well," JR says, "we never really got paid for it?"

"Somebody tell you to start complainin'?" Winston says. "Who?"

"Nobody," JR says. "Just thinkin' is all."

"Thinking's fine, just keep quiet while doing it. Like Willy. He's a good boy. I told you your work was an investment. I give you that van, didn't I?"

"Yessir," JR says, "a while ago."

"That don't matter shit," Winston says. "I'll take it back if you keep bitchin'."

"Yessir." JR nods. "But we're just workers, me and Willy."

"Hardly that," Winston says. "We're gonna hold this auction here, bid little Dusty fare-ye bye-bye, then we'll see where you and me are at."

"How much you think the ferry's gonna go for?" JR says. "We patched up that bottom and put a nice top on it, didn't we? Got all the electric wired. Didn't we? And the diesel runs strong."

Winston touches JR's shoulder with his rubber hand and nods as if in agreement with some faraway memory. "I'm thinkin' I might just keep it."

"But that wouldn't be sellin' it," JR says.

"Did I say I was gonna sell it?"

"Back when you hired me to work on it," JR says. "That's why we been workin' on it. To sell it. And that's what you been advertisin'."

Winston pulls his hand back as if bit by a copperhead.

"I don't remember that. This ferry's gonna stay right here, with me. Get it back to a useful purpose."

"Of being a ferry?"

"Something bigger," Winston says. "How about I let you and Willy help me operate it. We navigate the waters on it. Bring the message of our return. How's that sound?"

"Okay," JR says. "But Jesus said lyin's a sin."

"I think the message of the gospel spillin' out speakers from that boat goin' all up and down the river is just right," Winston says. "We can put signs on the sides and everything. No reason not to bring Jesus along with us into this. He walked on water, didn't he?"

"Course he did," JR says. "But you can't just have people doin' stuff for you and not pay 'em for it."

"I just agreed to your idea," Winston says. "I'm a man of compromise. I want to spread your good word far and wide."

"You mean it?" JR says. "Cause I know how we could reach more people than any speaker system ever could."

"I don't want nothing to do with the internet. They track you there."

"I'm talking about radio," JR says. "There's a transmitter sittin' in one of the piles. I could fix it. All you do is run a audio signal through a preamp and a modulator and power that out to a antenna. Then bang—the whole county's tunin' in. Next you know you're runnin' for office."

"I wouldn't say no to that," Winston says. "And we won't need a license because we're on the water."

"They won't be able to catch us," JR says. "Not after the engine I put on the back of that tub."

"We'll have us a little radio show kinda thing on the river. Broadcast to all the neighbors all your ideas about Jesus and the generals who fought around here who believed in him."

"You think it'll pay?" JR says.

"We'll take it all around, up and down," Winston says. "Into Lebanon and down onto the lake. Maybe even Nashville." He draws a dollar sign in the air with his rubber hand, almost as if making the sign of the cross.

"That's where the river goes?"

"All the way."

JR scans his surroundings like he just got hold of a key to the world. He goes over to the van and speaks to Willy.

"It winds a little bit gettin' there," Winston says. "But it'll get you there eventually. And there's all kinds of marinas and campgrounds down there all lookin' for entertainment."

"You're thinkin'," JR says, "like a genius."

"Write me a poem about it."

Willy sidles over next to JR. Even while he's slumped he stands taller than both men. He nods along to the movement of JR's finger writing across the skin of his palm as if there are new strange shapes emerging. Then JR speaks his poem: "We float the ferry, down the river, for their money."

"I like it," Winston says.

"How'll we get their money once we get there?" JR says.

"You'll recite your poems through the bullhorn," Winston says, "about the Lord's cavalry and General Winsaton. Then we'll *sell* your poems. We'll do some preachin', too. That's the one thing they ain't got down there. All that sin and no redemption? There's a demand for our services. Plus we'll bring all our junk. They like guitars down there. We got those. Guns too, many guns. But ultimately what they want from me is me, more and more of me, so that's what we can give 'em, really, more Winsaton."

"But how'll they pay us?"

"We'll be advertisin' it on the radio the whole way getting there. Then once we stop wherever we like, you and Willy start passin' a bucket around for offerings. I can only deal with cash. And for those out of immediate range, we'll have the broadcast station still running, always telling 'em where we are, where we're goin'. Voice of the people. Pirate radio."

"Can do," JR says. "We got all this stuff lyin' around here. You sure you don't want to add nothin' like Craigslist to any of this? We could do that, too."

"Maybe I'll try it, less there's too many questions and my subtleties don't come across."

"How big's the bucket gonna be?"

"Big as that pot on the fire there." He points to the cast-iron caldron over the coals. Next to it is an electric pan, fed by an orange extension cord and full of frying oil. Popping hot for something to drop in. "You'll take up a collection in it and keep it all. You and Willy both."

"All right then," JR says.

"And *my* payment," Winston says, raising his rubber hand to the sky, "will be with the Maker above. Plus a little auction talkin'." He rattles the bullhorn. "Sell them what they got, from the bottom to the top. Bid a dolla here, make a dolla there. Stand back and watch me make a circle turn square."

"Amen."

"A-men," Winston says. "Jesus did a lot of preaching from boats."

"Fishers of men," JR says.

"That's right," Winston says. "Now you and Willy go get to work. I ain't payin' you for *nothing*."

"Yessir!" JR salutes Winston like he's been taught to, then leads Willy by the arm up to the mill building where they'll be working the door.

James goes back down into the grass, face to the earth. He can see each blade shooting into the dirt. He finds a grasshopper and touches its striped leg. It jumps and flies away in the warm wet air.

Everything, always, away. James doesn't want Dustin to die. He closes his eyes. Last night was a long one. Let's just stay right here a second longer. Eyes closed. Breathe in the sun. Erase the thought.

The smell of wood smoke and frying fish wakes him up. He can taste it in the air and his stomach's an empty pit. All that drinking with Dustin. He lies there for a while longer in the sunlight. He can't believe there's a damn thing in the world worth anything enough to take a brother away from a brother. But Dustin's talked about leaving for what seems like forever, so it was only a matter of time, terrible time. In the yard, American flags and battle flags are hanging from poles and shuffling in the breeze. James wouldn't dare say a word to anybody here. Just let them keep thinking he's strong and proud of Dustin. Who can't even get out of bed right now.

Mandy is out at the fire pit, frying fish and greeting guests. "We're so happy," she keeps saying. "Just waiting for our hero to come out that door. Any minute now.

We're so happy." But the folks standing around sipping cold drinks are here only for the cookout and the auction. Winston struts chin up with his hands behind his back, greeting groups of people and hyping the piles of useless broken shit ready to be bid on. Some of it belongs to other folks, and some of it's his. All soon to be his profit and nobody else's.

And then there are the guns leaning back in guitar stands, the starting prices listed on little bright-colored tags and tape, all to be increased spontaneously by Winston and the sudden paranoid emotions of the bidders.

But there's a new attraction looming today: the old Rome Ferry. People who know boats keep asking how much it's going to go for, and Winston just says, "How much you got?"

"We'll see," they say. "We'll see."

And yes we will. James is interested to see how his old daddy gets himself out of all these expectations. The crowd will be pissed, least they ought to be.

It must be afternoon now. Everybody's drinking something except for Winston. He doesn't drink because it would muddle his sense of authority and make him look weak and talk like everybody else here. Keep them drunk and stupid and returning on Sundays to spend. That simple.

Mandy's pulling crispy filets out of the electric pan with metal tongs in her oven-mitted hand and placing them on paper plates covering the church table. Back and forth. She turns to the pot, puts in more, pulls out more. Ten bucks a plate and they're going fast.

James watches it all with an unsurprised understanding of Winston's pure genius at ripping people off. He's passionate about it and doesn't feel bad about it. James can see that. It's a natural gift the man possesses. And James, right here, is his son.

But where did all that fish come from?

Winston goes to the trashcan full of ice and cracks a couple of cans for some old boys standing around. James can't hear what he's saying, but he can guess. Chatting about the auction, building it up big, while everybody's getting buzzed.

He scans the scene for Shelly and finds her down by the tree line with some folks her age. Probably some friends from college, just hanging out. How's she have the nerve? This could all get out of hand real quick if Dustin wakes up. And speaking of, here he comes out the side door of their house and right past James. He's got one eye shut and doesn't even notice his little bro laid out in the grass like a snake. Some in the crowd start cheering and James ducks down.

Dustin wades through the grass with his arms held out and his fingers brushing the tips. Bugs and pollen and smoke form a wild halo around him in the hot glow. He stops and speaks to the crowd. "Last night," he says, "was a worldwind. You'll miss me more than I miss you. Now look at JR over there. He's like to massacure some booty while I'm gone."

Dustin's odd configurations of words have heads turning, but they make strange sense to James. His big bro's still drunk, and that makes him sound even more country.

"And Willy here?" Dustin says. "Dumber than dumb, supposubly. But I think he's got us all fooled. He knows, he knows. Now where's my breakfast? Gods peed."

JR hands him a popped beer, topped with a ring-slice of canned pineapple. "Here's to you," he says. "Cause nobody's like you and nobody likes you."

Dustin chugs the beer through the fruit hole.

"Looks like a hero to me," JR says. "Like he's back from the dead already."

Winston observes the conversation with his arms crossed.

Mandy comes over holding a handkerchief to her face. "Son a mine," she says. "So big and brave and... come, get some fish." She leads him over to the church table, where he dumps one plate onto another and eats. He's picking little bones out from between his teeth while chewing, and says, "What kinda catch is this? Skin's still on."

"That's fresh cleaned trout right there," JR says.

"Gettin' fancy," Dustin says. When his plate's empty, he walks over to the trashcan for another beer.

"Only the best," JR says. "Locally raised in fresh springwater."

Dustin's standing around the fire with a beer in each hand when the warped sounds of traveling music enter at the top of the yard. A three-piece string band on the bed of an El Camino, it cruises slowly down the grass with the musicians bouncing in the back. There's a mandolin, a guitar redeemed from Winston's last auction—the neon tape-tag still sticking off its neck—and an electric mini-bass with a battery-powered amp bungy-corded around the player's waist. It sounds like they're performing some version of "Dixie," except each player seems to be in his own unique key.

"Hell's this?" Mandy says.

"It's called en-ter-tain-ment," Winston says. "I'm paying them for it."

"Why?" Mandy says.

He studies her. "You take your medicine yet?"

She nods.

"Then act like it." He snaps his fingers at JR. "Come on, son. Show's about to start. Dance, you bastard!"

JR trips into a muddied flatfoot, arms swinging loose at his sides. Willy stands back and gazes through it all.

Winston takes up the bullhorn. "First in line is a couple of dimes, a pair of chairs, two lawn chairs, his and hers, blue and pink, Adam and Eve, how God made it be, his and hers, his and hers, make a holler spend a dollar, take 'em both only and never be lonely—biddy bid, biddy bid, biddy bid bid bid."

The crowd starts tightening around him now, waving hands and answering each price, not nearly as interested in the shit as in the seller selling the shit. "Starting right up with a ten biddy ten. Ten, ten, tenny ten—can I get a ten? Every rooster needs a little old hen."

"Ten for both," a woman yells.

"Ten on two, ten on two," he says. "Raise it by five and keep it alive."

"Five up," a man says.

"That'll make fitteen, how bout twunny? Twunny biddy twunny biddy, can I get a twunny? Ain't nothin' but a lill mo' money."

The woman waves a twenty-dollar bill.

"Twunny in the air, bidders beware. Take it higher still or leave it for the kill? Once, twice, three times the charm, SOLD to the lady with the golden arm."

She goes up to claim the chairs, and Winston brings her in close to him for an interview on the bullhorn.

"Can ya tell these folks here, such fine beautiful folks, about your most recent prize?"

"These chairs'll be perfect for me and my husband," she says. "When I get married one day."

"Ain't that sweet," he says. "And I'm sure you will, sugar. That's a lucky man who gets a front-row seat to you."

She blushes, folds the chairs up and carries them off.

The crowd follows Winston over to where the rifles and ammo are set up, and he begins with a bucket of hollow-point bullets. "Here we got some lead that could kill Death dead," he says. "The grim reaper himself tried to ban these off the shelf. Professionally homemade, military grade..."

James has heard enough. Keeping low, he crawdads backward into the house and chugs water directly from the kitchen faucet. It tastes as hard and minerally as the deep stone well from which it is pumped. Then he goes out to the porch and takes one of his poles, an ocean-worthy Ugly Stik Bigwater Shakespeare tricked out with thirty-pound test and a treble hook the size of a rooster foot. He follows the side trail down to the flood bottom where he hits the path that leads to the water.

He hikes downstream to that catalpa tree, greener than most, and starts collecting worms from under rocks. Carrying fistfuls of nightcrawlers, he goes back up the trail to his cottonwood, where he pops the points of the treble hook through their twisting wriggling bodies. A foot above the hook is a sink weight and he casts it all out, the hook and weight both spinning before splashing down into the river. He pushes a sycamore branch into the mud, rests his pole in the upturned fork and sits against a cottonwood's trunk. He'll wait here all day if he has to. When they ask him where he was for Dustin's party, he can tell them he was fishing, which is the truth.

A rustling comes up in the brush, and before he can turn to see what it is Flat's on top of him, licking his face and nibbling his ears. Breath smells like batter and slime, so JR's probably been feeding her fish heads. They play fight, the dog bowing and growling, then after a minute she curls up next to James and falls asleep. He waits like that for a long while, watching the line. The sun's now flickering sideways through the branches and casting a thick honey hue over everything. He puts a hand on Flat's side and can feel a dream running through her muscles.

The line pulls taut. He takes the rod up and tries reeling in, but whatever's on the other end is heavy and begins taking drag. Could it be a log down there? Or a coil of stray fencing rolling along the bottom? He's hooked both of those on trotlines, but this is just a treble with a sinker and some worms. He yanks back and sets the hook hard. Yeah, that's life on the other end, that low jittery tugging rhythm. It pulls out into the current and he begins guiding it while reeling in slack. And then a tailfin splashes, wide as a canoe paddle. The damn thing cruises back out into the middle and upriver against the current. He lets it take out more drag and when it stops he brings line back in. It goes on like this for a while—the fish coming in, then running straight out again. Once it goes downstream toward where a couple of sunk trees lurk, their wild root systems webbing ten feet out above the surface, this fish could tangle up in there and get gone. James leans on his heels and feels the fish out in the current again. The line slacks and when he takes it up, he sees the fish moving into the shallows, out of the stronger water and into a gentle place where it doesn't have to work so hard. It's getting tired.

When it starts turning and rolling, he sees this is a cat, a big damn cat. Let it be a blue.

Flat waits behind him on the bank like a good girl, whining and pacing, while James wades in up to his knees with the rod bent, trying to keep the fish from turning around again. Since he isn't using a swivel, the line could twist and snap at any point. No yanking now. Pull, gather line, pull, gather line, just gradual persuasion. It's a big one all right, and he won't try to bring it in any time soon. Need to wear this sucker down. His toes sink into the mud when he pulls back on it again and the line tightens and pulls him forward, deeper. The bank's slow on this side, so keep it right here. Any farther and you'll be chin deep with a throat full of trouble.

The water feels good on his sunburnt legs, though. The green Cumberland rippling around him and whirling away—a familiar dangerous invitation. When the line goes slack, James brings in more and more, keeping it tight so it doesn't get tangled or spit out.

When the whitish belly flashes to the surface, much closer than he expected, all the thinking goes away. Sometimes prayers do get answered. But when they do, as Winston's always warned him, they come with a price tag. And sure enough, when he brings the fish up to his side, as thick as his thigh, he hears the buzz of an outboard motor approaching. He puts his hand into the mouth of the catfish, careful to avoid the hook, and fingers his hand out through its open gill. The fish tries to shake him off, bulldogging its head right and left, but James holds on and drags it up onto the rocky mud bank.

He keeps his back to the water. He can hear the boat gearing down and coming up behind him. Winston has warned him never to talk to any warden, especially if it's about fishing the river, specifically their rightful stretch of it, which he's sectioned off himself with caution tape and orange cones. But when he turns around it's Miss Becka, her face in the slanted shade of a wide-brim hat and her eyes behind fishing glasses with polarized lenses the color of amber. She turns the motor off, glides in closer and lets the nose nudge into the shallows. "That's a big blue," she says. "Really nice one."

"It's all right," James says. In fact it's by far the biggest fish he's ever landed.

"Is she pregnant?" Miss Becka says.

"Who?"

"That's why she looks like that. Tight in the belly but with those short fins. Keeps her in the nest."

James studies the fish and it matches her description. "What made you so smart?"

"I stopped because I wanted to see the auction," she says. "When's your dad planning on selling my ferry?"

"He ain't gonna sell it," James says. "He's gonna keep it, just using it as bait."

Miss Becka looks upriver toward the little tributary inlet where the ferry now floats. After a decade of it being jacked up on the bank, it's strange to see it there, so still, the fresh paint job reflected in the green glassy water. It is magnificent. "What's he gonna do with it?"

"Put in a little radio station for advertising and float his auction up and down the river."

"Radio? How's he gonna do that?"

"JR's gonna help. I heard them talking about it." James wrestles the fish and rolls it like a log up the bank, covering its slimy sides in dirt and leaves. The gills are opening and closing, the fins waving and turning like fragile little hands.

Winston's voice, flat and battery-powered, is echoing over the water as he comes down to the ferry. "Folks, gather round now, for the biddy biddy why and the biddy biddy how, kick it right off with the lost and found: we got a pretty lady coat, a little lady coat, for a pretty little lady—chicky chicky dink, collar and cuffs lined with mink, how bout fitty, starting at fitty. Biddy biddy fitty, biddy biddy fitty. Do I hear fitty? Yeah, we got fitty. Sold and done, sold and done, pick it right up and gimme your mun."

Faint clapping. A couple of drunken hollers. "Wins-a-*ton*! Wins-a-*ton*!"

"That's a keep-'er-warm, folks," he says. "And there's more where that come from. Next up we got..."

"I saw a lot of cars out in front of the place when I was driving home," Miss Becka says. "All these folks showed up for the ferry."

"Why do you care?" James slips off his belt and loops it like a stringer into the fish's mouth, feeding the end through the buckle and pulling it tight. "I'm about sick of hearing about it."

"So why's he been advertising that the boat's up for auction if he isn't going to sell it?" she says.

"Brings more people out. The yard's full, front and back."

"It used to be my family's," she says.

"Maybe that's why he's keeping it." The catfish has turned itself against James's shoe, sliming the laces. "He's a history kinda guy, you know."

"And he's got it all backward," she says. "How old are you, anyway?"

"Sixteen," James says.

More noise from the auction, announcing, some cheering, a gun being discharged. "Fires good just like it should... gimme your best and forget the rest..."

"All those people hoping to get a deal," Miss Becka says, "while in the end they're just making Winston more money."

"You got it." James grabs the belt and begins dragging the catfish behind him up the path. "See you. I gotta go earn my keep."

"Wait," Miss Becka says.

James stops and looks back, a trail of glistening fish slime behind him.

"The mill?" she says. "And all that land? Even your house? It used to be mine."

"So?"

"And you want to know how he got it? Ask him about his hand sometime."

"You're full of shit."

"Ask him," she says.

James drags the catfish up the trail and across the yard until he stops at a circle of men hanging out around the above-ground pool. It smells like cigarettes and bleach up here. A couple dogs are swimming and chasing a basketball that some kid in the pool keeps tossing. Winston never let James or Dustin swim in there because "it's for payin' customers." Flat's down on the warm wet ground with James, sniffing the fish and jumping back when it slaps its tail. Winston and JR stand at the center of the circle with Willy behind them, talking about who bought what and who didn't but wanted to. "One man's trash is another man's treasure," Winston says.

"Yeah," JR says. "Yours."

"Tell me who in the county offers such a variety."

"Walmart," says an old-timer.

"Except them."

"Only you," JR says. "Ain't no other competition."

"It's hardly any kind of competition, either," Winston says. "I've got stuff and they've got stuff. But they ain't got *me*."

Willy turns to see what James has dragged up from the river, murmurs something, a thought bubbling up from his inner world and breaking the surface of his silence. The men quit talking.

"Say what?" JR says.

Willy says it again, a round-shaped word beginning and ending with an M. He points at James.

"What you got there?" JR says.

"This's a blue catfish," James says. "Prize winner, too."

Winston steps over and inspects it. "This auction just got a little more interesting. What you say, James? You wanna turn some profit?"

James notices Shelly and Dustin standing beyond the gathering crowd. She's whispering something into his ear and he's leaning in to hear it, his mouth open and his eyes sunken. When she's done saying whatever it is, she steps back and he stays there shaking his head.

JR brings out a pocket knife. "Let's strip her jammies off, then sell the meat."

"Dustin," Winston calls. "Bring your pistol over."

"No." James pulls the fish away.

"Get it in the oil," Winston says. "Sell it for double what they would at Cooksey's. Freshly caught, never store bought." He brings up his bullhorn. "Biddy biddy one, biddy biddy two—fish on land, dollar in hand."

Now James spots Shelly again, this time on a different side of the crowd and closer to him, looking worried. Of a sudden he sees her as he saw her last night. Skin shaped by nighttime shadows. That inward-pressing point between her thighs. He tried to forget about that. But he sees her.

Beware. Do not enter. Big brothers only.

"Why're you here?" he calls to her.

"Where'd Dustin go?"

"You tell me," James says. "You were just with him."

A loud bang behind him makes them both duck. The men start cheering again and he's still looking at Shelly. She's covering her mouth in surprise. James turns to see Winston standing over his catfish with the pistol in hand. A powdered smoking spot between the animal's wide-set eyes. It twists and pushes out a mass of jellied eggs. James drops the belt and steps back. Shelly's turned away from him now, facing a couple of friends she's here with.

"I said why're you here?"

"Guys," she says. "This is James. Son of the man who just shot that fish."

"What're you doing here?" he says. "Why're you back?"

"I'm sorry for what I said last night," she says. "I just came because I wanted to see Dustin."

"I don't believe you."

"Then that's *your* problem, isn't it?"

Her friends are a lady her age and a guy much older wearing glasses. From the college. That much is clear. They're both looking at James and then the fish.

"I swear," Shelly says. "I just wanted to talk with him."

"Any luck with that?" James says.

"I mean, not really. But I said what I said."

The older guy pats Shelly's shoulder.

They all quit talking when Dustin takes the gun back from Winston. He pours beer from a can onto the fish's head. The whiskered face seems to come alive, moving back and forth, gills flaring, like it's trying to swim, like it wasn't just shot.

"Look at him," Shelly says. "Look at him not looking at me. Pretending I'm not here."

"Shelly, you don't need this," the old guy says. "I think we should go. This is getting dangerous."

"I forgot you were even here, dude," James tells him.

"Come on, Shelly," the guy says.

James would love to hate Shelly right now, but he hates this guy even more. Shelly's just under his control. That's what they do in those old brick buildings—control you. "Why're you with him?" James says. "Why're you talking to him?"

"He's my teacher," she says. "Look, I'm worried about Dustin. And you. Y'all don't have to be like this. You're better than this."

"It's too late for all that." But James can sense something: here she is, here he is, the future's wild and unwritten, yet they're both bound together in it. He doesn't know what his responsibility is to her, or what hers is to him, only that it's there. Because they're here.

"You know what," she says. "Forget it. If he doesn't want me, I don't want him. Let's go, guys. Shit's getting crazy around here."

"Where y'all going?" James says.

"Cute," Shelly says. "*Now* he wants to play."

"I'll get Dustin to listen to you. But without them here."

"He can't listen," Shelly says. "That's the problem. And I don't want to hear Winston auction off a dying fish."

Over by the pool, the catfish is fanning its fins and slapping around weakly in the mud, pushing and smearing the eggs around. Somebody has given Dustin a capless bottle of Fireball. He lifts it to his mouth, swishes, gurgles, and swallows. His face is glazed and shining. "This fish is gonna be fine," he says. "Nothing to see here. Good and fine."

"Not in front of the families," Winston says, and knocks the bottle out of his son's grip. Dustin looks at Winston like he doesn't recognize him. He pulls a ten-dollar bill out of his pocket, hands it to his father, then bends down and picks the bottle back up. "Come on," he tells James, and goes dragging the fish away back down toward the river.

Willy makes the sound again, and JR says, "What you gonna do with it? Let's fry it, huh?"

James follows his brother and the fish, pausing halfway while Dustin tips the bottle up again. He doesn't want to come up on him too quick.

When they're down on the river path, James shouts, "Hey now!" but Dustin keeps on going. The air down here near the water is thick with the smell of late-afternoon honeysuckle and mulched fields. Dustin gets on his knees with the fish in the water and slides the belt out of its mouth. "It's just me and you now," he says to the fish. "Don't you worry none." He takes another drink and crawls forward. "Soon we'll have you right where you need to be. And me too."

Free from the belt, the fish floats belly-up out in the darkening water. The wind has moved the clouds in and little waves are making the current look like it's running backward. Dustin goes out deep, the water up to his chest, and pushes the fish back and forth. "Trying to wake up the gills."

James can't tell if he's drunk-crying, doesn't want to know. Winston has brought the crowd down to the ferry and is shouting through the bullhorn, raising the price higher and higher with every bid so nobody can buy it. And up past the ferry and the auction crowd, he can see Miss Becka in her boat. Looks like she's bringing in the anchor, and now pulling at the motor.

"Hey," James calls, "I'm taking the canoe. Let's go out."

"Nah." Dustin continues working on the fish. "I'm leaving tonight."

"We won't be seeing each other for a while," James says. "You hear me? One last ride."

The fish slaps its tail. Dustin's hands come out of the water and he backs away wobble-legged. "It worked! That fucker's gone! Alive and gone!"

The sun's settling between the hills, down into a

blurring bath. James takes the tarp off the canoe, flips it and pulls it into the water by the yellow nylon rope tied to its nose. Throws an extra paddle in, just in case. He's about to push off the bank when Dustin yells at him to wait a sec and comes stumble-splashing toward him.

"Yeah," James says, "but I caught it."

"It can't be killed," Dustin says, "because it doesn't want to die."

"I saw."

"You tried to kill it. Winston did too. Everybody tried to kill it. But they couldn't." His bloodshot eyes match the sun behind him. "Only me can kill me."

"You ain't gonna do that," James says, "cause you don't really want to." He walks out until the canoe's keel-line is up to his knees. Swings one leg over and sits down in the bow-seat facing the stern.

Dustin wades over and takes hold of the side. "Winston made these plans for me," he says. "I didn't have no choice. None."

"Yeah you did," James says. "You been talking about it forever. You had a thousand choices."

"Not like you do. Because you got this." He taps James on the head. "We're different."

"He doesn't believe in me like he does in you."

"Exactly," Dustin says. "Exactly. And that's a good thing for you." Dustin slaps the side of the canoe and pushes it upstream. "Just be careful with him. And JR and Willy. They're all fucking crazy."

And that's it. James looks back once, maybe to say bye, but the sight of Dustin standing there already feels like a memory. The river's near motionless up here among the trees, and James paddles on. The little folded waves moving with the easterly wind make him feel like he's gliding along at a high speed. It all feels like he's going faster than he really is.

TEN

Miss Becka's anchored just upstream from the auction, listening to Winston blare through his bullhorn as bets are placed on her family's historic river craft. Every time somebody takes the price up higher, Winston tops it with an absurd amount until the reality becomes clear: he's going to buy it from himself, right in front of all these people, with the money they just paid him for someone else's miscellaneous junk. It's an absurd situation, but they go along with it because of Winston's odd gift for keeping the attention on himself and nobody else. And as much as Miss Becka hates it, here she is—still listening to him.

She hangs out here until the sun smolders behind the hills and leaves the sky glowing and folded across the water. Down past the ferry, she sees Dustin wading into the river, and James bringing out a canoe. The separate directions and dysfunction of the entire family is complete in this vision of those two right here. How will they ever be brothers again? And why's she even worried about it? Maybe because she holds the answers to the escape they both deserve and therefore finds herself inadvertently complicit, inextricably linked, no matter how far they go. She brings her anchor up, then pulls the starter rope on the Evinrude. The recoil unit inside catches and coughs, and the current floats her closer down to the auction. Now it's just the sound of people leaving. She pulls the cord again, continues drifting, primes the motor, adjusts the carburetor knob for a richer fuel mixture, pulls again and it starts. She makes a wide, leaning U-turn in the river and gets heading eastward against the current and into the cooling air and darkening night. After a dozen river miles in under thirty minutes, she passes beneath the highway bridge and holds right into the mouth of the Caney Fork. She checks the fuel tank—still heavy enough—and buzzes back upstream at full-throttle. She never stays out on the water this late, when a floating tree trunk could be disastrous, but it's exhilarating to race through the night after completing her spy job. She hums a harmony to the drone of the motor. She can almost hear her father in it.

When she spots her parking boulder ahead, marked with white paint, she goes a little past it, shuts the motor off and lets the current bring her home. She can smell freshly released dam water in the evening air. Plus the gasoline from her engine. If you can ignore the environmental impacts for a second, there are no sweeter scents.

Before getting out, she checks her phone. It's supposed to rain tonight, so instead of tying the boat to the beech trunk she hooks the deck-plate rope to the winch-cable, monkey-arms herself across the aluminum gunwales, steps cautiously from the bow as it lifts from the relief of her weight and makes it out in a gitty-hop. Gonna break your ankle one of these days, old girl.

Normally she doesn't let her phone predict the weather—the clouds have that covered—but she's been scanning it every ten minutes, waiting to hear if Shelly's called. Nothing yet.

She goes up to where the winch is bolted to her untreated porch and cranks the handle. Like magic, the boat comes sliding up toward her. Rocks and sticks scrape its underside until she has it about fifteen feet above the bank. The water shouldn't get anywhere near that high tonight, but this is the only way she'll be able to fall asleep.

She huffs up each step and drops herself into the rocker, too tired to bend over and untie her boots. The night calms her, with a cool wind blowing in. With her eyes closed, she can hear the day-things quieting down and the night-things waking up. Then she hears leaves crunching on the side trail.

"Miss Becka?" a voice says. "You here?"

The little solar-powered security lamp clicks on and there's Shelly. "Well, howdy," Miss Becka says.

"Sorry," Shelly says. "I don't mean to interrupt."

"You aren't. I just got back."

"I know. I saw you at the auction. Out there in your boat."

"What a shit-show that was, huh?"

"I thought so," Shelly says. "I guess a lot of people like listening to how crazy that lunatic can get. They would do anything for him."

"I hope that's not true."

"I just went to say goodbye to Dustin." Shelly adjusts her bra. "Tell him a little something I think might be going on."

"Okay?"

"We had a fight." she says. "And when I got there today he was drunk. Or drunk again."

"It isn't your fault," Miss Becka says. "That family does it to itself."

"But for some reason I feel it's my responsibility." She pauses. "Can I come up?"

"Of course you can."

Shelly steps up onto the porch and says, "Sweet pad."

"Take that chair." Miss Becka lights tea candles on the little table between them. "So what's this thing that's going on?"

"Well," Shelly says, "I think I might be, you know. I haven't told many people."

"Your parents?"

"Hell no. They're hardcore Christians. Sent me to Cumberland specifically because they thought something like *this* wouldn't happen *here*."

"Where there's an Alcorn there's always a way. Winston is an insidious man. So are his insidities."

"Dustin and James are different, though. At least I think they are—or could be. I mean, I thought they were. Maybe they still can be."

"I know. Look, I'm sorry. I shouldn't get in it. So why'd you come here tonight?"

"I told you I was going to. And also because they were having a fish fry at the auction. And that guy JR kept saying he knew the best hole around."

"What kind of fish was it?"

"Trout," Shelly says.

"Fried trout?"

"That's what he said."

"I saw James pulling a catfish out of the river a little earlier. Couldn't it have been that?"

"No, James brought that up later. Then Winston

shot it with Dustin's homemade pistol-thing and then tried auctioning it off."

"Jesus H," Miss Becka says. "Course he did. So things *haven't* changed over there. They're just getting worse."

"I heard JR say something about you giving him permission to take some fish." Then she adds, "It was a whole load of trout."

"I didn't give anybody jack shit." Miss Becka gets up. "I'll be right back."

She takes her headlamp out of her vest pocket and follows the trail up to the spring-fed pool. At night the hemlocks smell of lemon rind. This is a grove she keeps alive. Most hemlocks in the state were killed by little sap-sucking bugs, but she keeps hers safe and healthy. They purify her spring and keep her trout safe and healthy. She walks through the trees until she can hear the water rippling and bubbling over the rocks. When her light hits the pond, she sees the net has been thrown over one side of the frame and there are muddy tracks across the moss. And then what's usually a thick swarm of smooth, shiny trout bodies now shows just a flash here and there in an otherwise dark empty pool.

Motherfucker JR must've netted them, that fucker of mothers.

When she gets back, Shelly's looking at her phone. "What's up?" she says.

"Looks like somebody borrowed a few fish," Miss Becka says. "No big deal."

"I have to admit I ate a little. I'm sorry."

"Well. But thanks for telling me."

"That's not really why I came, though."

Miss Becka can tell that Shelly's about to get into the heavy stuff, whether either one of them is ready for it or not. "Would you like some water or something?"

Shelly nods, staring off into the dark.

Maybe it's Miss Becka's imagination, but she can smell it coming off her: a motherly scent, gamey, feline, mushrooms, tree bark, belly-blood, ancestral oils seeping through her young body. Shelly keeps adjusting her bra. "You seen a doctor yet?" Miss Becka says.

"No. I figured you might know some stuff."

"And you can't talk to your mother?"

"I just told you," Shelly says. "And my father yelled at me one time when he found a box of tampons in the bathroom. He didn't want to have to see that in his own house, said they take your virginity."

Miss Becka shakes her head. "Men."

"They're not all bad," Shelly says. "My professor's cool. He says I have natural talent, and I'm trying to pursue that. But sometimes it makes me feel guilty, you know? Like I'm leaving behind what made me?"

Miss Becka bends over and picks at her double-knotted boot laces. These boots need to come off her feet. So another old washed-up professor paying too much attention to a female student. We've seen that movie before. "I need to get these boots off," Miss Becka says. "What's your professor's name again?"

"Professor Anders."

"Didn't he write about himself in the paper? Bragging about how he's teaching a course on the environment?"

"We call him Andy. He's an expert on stuff like this." She motions to the front porch and everything surrounding it. Miss Becka's life. "He writes about, you know, real stuff."

"I'm sure he does."

"But honestly," Shelly says, "I only really wanted your advice."

"So why don't you just ask for it?"

"Okay, first thing, my parents can't know about this. And nobody at school either. So please don't talk about it to anybody. I did tell Dustin because I thought he should know. But that's all."

A moth flutters crazily between them and lands on Shelly's shirtsleeve. "My parents' church has those signs out front?" she says. "How the number of dead unborn babies are more than the dead US soldiers in Iraq and Afghanistan combined."

"Makes it sound safer over there."

"Right?" she says.

"Why're you telling me? You hardly know me."

"Because you're old. I mean, in a good way. Like a hippie?"

"Winston's older than I am. Go talk to him."

"As freakin' if."

Becka opens her cigarette case and offers one to Shelly.

"I'm probably not supposed to be smoking," she says.

Miss Becka lights hers off the little tea candle and exhales. "You're actually gonna keep it?"

The noise of early nighttime is dwindling, crickets and cicadas and frogs winding down. Wind's pushing the treetops around and it's starting to smell like a shower's coming. Maybe her phone was right.

Shelly shakes her head. "Do you know any doctors around here I could talk to? Just to get an idea?"

"Sure. As long as *you're* sure."

"I want to stay in school," she says. "I have to."

"Excuse me for saying this, but I also think it'd be good to put a stop to their madness." Miss Becka stands up. "Let me get you that water. Or how about some tea? Fresh mint tea."

"Whatever you're having."

Inside, while waiting for the water to boil, Miss Becka takes off her boots and the pine floor feels good beneath her feet. She stuffs mint sprigs into a couple of mugs, pours in the boiling water and brings them back out.

Shelly takes her cup in both hands and blows into it. "This smells good."

"Apple mint," Miss Becka says. "Grows wild near the old outhouse. Makes good juleps, too."

"You got whiskey?"

"I like your style. I've got some if you want some."

"I think we know how this goes."

"All right then." Miss Becka fetches a jar of her favorite stuff, nice clear moonshine, and holds it out to Shelly. "You first."

"Okay." Shelly pours some into her tea. "Me first."

ELEVEN

Miss Becka's boat isn't between its posts when he comes up the Caney under the overgrowth. Something wild in the water here. Maybe the dam's releasing, or maybe it's raining farther upriver. James sits in his canoe, shuts off the little electric outboard and watches the waves splash against the snaky roots on the bank. Doesn't seem to be rising too fast.

He and his brother used to fish around here, Dustin always told tales about the witch who lived on the hillside. When he finally understood who he was talking about, it all started coming together.

He puts one foot out onto the bank and stands up. The overgrown bramble's obstructing his view, but when he leans right or left he sees flickering on Miss Becka's porch, probably candles. He smacks his thigh to make sure he's got his phone.

He crawls through slick mud and grasses onto a gradual rise with taller trees. In Miss Becka's yard, he pushes forward on his belly toward the porch and stops behind some old stone wall. Sneaking around never showed him anything this good before: Shelly and Miss Becka sitting there having tea.

"Me first," Shelly's saying.

Seems like Miss Becka's encouraging her to talk, like she's interested in helping her make something secret happen. James can keep a secret. Yes, he can.

"He did a favor for me once," Miss Becka says, "when I dearly needed it. Right in the clinic. Everything was clean. I was impressed. He was quick and efficient. I woke up with a couple of supportive women sitting there beside me. The man knows what he's doing."

"Was it your first time?"

"First and only," Miss Becka says. "I was probably ten years older than you are. But still."

"You won't tell anybody?"

"Not a soul," Miss Becka says. "Nobody needs to know. Nobody *can* know."

James is listening carefully. No, we won't tell nobody.

A squall sweeps in and the rain makes it hard for him to hear anything. But he's heard enough. The rain keeps falling as he squiggles back to his canoe and floats all the way down to the Cumberland.

When he finally gets home, lights are on in his folks' doublewide but Winston's Dodge dually is gone and he's probably taking Dustin wherever he's going.

On Dustin's bed there's a smooth oval spot where his duffel bag was sitting. The room still smells like his brother, liquor and puke, and a few of his things are lying around the room. Flat's curled up in the corner and won't even come to him when he whistles. Then he spots a small black safety case on the pillow and he knows what that is. He thumbs the hard-plastic snap open and there on the eggshell foam is the stubby homemade pistol that got Dustin kicked out of school. His now.

He takes it out and aims at his shadow on the wall, then spins around and aims at the light on the ceiling. "Who's there?" he says. Nobody.

It's so quiet in here, too much empty space, but the weight of the pistol in his hand makes him feel less alone.

TWELVE

Early in the morning after the auction, Winston drives Dustin into Nashville with Mandy behind them in the back part of the cab. They enter the city limits and the bright lights begin flashing in a bunch of different colors. Winston's clutching the wheel, squinting ahead like he's chasing a dream, looking older than ever with wrinkles clawing his face. A stranger could take him for Mandy's father.

When they pull up in front of the bus station, Mandy says, "My boy, my boy."

"He'll be back," Winston says. "Somehow, someday."

"We'll see," Dustin says.

"You be careful," she says.

"You got the papers they give you?" Winston asks.

"Sure, yeah. I got 'em."

"Finally making the family proud." Winston's still staring through the windshield, but his eyes are all lit up. "Infantry. At Fort Benning. Just like I did."

"Right."

Dustin gets out of the truck and slams the door shut with a little extra juice, while his mother stays in the backseat. He grabs his duffel bag out of the bed and tips his cap at them like in a cowboy movie. He's still drunk. He gets his ticket scanned, waits in line.

More than a week ago, after that final baseball game, and without telling anybody, Dustin drove himself to the recruitment center in Mt. Juliet. They asked him some questions, did a background check and gave him a general comprehension test, which he passed. A few days after that, the recruitment officer picked him up in Carthage and drove him to a motel outside Nashville, then before daybreak the next morning brought him to MEPS, where he took the official ASVAB test, more basic knowledge stuff, which he also passed. He identified his specialty as infantryman and submitted his application. He waited a few days, then went back to MEPS, where he did the duckwalk in front of a certified medical specialist.

He got more shots than he had in his whole life. He reviewed his application one more time with a counselor, who agreed the infantry was a good choice for him. He selected some dates, swore his oath and got assigned to basic training. Now here he is, on his way to Fort Benning.

It's going to be an eight-hour ride down to Columbus, so he might as well get comfortable. He finds a window seat, falls asleep with the AC blasting him in the face and wakes up to a lady shaking his shoulder.

"You're snoring," she says.

"Infantry," he tells her.

"Pee-ew." She fans the air with her hand. "Do you mind?"

"Thank me for my service."

He pulls his cap down over his eyes and leans back into the rhythm of the road. This whole trip is on the military's dime, which is pretty sweet. He's never traveled much because he never had the dough. But check him out now.

At the Columbus bus station, he waits in another line and boards the military shuttle. He spots a few other country boys, baseball caps with bent bills pulled low over their faces, and lots of black kids from Atlanta. When they get to the fort, the sun's a small white dot high above the compound.

A drill sergeant, in one of those Smokey the Bear hats, boards the shuttle and tells them all to get out and start doing jumping jacks. "Get off my bus," he says. "Y'all smell like shit."

The rest of the day is a bunch of running around and following directions and getting yelled at. Doing pushups as punishment for this and that. He's still dizzy and hungry from his hangover. "This one right here," the drill sergeant says, looking at him. "He's going to be a problem."

When everybody has to pick out a battle buddy, Dustin finds himself alone. Nobody wants to buddy with him. Not a single person out of the entire reception battalion. He finally gets paired with a kid who immediately reports him for smelling of alcohol.

The drill sergeant comes over, sniffs the air in front of Dustin's face and tells him to dump his duffel bag out. When he can't find anything, he says next time this happens they'll give him a piss test. In front of the other privates, women included, to demonstrate to them the effects of alcoholic shrinkage. "Do you understand me?" he says. "Female privates will be forced to witness your privates."

Everybody laughs.

"Now what's your problem?" the drill sergeant says. "Why're you just standing there? Don't you want to smile and show off those pretty teeth of yours?"

Dustin clenches his mouth shut.

"Your feelings are suddenly apparent. Make sure that never happens in front of me again. We don't need your attitude here." He crouches down, rummages through Dustin's bag and takes his phone. "You'll get this back when you start smiling for us."

During the rest of the week, it's just more of the same bullshit. The second week moves into the first phase of basic: physical exams and exercise, memorization of core values, plus rifle knowledge—the one thing he's decent at. After three weeks, he takes a test that he barely passes. The next phase is mostly marksmanship. He likes running around and shooting and rolling and stabbing fake bodies. The third and final phase incorporates everything he's been studying—a couple months of mind-draining drills and endless running. His stomach starts to flatten and tighten. If Shelly could see him now. He still doesn't have his phone, but that doesn't matter because there isn't anybody to call or send pics of his new abs to. He's in this alone. He wants to come out of this a new person with no past. Unrecognizable to everyone, even to himself.

One day toward the end of training, while standing at the toe-line in his barracks, that same sergeant calls him out and asks why his boots are untied.

"Because I didn't tie them, Drill Sergeant."

Some guys down the line snicker, and the sergeant gets up in Dustin's face.

"Start pushing," he says. "Fifty."

Dustin drops and gives fifty. When he gets up, the sergeant asks how many he did.

"Fifty," Dustin says.

"How do I know you're not lying?"

"Because I just did them in front of you."

"I wasn't counting," the sergeant says. "Were you?"

"Yeah," Dustin says. "I did fifty."

"I didn't hear you counting. Do them again and count them out loud. I want you to count each one. Now push."

Dustin does them again, but skips the counting. He can hear the people in line shuffling around and whispering, wondering what the fuck he's doing. When he stands up, the sergeant asks again how many he did and Dustin tells him fifty. Then he gets even closer to his face, and Dustin can smell shaving cream and coffee.

"There's a reason why nobody here likes you," the drill sergeant says.

"It's because I ain't like any of 'em," Dustin says.

"A snowflake. How about that?"

"And I definitely ain't like you."

"I thank Jesus Christ for that every single day. So does my wife. You're the most disliked person in here. It's quite an accomplishment."

And it's true, they all hate him. In his bunk at night, he imagines popping off rounds from a high-up hidden place and just watching them scatter and run for cover. So right here, right now, finally, in front of his bunk in the barracks, he decides he isn't doing this bullshit anymore. "I been following orders from a buncha fucking fools."

The drill sergeant's head tilts and makes a sound like leather tightening. "You don't want to leave like this," he says. "The quickest way out is through. Not around, not away. Just through."

"That's what your wife told me," Dustin says. He's in charge now. It makes him smile for the first time since getting here.

"Somebody ought to have straightened those teeth out for you a long time ago," the sergeant says.

And Dustin jabs him straight in the nose.

Instructors and privates rush him, pin him down and wait for the military police to get there. Lots of breathing and cussing and hard knees into his back. They get the cuffs on him, lift him up and walk him across the hard dry lawn toward the stockade. One of the female officers behind him says, "Don't you understand your career's over? Before it even began?"

"Story of my life," he says.

"I'll bet. Keep moving."

He's relieved when they open the cell door and he walks in. He's about to have some time in here to think things over. He doesn't want to go to Iraq or Afghanistan and kill people. He won't with this group. Not with any group. All he's got to do is make sure Winston never finds out about any of this. Take some time to figure out his new plan and keep it hid. Then he'll be fine.

In his solitary cell, the light's always on and never goes out. Nobody answers any of his questions, not even to tell him what time it is. He can't really sleep and he can't really stay awake. After a few days, maybe a week, the dull pain behind his eyes is almost comforting. He stops eating, which gives him a feeling of control over something again. He has the power to make his body shrink at his will. He can step outside of it and watch it.

He starts seeing things. Visions of battle. Of a war older than he is. Winston's somewhere in it, on a horse and above everybody else. Half-monument, half-man. He's yelling "Charge!" and pointing at the enemy with his rubber hand.

When they finally let him take a shower, he inspects the little bottle of Freshscent Baby Shampoo and reads the label. Tearless? Let's see about that. He pops the plastic cap off, tilts his head back and pours it straight into his right eye. He scrubs and scratches with his fingers, the soap foaming and running down into his mouth until he can taste his own blood.

He can hear himself laughing and screaming. Some guards rush in and grab him up off the floor. He hears them saying something about suicide watch. He tells them he's trying, he's trying. The visions are becoming clearer.

And finally he's able to see what Winston's been talking about for so long.

THIRTEEN

It wasn't always all work and no play. Back when Miss Becka's father used to take her out past the tracks and down into the floodplains to shoot clay pigeons, they'd sing country duets together while they walked, pretty old-fashioned stuff he loved: the Carter Family, the Monroe Brothers—especially those guys, Charlie and Bill. "Coonhound country," the old man called it, and she never was sure if he was referring to the place it came from, the people who made it or just the music itself. She asked him once about those distinctions, and he clasped his hands together, in some self-styled form of rugged prayer, and said, "One an' same, darlin,' one an' the same."

Those old family harmonies were bound by blood. You could hear it. And while singing with her father, she sometimes could find the magical vibrating closeness that she heard on his records, within which a phantom voice would emerge, a third presence, something turning the duo into a trio, a trinity almost holy—father, daughter, holy ghost—and proof that classic country was nothing short of alchemy.

Though she'd never shot anything living in her life, she had the sense from an early age that she might one day. She would, if she had to. Her father had taught her how, down there while singing near the river, a good place to learn the factual strategies of killing. How to load, cock, aim, fire, repeat. Otherwise, what was the gun and knowing how to use it good for? Her life became a strange sort of murder-mystery in waiting. The question not being who done it, but when she would finally do it.

As she got older, she was able to ignore that mystery of violence by reading books. She was able to escape certain inevitabilities of her own life here in this country—an odd yet irrevocably familiar place where everyone, even family members sometimes, seemed hell bent on eventually murdering one another—by going into imaginary worlds where words put order to chaos, where ideas and language were the ultimate currency. In books, she loved how everything was structured and in place, one word after the next. So satisfying.

When she went to college, her father warned her not to get above her raisin'—another of his bluegrass sayings that she would fully understand only years later—and so she stayed close to home, right here in Lebanon, enrolling at Cumberland University. Nonetheless she ended up elevating herself past the point of no return. Once you got up on that high horse of books and grades, it was impossible to get down. And it was there at the old university that Miss Becka rejected guns altogether, deciding that firearms were ultimately antithetical to a life of learning. Maybe they were the root of all modern problems everywhere. That's how far she took it. The belief hardened her and shifted her away from her father's traditions. She stopped going shooting with him. And in doing so, she was able to ignore the pull of what he had taught her.

Looking back on that change in her life, which she can only do through a side-eyed half-glance of shame and guilt, she regrets neglecting her father. It's too late to go back and make up for lost time, but there must be a path that leads back to those early roots of singing with him.

He'd been in slow decline ever since her mother's death, and because of that Miss Becka took over his cedar sawmill business. Not long after, they found him in bed, not really responding. It was a stroke, and she ended up taking him to live at the Second Wind Nursing Home.

Then Winston Alcorn showed up with his family and did what he did at what was for Miss Becka a moment of vulnerability. She was in the process of learning to let go of a lot of things. But she shouldn't have let the mill go like that. It should've been on her terms, not Winston's.

But what were those terms, and what are they now? That's what she's been trying to decide for more than a decade. Sometimes when she's particularly confused, she finds herself singing one of those old tunes—"What Would You Give In Exchange?"—in search of a higher harmony.

But that old habit hasn't been doing her much good lately, especially considering how Winston's been running his radio show on the ferry, what all he's been talking about and how many folks are getting riled up about it. He's been advertising his junk auctions, like always, while also going on about local politics, particularly regarding the Confederate Hatton Monument in Lebanon's town square. He raves about it's importance, talks about the old battles like they're currently happening and keeps daring people to just try to take that statue down. Almost like he wants it to happen.

This afternoon she's at the Bomb Shelter, getting the bar organized and ready to open. She hums in the quiet while restocking bottles and wiping down the counter. Once all that's done, she brings the lights up and turns the TVs on. The flatscreens show men arguing about sports. She doesn't care about any of that, but she knows what helps sell beer.

There's a long window beside the entrance door that looks over the back gravel parking lot. Through it she watches a little red pickup truck pull in and park. She knows whose that is. But didn't Dustin leave already?

Let's look busy when whoever it is walks in. She goes to the closet behind the bar, takes out a couple twelve-packs of Miller Light longnecks and sets them next to the cooler below the taps. When the young man walks in, she says, "We open in one hour."

"Sorry," he says. "But I'm looking for a job. If there is one."

And as soon as he says it, she recognizes him. "James Alcorn."

"Miss Becka," he says.

"Unemployment must run in your family," she says. "It's genetic with y'all."

"That's what I'm trying to fix."

"I gave your daddy a job once and he took everything." She snaps her fingers. "Just like that. Now I'm supposed to do the same with you?"

"Well," he says. "I didn't know that's what happened."

"You never heard? Didn't I tell you?"

"I mean, I heard the *rumors*. And what you said. But I still don't know."

"Then you know what happened."

"I'm not Winston. And Winston ain't my dad, not anymore."

"Yet here you are, begging for something from me. Like an Alcorn."

"I'm not begging."

"You should take a look at yourself in the mirror."

"Maybe I come from him," James says, "but I'm trying to move out. I'm here because Dustin was always talking about this place."

"Last time I saw you, you were pulling a catfish out of the water. You know fishing without a license is poaching and poaching's illegal?"

"I know *that*."

"So how can I trust you?"

James looks around the room. "I want to be on the right side of things."

"Then return to the other side of that door."

"Look," he says. "If there's one thing that'd piss Winston off, it's me working for you instead of him."

"Unless he put you up to this." Miss Becka studies the poor boy standing there in the middle of her empty barroom. He looks hungry and feral.

"He didn't put me up to nothing." James turns to leave.

"Here, put this beer in the cooler for me. That one right there. But not on top of the old ones, those go on top."

"Yes, ma'am," he says.

She orders him around the room and he wipes off

the tables, mops the floor, fills the napkin boxes, fetches buckets of ice from the machine in the kitchen and dumps it into the cooler. She watches for a while, then lights a rolled cigarette and is seized by a coughing fit. She leans over and then gathers her breath. "I'm only going to tip you a fraction of what I make, and that isn't much."

"Fine with me," he says.

She checks her watch. "Well, you're fast, that's for sure. We've still got fifteen minutes before Charlie gets here. He's the cook. If you want some food when he comes in, you're welcome to order some. Just put it in through the POS system."

"The huh?"

"Ah, Jesus." She gets herself up with the cigarette between her teeth and ashing onto her chest. "Come over here." He's probably never even ordered food in a restaurant before, much less served it. "You're an Alcorn all the way. How about we pretend you just aren't. How about that?"

"Works for me," he says. "Awesome."

She goes around the other side of the bar and takes a stool. "I'm going to give you some practice before folks show up. So listen good."

"Yes, ma'am."

"Just pretend I'm a customer. A normal person who doesn't want to be called ma'am."

"All right."

"So." She rubs her chin. "Let me see, what do I want to drink?"

"We've got Bud," he says.

"Perfect. I'll have that." She breaks character for a second. "But take it from the bottom rack you put in."

"You got it."

She takes a long drag from her cigarette, stubs it out in the ashtray and just sits there looking at him.

"Can I get you something else?"

"Am I gonna have to open the damn thing myself? Pretty little princess like me?"

"My bad." He twists the top off and the carbonation farts out between his knuckles.

"*That's* how I like it," she says. "Come on round here. I don't bite."

He goes around the bar and steps into her orbit. He smells like her old house, woodsmoke and mildew, mice and moths. That old world. She slips two fingers into the waistband of his jeans. "Get the fuck closer to me, goddamnit." She yanks him in. "When I order a fucking beer from a fucking bartender he not only fucking brings it to me but he fucking opens it for me. That's how I fucking drink."

"Yes," he says. "Yes, ma'am."

"Okay, good. When they act crazy you act less crazy."

"Got it."

"I know that might sound counterintuitive to you, considering who you come from, but that's how it's got to be. It's a big problem in this world, people going crazy because crazy people make them crazy."

"Right."

She takes a long swallow, then a drag, then another swallow. "And I'll warn you right now. If you ever try and fuck me over like your father did..."

"I promise I won't!" James says. "I swear. I ain't like him. I ain't."

Miss Becka's fingers are still hooked in his waistband.

The bottle sounds empty when she puts it down. "And what do you do once I finish the beer I paid you to open and bring to me?"

"Coming up." He brings her another one. She looks at the empty. "Sorry." He drops it in the trash below the register.

"Recycling! What kind of world do you want to leave for your kids?"

When she says it, they both look at each other.

He pulls the bottle out. "Where's recycling?"

"The blue bin over there with the recycling logo on it?" she says. "Try that one. Don't tell me you don't know what *that* is."

He tosses it into the bin. "Would you like anything else?"

"That's more like it," she says. "You get along with black folks?"

"I don't know any."

"You will," she says. "And you better."

FOURTEEN

There's a brief Saturday night rush, and when the bar finally gets quiet Miss Becka tips him out and tells him he's free to go. He drives out along the Caney Fork, up near where you start seeing signs for the dam. He could've slept in the Walmart parking lot, but the lights would've kept him up. That and the thought—the reality, really—of Winston spotting the truck while on a midnight run for something. So James keeps driving until he finds a clearing off the shoulder, where he cracks the windows and locks the doors. He stretches out across both bucket seats and digs into the to-go container the cook Charlie sent him out with. It's a sampler of everything they serve—hot boneless wings, nachos, fries, burger bites—and it's the most delicious meal he's ever had in his life.

    He checks his phone, but there isn't any service. He sits there eating and listening to a minor-league baseball game on the radio. The Sounds are losing, but it doesn't matter. It makes him feel safe, like Dustin's here with him. When he finishes his supper, he turns the ignition off and things go dark. Through the windshield, the night sky is shot through with millions and millions of stars. He checks the locks on his doors one more time and adjusts each window down about an inch.

The cab's small and the bucket seats don't go that far back. He stretches his legs across them and pulls his shirt up over his face. Sometime during the night he scrambles awake to the sound of men around his truck. It's still dark, but there's a haze to the sky that means sunrise isn't far off. He keeps quiet and listens. Low voices, whispering. Somebody tries the door. Then a bent hanger wire pokes down through the opening of the driver's-side window.

"What the *fuck*!" He grabs the hanger, yanks it into the truck and flips the cab light on. Like some perverse, voyeuristic moon, JR's round face is pressed against the window glass, staring in with his dirty mouth hung open in idiotic discovery. Willy waits silently behind him.

Someone bangs on the hood to get everybody's attention. Winston stands there with his arms out, the bullhorn hanging from his shoulder, the sunrise peeking over the hills behind him. "You done been found, boy," he says.

"Jesus fucking Christ," James says. "The hell are y'all doing?"

"Didn't know where you was at," Winston says.

"You never cared before," James says.

"Call us the Repo Team," JR says. "Here to take back what's ours."

Willy walks around behind the truck and starts wrapping what sounds like a chain around the truck's bumper.

"Dustin gave me this truck," James says.

"Wasn't his to give," Winston says. "Specially not if you're working for we-know-who."

"How the hell you know who I'm working for?"

"We know stuff." JR starts giggling and rubbing his hands together. "We pay attention."

"You ran straight into enemy territory," Winston says.

"But you can't escape," JR says. "Not from Team Repo."

James starts the truck up.

Winston triggers the siren on the horn, then speaks into it: "You can come back home. But only if you're working for me. Not her! We don't allow no traitors."

"That's right." JR's clinging to the window glass. "No traitors allowed."

Winston holds up his rubber hand and goes into auction-mode. "So let's make a deal and come out with a steal. Trade the traitor his truck for a bed, little tiny bed where he once laid his head. No use for wheels if ain't no place to park 'em, so come on back today where the auction'll soon be startin'."

Damn. It *is* Sunday. And there's an auction coming up.

The gear shift in the steering column is loose and slipping, and when James pulls it down into what he thinks is Drive, the rig jumps back and bumps into Winston's new used truck. The side mirror shows Willy leaping out of the way. JR's yelling about something when James whips around onto the road and the chain pulls his back bumper clean off. He swerves before going off the other side into a line of scrub, then floors it and keeps it whining for a couple of miles before realizing the thing must be in D2. He takes his foot off the gas and pulls the shift down a notch and drives on past I-40, heads east, then north across the river, where he hangs out at an empty campsite on a lake for a while, staring at the water, watching bluegills pop the surface. He sits there trying to figure out what the hell to do now.

Around lunchtime he decides to drive back home and grab a snack before his first real shift tonight. Winston's probably getting ready for the auction, too busy to notice him. James follows the highway back to the old house and raids the fridge and cabinets for anything that isn't spoiled: white bread, peanut butter, noodle packets, a bloated three-liter bottle half-full of flat Coke. He packs it all into his truck and goes out to the back porch.

He sits there on an overturned bucket and watches strings of sawdust descend from little holes in the boards supporting the porch roof. A carpenter bee crawls out of a perfectly bored tunnel in the wood and buzzes around like a drunk helicopter. It hovers in front of James, wobbling back and forth. Asking for it.

"Wait right there," James says.

He goes into Dustin's bedroom, looks under the bed and pulls out the pistol and box of shotshells Dustin left him. He returns to the porch, sets the box at his feet and flaps the cardboard lid open. Little brass caps are lined bottom-up in there, with their green tips pointing down. Pocket sprayers, Dustin called them. He packed the tips with his own secret mixture.

James takes out the pistol, slides a shell into the cylinder and pushes the cylinder shut. He leans forward, gets the bee in his sights and pulls the trigger. The little white puff blows the bee into another dimension. He gets up and checks where the spray colored the railing, pockmarks within a powdery compound. Just like with the blue catfish. He waits until another starts out of its hole, then stands up, gets the barrel right close and welcomes this one into the daylight, the shot popping and echoing. He lays the gun down, a satisfied overseer of the compound.

Out past the above-ground pool and the double-wide, the rocky red soil's dozed and flattened. Over that easy hill James hears a Bobcat going, and men yelling over the diesel engine. Pushing piles of junk around and getting ready for another busy day.

He slides more spray cartridges into the cylinder and fires them into the grass, not really aiming at anything. The dozer has stopped running and things are quiet now. James hears Winston coming through the side yard, calling "Hold your fire!" through the bullhorn.

"Clear," James calls back.

"My ass!" Winston comes around the side of the house. "That you discharging a firearm over here?"

"Just makin' sure it works."

Under the noon sun, his father's brow casts a tight shadow down over his eyes. He doesn't sweat because he takes salt pills, a trick he supposedly learned somewhere back in the military days. The smell of sweat's the smell of fear, he likes to say. Don't let them get a whiff of it.

"So what'd you decide?" he says. "You comin' back to work for me?"

"I don't know. I don't think so."

"Well, you can't work for her. You know that much, don't you?"

"Why not?" James says. "Something you need to tell me?"

"I don't owe you squat. Everybody wants something."

"Not me."

"Then why you here? You bringin' me my truck back?"

"Truck's mine now. You know Dustin gave it to me, just like this pistol here. Gave it to me."

"Bullets too?"

"Spray shells," James says.

"Generous brother. Could've made him some money off that."

James opens the cylinder, sends it spinning then smacks it shut. "I could fire straight at your face from here and you'd just feel a mist."

"That right? Then do it."

"It's rat repellant, is all. Dustin packed them himself."

"Come down and do some work with us," Winston says. "We're finishing up the pilot's cabin. JR's got the AM broadcast station running. He'll teach you how to use it. Come make a name for yourself."

"Nah, I'm gonna stay right here."

"Building yourself a solid foundation for your future?" Winston puts his hands behind his back in fake formality. "Sittin' up here on your ass all day every day, month after month, while JR and Willy and me been down at the ferry pushin' land and movin' mountains for you?"

"I could hear every minute of it, right from here."

"We got an auction today," Winston says. "Got a bumper for sale. Complete with tags. Heard your Ranger might need one."

James looks away and shakes his head. He can feel a bargain coming on. "I don't think so."

"You could help us build out the landing and the

loading dock," Winston says. "Very fine landing, makes for a smooth escape."

"What're y'all running from?"

"We're proud of what we're doin'."

"Nobody's arguing with that."

"Come on down and earn some calluses," Winston says.

"Nah." James smooths his thumb over the warm barrel, then lays it down on the porch.

"Get over it, Jebby," Winston says through the horn. "He's gone and he ain't coming back. Not for a while. Why aren't you like him? He wouldn't care none if you was gone. So why'd you care about him bein' gone?"

"It's all fine to you because you replaced him with JR and Willy."

"I had to replace you both. Because you're a useless son of a bitch."

"Yeah, and you're the bitch."

Winston takes a step forward. "How the hell old are you, son?"

"I ain't gonna play your game."

"Tell me. Say it."

"You know my age," James says. "Or maybe you don't."

"I'm asking because I think *you* need some reminding."

"I'm sixteen," James says.

"Then act like it."

"I'm old enough to work for whoever the hell I want."

"Not her, damn it!" Winston waves the bullhorn around. "How you're acting ain't how this out here works."

James spits onto the porch boards and smears it with his toe. "You're right, I shouldn't have to put up with this shit anymore."

"Got your mama's work ethic," Winston says. "Always knew it. Fly off. Get the hell out."

"Maybe I will then."

"So go on."

"I will."

"You ain't no damn son a mine."

"Took you long enough to say it."

"Get, I said."

"I am."

James picks up the pistol and box of shells and steps through the open door into the house. He gives a two-fingered whistle and Flat comes slinking out from under the bed frame. "You wanna come with me?" he says.

She tucks her tail and goes back under.

"Okay," he says.

Outside the window, he can hear Winston talking to JR, but he knows it's really directed at him. Bullshit about how much he could rent this old house for. Turn it into lodging for his workers. Give JR and Willy a place to stay. "Probably should've done that a long time ago," he says. "What you think, JR?"

"I think we could move in right now."

"Never too late," Winston says. "That's my philosophy."

"I'll write you a poem called that."

"Never too late for the startin' gate," Winston says.

JR stands there pretending to write words down on his palm.

"Now let's go get you back to work."

"Like a man," JR says.

"Like a man, son."

When they're gone, James takes the shells out of the cylinder and gives it a twirl. The cleaning supplies are under Dustin's bed where he left them, covered in dog hair and cobwebs and tiny little mouse turds, along with the safety case. He lays it all out across the mattress, sprays the gun with a can of multi-purpose oil and guides cotton swabs down the barrel with a cut of fence wire. He wipes it down one last time to get any fingerprints off the metal, rests it back in its fitted foam bed and locks the case.

The little Ranger's out in the yard. The missing rear bumper makes it look even crazier. It's body is red and lifted one foot above factory standard, with the white aluminum camper top bearing a red duct-taped X from corner to corner on the back. Dustin put that on, said it looked like a flag. Winston likes it too. But maybe James can scrape it off sometime. The truck has lasted through the past few auctions because of a bent frame from Dustin jumping it, because Mandy believes Dustin will come back for it someday and because of the inflated price Winston's been listing. James'll pay Dustin for it when he returns. Probably cost a fortune just getting the thing legal now, but time enough to worry about that. He tosses the truck keys in the air, catches them and steps out into the day. Good weather for leaving.

He hides the pistol behind the pullout jumper seat, packs his clothes and blankets in the truck's extended cab and throws all his fishing poles and tackle into the six-foot bed covered by the camper.

The truck bounces and bangs and squeaks as James navigates it up their drive toward the highway. Mandy's standing in the front lot at the end of the drive like she's been waiting there, and James stops. The sun's shining right in her eyes and she doesn't even use a hand to block it. He leans out his window and talks over the engine. "You want my sunglasses?"

"I'm sorry for what he's done," she says. "I'll make it up to you. I've got a plan."

"Don't worry about me."

"Is it true you're working for Miss Becka? That's all he's talking about."

"Maybe."

She nods and contemplates the fact. "Which way're you going?"

"You'll see when I pull out."

"Things are gonna change. Okay? Remember the plan."

"I'll check in," he says.

"Come back anytime."

"Can't. Not if I'm working for Miss Becka."

"You just be careful," she says. "I'll be here."

"I know you will." He bumps out onto the smooth asphalt and turns right to make her think he's headed toward Lebanon or Nashville, which is exactly what he wants her to tell the old man if he asks. The rearview mirror's blocked up with all his stuff in the back.

On its own, the truck pulls right, so in order to go straight you have to keep leaning left.

Flat Rock Road peels off after a couple miles, and White's service station is open at the intersection. They've got a Pepsi machine and a Coke machine out front flanking the garage doors, which are rusted open. An old-timer in overalls sits in the shady workspace on a plastic chair, with tires for sale all around him. James makes the turn and the road follows cedar posts strung with old steel wire. The gravel drives all have cattle gates. A little concrete bridge takes him over Salt Lick Creek. This far up, the water doesn't amount to much. He follows 55 alongside I-40, and his tires sing on the green metal bridge spanning the Cumberland, as he cruises into Carthage.

He passes a row of closed-up storefronts, then a couple Mexican restaurants painted in bright colors, both with plenty of cars parked in their lots. How the hell is Mexican food so damn popular if what Winston says about Mexicans ruining this country is true?

The overgrown bushes down near the entrance of the Bomb Shelter provide a nice place for him to hide. He parks there and waits for his shift to begin.

The truck's battery is crapping out, so he has to start the engine to listen to the radio, which is tuned in to 650 AM. He never thought he'd get into country music, but lately it's feeling appropriate. He cranks it up, rolls down the windows and just listens.

Then Miss Becka steps out of the little door upstairs. He taps the horn and waves, and she limps sideways down the wooden staircase holding the railing with both hands. When she gets to the bottom she stands on a patch of weedy gravel and motions for him to come over.

He turns the truck off and gets out. The day's quieter after what he was just listening to.

"What was that?" she asks, smiling at him. "I listen to Bill Monroe. Anyway, let's saddle this pony up."

Inside, while Miss Becka's behind the bar mumbling to herself over a checklist, Charlie's sitting at a table against the wall and waves for James to come over.

"It's James, right? That box I sent you home with last night? You study it?"

"Studied hard," James says.

"Good man. Hey, I'd like to show you a few things on the menu, all right?"

They go over what they're out of and what sides people can sub for fries. "And I only cook a burger three ways," Charlie says. "Rare, medium and done. I don't mess around with this medium-rare bullshit."

"Makes sense to me," James says.

"Okay then, I gotta go prep. But I'll see you on the other side."

Miss Becka comes over and takes Charlie's chair. "We're sitting pretty," she says, "stocked up on everything we'll need for a Sunday evening."

"Want me to sweep the floor?" James says.

"But according to this"—she taps the clipboard—"the last time I hired somebody, I wrote myself a note: *Give interview first.*"

James sits there while she asks him questions. The intended answers are obvious, and he answers all of them correctly with *No*.

Finally she asks, *How much do you drink on a daily basis?*

"Depends what it is."

"That's kinda two questions," she says. "There's how much do you drink? And how much do you *drink* drink? Like your brother. When he was just drinking, he was just drinking. But when he drank, he dranky drank."

"I know."

"Looks like we're done." Miss Becka lights a cig. "Good answering."

. . . .

James gets to pour beer behind the bar today, front of house and behind the stick all by himself, a big boy. Miss Becka lets him work the whole opening shift, from three until whenever the real bartender gets there, usually around seven. Dealing with a few day drinkers, particularly a retired pro bass fisherman named Randall, amounts to doing what James did with Miss Becka the other day: ask what they want, pop bottle tops and ask if they'd like another, which they always do.

The register's cash only and the tips go in a jar. When the regular bartender arrives, an older bleached lady named Madison who also owns the place, James is counting out the jar in front of Miss Becka. She's watching him, and it's a good thing too, because if he got the chance he'd slip a twenty in his pocket. He isn't proud of that, but he needs the money.

His shift leaves him with thirty-five bucks in tips. Miss Becka pulls out two fifty-dollar bills and sets them on top of what James has in front of him. "What's this?" he says.

"That's so you can get a place for a couple nights until you figure out where you're going to be sleeping."

James could ask how she knew, but it's probably obvious.

. . . .

The free Wi-Fi at the Red Rooster Inn allows James to prowl around on his phone long into the night. He keeps searching his brother's name and nothing comes up until something useful does: some message board for military conspiracies.

He starts chatting with people who tell him it's weird that he hasn't heard from his brother yet. But they say also that secret operations have been increasing recently, and they're using mostly poor white guys as disposable pawns in deadly assaults.

But if he's dead, James messages, *why don't I know?*
Exactly, is the first answer.

. . . .

When James checks out at eleven, the lady at the counter says, "We hope you come back."

"I do too," he tells her.

Again he waits in the truck for his shift to start, listening to the half-static country radio. He starts scanning around after a while but stops on a strange, weak signal with a familiar voice, thin and angry, announcing next week's auction that's taking place on the world's only floating radio station, their newest attraction. *Pretty biddy who, pretty biddy who? Wanna make a deal, how 'bout you?*

Then a voice behind Winston's, must be JR: *Yessir! I do, I do! Takes money to make money!*

So bring the whole family and your whole wallet, because, remember, here at Rebel River Auctions, when you win a little, I Wins-a-ton.

All this sounds far away, at once blown out and way too close. They got their shit working and they're on the move. James clicks off the radio and just sits there thinking until Miss Becka comes down and waves him in.

He's filling up the ice bins when she leans out of the backroom doorway. "You know who was in here last night?"

"When? After I left?"

"Your daddy," she says.

"Shit."

"We had a late rush. Winston came in with a bunch of his auction fans. Had everybody buying stuff for him. Snacks and drinks, which he wasn't even drinking."

"Yeah, he don't drink."

"He was looking for you," she says. "Said he was here to pick you up. Did you know he was coming?"

"Should've."

"How'd he know you were here?"

"Look, I'm sorry," he says.

"You told him?"

"They been following me around."

"Where? When did you see them?"

"This morning. Before I came in."

"And you didn't call me?" she says. "Aw, Jesus."

"He doesn't want me working here."

"Yeah, no shit," she says. "He wouldn't shut up about it. Talking about, *Blah blah blah, where's my son at?* and threatening kidnapping charges."

"He won't do that."

"I wouldn't put it past him."

"He ain't about to get the law involved," James says. "He hates cops."

"I told him to leave," she says. "Straight up said it."

"Seriously?"

"I told him and JR and Willy to get out and never come back."

"You think he's gonna listen to that?"

"He'd better," she says. "I just don't want him taking any more of my shit."

"Maybe you finally got some of his," James says.

"Poof." Miss Becka licks her thumb and rubs at a smudge on the countertop. "That's one way to look at it."

They start getting the room set up. After restocking the bottled beer, James goes the extra mile and wipes down the tracks inside the cooler's lid. "So I think we're set here," he says.

"I'll unlock the door," Miss Becka says. "You just stand there and look pretty."

"Can do."

A regular who was waiting outside walks in. He sits down, orders a beer, drains it and orders another one. "Fucking hot out," he says.

"That's why we keep 'em cold." James tosses the empty into the recycling bin. This is only his second full shift, and he's already finding a rhythm. Oddly at home back here. The cooler slides open easy on its clean tracks, and in one motion he pulls out another longneck, pops the top and sets it in front of the man.

"Two-fifty," James says, and Miss Becka nods.

Madison's supposed to be closing again, but she calls in and says she's still feeling rough from last night. Miss Becka asks James if he's comfortable handling an evening solo. "It's just a Monday, won't be too crazy."

"Okay." He pats the bar. "I got this."

So Miss Becka heads out early. But tonight's

apparently the new Friday, and the place is real loud by six. That's when James sees Winston standing at the door. Talking into JR's ear while looking straight at him.

FIFTEEN

Winston spots the lifted truck in the back lot outside the bar, its camper top poking up over a trimmed hedge. "There we go," he says.

JR's riding shotgun in the cab next to him, and Willy's napping across the backseats. They've been cruising around for a while now, and when Winston speaks, he sits up, rubs his eyes and looks around, a sweaty dollop of yellow hair pasted across his forehead. He scratches at his tongue with a forefinger.

"He's thirsty," JR says.

"Give him some water then."

"We ain't got none."

"All right then," Winston says. "Problem solved."

"Let's get him some at the bar," JR says.

"Boss lady told us to never come back," Winston says.

JR starts cracking up. "Turn in here."

"What I'm doin'," Winston says.

The trio enters the crowded room and a few people come over to shake Winston's hand. They take selfies with him as he stands there scowling gratuitously, theatrically mugging for the phones, this smalltown celebrity, this up-and-coming radio river pirate, much like a politician surrounded by his backwoods supporters. One woman even asks him to sign her purse, which he does, then charges her for it. "Five bucks for any autographed item," he tells her. "This'll go for twice that much now that I inked it. You can thank me later."

"Oh, I will," she says. "I'm your biggest fan. I listen to you all the time." She leans in close. "And I agree with you about our statues. We need more men like you in this country."

"Go tell my son that," Winston says.

"You're a rare dying breed, you are."

"Ain't dead yet." He turns to JR and Willy and the guys around him. "Y'all boys hear that?" he says. "More men like me."

They all nod and mumble in agreement. Everybody's problems would get solved if the leaders of this constitutional republic had half the backbone of Mr. Winsa-ton here.

"He speaks his mind," JR says. "You gotta respect that."

"He believes in *history*," the woman says.

"That's cause I *am* history." Winston puts his rubber hand over his heart. "Here and now."

"True." JR's messing with people's phones, putting in the call-in radio number.

"Livin' breathin' proof of it, friends and neighbors, and it ain't over yet. We still got time."

"He isn't trying to silence us," one of the guys says, "like all them other people are. He speaks up for us. *Sounds* like us. That's why I like him."

"He's here to save us," the woman says. "It's our heritage. Who we come from."

"He sticks up for the workin' man," JR says. "Yessir."

"Speaking of working," Winston says.

James looks up for a moment, right at Winston, like he can hear them talking, then goes back to serving his customers.

"Go ask him for a drink of water," Winston tells JR. "See if he'll do it."

JR wanders over to the bar and comes back with a pint glass, a paper-tipped straw sticking out the top. "He told us to leave if we ain't drinkin'."

Winston takes the glass and hands it to Willy, who drops the straw to the floor and chugs the water, spilling it all down his chest. When it's empty, Winston takes the glass and hands it back to JR. "Go ask him for another one."

JR waits at the bar, but James ignores him. Winston watches James go back and forth, pouring drinks and making money. Never seen the boy be so damn useful. Who knew. He's almost proud of the kid, except for the fact that all the money's flowing away from him and into the enemy's pocket. Eventually JR returns empty-handed.

"What'd he say?" Winston says.

"That he ain't playin' our game."

"It's no damn game." Winston pushes through his cheerleaders to the bar and stands there until his son comes over.

"Can I get you something to drink?" James says.

"I'm telling you," Winston says, "this is your last warning."

"I doubt it, but that'd sure be nice."

"You're working for somebody I can't trust."

"I trust her just fine."

"You don't know what you're talking about," Winston says. "When shit blows up, you can't come crawlin' back."

"Deal," James says.

"Why you doing this?" Winston puts his hands on the bar. "Working here and bringing shame on me and our family?"

"I do what I want."

"You know how disappointed your brother would be in you right now?"

"I found Dustin last night." James decides to tell some lies, just to see what it does to Winston. "On some message board. People are saying he went missing. Or might be dead. Got caught in a secret mission."

"Who all's saying that?"

"The Zone," he says. "Some marine guys on there claim they have information."

"Is this some conspiracy crap?"

"Thought you'd be interested," James says.

"Well I am now."

"It happened during a classified operation."

A guy knocks on the bar between them. "Speaking of classified operations," he says, "can I get a beer?"

James goes and pours him a draft. When he brings it back and collects the money, Winston's gone. He serves a few more people, looking around the room between orders, but doesn't see the old man anywhere. Then he notices a familiar face, the lady up on a stool in front of the taps.

"Shelly," he says.

"Thought I'd never get your attention, you and your dad talking all that nonsense."

"I was just trying to get him to leave." He laughs but knows it sounds false.

"Well, it worked." She fans herself with both hands.

"You see where he went?"

"Shot out of here like a bat. Went out with his creepy little crew."

"Can't have them around," James says. "That's Miss Becka's rules."

"He's your father."

"And you're not my mother."

"Do you actually believe what you were saying?" Shelly says. "About Dustin?"

"Not really." James repositions the napkin box on the bar. "I just knew it'd get Winston going. Me saying it, you know?"

"Oh, God."

"But it is weird nobody's heard from him, right?"

"I mean, no?" She looks at her phone, then puts it on the bar. "He joined the army to get away from all this."

"Including you."

"And you too," she says. "Sorry." She shakes her hair loose over her face. "Can I get a beer?"

"What would you like?"

"Coors Light."

"Bottle?"

"Draft."

James fixes it up and sets the tall foaming glass on a clean napkin in front of her, just like Miss Becka taught him.

Shelly takes a sip. "My God, that's better."

She sounds like Dustin used to. "Are you hungover?" he says. "Where were you last night?"

"Where else would I have been?" she says. "After an auction like that?"

"You aren't serious."

"It's the biggest thing happening around here these days," she says. "I wanted to see the old ferry, now that he's got his radio station on it. I've been hearing his crazy talk about the statue and can't believe people buy into that stuff. But there I was." She checks her phone, texts somebody, then puts it back on the bar next to her beer, which is going down fast. "So where are you staying? In Dustin's truck?"

"No."

"Sure looks like it."

"I'm at the Red Rooster."

"Ooh, fancy." She blows on her nails and pretends to polish them on her shirt. "Free breakfast."

"All-you-can-eat muffins."

They keep talking, and something about how Shelly sips her beer between thoughts makes James realize how much older she is than him. Not just in years but in something else, that specific something-else he saw her doing with his brother that one night.

The place starts to clear out and Shelly sticks around texting on her phone.

Charlie comes from the back, checks the room and tells James the kitchen's closed. "You want fries or anything?"

"Whatever you got."

"I like the loaded tater-skins," Shelly says.

"Everybody does." Charlie steps back into the kitchen and returns with a to-go box.

James has almost finished cleaning the back bar

when Miss Becka shows up. She walks around the place looking pissed, sniffing and sparking a lighter in her hand. "I heard he came back, is that true?"

"*Somebody's* been drinking." Shelly grins.

"They were here a while ago," James says, "but I got them to leave. Wasn't no problem."

"Them being here *is* the problem," Miss Becka says.

"They weren't here long."

"Is he lying to me?" Miss Becka asks Shelly.

"He's telling the truth, I was right here. He kicked them out."

"Good." Miss Becka pats her waist and right there James can see she's got a buck knife on her belt. "I tell them they can't be here, then they come back? Acting like they own the place? I don't think so."

"How'd you even know they were here?" James asks.

"Charlie told me," she says.

Charlie's back there mopping the floor, ignoring all the front-of house drama.

"You could've texted me," she says. "The least you could've done."

"It was busy," James says. "I was serving customers."

"Seriously, Miss Becka," Shelly says. "They came in when it was slammed."

"That's when it always happens. I guess that's an excuse." She pulls out a hand-rolled cig, lights it up and blows a thin, contemplative cloud into the room. She's definitely been drinking. "I'm outta here," she says. "And you two need to wrap it up. Charlie will lock the door behind you."

"I got this," James says. "You don't need to worry about me."

"Too late for that," Miss Becka says. "Next time, call me, even if it's busy. Okay?"

James wrings a rag into the sink. "I will."

When Miss Becka leaves, Shelly makes a crazy face and puts her phone in her back pocket. "She really hates Winston, doesn't she?"

"Oh yeah," James says. "I do too."

"But he does something extra special to her, doesn't he?"

"They go way back."

Shelly gets off the stool and hikes up her tight-fitting jeans.

James forces himself not to look. He doesn't want her to see him looking. Thou shalt not enter. Big brothers only.

She walks across the barroom, stops at the door and turns around. "So what's up?" she says. "You wanna show me the Red Rooster?"

SIXTEEN

The next morning Miss Becka spots James Alcorn's crazy-ass truck in front of the motel. And what's that next to it, Shelly's maroon Saturn? God help us. She keeps on driving. Normally she'd stop and give everybody hell, but she can't get into any of that right now. She's going to Second Wind to see her father.

The two-lane takes her around a dynamited shelf of gray limestone, and up ahead, past the guardrail, the river reflects a duck flying upstream, so low that its wings tap the surface with every flap, briefly connecting the bird to its reflection, making a circle.

When she gets there, he's waiting in a wheelchair behind the sliding glass doors. His hands are so white against the dark blanket over his lap that *from here*, just for a gentle second, Miss Becka imagines that he's been baking bread. Like he and her mother used to do on Sunday mornings in that old house they once lived in.

"Hey, Daddy," Miss Becka says, "you're looking nice today."

The assistant who wheeled him out is a young lady who doesn't yet realize she's looking at her own future here every day. "After church this morning," she says, "he had coffee with his friends and ate two pieces of cake. Isn't that right?"

He doesn't answer because he can't. Miss Becka hates it when people speak to her father like this. "I'll take him from here," she says. "Okay if we go out to the gazebo?"

"Fine with me," the assistant says. "I'll unlock the back doors for y'all."

Miss Becka wheels her father along the pebble-stone walkway through the sun and up the ramp into the gazebo. She sits down on the bench across from him and hums one of their old tunes. She can almost hear his lower voice coming from somewhere in the cave of his chest. She sings the lyrics, as best she can remember them—*Brother afar, from the savior today, risking your soul for the things that decay*—and stops when she runs out of verses. He's definitely humming along. Nearly inaudible, but it's there. She watches him until he's quiet.

"I've got something to tell you," she says.

He just sits there, unresponsive.

She lights a cigarette. "You see, still smoking," she says.

Nothing.

"You aren't even going to moralize at me today?" she says. "How're you doing in there? Can't you give me something, maybe a nod?"

He blinks. Then blinks again.

"Two means yes," she says. "Yes what?"

There's a breeze moving around, and they stay out here for a while. She tries to get him to blink like that again, but he won't. During the visit her phone rings and it's Madison Gentry, who says she can't make it in tonight again. She sounds seriously hungover. Does Miss Becka know anybody who can cover the shift?

"Yeah," Miss Becka says, "I know somebody."

When she hangs up, her father's watching her. Hard to read him, but he seems aware.

"Okay, I really do have something to tell you. It's about the mill."

He blinks twice. Maybe this *is* real communication. Who knows? She pulls the little box of sawdust out of her pocket, then opens it, and holds it to his untrimmed nostrils.

"I don't know why I need to tell you this," she says. "But I gave it away."

He blinks. Once.

"I'm sorry," she says. "A man took it from me. I got played. I didn't know what to do. And now it seems like he's taking stuff from everybody. What do I do?"

He brings his hand up to his face. Touches one eyelid, then the other.

SEVENTEEN

She follows him back to the motel. They talk for a while, but really it's just her talking, trying to get him to as well, but he won't, because he doesn't know what to say, so she just keeps talking. She's also sipping from something in a paper bag in her purse, a flat plastic bottle of vodka that keeps her talking.

She talks about how Dustin left her high and dry. "Would you do that to somebody?" she says. "Just up and leave?" When he doesn't answer, she goes on about how she went and did what she did with the baby because she had to. James acts like it's the first he's heard about that. She asks him if he hates her, and he says no, he doesn't hate her. "Folks should be able to do whatever they want," he says. "Free country."

But he's not sure if she even heard him. She's drunk enough by now to go in circles around ideas until she falls asleep in his bed. He takes one of the pillows and sleeps on the floor in his clothes.

He wakes up before her but lets her sleep. When she starts waking up, he gets back down on the carpet and pretends to be asleep. He listens to her gather up her things and leave.

He spends most of the day in bed staring at his phone

while the TV on the wall shows Fox News on mute. He glances up at it every once in a while, in case a breaking news headline might pop up about Afghanistan or whatever. The message board on his phone has been talking about a botched mission, and if you haven't heard anything about it that's because the military state is covering it up. Nothing directly about Dustin, and after a while James taps on an ad that says there are young women looking for love in his area. He's never seen any women who look like this around Carthage. One click leads to another, and pretty soon he's under the blankets with his jeans around his ankles, squinting to see closer. When he shuts his eyes, there's maybe a flash of Shelly somewhere in there. He turns over and smells the spot where she slept.

Forgive us our trespasses.

He lies there afterward, holding a sock over his crotch like he's staunching a wound.

It's about ten till three when his phone rings.

"What're you doing tonight?" Miss Becka says.

"You know," he says. "Staying out of trouble."

"I doubt it, not at the Red Rooster. I drove by this morning and saw your truck there. And Shelly's car."

"Nothing happened," he says.

"Did she sleep over there?"

"She was drunk. She had to."

"Your two cars were the only ones in the damn lot," she says. "Everybody saw it."

"Are you seriously calling me up to talk about this? Like, seriously?"

He can hear the click of Miss Becka's lighter. "I'm calling because Madison's sick," she says, "so I want to know if you can cover the bar?"

"When?"

"Tonight," she says. "Now."

"You gonna be there?"

"I'll stop by," she says. "But I'm not working. It's all yours."

. . . .

He's straightening bottles and looking at himself in the long mirror—James, the bartender—when somebody knocks on the front door.

He turns around and waits for another.

Silence.

First his mind goes to Dustin—like it always does—but that's not possible. Maybe Miss Becka forgot her keys. He goes around the bar and looks out the window beside the door. There's movement out there, somebody peeking around the side. It's JR, pointing straight at James, and then he backs away, still pointing. By the time James unlocks the door and steps out, he's gone.

Then Miss Becka pulls in and parks. She sits there with a cigarette in her mouth and her window wide open, fumbling with the car's lighter.

"You need help with that?"

"My hands just aren't working yet," she says.

He fans away a fly, takes the glowing lighter from her fingers and touches it to the tip of her cigarette. "There you go."

"I knew I hired you for a reason. What're you doing out here, anyway? You all set in there?"

"Ready to rock," he says. "The floors are dirty, but I figure I'll just sweep tonight after we close."

"Bingo," she says. "No use in cleaning before a shift."

"Actually, I came out because I saw somebody looking in the window."

"Somebody who?"

"I—JR."

"America's handyman," she says. "Just what I need. Was Willy with him?"

"I didn't see him."

"Winston?"

He holds out his hands, palms up. "I really don't know."

"Stupid question," she says. "Sure he was there."

"I only saw one by the door."

"Don't get smart with me. Where there's one there's more. What was he doing?"

"Pointing at me? Maybe Winston sent him. He was shaking his head."

"He used to work for me."

"No shit?"

"Now he's Winston's. I don't want any part of this."

"I need to keep this job," James says.

"I've had enough of Mr. Wins-a-ton to last me a lifetime. And now he's fucking with me here? I don't think so."

James can feel a rant coming on. "I'm sorry," he says. "Whatever good that does."

"It's all right. You got out of there and you're trying to do better. Which you are." She inhales smoke with her mouth open. "Except for the Shelly stuff. What the hell were y'all thinking?"

"We weren't." He kicks some gravel around. "I appreciate the work."

Two cars pull into the lot with a black couple in both.

"Better get in there," Miss Becka says. "You never want your customers walking into an empty room."

"Yes, ma'am."

"I'm right behind you," she says. "Set me up a cold one."

The two couples scoot stools around the high top, dressed up all nice and clean unlike the white folks who come in straight from their jobs with name tags still on their shirts. He pops Miss Becka's bottle, places it on the bar and brings menus over to the group. Winston used to tell him you couldn't trust black folks, never told James he could trust anybody. Lebanon has a black community, but they didn't mix much with his family—except at the Sunday auctions, where whites and blacks kept mostly to themselves.

When he goes over to take their orders, they're wanting food but he tells them the kitchen isn't open yet, and they're willing to drink happy-hour pints and munch on a couple bags of chips from behind the bar.

James brings it all over on a tray and says, "That'll be eighteen dollars, with the chips for free."

The nearest guy pulls out his wallet and hands him a twenty and a five, then says, "Keep the change."

"Thank you."

Back at the bar, Miss Becka finishes her beer in a gulp. James opens another one for her, then walks a couple more pints over to the folks at the high top. "On me."

"Whatever you say," the man says.

"All right," Miss Becka says, "let's get some music on."

"I got it," the other man says, then starts typing something into his phone. James didn't know you could connect your phone to a jukebox.

"This one's for the kid," the guy announces when

the music comes on: *Now, I'm just a bartender. And I don't like my work. But I don't mind the money at all.*

"There you go," he says, "told y'all!" And his friends start laughing.

The song and the voice are so perfect that James wants to have a beer with these people, but Miss Becka wouldn't like that. There are rules in here.

Then Charlie texts Miss Becka that he can't handle his shift because he's helping Madison who's been having it rough.

James delivers this news to the high-top table.

After they leave it's quiet again, just James and Miss Becka. He washes and dries people's glasses and stacks them on the shelf below the taps. Carefully, taking his time. "So," he says. "How'm I doing?"

"Pretty good," she says. "But I'm still wondering about JR and Willy and your damn dad. What's he doing with them?"

"I think I'm being watched. They're spying on me."

"Why?"

"Betrayal, I'd guess."

"What the hell does that mean?"

"It's about loyalty," James says. "That's all Winston cares about."

"How does your mom put up with it?"

"I think she's got a plan. Might take the rest of her whole life, but she's gonna get out of there."

"How?"

"I don't know." He looks at her. "Would you mind if I had a beer with you?"

"Just don't let all these privileges go to your head, little man."

One becomes two becomes three becomes more. By then Miss Becka has him pouring shots of freezer-chilled peppermint schnapps. He's starting to feel what Dustin must've felt here, everything crystalizing around you into one happy falsehood: your brother might be okay, your father might be looking for you just to make sure you're okay, your mother might escape from her monstrous husband and be okay. This stuff's *good*.

"If anybody ever asks if you want fruit on your shot," Miss Becka says, "tell 'em fruit's for flies."

"Becka, I respect you a whole damn helluva lot."

"*Miss* Becka."

"But I got one question for you."

"Does it come with a beer?"

He pops her another one. "Tell me the truth, please. You think I got a chance with Shelly?"

Miss Becka spits foam. "I think she's already had enough trouble out of one of you."

"Never mind I said it."

"How about this," Miss Becka says. "Instead of trying to get her knees apart, how about just listening to her and seeing if she needs anything."

"That's all I did last night."

"Maybe a little bit of help, a little bit of care. Which Dustin obviously didn't give her." She finishes her beer. "All right, you talked me into it. One more shot."

"I gotta go outside for a sec."

"I bet you do," she says.

. . . .

Back in his room he sends a riot of drunken texts—*where*

u at, been thinking bout u, remember that night we first met, I can still smell you—but Shelly doesn't text him back, so he fires off one more: *they mighta got dustin, he might be dead...*

He's drunk-sleeping in the chair when somebody knocks on the door. Shit. He drops onto the floor.

"Come on." It's Shelly's voice. "Let me in."

He crawls over and unlocks the door.

She pushes it open and takes a look at him. "What's wrong with you? Are you drunk?"

"I was."

"Dustin isn't dead," she says. "You don't know that."

"I don't know nothing." He starts weeping and can't even guess what that's about.

"You need to get your shit together." She comes in, slams the door shut behind her and pulls him up onto the bed. "Why were you texting me all that?"

"I just wanted to see you."

"Well," she says, "take a good look."

"You about to leave?"

"Definitely."

"But you just got here."

"I can't be here twice," she says. "I think they're watching."

. . . .

He goes the rest of the week pulling doubles, opening and closing. Tending bar's interesting at first, all the stories and people, but it gets old quick—same folks, same problems. That there's been no sign of Winston should reassure him, but instead it just makes him more nervous.

He checks his phone whenever he gets the chance—often enough—and does shots with Miss Becka at the end of every shift. Which is illegal, but whatever.

"I shouldn't have fired Madison," she tells him. "The lady *owns* the damn place. What am I going to do when you leave? Because you *will* leave. And you won't be wrong to."

Early one Saturday evening, before it gets busy, a woman comes in and takes a stool at the bar. James lays a menu in front of her, starts telling her what the kitchen's out of, then sees it's Shelly. "Oh shit," he says. "My bad."

"Look." She's pissed, but at least she's here talking to him. "You see the news tonight?"

"I been working."

"There was a whole thing on Winston."

At the end of the bar, Miss Becka looks up from the paper she's reading and slides her glasses down her nose.

"What happened?" James says.

"He's okay," Shelly says. "Better than ever, really. He's just been promoting his auction on the radio station. And running for the general fucking assembly."

"General who?" James says.

Miss Becka comes over and waves for another beer. "I heard folks talking about this."

James pops a longneck and slides it in front of her without a napkin. "I don't even understand what y'all are saying."

"Apparently some folks're calling for your father to run for office," Miss Becka says. "Word's out about his tenacity, his vivacity. Especially in regard to the damn monument, which he's made all the latest rage." She flutters her fingers like she's impressed, then takes a couple deep swallows of beer. "So they want him to run for member of the house."

"Whose house?"

"House of Representatives," Miss Becka says.

"They make laws," Shelly says. "Right?"

"Among other matters. And this district in Lebanon, they make decisions about public spaces as defined by the state, which is what this is all about."

"My old man doesn't want anything to do with laws."

"I wouldn't be so sure," Miss Becka says. "If he's the one making them—"

"Or getting rid of them," Shelly says.

"I guaran-damn-tee you this has everything to do with the monument on the square."

"Oh, for sure it is," Shelly says. "Winston's railing on about it all over the radio all the time. You know, how the Confederacy's our family history and that no statues should be removed."

"He's always been saying shit like that," James says.

"But now it's for real." Shelly starts typing something into her phone. "People are calling for Winston to replace the current representative. They're saying he speaks for the people and will keep history alive."

"Why would anybody want him in charge of anything?" James slips a white napkin under Miss Becka's bottle. "That's just crazy."

"They come to his auctions and they love him," Miss Becka says. "He's the town mascot, if there ever was one."

"Read this." Shelly holds her phone up and shows James an article on the local news site. The Sons of

Confederate Veterans, Camp #723, are voting for Winston Alcorn to represent the 46th District. They believe he'll stand up for their statues. They plan to hold a rally about it at his next auction.

"That's tomorrow," James says.

"Let me see that." Miss Becka reads the phone and hands it back to Shelly. "Jesus."

"He hasn't won anything yet," Shelly says. "We should go mess with them."

But Miss Becka isn't listening. She's off somewhere by herself, staring at something only she can see, then heads out with a vague wave.

James hefts her bottle of beer and says, "Only half finished."

EIGHTEEN

This ground has ghosts.

From her porch Miss Becka watches the colors of the evening sky mixing together in the river eddies. Pink, silver, purple, black. On land, broken branches, bare and bone-white, among the porous jutting outcrops of rock, like unmarked headstones.

She's been drinking a lot lately, to keep the spirits off. And tonight will be no different, especially because of what she just heard about Winston. She's too old for this. The only way to keep the voices quiet out there, to ignore what she's surrounded by, is to set the old blue Ball jar next to the cut-glass tumbler engraved with her mother's initials.

Soon today will be tomorrow, while the future was yesterday. And so on. There's a six-pack chilling in her hemlock pond, where the trout used to live. The labels on the bottles will rub off under your thumb once they've been in there long enough. That's how you know they're cold.

The weekend's here again, a Saturday night, and the bar's probably getting busy. Little James, still a teenager, in charge of everything because Madison can't make her shifts. Charlie calls to ask her why it's just James working out there tonight. "He needs to be selling burgers," Charlie says. "We've got a bunch of meat that's about to spoil."

"So set up a burger-stand outside and just give it away," she tells him.

"I'm a nice guy," he says, "but I don't work for free. Especially not for Madison Gentry. Not anymore. You might've fired her, but she still owns this joint. She needs to get it together."

"Well, Happy Saturday then," Miss Becka says.

She'd normally go back in to help out, but she just doesn't feel like it tonight. She's got some thinking to do. A few months ago, a petition was going around, asking voters if they wanted the General Hatton monument removed from the town square. She signed *yes* and sent it along to Charlie and everyone at the post office. It got her feeling hopeful, for the first time since she was young, that the damn thing might finally come down. But who started this conversation in the first place? Yeah, Winston.

Decades ago, when, as a college kid, she'd written a letter to the editor of the *Lebanon Herald* about this very issue, saying the statue should be replaced with one of DeFord Bailey blowing his harmonica, she'd been laughed at and mocked by most everybody. And here it is again, coming back around. But this time it feels different, somehow co-opted. She's worried it might elevate Winston to a status he never would've had otherwise.

She pours a jigger from the jar into her mother's old glass—cheers, Momma!—then shoots it down, pours another and goes up to the pool to grab some beer.

It's dark when she gets back and sees a flashlight coming down the trail through the trees.

When Shelly gets in range of the porch light, she clicks her flashlight off and comes up the steps without a word.

"Howdy," Miss Becka says.

"Why'd you run off like that?" She stands in front of Becka. "Because of the Winston thing? What the hell?"

The bottles in Miss Becka's hands are cool and dripping wet from the spring. She sets them on the porch next to her chair. She sits down, shoots the shine from the tumbler, twists the top off a bottle, then stretches out and crosses her ankles.

"Crickets," Shelly says. "Are we not talking?"

Miss Becka closes her eyes.

"Have you been getting drunk with James every night? Just like you did with Dustin? You have, haven't you?"

"Ah," Miss Becka says. "The queen has been disturbed."

"Quit that," Shelly says. "You don't know me."

"Please." Miss Becka raises her little glass. "Sit down."

Shelly crouches onto a sawed stump of oak. "You can't just ignore what's happening. What Winston's up to. You can't pretend it isn't there."

"What the hell am I supposed to do then?"

"I think we should go to Winston's auction tomorrow."

"It's a rally," Miss Becka says, "for a racist monument. And a racist man."

"Exactly. We should show up and protest or something."

"Please." Miss Becka sniffs the clear corn whiskey in her glass. "You want a beer or something?"

"Wow," Shelly says. "Not in the least."

"Then what can I do ya for?" Miss Becka says. "Because I'm here to drink. It's Saturday night and I'm not working and I'm here to have a good time with *me*." She pours another shot. "Just come on, will you?"

Shelly shakes her head. "I'm tired of studying at Cumberland. Sick of just reading books. I want to make a difference."

"You never even wrote that paper on me."

"*On you*," she says. "What was I thinking?"

"You weren't," Miss Becka says. "You had ideas about me that weren't accurate. When what you were actually searching for was yourself."

"Deep," Shelly says. "I was just curious about you. That's all."

"Doesn't make you innocent." Miss Becka picks a dried bean pod off the porch floor, turns it in her fingers and sets it on her knee.

"I had no intentions. I just thought you were different."

"How?"

"I thought you'd stand up to somebody like Winston," she says. "When the time came."

"You have zero idea what you're talking about." Miss Becka tosses the pod into the yard. "I don't want anything to do with him. And if you and James get involved, I don't want any part of y'all either." She picks up another longneck and rubs the paper label off. "So you need to figure out what you want."

"I know what I don't want. Winston going around—"

"I respect that," Miss Becka says. "I do. But you can't just stop people."

"Yes you can. Listen to yourself!"

Miss Becka swigs her beer and lights a cig. "You wanted to use me to get an A. Everybody wants something from me, and I'm tired of giving it away for free."

"I was listening to my professor," Shelly says. "You were his idea. Anyway, it's all over and done with. I'm going to the rally tomorrow and I'm taking James with me."

Miss Becka sits up straight. "If you do that, tell James he isn't working for me anymore. I won't have it."

"I'll help him find a new job."

"You hardly know each other."

"He knows more than you think," Shelly says. "And so do I."

Miss Becka shakes the thought out of her head. "Where would he go? Who'd hire a kid like that?"

"Look around. There's a hundred shitty jobs out there."

"Mostly factories and department stores. You don't know what he wants."

"Winston's about to run for office," Shelly says. "On the craziest most backward issue you could imagine."

"I know."

"So who better to speak out about it than me and James?"

"I hear you. But I'm not doing it." Miss Becka exhales smoke and stubs out her rollie in the cast-iron ashtray. "Just be careful. I'm warning you." She unscrews the jar's lid and drinks straight from it. Shelly steps off the porch, clicks the flashlight on and shines it into the dark woods.

"Don't worry," Miss Becka says, "nobody's out there."

"That's what scares me."

NINETEEN

Scrolling through Craigslist, James comes across some ads that are obviously Winston's. Each one is the same, just listed under different tabs and in different type. *CHEAP $TEAL$ & DAM GOOD DEAL$+GUN$ n AMMO~HI$TORIC FERRY AUCTION!++something for everybody cuz everybody needs something+++When u win, I Wins-a-ton...* One has a picture of Winston standing on the ferry's deck with the bullhorn slung over his shoulder and some flags flapping behind him. Damned if he didn't get that old rig looking good. Others show piles of random stuff, clothes, shoes, a lamp, a blender, baby toys. MYSTERY MOUNTAIN! $10 ARMLOAD! HOW MUCH CAN U HUG? Guns are laid out on a table. And under the table are piles of yard signs in the style of the flag, promoting Winston for Representative of the 46th District. PROTECTION IS PRICELESS! HISTORY IS NOW! The old man hasn't slowed down any. Good for him. Bad for everybody else.

James puts his phone down on the bedside table. He's got his motel door cracked open with the chain-lock holding it secure. He can see a strip of pavement outside, then some trees along the river, and above that a line of bright morning sky. It's the kind of Sunday that must feel like church. Calm and clean. He's staring out the door's opening, but then a shadow blocks the light and fingers reach in and rattle the brass chain.

"Ready to go?" Shelly says.

James grabs the covers and pulls them up. He's been lying around in his underwear.

"Come on," she says. "We're going over to your folks' place. I want to watch the auction with you and see if they're actually having a rally for the statue."

"I don't wanna go. I'm not even dressed."

She peeks in and whistles. "How do they even let a minor rent a room on his own?"

"I lied. Said I was eighteen."

"Didn't they ask for ID?"

"I showed it to them," he says. "but I don't think they're good at math."

He can hear her laughing. The smell of her shampoo comes in on a breeze through the doorway.

"I'm going to go get us some breakfast. When I come back, you better be dressed."

"Grab me a blueberry muffin and orange juice."

"We'll see what they have," she says.

"That's all they ever have."

When she comes back and knocks, he's ready and steps out into the daylight squinting and holding a backpack. He locks the door behind him, gets in her car, puts the bag between his feet and feels a rush of excitement he wasn't expecting. Low humidity and a clean blue sky. Trees on the hillsides brushed with old-timey colors. Did all that happen overnight? She hands him his plastic-wrapped muffin and a styrofoam cup of juice. She sips coffee from hers as they follow the river along a two-lane highway, sometimes glimpsing the water through a break in the tree line, and every now and then the abandoned nuclear reactor's tower pops up over a field.

"That's where I'd be working," James says, "if they ever got it running."

"What a waste."

"You know this road puts us on the other side of the river from Winston?"

"I know where your house is," she says. "And I know where we're going."

"Just checking."

"What, you want to be closer to your people? I thought we'd observe from a distance and have an easy getaway."

"I was just saying—"

"Perfect," she says. "We'll stick to this radical plan of me being the driver and you being the passenger."

James holds up his hands in exaggerated neutrality. After an awkward silence, he decides to change the subject. "You think Dustin's ever coming back?"

"Dustin was scared about having a kid," she says. "So he decided running was safer than being a father. He'll come back when he's ready."

"Maybe," James says. "Can you blame him?"

Shelly glances over her sunglasses. "I made a decision after he left. I decided that I wasn't gonna have anybody's damn kid alone. I didn't want to be a single mother. Anyway, it's all in the past."

The tip of Beasley's Bend is accessed by a washboard gravel road that winds through miles of soybean fields and then drops off into a tractor path down to the river's edge. Shelly's car bottoms out a few times and they decide to park before they get stuck. They leave their doors open as they stand there gazing out over the water at the Alcorn complex.

"Pretty quiet," Shelly says.

"That'll change," James says. "Follow me." A muddy footpath leads to the inner bend of the water's edge. "This is where the old ferry used to let off. Also where a band of rebels escaped."

"Who cares?" Shelly says. "You sound like Winston."

"All the stories I know are from him," James says. "So there ya go."

"Look!" Shelly points across the river at the short fiery bursts and colorful glittering arcs of a roman candle. The delayed reports come echoing across the water. Then the sounds of men talking. The ferry—seventy feet long, painted in glossy red and white, with a tall CB antenna sticking up off the skipper's cabin—is anchored in the green water against a clearing on the bank. Two men stand on the deck lighting fuses.

"What the fuck?" Shelly says.

"JR and Willy," James tells her. "Definitely."

JR turns around holding another roman candle. Willy lights it and it begins spitting little balls of fire out over the river, reflecting on and dropping into the water.

James and Shelly settle down in some high riverbank brush and watch people trickling down the cleared hillside to gather around the ferry. Most of them are older and white, but Shelly points out a few young freaks among them. The one thing they all have in common is Wins-a-ton. They're carrying signs with his name, flags with his name, wearing shirts and hats with his name. They set up chairs and coolers along the hillside like it's an amphitheater about to stage an old-school country variety show.

When JR goes into the ferry's cabin and gets Greenwood's "God Bless the USA" playing, a convoy of ATVs comes riding over the hill. On the rear platform of one four-wheeler, Winston's perched on some sort of royal throne and wearing a W cap while pumping his bullhorn in the air with his good hand and waving to the crowd with the rubber one. People stand up and cheer as the caravan goes down the slope to the ferry and Winston's rig goes up the loading ramp onto the deck.

Flanked by two men in suit jackets, Winston greets the crowd, his voice eerily clear through the megaphone even across the river to where James and Shelly are sitting. "My lovely beautiful people," he says. "I know you wanna deal cuz everybody's looking for a steal..." Prompted by his redneck rhyming, the crowd gets to its feet and erupts. "But right before we get to that, I wanna get to this." His tone turns serious and solemn. "I have some friends with me today, the Sons of Confederate Veterans. Very brave people. And they love their history, yes they do. So very much so. Buffs is what I call 'em. Buffs! They'll buff your history right up. And they're here today to tell us all about something we've been very concerned about, something I've been talkin' about a lot."

"We love you, Wins-a-ton!"

"Wins-a-ton loves you too," Winston says. "But first let's hear from this great man, whose great grand patriarch was a heroic rebel soldier."

This summons an uproar of applause.

A stiff man in a tan tweed suit walks up the ramp with a cane, removes his wide-brim hat and bows to the crowd. Winston hands over the bullhorn, something James has never seen him do, and the man begins speaking with what sounds like an antiquated Southern accent, maybe aristocratic with something almost European about it.

"They killed our boys and it wasn't enough," he says. "They took our land and it wasn't enough. They destroyed our economy and it wasn't enough. They rewrote the history books and even that wasn't enough. They did let us have one little statue," he says, "and now they want to take that from us." People start booing and hissing and shouting. "When will enough be enough?"

"Never!" Winston yells.

"Well, I'm here to tell you folks, enough is enough is enough!"

"That's right!" Winston shouts, and the crowd goes crazy.

"And this gentleman by my side will give us our best fighting chance. He's pushed back against the communists who want to erase who we are and where we come from. The blood we shed on this very soil. He's given voice to the monuments and the men of our past, and because of that he's the man for our future! We need a leader like Winsaton," he says. "Not only will Mr. Winston Alcorn preserve our history by keeping our statues where they stand—and I mean *right* where they stand today—but he'll also build new ones and lead our course forward! This is why we're putting Winston at the top of the ticket, for the General Assembly of the House of Representatives to represent the 46th District, which includes Lebanon, Tennessee, the home of General Robert H. Hatton and his military unit the Lebanon Blues, not to mention the very land on which John Hunt Morgan raced his horse and led a running battle against the invaders right to the ground upon which you now sit. Are you with me, fellow patriots? Together we can put Winston in power and make the South great again!"

The frenzied crowd tosses signs into the air and waves flags back and forth.

"Can you believe this?" Shelly says, turning to James. "It's fucking nuts!"

"Home sweet home," he says.

"All these people can't be serious, can they?"

"Oh, they're serious." James unzips his backpack and takes out the plastic safety case. He clicks open the latches and shows Shelly the pistol resting on the egg-crate foam.

"Is that real?"

"Want to find out?" He takes it from the case, spins the chamber, spanks it shut and offers it to her.

"I'm not touching that thing."

"Fine." He cocks the hammer back. The crowd's going wild over there and it sounds like Winston's back on the horn. "Let's just disrupt this bullshit."

"You're not serious."

"They won't even know who did it," James says. "Probably just think it's one of JR's firecrackers."

"But they'll see us."

"Then it's a good thing you parked us on the other side of the river, isn't it?" He points the gun out over the water in the general direction of the rally and fires, then again. Pop, pop. He watches himself doing it. He can hear it as if he's not a part of it. People gasp and scream, but they don't run. They stand their ground. Willy comes running from the ferry's cabin and tackles Winston, shielding his body with his own like a genuine security guard. The men in suit jackets are pointing across the river. Then people in the crowd start pointing too.

"They see us," Shelly says. "We have to fucking go." She takes James by the arm as he puts the gun and its case in his backpack. When they race up the bank, a spot of dirt explodes in front of them and James hears the ringing crack of a rifle. He looks back and sees JR standing by one of the auction tables and aiming a scoped rifle in their direction.

They make it up the bank and jump behind Shelly's Saturn. No more shots. James peeks over the hood and sees Winston standing back up. His pink rubber hand must've got knocked off when Willy he took him down, but Winston puts it back on, slightly bent over as he attaches it, a surprisingly vulnerable posture. Then he picks up the bullhorn and says, "I wasn't hit. Fine as a dime. You show me your luck and I'll show you mine."

"Wins-a-ton! Wins-a-ton!" the audience starts chanting.

Winston waves the bullhorn at them and then announces, "The threat's been neutralized so put the rifle down. I ain't hit so you best quit. One more round and you're putting money down." The crowd laughs and cheers and chants. "I want everybody to know what they just saw." Winston straightens up in solemn formality, and everyone hushes. "That was a God-honest assassination attempt, it was. They tried to get me. But guess what? They can't get me. And y'all know why they can't get me?"

"Why?" they shout. "Tell us, Wins-a-ton!"

"Because of the big man upstairs."

A woman raises her hands to the sky in worship. "Praise God!"

"He ain't played my card yet," Winston says. "We still got some votin' to do."

"We sure as hell do!"

"Never thought I'd say this, but we gotta get out there and vote for me in the 46th District. We gotta stick up for what's ours. Save history and bring back the past."

Whoops and hollers and shouts of "Amen!" echo and swell across the water, as if there were even more people over there than there actually are. Then a saccharine patriotic song starts, blasting from the system, filling the river basin with rageful celebratory noise.

. . . .

They drive around for a while without talking. The windows are rolled up and the quiet interior of the car is all but vibrating from their adrenaline. When James goes to say something, she tells him to hush. "I don't want to hear it right now. I've never been shot at before," she says.

"First time for everything," he mumbles.

"Like this is part of your daily routine or something?" she says. "Quit acting cool. You're still shaking."

James slides his hands under his legs.

It's early evening, which gives everything a saturated look. The rust-bitten roof of a tobacco barn, the plastic grocery bag up in a tree—all of it deep with meaning.

But what's the meaning? James can feel that it lies in whatever Shelly isn't telling him. And whatever's in front of him that wasn't there before. Something is there that wasn't there before. Is it what Dustin felt when he left? What is it?

On the drive back into Carthage, Shelly turns on the radio and jogs through the channels. James knows what she's looking for. He switches it to AM and tunes in. The rally is still going, Winston sounding stronger than ever: ... *y'all done heard it live, and there ain't no denying the truth now, they want me dead, dead, dead, but I'm back from the dead and they can't stop me now, my woulda been shoulda been coulda been killer's out there on the loose right now, and there's only one thing to do at this point and that's put your checkmark right next to my name, Winsaton Alcorn, and let them know you want the rule of law back in this great land, and the only one to do it is the man with the rubber hand...*

They listen to it and shake their heads in disagreement and disbelief that anyone might actually believe any of what he's saying. The rally speech, or whatever it is, ends with the man who spoke first speaking again, reminding everyone that the monument is being taken away and the only man to stop it is Winston. Then Winston takes the mic and goes into his auctioneering standards: ... *and because this operation don't run on nothing, I'm askin' you for a little biddy something, talkin' one biddy one, biddy two biddy two, biddy shoota fella whose a sella, how bout two, two two two, two guns for the price of one, can I get a one, one hundred tops for a long range couple pops...*

The station finally cuts out, and they roll back into

town with the static. She turns into the Red Rooster and parks next to his truck.

"So are you pissed at me?" he says.

"I'm super pissed," she says, and adjusts the rearview to see herself. "But I'm also kind of impressed."

He turns and looks at her. "Then what the hell's the problem? What's going on?"

"Something I need to tell you," she says. "I spoke with Miss Becka last night. She said you couldn't work for her anymore if you went to the rally with me."

"She already told me that," James says. "We don't need to tell her anything."

"She's definitely gonna know. She'll find out. And Winston will be back around soon enough, looking for us."

"So?"

"I think you need a new strategy," she says.

"Like what?"

They sit there for a while, and eventually Shelly proposes the idea that they find James a rental. She'll put it in her name and pay for it until he finds a job. "I feel kind of responsible for you? And honestly it isn't the first time. I'm just worried."

James gets his phone connected to the Red Rooster's Wi-Fi, and they both search for month-to-month deals. When Shelly finds a vague yet affordable listing on Facebook Marketplace for a duplex in Lebanon, she calls the number. A guy answers and tells her it's still available, but might not be for long. Can they come over tonight to look at it?

"Hell yeah we can," James says.

Shelly tells the man they'll be there in an hour. James

gets out of the car, goes back into his hotel room and packs all his things into his truck.

"You ready?" Shelly says.

"One more thing." He reaches into her backseat and grabs the backpack. "Don't want to forget this."

"You don't think you should get rid of that gun?"

"Nobody knows I have it."

"Let's go," she says. "I've got the address."

"Following you."

. . . .

It isn't a great part of town, but anything will do. The river's somewhere over there, and James can smell it mixing with factory exhaust. This area's overgrown and run-down. Used tire places, a liquor store, shipping warehouses. They stop at a Piggly Wiggly with a *Hiring!* sign in the window.

James parks the truck and Shelly tells him to get in the car with her. "We're almost there," she says, "and I don't want them seeing that truck of yours. Bad first impression."

He locks it up, gets in her car and they pull out onto the road. "That grocery store's looking for workers," she says.

"I saw the sign." He can already feel her trying to run his life. Maybe that's what he needs.

The neighborhood's across the street from a freight-company warehouse. They drive up and down Forrest Avenue looking for the address Shelly saw on the internet. "I just don't see it," Shelly says. "It's supposed to be right here."

"Stop. What's that?" He's pointing at a house they've already passed a few times. The unit on the right side of the place is burned out with a tarp covering the roof. A man emerges from the left-side unit, which seems to have survived the blaze, and waves them up the drive.

"Are you freaking serious?" Shelly turns in.

The photos they saw must've been taken before the blaze. The guy gives them a quick tour, and everything still smells charred. It kind of reminds James of his old home, that smell of woodsmoke and ash in the walls. But things aren't as bad on the inside as they are on the outside. As long as you don't breathe through your nose.

They walk out to the driveway and Shelly says, "I don't know."

"I bet he'll come down on the price. Nobody else could want to live here. You should just make an offer."

"Why don't you? You're the one who grew up with a big dealmaker. Let's see what you got."

"It's your money," James says. "I don't want to go around spending it."

"We're in this together. I'll be paying for it, so you should go negotiate it. Like, you know, teamwork?"

And she's right, it's the least he can do. He goes back into the house, ready to drive a hard bargain. What he was born to do.

The guy's in the kitchen, sitting on the stove under a bare lightbulb. "So?"

"Four-fifty a month," James says. "That's as high as we can go. We didn't know half the place was burnt down."

"Yeah, that," the guy says. "I don't know. Four-fifty? Whatever."

"Can I move in tonight?"
"Why not?"

. . . .

Shelly helps James unpack his truck, then tells him she'll be back in the morning to help him look for a job. He spends the night on the floor with the lights off, tapping into the warehouse's Wi-Fi and looking up on his phone who used to live here. Well, it made the news. When he turns over and puts his face against the wall, he can smell what happened on the other side to that guy and his cats.

. . . .

James wakes up when Shelly starts bringing boxes of her own things into the house. "Got in a fight with my parents last night," she says. "You don't mind if I crash at the place I'm paying for, do ya?"
"I thought you lived at the college."
"Nope."
"You live with your parents?"
"Not anymore." She drops the box on the floor and sends dust into the air. "Plus this is a lot closer to the university."
"You got any food? Maybe some coffee?"
"We need to go shopping."
"Cool," he says.
Shelly pays for the first two months after James promises that he'll find a job and start pulling his own weight.

. . . .

The one he lands is at a new Petco across town. There were a couple other places in the same shopping mall—Kroger, Little Caesars Pizza—but he likes animals, and Petco was the only one hiring. The manager asked if he could lift seventy pounds and use a ratchet wrench, so two weeks into it he's putting together metal shelving for the dog food bags. Grand Opening's in a week and they're behind schedule. He hasn't heard anything from Miss Becka, or seen anything of Winston, except for a few yard signs. Is it possible to just leave all that behind, like Shelly did with her parents?

He's lying down on top of one of the shelves with his eyes closed when he hears his boss in the aisle below.

"King James?"

"Sarge," he says, "in attendance. Up here."

"Did you clock in?"

"Yes sir."

"Then why aren't you working?"

"I have been, sir."

"I said why *aren't* you."

James rolls onto his belly and looks down at him. "Just making sure this thing's stable."

This boss made the mistake of telling somebody he used to be in the Army, so all the workers call him Sarge. He's a nervous guy with razor scrapes on his jaw. His office has a one-way mirror that looks out at what will be the ferret station, and on his desk is a book called *How to Manage People*.

"We've got a situation," he says, "and I need your help. The animals just got delivered."

"I thought they were coming tomorrow."

"This is how Petco runs their new stores."

Snakes, rats, birds, lizards, spiders—they're all outside, waiting in an air-conditioned tractor-trailer. All James has to do is go out there, open the door and start bringing them in.

"That's cool," James tells him.

"Great, that's what I like to hear," Sarge says. "Let's go unload these fuckers."

James climbs down and dusts himself off.

"One more thing. There's tarantulas out there bigger than this." Sarge shows James his open hand. "Snakes thicker than *this*." He grabs his forearm. "Can you handle that?"

"Yes sir," James says, "I'm gonna *own* it."

. . . .

Out behind the store, the truck sits idling near an embankment of neon-green grass. When the driver sees them come out, he climbs down from the cab. "We ain't got much time. The generator broke, so there's no AC at all."

"Shit," Sarge says.

They all three stand there looking at the side of the tractor trailer, baking in the sun.

. . . .

When James gets off work, he finds Shelly out in their little backyard at their picnic table. A guy's sitting across from her, and a book's on the table between them.

"Hey," James says. "It's me."

Shelly turns around. "Oh, you."

"What's going on?"

"You get off early?"

"Nothing much to do. The animals showed up but most of 'em were dead."

"This is my professor," Shelly says. "Professor Anders."

"So you're Dustin's brother."

"How you know Dustin?"

Anders looks at Shelly, she shakes her head and now James knows what's going on. He isn't a fucking fool. He walks back into the house and out the front door. They've both been living here for two weeks, but they aren't *together*, right? They sleep in separate rooms and they've never even done anything. But he still feels an embarrassing sense of possession and protection.

Earlier today, when James had to cut dying ferrets out of a congealed mess, he was thinking about his brother. And here he is in his front yard, wondering what to do about what he just witnessed. Were their hands touching? No, so calm down. Deal with it like a big boy.

His Ranger's parked in front of the house and it's leaking oil or gas or both from underneath. He stands there watching it drip and drip and drip. Look at this place. The little tree in the side yard that's never going to grow. Stuck here not knowing anybody. Fuck this.

Shelly and her professor are still out back. James wants to make sure he saw what he saw before he goes and does what he's going to do. And yeah, there it is. They're sitting together, an open book between them.

There's a twenty-dollar bill in his wallet. He earned it. He drives to the bank's drive-through, asks the teller for a roll of quarters and sends the bill up the chute. The windows are down driving back to the house, so he keeps the roll of quarters on top of a crisp tenner. He parks over his fresh oil slick and goes back to the picnic table. They're still there, doing whatever they've been doing.

"So," Shelly says, "let's start over. This is James. James, please say hello to.."

Anders stands up and offers his hand.

But James's gripping the roll in his fist. Before the professor can get in a smart word, he steps forward, ready to crack him right on the damn nose. Dustin sure would. "What's going on here?" James says.

"He's helping me study. What's going on with you?"

"Nothing," James says. "I'm good." And he goes back into the house.

. . . .

The next day the parrots come in. One cage holds a young African Gray, and he feeds it from a syringe full of a warm grainy mixture. The bird room's a glass hallway, warm from all the lighting. The birds need space to flap and scratch, and in here they send the food and litter all over the floor. When the store finally opens, it'll be his job to keep this space clean.

"Morning," the African Gray says, turning its head toward him.

"What'd you just say?"

The bird scratches its beak with a talon, shakes and fluffs out its feathers.

"I know you just said something." James gives it the last of the breakfast mixture and begins packing up the supplies.

"Morning."

"All right," James says. "Morning it is. Good morning."

The African Gray bobs its head, does a rhythmic sidestep across its perch. "Morning, morning."

"Think you're so smart," James says. "We'll see."

His muscles feel tight from all the lifting he's been doing. Sarge said they were going to hire another person, but that was before he saw James hauling the supplies across the dusty tiled floor all by himself. Building the high metal shelves on his own. Even the cross-shelves, which the instructions said required two men to put together—he just took the long square rail and lifted it with one hand while ratcheting it into the mainframe. So that's what he's been doing ever since. The birds are a nice break.

. . . .

"Would ya lookee thar," Sarge would say, in an accent meant to mimic James's. He probably learned on TV. But Sarge is no longer impressed with his strength. He doesn't even talk to him anymore. The animals are all on display in the store and all the shelves and aisles are full, so James wonders how much time he's got left here. He's been working six days a week for nearly a month.

On the drive to and from the job, he's seeing more and more Winston signs, especially around the famous monument. He hasn't tuned in to the Wins-a-ton radio station because he's usually working. But those signs tell him everything he needs to know.

When he arrives this morning he isn't able to clock in. The goldfish girl who's sweeping the floors tells him Sarge called to say he was going to be late. James goes ahead and feeds the Gray, and now he'll just wait for the axe to fall.

He takes a seat on the bench near the registers. The front of the store's all windows and the sunlight's making it hotter than a reptile terrarium in here.

Sarge finally walks in. "You're in my store."

"You weren't in the military," James says.

Sarge glances around. "Are you talking to me?"

"My brother's in the Army." James stands up "You ain't got half an idea what it takes."

"Well, if you're any indication—"

"Tell me why I couldn't clock in today."

"Because you're fired," Sarge says. "F-I-R-E-D. You do know how to spell that, right? We hired you to build the shelves. And you built them. Good job. Now you can go."

James tries to channel the calmness that Miss Becka taught to him. He doesn't need to ruin another day or opportunity. "Just let me get my things and I'll clear out."

"What things?"

"Back in my locker."

"You've got five minutes."

James walks over shiny red and white tiles that he's mopped so many times, then goes down the aisle between shelves he put together, running his fingers along the smooth painted metal, and goes into the bird room.

"You ready to get outta here?" he says.

"Morning." The African Gray bobs its head and holds onto the cage door and rides it out as James swings it open.

. . . .

When he gets home there's a note from Shelly. *Went for a run. Be back soon.* He eases the parrot out of his backpack and sets it on the kitchen table, where it wobbles around pecking at crumbs. The windows are open, and when he hears footsteps, he looks out and sees her jogging along in brand-new shorts and sneakers, then holds the Gray behind his back.

She comes in breathing heavily, looking happy. When he tells her he got fired, her smile drops. And before she can say anything, he swings his arm around and presents their new pet on the palm of his hand. "But I got this."

"You've got to be kidding me."

"This parrot's worth a full month's pay," James says. "If I don't find another job soon, we can sell it."

"Sure," she says. "Or maybe your dad could auction it off for us."

He lifts the parrot higher. "Morning," it says.

. . . .

After that day, he and Shelly start drinking at night. Especially on the weekends, when she doesn't have classes. He wakes up on the floor each morning with the parrot right next to him, tied to and perched on the back of a chair, calling, "Morning, morning," no matter what time of day it is.

TWENTY

She did the right thing by deleting what Dustin deposited inside of her, of course she did, but sometimes she worries about her ability to make other right decisions in life. She went to college to improve her possibilities, and now here with James she's sunk back even deeper into whatever she thought she used to be.

But this could be her own hangover talking. She's been drinking with James since he lost the Petco job, going one for one with him, teaching him how to hang with the big kids. And last night they really got into it. Classes were over for the week, and with final papers looming she decided to bring home a bottle of vodka and put his bartending skills to use.

This morning, when she peeks into his room, James rolls over facedown, the synthetic sleeping bag twisted around his ankles. "What kinda man am I?" he says, crying the blues about not being able to pay his share of the rent.

"You're just a kid," she says. "You don't get to be a man yet."

"Well, I'm sure useless."

"Look, let me fry you up some breakfast."

"Can Paycheck have some too?"

On the chair, the parrot bobs its head, ruffles its feathers and whistles.

"Is that its name now?"

"It's the only thing I could think of."

"Aw, poor baby," she says. "All right, everybody gets breakfast."

"Who's there?" the bird says.

"Excuse me?" Shelly says.

"Was that Paycheck?" James says.

"Morning," Paycheck says. "Who's there?"

"I'll be damned," Shelly says.

"That's a new one," James says.

"Maybe he heard me say it last night?"

"You're always saying that, Shelly."

"Yeah, because it always sounds like somebody's at the door. It *does*. Then when I go to look there's nothing out there."

"Who's there? Morning."

"That bird's definitely getting some breakfast," Shelly says.

Once the butter's smoking in the skillet, she cracks in a couple eggs. They sizzle and pop while she brews a pot of coffee, double strong. This coffee maker's one of the appliances they bought at Target with her credit card.

James comes in with Paycheck riding on his shoulder.

"You look like some crazy pirate." She slides the eggs on their plates and sets them on the table, and a saucer with toast bits for the bird.

"I just need me a boat," James says.

"Then call your dad."

"He isn't my dad. Not anymore."

"You're still his son, though."

"Morning," Paycheck says, and retrieves a shred of toast with his beak. "Who's there?"

. . . .

After they eat, she watches him wash the dishes, then they both go back to their rooms and fall asleep. James wakes up with the sun in his face, then goes into the bathroom. The mirror's flecked with toothpaste but he can see himself yawning between the whitish dots. There you are. If there's one thing he's learned since moving here, it's that time won't improve you unless you change yourself, which is pretty much impossible. Unless you go out and apply for jobs again. Paycheck needs a real cage and some toys. And he needs to pay his half of the rent.

But it's hard to get motivated. Maybe the game's rigged, like Winston always says it is. But don't you start thinking like that. You know where that leads.

He turns the shower on and lets it run.

In the bottom corner of the cloudy little bathroom window, he spots a face peeking in at him. JR? He pulls on his jeans and runs around outside, but whoever it was is gone.

Maybe his mind's just playing tricks on him. Or not? He's heard the neighbors talking about somebody creeping around. When he goes back into the bathroom, it's full of steam.

Shelly knocks on the door. "Take a shower or give it up."

"Got distracted," he says, stepping out of his pants. "Just a minute."

She opens the door, slips in and shuts it behind her. "Warning," she says. "Forbidden shower-sex scene ahead."

"Jesus." James pulls a towel off the rack and covers himself. "What the hell?"

"You can't see me, and I can't see you." She bats at the steam between them. "It's like we're not doing anything."

"Are you drunk or something?"

"I did have a little sip. Hair of the dog."

"Yeah, I can smell it."

"Well, so come take a closer whiff." She opens her mouth.

"I'm good,' he says.

"Look at you." She takes off her shirt, then her sweatpants and presses herself against him. "You've been needing something," she says. "We both have."

"I ain't really never..." Against the back of his hand he can feel her soft bristly pad.

Her hand squeezes him. "There you go," she says.

He looks down at how she's holding him, lightly yet with her fingernails. It's kind of like what he's seen on the internet, but not at all. She fingers spit from her mouth and spreads it around the tip of his erection, then turns around and puts a foot up on the toilet seat. "Try it like this here."

"I don't know," he says.

"Come on, you can do it."

He does. Then they try it in the shower with shaving gel somehow figuring into the mix, but she says it's making her dizzy and then she slips, bringing the shower curtain down with her.

They both start laughing and cussing with water spraying everywhere. James helps her up and walks her into her bedroom, leaving wet, staggered footprints on the hallway carpet.

She falls back onto her bed and says, "Let's try that one more time." Her ankles lock together around his back, her legs strong from all the jogging.

. . . .

"Tell me when you're close," she says, and when he says he is, she scoots back and he releases a line across her inner thigh. "That was worth it," she says, then closes her eyes and drifts away as she hears James saying something...

. . . .

So this is how it feels to do what everybody's always talking about doing. One wall in her bedroom has pale squares where pictures used to hang. The rest of the wallpaper's stained black and yellow from the smoke. James starts making up stuff he could tell Dustin, if he ever shows back up.

Shelly's snoring softly in the new bed she's still paying off. The sheets have creased squares from how they were packaged.

He goes into the living room, where his phone's charging, and sees there's an email from Fidelitone freight company, whose warehouse is in the gated lot across the street. They'd like an interview as soon as possible concerning his interest in the position of Materials

Handler. He doesn't even recall putting his application in but he calls the number, gets transferred to the correct department and says he'll be there for the interview within fifteen minutes.

After he has a quick shower and gets dressed, Shelly's still sleeping and he leans down close. "Be right back," he whispers. "Wish me luck."

. . . .

The man giving the interview has gelled yellow hair and a tight reddish beard. "Operations Manager," he says, then taps his name tag. *Terry.*

"Yes, sir," James says. "Good to meet you, sir."

A guy leans into the room. "Yo, Red. The verification system's down again."

"Is it?" Terry says. "Or can you just not log in?"

"Yeah." The guy shuffles his feet. "That's it."

"Forgot the passcode, didn't we?"

"Yeah."

"All right," Terry says to James. "Let's problem-solve together. This will be a good intro." He looks back at the guy in the doorway. "First, never call me Red again."

"But everybody calls you that," the guy says.

"I noticed," Terry says. "But not any more they don't. Starting right now." He stands up, just his shoulders back, tucks in the front of his shirt. "This is about new beginnings," he says. "Starting with this new hire here, Jason."

"It's James, sir."

"The first problem with your problem," Terry tells the guy, "is in fact the basic problem of y'all not knowing what the *problem* is."

The guy shrugs, holds up his hands and leaves.

"There used to be rules here," Terry tells James. "Followed to a T." Terry makes the letter with his fingers. "See what I'm saying?"

"Yes, sir," James says. "I do see."

Terry nods as if they're in on a secret. "When can you start?"

"Today? Right now?"

Terry speed walks out of the room and comes back holding a button-up short-sleeve shirt. "XL do ya?"

"Maybe a large?"

Terry tosses the shirt at him. "You'll grow into it, big dog."

"Yes, sir."

"You'll need some boots, too."

"I got boots."

"With you?"

"In my truck."

"Me like this kid very mucho," Terry says. "Go put them boots on and we'll get you in that warehouse el quicko."

"Yes, sir," James says.

"Today starts the placement process," Terry says. "Materials Handler is no joke. So now we just need to determine what kind of materials you're going to be handling. Which corner of the box you'll be master of. You see? I want to find something that fits your personality. You know why?"

James cocks his head.

"Because I'm a professional."

On the crushed gravel of the outdoor lot, it feels like it's about two hundred degrees. Terry gives James a tour of the mostly empty area, then waves at the line of forklifts along the back wall. "You ever drive one of these bad boys?"

"Always wanted to," James says.

"Well, bud." Terry holds up a single silver key. "Call me the dream maker."

"You kiddin' me?"

"Do I look like a bullshitter?" Terry puts the key in James's palm and closes his fingers around it. "Now shut your eyes."

"Why?"

"Just do it."

James does it.

"That forklift?" Terry says. "Envision it. Can you see it?"

"I think so."

"Go ahead and get in it. Turn the key."

"Okay."

"Now repeat after me," Terry says. "I'm driving a forklift."

"I'm driving a forklift."

"Louder."

"I'm driving a forklift."

"I can't hear you."

"I'm driving a forklift!"

"Feel that wheel?" Terry says.

James puts his hands out in front of him.

"Now turn it. There you go. That a boy. Now test the lift levers. Make it go up and down, tilt it left and right. That's perfect. Good job. Now open your eyes."

James is back in the brightness of the day.

"We'll work on getting you your license tomorrow,"

Terry says. "Until then, if somebody asks you if you've ever driven a forklift, you say, *Yeah, sure.*"

"Is anybody gonna ask that? I don't want to lie."

"It isn't a lie because you just did it." Terry cups his hands as if he's holding vibrating energy. "Mind power. That's all this is. And it's why I'm so fucking good at what I do."

TWENTY-ONE

She's still dizzy when she wakes up trying to decide whether or not she should feel guilty about what happened with James. She sits up and her brain starts pounding behind her eyes. Just focus on that.

She gets out of bed and feeds the bird, who's telling lies about it being morning. She gets a cold can of Diet Coke from the fridge, washes down three ibuprofen tablets and sits at the kitchen table.

When James pulls up outside, she's still sitting there. "Where'd you go?" she says.

"Just down the block."

For the first time in while, she's the one who's in bad shape with a puffy face and watery red eyes. "What's going on there?"

"They hired me."

"Who did?"

"Fidelitone. That warehouse outfit across the street. They emailed me, then I called them back and they had me come straight in for an interview. And yeah, they hired me just like that. Boom. Done."

"Oh my god! The position right here? For Material Something?"

"Materials Handler." James puts his shoulders back

and straightens up. "How'd you know that?"

"Dude! I sent that application in for you after breakfast this morning."

"You serious?"

"I put a fake resume together. Told them you were eighteen. I was feeling ambitious. In the zone."

"I was wondering," James says. "I couldn't remember anything about that place."

"Yeah, no. *You* didn't apply."

"What's wrong?" he says. "School again? Your forehead's doing that school thing." He scrunches his up to show her.

"I'm just hungover. And I've got a paper due. And it all starts to feel so stupid. Like, you have a real job now. And I don't. I just have more school."

"How about this," James says. "How about I start paying the rent? All of it."

"That's crazy talk."

"I'm serious."

"It's *your* job. I'm responsible for me."

"You found me the job. So it's yours, too."

"That *is* kind of true." She takes his hands in hers. "You mean that?"

"Are we touching now?" he says.

"Do you remember what happened this morning?"

His cheeks glow hot, like he got caught doing something wrong. "Guess I do."

"Good. Because I don't."

"Was I that bad?"

"I'm kidding," she says. "Just don't tell the cops."

"Did we do something illegal?"

"Not if we don't tell anybody about it."

"I never thought—I mean, thanks?" He bops around and punches the air a few times. "I owe you one big-time."

TWENTY-TWO

They share a banana split and onion rings at the Snow White Drive-In. It's a warm fall day with a clear sky and they sit at a painted picnic table in the sun. There's a little stage off to the side of the parking lot, where a bluegrass band is setting up. "It feels good to be out here with you," she says. "Like we aren't hiding anything."

"I hear you," James says, but he's distracted by the band. "I think I recognize that guy, the guitar player."

She squints across the bright lot, hooking a hand over her brow. "Where from?" "Maybe Winston's auctions," James says.

The man has the recognizable look of a local good old boy, big hot face and trimmed curly hair. Polo shirt tucked into washed jeans with a belly hanging out. Permanent half-smile. He comes walking over to them with the guitar around his neck. "You Winston's boy?"

"Nah," Shelly says. "You got the wrong person."

"I'm talking to the kid here." The guy laughs and strums a quick muted chord. "You're James Alcorn. I used to watch you and Dustin while Mandy and your daddy was busy selling goods."

"Ray," James says.

"Yessir, yessir. Can't tell you how happy I am about

what your old man's doing. When he called up and asked me to play for this fundraiser, you know I said yes faster than a polecat on stink." He flat-picks a run up the neck. "They want to take our statue down, and Winston's the only man standing in the way of that. You must be proud of him. We sure are."

James and Shelly lock eyes with a mix of disbelief and panic. Scanning the lot, they see folks pushing yard signs with Winston's name into the grass all around the stage. A couple men are hanging up a banner: WINSTON WINS-TN 46.

"Shelly, you ready to go?" James says.

She's already tossing their trash into the can and heading for her car, and James is right behind her. They pull out with the man still standing there holding his guitar, smiling that smile, hollering, "I'll tell him I seen ya!"

. . . .

The whole next week, while she's studying and writing, he's moving boxes from here to there in the warehouse for thirteen dollars an hour. He usually works six days a week, sometimes even seven when he picks up an extra shift, which's what he's been doing lately. After his shifts, he learns to shop and cook. Hamburgers with oven tots. Spaghetti and bread. Beef stew. One night he gets fancy and makes a tray of chicken parm. They sit at the little table in the kitchen with one candle between them. It's cold outside, but warm in here from the oven.

Except for supper, they don't see each other much. A couple more weeks go by and Shelly's on track to pass all her classes. She's studying for a future, while he does the same thing over and over again with no sign of ever moving forward. Thirteen bucks felt like a lot at first, but now it feels like too little. Funny how that happens.

She never talks about school with him. He wouldn't understand. That part of her life's separate from this part of her life, because that's just how it is.

One night she tells James he's working too much and it's stressing her out. And it's true, James is working a lot. But so is she. And the county election's coming up too, so all around town are Winston signs paired with Confederate flags and redneck propaganda. James figures she might be wondering how things would've turned out if she hadn't ever met her ex-boyfriend's little brother. And how nice things would be if she could free herself from the Alcorns for good.

But she surprises James one evening when she mentions how cold it's been getting in her room. "Would you mind sleeping in bed with me?" she says. "Just to keep me warm?"

Happy to, he's here to help. And sometimes they do more than keep each other warm. Sometimes it gets hot.

One night, she tells him she's scared. "I feel like somebody's been watching us."

"Probably just in your head." He doesn't want to freak her out with what he thought he saw that morning in the bathroom.

The next morning, before getting up for work, he looks at her while she's sleeping. She's on her side of the bed and he's on his. He gets up, stomps around the room a little too loud, and she says, "What's *your* problem?"

But she really doesn't want to know the problem's that he's already sick of this job. That he's been thinking about calling Miss Becka, checking in on her, asking if he can come back to the Bomb Shelter.

At Fidelitone, he's been moving material around the warehouse just long enough to get sick of it, love it, then get sick of it again, which is where he's at right now. They hired him for this position mostly because he was strong. Every day he has to get out of the forklift and reposition boxes that weigh hundreds of pounds and are stacked far above his head. He does it for the paycheck but no health coverage. How they stagger his hours somehow keeps those benefits out of reach.

Each week ages him by a year. Meanwhile, Shelly seems a little too beautiful for what surrounds her here on Forrest Avenue, including James. And that's quickly turning him into one of these jealous protective meatheads he saw in the Bomb Shelter. Jacked up roosters just waiting for you to look at their chicks. But is Shelly even his chick?

While this little duplex thing isn't that bad, with the Piggly Wiggly just down the street, it isn't all that good either. There's still a tarp covering the missing half of the roof and the charred framing. At night in bed with Shelly, he rolls over to face the wall and listens for something on the other side of it.

. . . .

This week he's pulling a full weekend shift. Saturday evening when he gets home from work, he finds Shelly crouched in the hallway, with the parrot perched on the chair screeching, "Morning! Who's there?"

"What the hell's going on?" he says.

"There was somebody outside my window."

"Which window?"

"The one in my study," she says.

Her study is James's old room. He'd never heard the word "study" used for a room before he met her, and something about how it sounds pisses him off. "Studying in the study," he says.

"That isn't the point," she says. "This dude, like, came up to my window. While I was right here. In my own house."

"Did he see you?"

"Why else would he be there?" she says. "To clean the gutters? He said nasty things to me."

"What were you wearing?" He warned her once about walking around topless like she does sometimes. The blinds she put up aren't really blinds, just see-through roll-down things made out of bamboo.

"Clothes," she says. "Okay? I was wearing clothes."

He does like how she looks walking around in only underpants, the ones with the eyelets in the fabric. He can't blame somebody for peeking. In fact, last week he watched her through that same window. She hadn't heard his truck pulling in and was doing the dishes in her undies. And there he was, spying. He doesn't plan to tell her about any of that right now.

"So what did he say to you?"

"He told me to..." She pretends to pull up her shirt and flash him.

"So did you?"

"I didn't want to piss him off."

"Motherfucker." James stomps into his old room where she now studies and stomps back. "What exactly did he say? I want to know."

She puts on a man's voice and says, "Show me your tits."

"Was he white or black?"

"I don't know. It all happened so fast. Anyway, he had his face covered. And what difference does it make?"

"I don't have anything against black people," James says. "I got a black friend at work. His name's Ed."

"Here we go," she says.

James follows her into the bedroom. She gets under the blankets, and he lies down next to her on top of them. He's been working all day and stinks of propane fumes from the forklift. He still kisses her shoulder and holds her. He acts gentle and understanding, because he is. "Calm down," he says. "Everything's safe now."

They must've both fallen asleep because when James opens his eyes it's dark in the room. He watches the glowstar she stuck on one of the ceiling fan's blades. She put it there because she likes the swirling green circle it makes above them.

Her hair smells like shampoo and he runs his fingers through it. She wakes up and after a while of getting spoony with her, he figures she's back to normal and hunches in, hoping she's interested in trying to stay warmer. She sniffles. Well, shit—now she's crying.

"I'm gonna go find this fuck," he says. "And when I do, I'm gonna put him in my sights and tell him to show me *his* titties."

She turns over with a worried look. "That really isn't what I wanted to hear right now."

James gets out of bed. "Dude fucked with the wrong dude."

"You don't think it's your dad, do you?"

"He doesn't know where we live."

"They could find out. That's easy."

"They're busy with bigger stuff. Winston's about to get his ass elected. They don't want anything to do with us. Anyway, they'd only be after me. This is about you."

"You don't still have that gun, do you?"

"A gun would only be dangerous if there was a kid around."

She puts her knuckles in her eyes. "Thanks for bringing *that* up."

"Sorry," he says.

"This isn't about you," she says. "*Or* him. It's about me. What happened to *me*. *Tonight*. Okay?"

"You aren't supposed to give these sickos what they want. They'll come back looking for more. They're like raccoons."

"You're making it sound like I did something wrong."

"You remember what he looked like? Was he handsome?"

"I *told* you," she says. "He had something covering his face. A shirt or a mask or something. So yeah, I about creamed my pants."

"Yeah, but you weren't *wearing* any pants, were you? Give me one identifying detail. Just one."

"It doesn't matter what he looked like. He's gone now."

"You said that already." He stomps into the kitchen and slings the fridge door open. Great, she hasn't done the shopping. But he guesses it's fair to say he hasn't either. There's an old box of Chinese take-out on the middle shelf that she's been picking at for days. The meat's gone and all that's left are little corn-things in brown sauce. A half-gallon of milk in the door. Three cans of Busch in the crisper. Lately they've been sticking to beer. They made an agreement to drink only if they were celebrating something. Never if they were angry. Which means they'll never be able to drink again.

He drops the Chinese box in the shopping bag of trash hanging from the pantry doorknob. "I'm hungry," he says.

She says something back, but he's already had another idea.

"James?" she says.

"I'm thinking right now."

"Won't you come back in here with me? I just need somebody near me right now."

"I'm taking a drive," he says. "I don't like what he did to you. I love you and you didn't deserve this shit."

He walks out to his truck and notices the passenger door's unlocked. Then he sees the glove box is open. Napkins, receipts, a lighter, soy sauce packets, his flashlight—all scattered across the seat and on the floor.

He cleans up the mess and drives to the liquor store, where he sits in the parking lot, watching people go in with nothing and come out with paper bags. Seems like a good deal. When they ask for his ID, he shows them his warehouse access card. Good enough. Back in the cab, he opens the bottle. The first gulp gives him the courage to pull the jumper seat down and reach around until he feels the hard-plastic safety case. Thank God the crackhead or whatever was too stupid to poke around back there. He opens the case, and inside lies the little homemade pistol, loaded and ready for debate.

He puts it back under the jumper seat with the bottle. He doesn't want to get drunk, just calm down. Then he drives around their neighborhood, looking for somebody doing something. Anybody doing anything. But the streets are deserted.

When he gets back in bed she's either sleeping or pretending to.

In the morning, his eyes open before his phone starts going off. There she is on her side, him on his. He goes into the kitchen, turns the radio on and gets some coffee brewing. They stay tuned to an AM station that plays recycled country music. A few turns to the right, depending on where on the river Winston's ferry is, sometimes you can hear him preaching about the Lebanon statue and the upcoming election. He goes there now and finds him saying, *That's how the working class is getting robbed, and that's why everybody deserves themselves a good deal so come on down to Rebel River Auctions and get you one, right here on the day of the sun, the day of Lord as tough as a Ford, and while you're at it, feeding that buying habit, don't forget they're trying to topple Mr. General Hatton, but me and the Sons of the Confederate Veterans ain't gonna have it, we can put a stop to it all, if you'd just check that box next to my name, we can keep everything the same, our flags flying tight, and our history standing upright...*

Extremely offensive stuff for Shelly. And Miss Becka too. James also used to think those old backward conservative guys were crazy, and while he still does, maybe they have a point. Why *not* be pissed off about everything?

Whatever, you've got to give it to the old man. He went and started up his own little riverboat radio station. He did that. And now he's campaigning at the ass crack of dawn before one of his auctions because he's got an election to win. Will he be in charge of passing laws? James grew up listening to all his bullshit plans but never once thought any of it would ever come true.

Across the driveway the neighbors are already sitting out on their porch listening to their music. Some folks have to go to work, Winston would say, but not them. Well, it *is* Sunday.

Today's a Sunday shift, which means James will be loading cargo onto trucks on the outdoor dock. Tomorrow he'll be back inside the warehouse, driving his forklift. He needed an operator's license for it and passed the test on his first try. He knows it's a privilege to be working here. They remind him of that every day.

At work, he spends the morning organizing pallets with a hydraulic dolly. For lunch he has a bag of Doritos and a Mountain Dew. In the afternoon he helps load the pallets and wheel them into the beds of tractor trailers. Some of the guys try joking with him, like, *What's the similarity between a hippie chick and a hand-rolled cigarette?* The punchline's a guy pretending to pick loose tobacco or pubic hair from his teeth. All the dudes crack up, but James isn't in the mood.

What would his mom think about these people? And that gets him wondering how her plan's working out so far.

He's in the break room clocking out when Terry comes up. "What're you doing tonight? Wanna go somewhere? You know, Sunday Funday."

His timecard reads 17:13, and something about that number gives him the creeps. He drops it into its little slot and says, "Where you thinking?"

"I know this place up the river?"

"How far?"

"Not too bad." Terry looks around to make sure nobody's eavesdropping. "You into politics?"

"No," James says. "Why?"

"Here, maybe this'll change your mind." Terry takes a flyer from his back pocket and hands it to James: a shiny piece of cardstock decorated with all sorts of Confederate symbols and images—each one floating in its own nostalgic haze—and advertising one of Winston's rally-auctions.

"Happening tonight at an old sawmill. Crazy cool spot, and it's always a real party. You know this guy, Wins-a-ton?"

"Heard of him," James says.

"You gotta see him in person," Terry says. "I'll give you a lift up and back."

He pulls his phone out and calls Shelly. "I'll be late," he says.

"But it's your favorite we're having for supper."

"What's my favorite?"

"Chinese? General Tso's with extra sauce?"

Though he wants to tell her where he's going, he just can't and doesn't know why. "Here's a hint," he says. "I don't really got any favorites." Then he hangs up.

"My man!" Terry slaps him on the back. "Don't let 'em run your life. Let's do it."

He gives James a lift to his house, where a bunch of boys are in the yard trying to catch a dog. It's a little neighborhood not too far from James's house, just on the other side of Lebanon. James could leave right now and walk home for supper. Tell Shelly he's sorry, doesn't know what got into him. But instead he steps into Terry's place.

Terry's got ninja swords all over the wall in front of them. He asks if he smokes weed and James says, "Sure."

They go into the bedroom and it looks like James's, which also gives him the creeps. Only difference is they've got heavy drapes over their windows, and it doesn't smell charred. "Where's your wife at?" James asks.

"Good goddamn question." Terry takes a bowl off their dresser, lights it up and hands it to him. "You ever feel like, you know... Shit, I don't know what."

James blows out the smoke. "Sometimes."

Terry goes through their top drawer and takes out some cash. "Me and her's been saving up, and I'm gonna buy *me* something tonight."

They step back out onto the front stoop, and all the boys are gone except one who's kneeling and offering something to the dog.

"Try baloney," Terry calls. "That's the only way she'll come." He turns to James. "That dog used to be mine."

They go east along Lebanon Pike toward the hills and stop at a liquor store with a bug-zapper hanging over the front door. He and Dustin used to empty it out for the owner, then use the dead insects as bait for panfish.

Terry comes out with a bottle of Jack. "You know why they make 'em square?"

"So they don't roll around on the floor while you're driving. Cause that'd be dangerous."

"You're a smart son of a gun," Terry says. "I don't care what they say about you."

As they get closer to where James comes from, he

starts spotting pieces of the river. The glittering green, then the shacks and trailers, the tugboat pushing flat-bottom barges loaded with coal, the tributary inlet where he and Dustin used to fish.

Terry passes the bottle. "Take a swig."

It's starting to return—that sad, warm feeling—and James can almost smell it now, his childhood, the small little sunny prairies on the shore, clumps of giant grasses taller than you'd ever be, river rocks cooking in the sun, a bare bone-gray tree grotesquely contorted on its side. You expect to see yourself down there with your brother in the canoe, casting a jig or a swimmer, pulling in a crappie or a striper, brothers being brothers. But so much gets lost. And how quickly it happens. Dustin's not down there, and neither are you.

Rows and rows of signs and flags and banners line the road leading to his old homestead. Home sweet home. They pull in and park in the top lot.

"I don't know why," James says, "but I've never been around here." He doesn't need to lie, but for some reason he wants to cover up his history, to keep it from springing back to life. He wants to see what's happening through a stranger's eyes.

"I've only been once." Terry hits the bottle and passes it to James. "But I listen to him all the time. I like what he's saying. He isn't afraid of them, you know?"

James takes a sip. Terry brings out a bowl from the middle console and lights it up. They trade back and forth, while more and more people pull into the lot. "What're we smoking?" James says. "What's in this?"

"Little bit of everything."

James doesn't answer him.

"What's the trouble? Is somebody upset?"

"I'm good," James says, and it sounds hilarious. "My brother was in the army. Or the military or the navy or whatever. Damn. This shit's working."

. . . .

They walk down the sloping yard, and it feels like he's floating over the dry grass. There's the house he and Dustin grew up in, the double-wide next to it. The pool's been drained and filled with random crap. Pay five bucks to jump in and keep whatever you can carry out.

Down on the river the ferry's anchored to the bank, serving as the stage, and the show's just beginning. Winston stands with his bullhorn raised, flanked by a crew of nicely dressed government-looking men. Probably the Sons. Mandy's on the ferry too, sitting in a chair to his left. She isn't smiling or waving like the others are, just looking blankly out into the crowd, her face unreadable. If there's an answer to any of this, it's his mom. James thinks he can see the hidden plan now.

Winston beeps the siren button a few times and people start cheering, then falls into his regular galloping rant, seething about the statue that some traitors want taken down. He's the only one brave enough to stop *them*. Anybody who was sitting down is now standing up and yelling and clapping. And all of it, for the first time, seems hilarious. He starts laughing and can't stop. When he trips into a man wearing a t-shirt with his father's face on it, he totally cracks up.

"You okay, dude?" Terry says. "You need to calm down. What the hell?"

"I'm good, I'm good." But he can't stop laughing. So Terry leaves him there and goes down to the foot of the stage.

That's when somebody grabs his shoulders and spins him around. It's JR, with Willy right behind him. "What's so funny?" JR says.

"You guys, the two of you." James hold up two fingers at them and accidentally spits on JR's face when a burst of laughter escapes.

"Assaultin' security," JR says, wiping the spit away, "is grounds for removal."

"I'm just here to see my dad," James tells him.

"He told us you can't be here."

"It's my fucking house," James says. "I can be wherever I want."

"Not no more," JR says. "We live there now. We done moved in."

"Quit fucking with me."

"Why're you really here?" JR says. "You lookin' for big brother?"

James is trying to stand straight but can feel himself wobbling.

"You're here lookin' for him, ain't ya? Yeah, you sure are. I can tell. But you're not gonna find him. He showed up lookin' crazy as hell. One of his eyes was weird. He kept askin' about you. But you ain't gonna find him."

"The fuck are you talking about?"

"Should we tell him?" Willy nods insistently, so JR says, "Your brother's back."

"No he isn't."

"He was just here."

And before JR can say anything else, James lunges

forward and swings on him. A couple blind punches connect, then James gets tackled and held to the ground. He can taste dirt and blood in his mouth. A bunch of people gather around, stepping on him, kicking him. Somebody says, "Don't move."

"I ain't," James says.

After some deliberating, JR and Willy and a couple other guys pick him up and walk him to the lot. He can hear Winston and some other man down there raging about something. The crowd's so big and the system so loud that not many people even noticed the scuffle.

They shove James out into the street. "Start walkin'," JR says.

The sun's setting and it's getting cold. James doesn't see Terry's car, just the empty bottle where they were parked. He walks until it's full dark. He smacks his pockets—no phone. Must've fallen out. But he's still got his keys and his wallet. He trudges down the highway for a couple hours. When cars come flying past, he sticks out his thumb, but no luck. His truck's in the company's lot. If he can just make it there.

. . . .

He got sick behind the tire place—or he guesses he did, because that's where he wakes up on a stinking patch of caked grass and puke. His phone's still gone. He's proud of getting this far, though, which puts him probably a little more than an hour's walk from work. The tire place isn't open yet, so he's probably still got time. He could stop by to see Shelly first, but he's too embarrassed to show his face.

The road feels too hard beneath his feet and the day too bright, even though it's cloudy. After ten minutes or so he gets dizzy and has to sit down on a guardrail until his balance returns.

At the Waffle House, he goes into the bathroom and washes his face and mouth. There's no mirror in here, and that's a good thing. He takes a stool at the counter, sips coffee until it cools, then tells the counterman to fill the cup with milk, and bring him a plate of bacon and scrambled eggs with grits and hashbrowns.

He holds back the shakes while bringing the fork up to his mouth, eats as much as he can and there's still half a plate left. The guy brings the check and James tips him five bucks. Maybe it's possible to buy back a little bit of mercy.

His truck's where he left it and he gets in and then pulls the bottle out from behind the jumper seat and takes just a little nip to clear his head. He turns on the ignition, blasts the heater. The digital clock on the dash reads 7:56. He checks his face in the visor mirror, and they fucked him up pretty good. He licks his palm and pats his hair, breath's a little boozy, but no big deal. He's ready for work.

Ed—a black guy who's Terry's boss—is waiting for him at the time clock. "Left your truck here overnight," he says. "You know you can't do that."

James won't talk to him without getting paid, so he punches his card before saying, "It wasn't starting. Terry gave me a lift."

"But you just had it running out there," Ed says. "I saw you."

"Don't you got anything better to do?"

"Who do you think you're talking to, sir?"

Then Terry walks in, carrying a paper lunch bag. He lowers his eyes when he sees James. "Gentlemen," he says.

"Nice of you to give James a ride last night," Ed says.

Terry's face goes rosy. "Oh, yeah. We had some fun."

"It's Monday," Ed says. "You're on forklift. You know that, right?"

"Yes. I do know that," James says.

Ed walks him into the warehouse. James knows what's happening. The forklift won't start until you blow into the interlock device. Legal stuff the company follows. He should try to talk his way out of it, but his head isn't working. He sits down, pulls the mouthpiece free from the Velcro pad under the steering column and gives it all the fumes he has.

The little red light flashes and the device buzzes. James puts the mouthpiece back without looking at Ed. Just stays sitting there.

"Maybe that was a malfunction," Ed says. "Want to try that again?"

"I'm good."

"Come on, James. You know what this means."

"I know."

"We have policies here. And this is one of them."

"I know."

"You know who's been calling?"

James closes his eyes.

"Go home," Ed says. "Just go home. You be okay to drive yourself?"

. . . .

The parrot's hanging out on the table in the kitchen when he gets back. Then he hears the bedroom door opening, her footsteps in the hall. When she walks in, he can tell she's pissed.

"I was up all night," she says. "Where've you been?" She comes over to hug him, then steps back. "God, you stink. What happened to your face?"

"Sorry, okay?"

"What's that even mean to you? Like you're going to change? Why haven't you been answering my texts?"

"I lost my phone."

"Then let's find it." She picks hers up, taps the screen and brings it to her ear.

He doesn't want to hear that conversation, so he goes into the bedroom. After a minute she comes in. "Are you serious?" she says. "JR just answered."

"I went to the auction last night with Terry."

"Why the hell would you do that?"

"It was Terry's idea."

"Of course it was. It's never your fault. Somebody's always making you do something. Poor you."

He's in no shape to argue. And what would he say? She turns the light off and shuts the door on him.

. . . .

His heart wakes him up. The green circle's going. Another day gone. He reaches for his phone on the bedside table, then remembers.

On the kitchen counter there's a note from her. He isn't about to read it. If she even comes back, she'll be leaving again just as soon as she hears he got fired.

He goes and sits in his truck. His brother left and joined the service, because of what Winston always told them, that there wasn't any opportunity anywhere for boys like them. His forklift license won't be any good with Fidelitone as his only reference. They take that shit serious. And there isn't much else he's good at.

Piggly Wiggly has a line of shopping carts in front of their entrance and an employee's mopping the aisles. He parks his truck in the lot, turns on that station and gets out the bottle. He watches everybody in there doing their little jobs. It gets him thinking about how hard you work for nothing. One more swallow leads to an idea. He reaches back and unlocks the safety case.

He drives around their block and others nearby, trying to figure out how to make it all up to her. Up and down their little street. After what must be the fourteenth drive by their duplex, he sees her car is back in the driveway. And there's a guy in a hoodie standing outside her window.

James hits the brakes, pulls over and checks the gun's chamber. The guy just stands there, doesn't even move. James gets out, leaving his door open. The guy turns around and watches him coming, like he lives here, then pulls a pair of headphones down around his neck. "What's up?" he says.

"This." James shows him what's in his belt, then grabs his sleeve and pulls him in close. Exactly what he should've expected. One of the neighbor boys. He pushes the pistol into the kid's stomach. "So it was you."

"The fuck?"

"This's a real gun," James says. "It's real. My brother gave it to me. He's a sharpshooter for the Marines and he taught me how to use it."

"Don't," he says.

"And it isn't registered," James says. "Nobody knows I got it."

He hears her step out onto the front stoop. "What's going on?" she says. It isn't Shelly's voice. It isn't Shelly.

The lady moves in between them with her eyes hard on James. He can't look into them. She leads her boy away, and only now does he see he's in the wrong yard. His place is the next one over.

Shelly comes running. She sees what he's holding and stops. "Jesus," she says. "What is your *problem*?"

"Where you want me to start?" he says.

TWENTY-THREE

The first thing Shelly did was take the gun from him. Or maybe that wasn't the first thing, but it's what she remembers first when typing out everything that just went down. She's in her study making a record, just in case James goes out and causes even more trouble, wherever he ends up. The police will want a timeline.

She hadn't thought about it, just snatched it, and he hadn't barely even noticed. He was in some kind of unblinking deadeyed rage. She'd never seen him like this. Then she told him to get lost. She'd never said that in her life. *Get lost*? Come on. He was already so lost. She'd seen him drunk before, but this was also something else that was coming from way far back. She saw promise in James, but he was still an Alcorn, and she couldn't change that. Never should've tried.

So what does that make her now? Who is she really? And what was she after, anyway? Was it the fight with her parents that brought her here? The chilly weather coming on, and the fear of being alone through it? Partly, sure. But maybe deep down it's also always just been about Dustin.

Sitting there at her desk, alone with the dark night outside, she picks up the gun again. It's not very big.

Looks kind of pieced together, probably one of Winston's auction projects. But boy does it have some weight to it. All these movies with people waving guns around like nothing? Not true. They're heavy. Should she empty the bullets out? She doesn't even know how to do that. Plus she better leave it how she found it. In case the cops get involved.

James went and got back in his truck and drove off. Shelly asked Mrs. Glenda if her son was all right. She said her boy didn't do anything, and Shelly said, "Of course he didn't. I know that. Do you want to call the cops?" The lady already had one foot inside her door. "We don't need more trouble," she said.

That's as good an answer as Shelly could piece together.

. . . .

There's a calmness in the house without James being here. Take it in while you can. She goes into the kitchen and cracks open one of the last cans of Busch. Then she hears a knock on the front door.

She turns out the kitchen light. Maybe it's just the cops. Or Mrs. Glenda. She's got nothing to worry about, right? She sneaks along the wall and puts her ear to the door. Nobody.

She checks on the parrot. It's perched atop its cage, not saying a thing. Maybe it finally knows who's there.

She goes back into the darkened kitchen and gulps down half the can. Then the knock again. Is it James fucking with her? She isn't going to stand for this shit anymore. She sneaks over to the door and flips the porch light on. Nobody there. Okay, breathe. She unlocks the door and opens it just a crack. Nothing. A little more. And that's when the door gets kicked in.

A man forces himself inside. He's got his shirt pulled up over his nose and a trucker cap pulled down low. It's the dude who was at her window. He shuts the door behind him, careful not to make a noise. Shelly's up against the wall and can't get herself to move. She watches the guy standing with his back to her while he locks the deadbolt.

She recognizes those shoulders.

The guy turns around. "So, what do you got to say for yourself, my baby?" He pulls the shirt down.

"You," she says.

"Tada," he says, "it's Dustin!" He bows like a bad actor.

"What the fuck?"

"Sshhh." Dustin puts a finger to his mouth, looks around the living room, then goes into the kitchen.

Shelly follows him. "Where've you been? What're you doing?"

"Questions! All these fucking questions! I can't get away from them." Now she sees that one of his eyeballs is glass, rotating up at the ceiling. "I'm just looking for our little baby boy. Where's he at?"

"It's been like a year," Shelly says.

"Seven months and three days," he says.

"But like—"

"Like, like, like," he says. "Then that would make him, like, like, like, like... seven months and three days old or something?"

Whatever used to be wrong with him has gotten much worse. He's still got that hyperactive tic, but it seems to have been exacerbated by what she can only guess was a psychotic break. Sometime during his stint with the military. "Are you okay?" she says.

"That's the thing, I'm getting better by the minute. I'm practicing self-care for a quick recovery."

"How'd you know I live here?"

"I been watching," he says. "C'mere." She follows him into her study, and he puts his ear to the wall that separates their place from the duplex that burned up. "Come over here and listen to this."

She leans against the wall and listens. "I don't hear anything."

"Course you don't," he says. "That's because I'm not in there right now."

She tells herself to take a deep breath, but she can't. "How long?"

"Much better question," he says. "Now you're starting to get it." He knocks on the wall, locates an interior framing stud, then punches between the two-by-fours and through the drywall. He tears and rips pieces away, pulls out ratty old charred insulation and finds the other side and starts punching again until there's an opening big enough to see through.

Shelly can make out Dustin's old duffel bag there in the dark. "I said how long?"

"Ain't been back but a week." Dustin's still looking through the hole. "It's nasty in there, isn't it?"

"What happened to your eye?"

"IED," he says. "Get it?"

"Oh my God."

"Not really," he says. "Nobody tells Rusty Dusty what to do. You know what I'm sayin'?"

"So you know James and I have been living together here? You know that."

"Look at my new eye."

"I don't want to see."

He digs a finger in his socket and pops out the prosthetic eyeball. It's a scooped and rounded sort of thing. The socket it was in is still raw and terrible. He makes her look. When he starts trying to fit it back in, she figures now's her chance.

She races to the desk in the study and grabs the pistol, her hand shaking like crazy. "I need you to leave."

"You don't know what you need." The eyeball's back in and pointing crazily sideways. He steps toward her.

"Stop." She aims it at him.

"If you're gonna shoot me, you gotta pull the hammer back first."

"I'm not gonna shoot you," she says. "I just need you to leave."

"That thing used to be mine. If you ain't gonna shoot me with it, give it here." He snatches it from her. "You shouldn't point a gun less you aim to fire it."

"I told you. James and I've been living together. You need to go."

"There's certain shit I just don't like to hear." Dustin cocks the hammer back and squints down the barrel. "You know what I'm sayin'?"

"I'm sorry," she says. "I shouldn't have said so."

"But then you would've been lying," he says.

"Okay, you're right. Please don't hurt yourself."

He releases the hammer, then stuffs it in his pants

pocket. "Where's my bro at? And what about the baby? What in the hell's going on around here?"

"James left. He started some trouble out there, then just drove off. I don't think he's coming back."

"That must've been what woke me up," Dustin says. "I was trying to fucking sleep."

"Morning," a voice says from the bedroom.

"What was that?" Dustin says. "I been hearing that thing."

"It's Paycheck," she says. "The parrot."

"I thought it was the baby. That's badass. Lemme see."

She leads him into the bedroom, where he goes up to the bird's stand and convinces it to perch on his finger. "Cool," he says. "Fuckin' awesome." He unhooks the chain from Paycheck's ankle.

"Don't do that," she says.

"Why?" Dustin lifts the bird up and down, making it flap its wings. "Can it fly? Or did y'all rob it of that, too?"

"I really think you should just please go. That's what I need from you right now."

"You already said that," Dustin says. "Needy, needy, needy. This's all about you, isn't it? Now where's our baby? Did James take him?"

"I don't know where he went. Why don't you go find him? He's driving your truck."

"Maybe old Paycheck here knows where he went." Dustin walks to the front door with the parrot on his finger.

"I can't let you do this," she says.

"Can you stop me, though?"

When she reaches for the bird, he smacks her hand away and the parrot screeches. "You scared it!" he says.

"How're you even here? How'd you find us?"

"You want the short or the long version? I'll just put it like this. Nobody tells Rusty Dusty what to do. Now I'm here. I came back home."

"To your parents' house?" she says.

"Yep, back in the old homeplace. JR and Willy are living in there now. JR told me a little about what's been going on. He's keeping track of things, told me where y'all ran off to. He's been following y'all," Dustin says. "I ain't the only one. He even let me take his van. I been parkin' it at the end of the road. Nobody bothers you down there."

"This is so fucked up."

"How about a thanks? I'm spillin' out all my secrets for you."

"Please just go find your brother," she says. "He's probably still driving around the neighborhood."

"Ain't no thing." Dustin opens the door. "I'm going."

"Thank you."

"Now go find Jimmy!" he tells the bird, and tosses it into the air.

"Don't!" Shelly cries.

But the African Gray takes flight, its tail feathers a smudge of red in the inky sky.

TWENTY-FOUR

The door of the Bomb Shelter's propped open with a traffic cone and letting rain in. James is sitting in his truck out in the parking lot, like he used to do before work, trying to guess who's tending bar in there. He'd bet it's Miss Becka. Who else could it be? His bottle's all gone, so he might as well have one last drink before this night's done with.

He recognizes Randall the regular hunched over the bar. Corona plus Patrón. He's always drinking by himself, even when surrounded by people.

Sometimes James talked to him about bass fishing—like what knot to tie when connecting braided line to a mono leader with a weedless craw jig at the end. Obviously the man had done a lot of fishing at some point, but now he was always here. Miss Becka would often pitch in and start yelling at them about the environmental hazards of barbed hooks and lead weights. And while none of that was very long ago, it sure feels like a different life.

He steps out of his truck. Big fat drops are falling past the amber streetlamps and splashing in the puddles. He looks up at the sky and sees this rain isn't about to quit—but what the hell is that? A bird flying low through the storm, maybe a pigeon? But it's flapping like a parrot. Paycheck? He must be drunk.

He goes in, takes a stool a couple down from Randall, mops rain from his face with a napkin and leaves it crumpled there in front of him.

The clock behind the bar is slow and almost never shows the right time, but when it does, everybody gets a free drink, if Miss Becka's pouring, to celebrate the outside world finally lining up with this one.

A young couple at one of the high tops is ordering pints of Bearded Iris Homestyle IPA, the most expensive stuff here. They're around James's age, but in clean shoes and slim-fitting jeans they seem different—college kids with cash to burn, laughing at themselves for being in this blue-collar bar. For them, hanging out in here is just a game.

Miss Becka's recording keg levels on a little clipboard. She asked James to do it once and he accidentally ordered a closet-full of Bud Light Lime. They're probably still working through that.

"How's it going?" James asks Randall.

Randall pretends to cast a line behind the bar and starts reeling it in. "Where you been?"

"Working."

"Ain't for me," Randall says. "But whatever tickles your kitten."

"I need a drink," James says.

"She might be able to help. If she's in the mood. Becka, darlin'?"

"That's Miss to you." She tuns around and looks at them both. The tin case of rollies in her shirt pocket. Her hair pulled back loosely and frizzing out wildly at the sides. She squints at James. "Why, honey," she says. "I've been thinking about you. With all this talk about Winston getting shot at. You really think he's gonna win the district because of that? I wouldn't doubt it. I've been wondering where you went." She steps closer to him, takes the glasses hanging from around her neck and balances them on her nose. "Are you okay?"

"I'm good."

"Randall, doesn't it look like he's seen a ghost?"

"Maybe," Randall says. "I ain't looked at him yet."

"When you do, you let me know."

"I'm going out to smoke," he says.

"Are you okay with me being here?" James asks her.

"Why wouldn't I be?"

"I went and saw Winston. Twice now."

"Long as you're not working here and he isn't following you around." She puts a glass of water in front of him. "Can I get you something?"

James twists his fingers together. You can't be drinking hard like he was and then just straight up go and quit. "Beer?"

"Preference?"

"Yellow?" he says. "Cold?"

"I think we've got something for you."

She pulls the Bud Lime tap handle and bright yellow beer turns and swirls in the pint glass. She sets it down in front of him and the foaming head spills over the lip.

"You want a lime with that?" she says.

"Fruit's for flies."

"That's my boy." She winks at him. "Taught you well."

"Can I start a tab?" he says.

"On me."

Half the beer is gone before he realizes he's drinking. Above the bar there's a UFC cage match about to get underway. Charlie must've turned that on. James settles in, bellies up to watch the men in tight shorts bumping fists and hopping around. Somebody's winning, somebody's losing.

"Need a yank with that?" Miss Becka sets a plastic glow-in-the-dark shot of tequila next to his beer, and he shoots it. She's turned around drying glasses when two guys come in and take stools on either side of James. He doesn't look at either of them, but after a while of them just sitting there he glances ahead into the mirror. And there they are.

"We been looking for you," Winston says.

"And we found you," JR says.

James slowly tears the wet napkin in half, then goes back to looking at the fight. What's he supposed to do now? A guy's nose is getting crushed by an elbow in slow-motion.

"There's what justice looks like, son," Winston says. He holds out his hands, palms up, the real one and the rubber one, as if he's weighing two invisible things.

"I ain't your son," James says.

"Yeah?" JR says. "Well, Winsaton's the daddy."

Randall comes back in, smelling like cigarettes. Before he sits down, Miss Becka sets him up with a shot and a beer. "Lemme have it down at the end," Randall says, "and give these guys some room. I got me alone to worry about. That's more'n enough."

"Can I get this kid a pitcher?" Winston says to Miss Becka when she comes back. "And a Coke for me. And a Diet Coke for my boy JR here. He's on a diet."

"I'm not serving you," she says. "I told y'all this a hundred damn times."

"I know that was the rules of engagement," Winston says. "But then James, your worker, snuck in as a spy yesterday. To *my* place. He broke the rule once, so we break the rule once."

"Dear Lord God," she says. "I cannot even—"

"I just need to talk to him," Winston says. "Just this once. The quicker you serve us, the quicker we leave. Deal?"

Miss Becka looks at James and James looks at her. He nods. She throws her hands up, shakes her head and starts filling a pitcher with Bud Lime.

"Guess I better tell you," JR says.

Winston waggles his rubber hand. "The fields with the horses and the men," he says. "Brother against brother. Father versus son."

"Ah, shit," James says. "It's story time already?"

"You know your brother's back, right?" JR says.

"That's what you said," James says. "But that's bullshit. Dustin's gone."

Winston puts his hands together as if in prayer, but his eyes are open and he's looking at something in front of him that nobody else can see. He looks so old right there, a raggedy pieced-together doll of an old man come to life. Here to deliver a riddle, enact some spell. "Your brother," he says.

"He messed up bad," JR says.

"Is he okay?" James asks.

"You tell *us*," JR says.

"I don't know," James says. "He isn't anything. He's nowhere. That's all I know."

Winston motions to the barroom around them. "Now *this* is somewhere. Which is something. And something's everything."

"I don't know what the hell that means," James says.

"Exactly," Winston says.

"And I don't know where the hell Dustin's at."

"But he knows where you're at," JR says. "He does know that."

Miss Becka sets the drinks in front of them. "Y'all starting a tab?"

Winston slaps a pile of crumpled bills onto the bar. "When this kid drinks," he says. "Daddy pays for it."

"Don't we all." JR's bouncing his knee. "You stay quiet, Mr. Winsaton. Let me tell him how it happened. It's my van we're looking for, you gave it to me, so this is my problem."

"The battalion began fighting amongst itself," Winston says, "for differences in opinion over the most direct path to victory."

"Dustin showed up about a week ago," JR says. "Don't know how he got here. But I sure know how he left."

"He was a soldier in the infantry," James says. "He was supposed to be a hero."

"Well he showed up lookin' like a damn bum," JR says. "He was walkin' round the house, sittin' in y'all's old bedrooms, talkin' bout how he lost his eye in battle. And that's when I seen he only had one workin' eyeball up in his face. Other was screwed in tight like a fool."

"The invisible will become visible," Winston says. "Showing that the world we lost was never lost at all, but only waiting."

"Huh?" James says.

"I thought I got it back," Winston says. "The house you grew up in and the land it sits on. I thought it was mine. I *earned* it. I bled for it, didn't I?" He holds up his rubber hand.

Miss Becka's standing there, visibly enraged. "I'm going out to smoke with Randy. Y'all got five minutes. Then the bar's closed."

"You might like to hear what I'm about to say," Winston tells her.

"Is it about you stepping down from the General Assembly election?"

"Far from it."

"Then, like I said, I'll be smoking outside with Randy. Five minutes." She shows them her fingers. "Five."

"Got it," James says and turns to Winston as she stomps off. "You bled your own blood for what was rightly somebody else's. Hers. It's all a crazy joke, every damn thing you do."

"I identified the enemy and reclaimed what was rightly ours."

"I know Miss Becka. She's a good woman."

"Ain't no such thing," Winston says.

"I'm more her than you," James tells him. "She's taught me decent things about how to get by without putting other people down."

"Ain't possible. Mandy had that lawyer of hers who I should've known, I *did* know, not to trust. She showed it to me. Right after Dustin showed up and ran off again. She showed it to me."

"Go on, tell him the rest," JR says. "Then I'll finish mine. Let's tell him everything. If he wants to know so bad."

"*Mandy's* name is on that deed," Winston says. "And it's only *her* name on there. Not mine. *Mandy* Alcorn. No Winsaton."

"What, she kick you out?" James says. "She oughta done it sooner."

"People take from me and take from me and that's all they do," Winston says. "Just like you and your brother. But it's all fine." He slaps down one of his flyers. "I hope you'll be voting for me."

"Not a chance."

"Dustin kept on askin' for you when he showed up," JR says. "Kept sayin', 'Where's Jimmy at?' like no time had passed at all. Like you wasn't livin' in Lebanon with the mother of his woulda-been baby boy."

"You don't—"

"So I told him everything. Told him what you was doin' and where you was doin' it at. We all been watchin'."

Winston fills James's pint glass from the pitcher.

"So I was gettin' about sick of it," JR says. "Him goin' round scarin' people and actin' crazy. He was makin' Willy nervous."

"Willy here too?" James says.

"He's around," JR says. "Keepin' an eye on things."

"Where?"

"He's out there." Winston points toward the open door. "Keepin' dry beneath a cedar and standin' picket."

"So with Mr. Winsaton's blessing," JR says, "I tell Dustin he's gotta get himself fresh the fuck outta there. Because that house is mine now."

"That's right," Winston says.

"No it isn't," James says. "Dustin made it back home in that kind of shape and you had JR kick him out?"

"And then your mother Mandy tells me to go," Winston says. "Just like that." He snaps with his good hand. "She shows me the deed. Tricky-ass bitch."

"So under orders from the captain," JR says, "me and Willy go and pack everything up and put it on the ferry. We didn't fix up that boat for nothin', did we?"

Winston's nodding along to JR's story, looking off at the big slow clock.

"I told him to get the fuck out," JR says, "and that's exactly what he done. Shit. Then Mandy gets in on it and does to your daddy what he just said she done. Meanwhile Dustin's takin' the keys to my van out the kitchen and we hear the motor startin' up. Ain't that right?"

Miss Becka comes back in with a cigarette hanging from her mouth and announces last call. The young couple glances at these weird people sitting at the bar. Randall asks for his tab. "You already paid," Miss Becka says. "Before you started drinking. I'm not about to take your money again."

"Why not?" Winston says. "If he's—"

"I wouldn't ever do that to Randall," Miss Becka says.

"And that's why you'll be babysitting him for the rest of your life." Winston slides his flyer down the bar toward her.

"I've seen it," she says. "Time to go."

"She's still mad about the mill," JR says. "You lose what you don't take care of."

"You got that right," Winston says.

"Five minutes was up five minutes ago," Miss Becka says.

"You sure you don't know where Dustin's at?" JR asks James.

"I got nothing for you," he says. "Seriously."

"But I'm gonna *get* my van back."

Without another word, Winston and JR get up and leave. Miss Becka follows them to the door and locks it, then she comes back around behind the bar in front of James. "So," she says. "Would you look at that." She nods to the big clock, then shows James her watch. She pours him and Randall each a shot and they down them.

"Thanks." James slides off the stool and steadies himself. "What put you in a good mood?"

"I was listening," Miss Becka says. "So your mom took the place from him?"

"Sounds like it."

"Goes around comes around," she says, rubbing her jaw in thought. "But I wonder what this means."

"For what?"

She picks up the flyer. Winston's face superimposed above the General Hatton monument, like some crazy auction-god looking down over it. "Is him losing at home going to make him keep losing everywhere?"

"I don't think so," James says. "Just like me shooting at him, it's gonna help him win."

"You *shot* at him?"

"I figured everybody'd heard about that."

"I mean, I heard about it, but I didn't know it was *you*."

"Yeah, I was with Shelly."

"I'll pretend, James, I didn't hear about the shooting part, because it shocks me. I thought you were better than that. But don't assume he's gonna win, it's putting bad vibes in the atmosphere. I'm feeling hopeful."

"You keep feeling like that," James says. "I got a brother to find."

. . . .

The low clouds are glowing purple out on the interstate and over Lebanon. Somehow James feels sober now and he starts driving around, up and down and around the square, watching for that van.

It gets so late it's early. He pulls into the Piggly Wiggly parking lot and sits there looking at the sign: still lit up in these final hours of morning-dark, the storefront lettering reads Piggl Wiggl—both the y's blown out. He says the illuminated words aloud, stares at what's there, then realizes he's focusing on the wrong thing. What used to be there and now is gone—that's what's up. The same missing letter twice, doubled in absence. Does the word that a letter's part of make it a different letter if it's a different word? He sits there repeating the question, then the letter twice, until the letter splits into different words, answer and question, all in one:

"Y?" he says.

"Y," he says.

"Why?" he says.

"Why," he says.

Maybe he should just go back to the duplex and see if he can start over with Shelly. But he's a mess right now and that's exactly what she's sick of.

The sky's starting to brighten when a van bumps into the lot and stops right beside his truck. And James sees who's behind the wheel.

"Hey, nice ride," Dustin says.

"What the fuck?"

"Watch your fucking language," Dustin says. "You

better get in here, we gotta figure some shit out. And one more thing. You got my pistol in there?"

"How'd you know?"

"I don't know shit." Dustin grins. "Just guessed."

"Fuck, man." James leans into the truck, pulls up the jumper and finds only the empty case. He feels all over down there, shaking his head.

"You..." Dustin gets to laughing, "should see your face." He holds up the pistol. "Here it is," he sings.

"How'd you get that?"

"It was at your house. With little Shelly Belly."

"Shit," James says.

Dustin pops open the cylinder and checks each chamber. "And it's still got the little spray cartridges I made. Sweet." He spins the cylinder and snaps it shut. "But don't worry. I was just testing your memory facilities. Old Army trick. You fail."

"Is Shelly okay?"

"Why do *you* care? Nah, relax. She's back there, never been better. Come on, bro. Let's ride."

James goes around the back of the van, the hot exhaust huffing against his pant leg, passes the wide-open doorless side, opens the passenger door and gets in the bucket seat. And there's Dustin, in real life, alive, up close—his buzzed head, his stubbled jaw, the high, sunburned cheekbones, the clothes that don't fit him right. But he's got a glass eye, like JR said. On the right side.

Hard to believe JR and Winston haven't found him yet, driving around in this thing. God must love him.

Out on the street, he gives it too much gas and the engine coughs. The steering's loose and exaggerates every little turn, making him seem like even more of a maniac than he is. That stupid buzz cut on top of those wide shoulders.

"They're looking for you," James says. "You know that, right?"

"Can't imagine who you mean. Wanna listen to some radio?" Dustin turns it on and finds some guy singing about a truck and a girl and a cold beer and a river.

"This is shit," James says, and turns it off.

"No it isn't," Dustin says. "It's a prayer." He turns it back on and gives James a crooked smile that seems to contain a secret. "How long you guess we got together?"

"No telling."

"That's the attitude."

"We better ditch this van," James says. "Find you somewhere safe."

"So you're gonna be my accomplice."

They hit I-40, and the wind takes the hat off James's head and spins it out the window. He grabs for it, looks back to see where it went. The early morning light's flashing in through the open door. They drive in circles around the town.

"There's actually some good tapes in here somewhere," Dustin says. "Check your door. And quit staring at my eye."

"I'm just trying to assess."

"Assess this," Dustin says. "Whatever you're doing right now in your head, just quit it."

"Why are you back? What happened?"

"I just want to live, man, that's all I want to do. That's it. You gotta respect that."

"I respect you," James says. "I do."

"Good, because I earned it," Dustin says. "The army was awesome, man. I ran that place. Everything went according to plan."

"What was the plan again? Did you actually even go?"

"Never mind," Dustin says. "I don't feel like telling."

"So what happened to your eye then?"

"Battle."

James turns away from him and watches the signs of shopping centers float by.

"There you go again," Dustin says.

"What's going to happen to you? You know when JR finds you, he's gonna try to kick your ass."

"And how do you think that's gonna go?" Dustin says. "Fighting's a funny thing, man. Kinda like *fucking*." He drums on the steering wheel. "I know where you been sleeping. I been watching y'all. From the other side. In the burned-out place?"

"Don't do this."

"I already did," Dustin says. "It's cool. You deserve everything you got. Even if it was mine in the first place."

"I'm sorry," James says. "I disrespected you, man. I thought you were gone. You left us. I thought you were out for good."

"So you went picking through my trash. That's cool."

"No it isn't. Please."

"Don't beat yourself up," Dustin says. "Cause I got some news for you. About Shelly."

"She's done with me. I been nothing but a problem for her."

"Like bro, like bro," Dustin says. "But listen here. What if she was just as bad as either one of us? Maybe even worse."

"Un-fucking-likely."

"There's this older dude," Dustin says. "This teacher of hers from Cumberland."

"What about him?"

"Everything, man. She was fuckin' him. I watched it."

"No way. I don't believe you. You're lying."

"Maybe, maybe not. But let me just say this." Dustin takes his hands off the wheel. "I squashed her first. Which is true. So somebody needs to give me the props."

"I don't believe this shit," James says.

"And after I watched them do that in your bedroom—your own damn bed, bro!—I knew I had to make myself known. See what I'm saying?"

"She knows you were there?"

"Now she does."

"Put your hands back on the wheel," James says. "I don't even understand."

"Let me help," Dustin says. "We got zero control in any of this. Sometimes what we didn't want to happen is what we needed to happen."

It's bright daylight now and getting busy with traffic. People going to work.

"We could drive into the mountains," Dustin says. "Live off the forest. Start our own survival pack."

"First thing, we got to get rid of the van. Let's go back and grab the truck."

"And then where? Your and Shelly's house? I like that place."

"Jesus," James says. "That's the last option."

"I ain't joking. We gotta make this right. We'll show up there in solidarity. Show her she can't come between us. Unless she wants to." He tries to elbow James in the ribs and James pushes him away. "Maybe we could all live together. Happy ever after."

"She'll call the cops," James says.

"Nah, she won't. We both love her. She can't do that to *both* of us."

"You don't know *what* you're talking about."

"I know a lot more than—hush." He points ahead to a cop cruiser parked in a lot. They pass it doing exactly forty-five.

. . . .

There's the small, overgrown yard, nothing in it but a scrub tree. The gas gauge is on red when they make it back to the house. Shelly's car is there. And parked next to it is a Subaru.

"Looks like school's in session," Dustin says.

"That his?"

"Go check."

"What if he's in there?" James says.

"Tell him everything's just fine. Tell him we just want to talk to him. Tell Shelly we love her. And then," Dustin says, "tell 'em both to come outside."

. . . .

She opens the door right away. Her hair is tied on top. "Jesus," she says.

"Can I come in?"

"No!"

"Who's in there?"

"Nobody." Then she just starts crying right there in the doorway. "I've been so alone," she says. "And you pulled a fucking gun on Glenda's boy? And now Dustin shows up? You probably knew about that, didn't you? And then *he* takes the gun? I can't do this."

"Who's car is that out there?" James says. "The one who was teaching you?"

"Me and him are nothing," she says. "We're friends. Is that a problem?"

A voice comes from behind her: "Everything okay out there?"

"Who the hell's that?" James says.

"You know JR and Winston came by here too? Late last night. Looking for Dustin. Saying he stole their van."

"That's not what I asked," James says. "Who's in there? Tell me."

"I haven't seen Dustin since last night. Since after you left."

"That isn't what we're talking about."

"Then what, James? What *are* we talking about?"

"Me and Dustin. And you."

"Just what I thought." She slams the door and locks it.

. . . .

Dustin's parked in the ditch with the engine off and the radio on, the music coming out the wide-open side. James stands there on the shoulder, watching him sitting there, nodding along to a tune. He goes over and taps on the window. "She doesn't want us here."

"She doesn't know *what* she wants," Dustin says. "That's her problem. Is that dude with her?"

James nods.

Dustin gets out and walks around to the open side of the van, takes his shirt off and tosses it in. The butt of the pistol sticks out the waist of his jeans. "Let's go." He walks so fast up the driveway that it's hard for James to keep pace. "Man," he says. "Sometimes I wish I had, like, a family? People taking care of each other and shit."

"I'm here," James says.

"I know that. But now it's too late."

Winston's dually Dodge comes rumbling into the driveway behind them, then stops in a heavy idle and their father leans out the driver's-side window. "Charge!" he says.

JR and Willy hop out of the bed and trot toward the brothers, almost mirroring them in front of the half-charred duplex.

JR's carrying Dustin's old baseball bat. "I want my van back."

"Come and get it," Dustin says.

"Charge!" Winston says.

James calls out for Shelly. He's yelling her name when she opens the door. Anders's standing behind her with no idea about the shit he just stepped in.

"You want some too?" Dustin asks. "Everybody come over here. I got somethin' for everybody."

"Let's do this." JR slaps the bat into his palm. "You ain't got shit."

"Get a little closer then," Dustin says. "You can't fuckin' touch me." He pulls the pistol out and points it at his own face. Shelly yells for him to stop. The shot cracks and echoes off the houses and James sees his brother stumble backward and then collapse on the ground.

TWENTY-FIVE

James takes off running down the street. "Deserter!" Winston shouts. "Fire!" But there's only one gun on the scene and it's lying in the grass next to Dustin.

Willy shuffles over to the body and kicks the pistol away, like Winston taught him to do in security training. JR goes through Dustin's pockets and finds the keys to the van. "Bingo," he says. "What's mine is mine."

"And what's yours once was *mine.*" Winston gets out of the truck, takes the keys from JR, then goes back and drops the tailgate. "Retrieve my brave son off the battlefield," he says. "We'll deliver him home to his mother."

JR and Willy carry him by arms and ankles over to the truck and lift him into the bed. Some wind's pushing the treetops around, blowing colorful leaves from the patched canopy of hickory and poplar, the distant threat of an unseasonal thunderstorm.

Winston takes his cap off and places it over his heart. "I always knew," he says, through a tearless emotional puffing. "I seen it. And I always knew it."

"Knew what?" JR says. "Tell us, Mr. Winsaton."

"I seen it before," he says, "and now I see it again." The heels of Dustin's sneakers are touching, the toes pointing apart. "Hurry now and hush," Winston says.

"Honor him as we done our heroes past."

"We gonna make a statue for him?" JR says.

"We already got us one a them," Winston says. "First we need a proper burial on his native ground."

Shelly's peeking out the front window with a phone to her ear, her face red and crooked. From outside the frame, a hand reaches in and touches her shoulder.

"I said now," Winston says. "Get on up in there and see to it his body doesn't get messed with on the ride home."

JR and Willy climb up, push aside ratchet straps and fuel tanks, slide Dustin forward against the cab and sit either side the body to keep it from rolling.

Winston slams the gate shut, picks up the pistol and checks its chamber. "Huh," he says, "handmade artillery." He gets back in the truck and pulls out onto the street, takes a couple turns and goes back toward the river.

JR pushes the rear slider-window open and looks into the cab. "Mr. Winsaton, can we go back and get my van?"

"Negative," Winston says. "We continue on and will count collateral later. Our time's run short. The enemy's on us."

"But that's why we come down here in the first place," JR says. "My van."

"That's *my* van," Winston says glancing in the rearview. "Been so from the start. My son's been shot by the enemy and we gotta return him."

"He shot hisself."

"We got a mission to fulfill and are bound to keep going."

"I don't mean nothin' by it," JR says, "but you're losing it, sir."

"The enemy's out there," Winston says, pointing around. "And we're here. That's the difference."

JR's looking down at where Dustin's lying. Or was. Now he's sitting upright.

Willy backs against the edge of the bed with eyes wide in disbelief and mouth moving silently in slow tremors. Winston's watching it all in reverse and slows down as the back of Dustin's head comes up into view, his son's complete skull covered in an uneven buzz cut with no exit wounds. He's sitting there touching his face. Then he motions vaguely and talks quietly. "Where am I? Am I dead?"

"Not quite," Winston tells him.

"I think you'd best pull over," JR says.

"Praise be. My soldier son's returned." Winston stops right in the middle of the road, gets out and comes around to see his boy sitting there not dead, with one glass eye skirled sideways at the warped sky and the other just a blasted socket that's bloodied and busted, a shock of white powder covering that side of his face.

"You back with us?" Winston says. "You back here now?"

"He tried killin' hisself!" JR says. "That's what he done."

Dustin fingers the area around the exploded eye. "It burns."

"Can you see?" Winston says. "How many fingers am I holdin' up?" He lifts his rubber hand in front of his son's face.

"Only lights and shadows." He reaches around in front of him.

"Onward, men," Winston says. "His sight's gone but his vision's true."

"How the hell's he even talking right now?" JR says.

"Describe what you seen," Winston tells his son.

"I can't think," Dustin says. "It hurts."

"You're gonna be all right. They tried to make you kill yourself because you saw too much but they can't. We'll win this battle. Just hold on." Inspecting his freshly deformed boy, Winston realizes this is the final gift he might've been needing. Kinda like getting shot at. What doesn't kill you helps you win elections. "He'll be all right, JR."

"Yessir."

Dustin leans back. "Okay, okay."

"What's all this white stuff on your face?"

Dustin runs a finger through the powder and licks it. "Kitchen salt," he says. "I packed these shells myself. Nothing fancy."

"Wrap his face with your shirt," Winston tells JR, who pulls it off, rolls it up and ties it like a blindfold across Dustin's eyes.

"Goddamn," Dustin says.

"That's just the salt talkin'," Winston says. "Now let's move, boys. We got to get off the road and back upriver."

"We goin' back to Mandy's place?" JR asks.

Winston blinks, looks at him like he's trying to recognize him, blinks again. "Whose side are you on? Is there a spy among us?"

. . . .

They pass fields and creeks and head toward the filtration plant. Soon they'll be at the Hunter's Point access area and boat launch, where their ferry's stationed.

Trucks pulling boats on trailers are passing them by in the other direction. With the storm rolling in, everybody's leaving the river. Except for Winston and his men.

The ferry, twenty feet wide and seventy feet long, is tied off near the boat launch with its loading ramp lowered onto the grassy bank. A tall radio antenna rises above the metal roof of the wheelhouse, and hand-drawn signs are duct-taped to the side railings: AUCTION DEALS NOW! THE LORD COMETH SOON BUT NOT SOON ENOUGH! VOTE WINS-A-TON DISTRICT 46! SAVE THE STATUE! PROTECT OUR CHILDREN! HONOR HISTORY AND THOSE WHO DIED FOR IT! On the back deck a flagpole dangles a curling mullet of Confederate and American flags. A plastic water jug labeled TIPZ is zip-tied to one railing and stuffed to the mouth with dollar bills, offerings from fascinated folks at each marina fuel-stop.

Winston puts the truck in four-wheel-low and rolls down the soft grassy slope, then up the pressure-treated plank-board ramp and onto the concrete deck. JR and Willy hop out of the truck bed, reel in the ramp on a hydraulic winch and pull up the front and rear anchors. Winston turns on the engine, an enormous diesel connected by a drivetrain to the paddle-wheel and it burps clouds of black smoke into the air and begins churning and boiling the water, a cavalry of horsepower.

"Black Bessy!" Winston yells over the noise and beneath the rolling storm scud. "Let's ride!"

The boat steers out onto the Cumberland as a solid wall of clouds moves in, darkening the surface of the river and roughing it up with white caps. Winston plows them through in full forward drive, carving a wide path and leaving an arrow-shaped wake behind them.

Distant thunder rumbles and rain pelts down across the deck and scatters over the cabin's tin roofing. Winston opens the door to the noisy little room, and JR and Willy lead blind-folded Dustin inside, carefully and calmly as if he were some beloved hostage. They stand there in the cramped space of wires and motherboards and microphones, switches and lights and amplifier gauges, all of them around the large helm's wheel. After steering around some bends, Winston gets them out into an open stretch. Linked together and posted along the far shore are two barges loaded with small mountains of aggregate. Above that, on limestone bluffs and rolling hills rest some large houses, middle-class mansions. Winston studies them without saying a word, then clicks a button, slides two fader channels up on the soundboard and speaks into the microphone: "Hidy, neighbors! We are live on air and alive on the water, so tune it in and turn it up, whether you're looking for a deal or a steal, or just a little biddy bid of history come to life, you found the right station on a waterborne location, provideth not provocation and be spared eternal damnation, right here on the historic waters where most folks don't know so many of our battles were fought, and some won... It's yours truly, Winston Wins-a-ton Alcorn, whom many of y'all know and love by now and all of ya should because, yes, he's running for office, member of the House of Representatives of the General Assembly, here we come, can we get it done, I think we can with the help of my—"

A flash so bright that everything is nothing but blinding light, and then a cracking explosion. Winston's reeling and steadying himself against the helm with his rubber hand. He checks the microphone and says, "Ladies and gents, we done been struck by a bolt. Are we still with y'all?"

JR's checking the connections. "Yeah, we should be. But we might gotta stop at the next marina at Pine Cove. It's dangerous out here."

"Dangerous?" Winston shouts, sending the analogue meter rightward into the red. "You can't run away from that."

"Willy's scared," JR says.

Winston mutes the mic momentarily. "Don't use him as an excuse," he says. "But we're low on fuel so we'll make a stop."

"I saw it!" Dustin says. "I saw it and it was *wild*."

Winston slows the boat, spins the big wheel and steers them toward the small Pine Cove Marina—while dictating their real-time progress into the microphone. They approach floating docks, a couple pontoon boats, little homemade tiki huts over picnic tables where people in jackets sit around iced buckets of beer. Two women holding umbrellas are standing at the end of one dock and pointing at the boat coming in.

Guys at the beer huts start clapping. "Rebel River Auctions!" one hollers. "Woo!"

"Wins-a-ton! Wins-a-ton!" shouts another.

Winston grabs the bullhorn with his real hand and steps out onto the decorated platform. "My people," he announces. "You gotta lose a ton..." Then he holds his rubber hand up to his ear.

"To Wins-a-ton!" they begin cheering.

"We're bound by God to win this!" he tells them.

A young man in a sports hoodie is dancing spastically

atop a picnic table to the beat of Winston's promises.

JR and Willy come out and look around and without even tying the boat to a post they race off down the dock past the marina and out of sight.

Winston steps back into the cabin, where Dustin's crouched and holding his head in both hands, rocking back and forth. "I need you now, son," he says. "We've been abandoned. Are you ready?"

"I don't know," Dustin says.

"Answer me."

"I think so," he says. "Yeah."

The rain's slowing and the clouds are clearing. The lingering colors in the trees are rich and scattered. People wander out of the lakeside tavern holding phones in their hands and recording the scene for posterity.

"Good," Winston says, "they wanna hear it." He turns on the power to the sound system so his live broadcast can be heard all around the boat and as far as the radio waves will carry. He helps Dustin stand up, then speaks into the microphone: "This here's my dear boy, the son I've loved and missed the most. He's come home from war."

Some scattered applause, plus "Thank you for your service!"

"Now Dustin?"

"Yessir."

"Kindly tell these folks where you been," Winston says. "Tell them what you seen. And tell them a little bitty bit about what they're gonna be bidding on today. All proceeds are dedicated to my personal efforts to become your representative so we can keep our statue."

Dustin takes the mic and speaks uncannily in his father's auctioneering rhythms. "My old man is a good old man who sacrificed his hand for our glorious homeland."

And Winston proudly stands back, maybe for the first time ever, and listens...

TWENTY-SIX

It's been two weeks to the day since Miss Becka put her father in the ground. Second Wind had called to tell her he wasn't doing well—*decreasing blood pressure, low oxygen saturation*—and when she got there he was already gone. Cold skin, blue lips. She spent the next few days making arrangements with the funeral home, putting it all on her credit card and trying to ignore the fact that she'd missed his last big moment, their final duet.

Today she's standing in her backyard, barefoot on the cool pine needles and wet leaves, looking down at the Caney Fork and trying to understand what she's been feeling. It isn't surprise or grief. No, it's something else. Maybe relief? But not quite. She spots a barred owl on a branch, watching her, and for the first time since his death she understands the strange thing in her chest, this newfound freedom of orphanhood.

She tries singing one of their old songs, "House of Gold," but can't quite find the harmony without his lead.

She goes up into her cabin. None of the lights are on, and everything's motionless in paper-cut shadows. The mortared stone wall in the back, the hand-hewn beams flanking the length of the room. With the eyes of a stranger, she looks around at all her stuff. Chair, couch, coffee table, newspapers, mugs, medicine bottles and beer cans. It's time to do what she's been meaning to.

. . . .

After a few rings, Mandy answers in the Kentucky accent that Miss Becka has a hard time hating. "No auctions this week, or next either."

"This is Miss Becka. I'm not calling about the auctions."

"Miss *who?*" Mandy says, but she knows. "I don't owe you anything." But she does. "Winston isn't here right now."

"I'm not calling for him. I want to talk to you."

"What do you wanna talk about then?"

"I need to give you something," Miss Becka says. "In person."

"I don't need anything, I got everything I need. And then some."

"I know, I know. It's more for me. Just this once."

"We can't meet here," Mandy says. "If he tries coming back, he'll likely be madder than hell."

"Why's that?" Miss Becka says, but she knows.

"When he kicked Dustin out, I told him to get out too. And he did. But I know it isn't permanent. Nothing with him ever is."

"Okay," Miss Becka says. Now they're getting somewhere. "You got wheels?"

"Course I do."

"Can you come over to my place? You know the Razor Branch boat ramp? Cross the bridge there, then go a quarter mile and you'll see my car on the shoulder.

Park behind that." "I'm busy for the next couple hours."

"Perfect," Miss Becka says. "I'll see you later then. Just text this number when you get here. I'll take you fishing and we can talk. Do you like fishing?"

"Used to, but Winston ruined it for me. He doesn't like having me out on the water."

"Let me take you out then," she says. "What's your foot size? I've got some waders for you."

"You mean I'll be standing up to my ass in the middle of a river?"

"Not just standing," Miss Becka says. "*Fishing*. On the Caney Fork. I've got an extra fly rod, too. I'll teach you how to cast, mend line, set the hook, all that."

"Lord God help us."

"You're gonna love it. The feeling of catching a trout on a fly? There's nothing like it."

"I'm sure."

"And we'll have some drinks after. Do you drink? What do you like?"

"Whatever you got'll be good," Mandy says.

"We'll be safe," Miss Becka says. "I promise."

"Why're you doing this?" Mandy says. "Why me?"

"We'll talk about that when you get here."

. . . .

With some time to kill, Miss Becka drives over to Al's Foodland in Lebanon. In the entrance, the *Lebanon Herald*'s displayed on the front rack, with the front-page photo showing people protesting against the town square's monument. It's been going on for weeks now, in response to Winston's growing popularity, and while she wouldn't ever march or wave a sign, she did *sign* that petition about removing the monument. It was the least she could do. And also the most.

She just wishes they'd talk about who they want to put up in its place. DeFord Bailey would be nice.

She walks the aisles, picking out snacks that Mandy might like, and after paying for the crackers and cheese and chips and dip, she decides to circle down to the square and see what's going on. As she approaches the roundabout, a loose group of people are standing around in the Antiques parking lot chanting slogans. Back in the day, Confederate cavalry had camped out here, until they got chased off by Ebenezer Dumont and his Union boys. And now rising above the traffic circle stands a rebel, a traitor, old General Hatton himself, his eyes hard under a wide-brim hat—bravely, oh, so very bravely. She honks, gives a thumbs up, and the protesters cheer, but she needs to get home.

She parks in her spot off the highway, lugs her groceries down the worn path, fits the boxed wine in the minifridge and lays out a little snack platter. She's never been an hors d'oeuvres kinda gal, on this occasion she wants to be hospitable.

It rained a lot yesterday, with a freak lightning storm to the west, so she checks the dam's release schedule on her phone. The water won't start rising until later tonight. "We should be good," she says.

A few minutes later, Mandy texts *here*.

Miss Becka goes up and finds Mandy standing next to her car checking her phone, dressed in jeans and a canvas jacket.

She looks at her and says, "You made it sound like you're living out in the middle of nowhere—but here we are."

"Not there yet," Miss Becka says. "Come on." She takes the tote bag from Mandy and peeks in. "Oh, good. Whiskey."

"Girls' day out," Mandy says.

"That's what I'm talking about."

On the front porch, after one respectable splash each, and then another, Miss Becka brings out the waders. Mandy takes her shoes off, showing socks with holes, steps into the long rubber booties and pulls them up. Then Miss Becka does the same but slips off balance, and Mandy catches her with a hand. Miss Becka allows it—not because she needs the help, but because she figures she will sooner than later and might as well get used to being helped out.

The rods are leaning up against the boat down near the river's edge. Both are nine-foot five-weights with ten feet of leader. On the end of Mandy's line is a beadhead Pheasant Tail nymph with a strike indicator, which will work like a bobber, allowing her to sink the tail into the deeper columns of the current. That's where most of the fish are hanging out this time of day. And on her own she's tied a streamer that she made herself: a trimmed bluejay feather with deerhair along the body and red sewing thread making gills at the throat. It's supposed to mimic a shiner minnow, which it does when streamed correctly. She'll use this to cover the upper columns. If she needs to, she can even fish it dry right on top. A floating dragonfly, maybe. Between the two of them, they ought to land something.

In felt-bottomed boots, the two women step out into the current together and walk carefully over grassy rocks with water rushing around their legs. Out here the world's fast and powerful and pushing as they move slowly through it. They wade up onto a gravel bar and follow it downstream toward the bend, where the water turns and slows and deepens against a limestone wall. And here they stop to cast.

To keep Mandy's line from tangling, Miss Becka holds her wrist and shows her how to throw. After a few tangles and a snag behind them, Mandy pulls back and releases the line and lays it straight out in front of her, across the slow water.

"Nice," Miss Becka says, "that's it. Now just let it drift. And keep an eye on your indicator there. If it tugs or dives, just lift the tip of your rod."

They stand knee-deep in rubber chest-waders in an easy current on a slowly sloping gravel bar. For almost an hour they throw line, let it drift, mend, bring it back and throw it again. It's a calm day with the distant rush of I-40 over the hills. The sun's sharp and the river air's cool and mossy. Mandy's line goes tight and at first they think it's a fish, but it's just a snag. Miss Becka breaks the line and tries tying another nymph onto the end of her tippet, but there's glue or something in the eye of the hook, so she takes a snippet of barbed wire from her breast pocket and pokes the hole clean. Once the leader slides through the metal eyelet, she brings the end of the line back up, wraps it seven times around itself, loops it and threads it and loops it again. She spits on the knot to kill friction and pulls it taut. Christ, her hands are getting a little shaky. How long will you be able to tie these tiny damn flies?

She hears a familiar sound and turns to see Mandy unscrewing a flask and having a sip. "Rascal," she says. Mandy hands it to her and she swigs, then hands it back. "Bourbon on this river's almost perfect. But we still need a fish."

"That isn't what this is about, though," Mandy says. "Right?"

"No." Miss Becka can feel the whiskey warming her face. "So yeah. My dad died recently and it got me thinking about stuff. He's the one who gave me the mill."

"Ah. Okay, now. I get it," Mandy says. "You want it back."

"No, no, no." Miss Becka reels in her line, holds the rod under her arm and turns against the current to face Mandy. "I want to give it to you."

"You crazy? It isn't even yours."

"Because y'all took it. But I never *gave* it to you. And that's why I've been holding on to it right here." She pats her chest. "I need to release it, you know? I don't have kids. I don't have any family left. I want to let go of the mill and what happened there—morally, spiritually, whatever."

"This is getting too weird for me."

"I want *you* to have it. Not Winston. Just you. Will you accept it from me?"

"Sure," Mandy says, "whatever. But yeah, thanks."

"Then it's done," Miss Becka says. "Thank you." She brings line into the air, guides it back and forth and casts out.

"The mill already belongs to me, though," Mandy says. "Not Winston."

"I know. That's partly why I called you."

"How the hell you know that?"

"James," Miss Becka says. "He came down to the bar last night. Then Winston followed him inside. They were talking about it."

"When Winston injured himself, I was the one working with the lawyers. And I put my name on the deed. Your old place belongs to Mandy," she says. "Signed on the dotted line."

"That's incredible."

"And it's been my plan all along," Mandy says. "Just sometimes it takes a lot of patience."

"Good for you." Miss Becka drifts the deeper run and casts up it again. "But how's he taking it?"

"He likes your ferry," Mandy says. "And he has much bigger plans with the government stuff."

"You think he'll win?"

"Definitely," Mandy says. "Look around."

"You think he's right in what he believes?"

"I don't know what he believes. But I do try not to think about it." Mandy takes another sip. "You ain't pissed at me, though, for your family's mill?"

"I would've been. I used to be. But not anymore. The mill was never for me anyway. It was my dad's business. I'm free of it now."

"You don't mind me keeping it and doing what I want with it?"

"By all means," Miss Becka says. "What're your plans?"

"I'm not sure," Mandy says. "I always wanted horses. Or maybe get the mill actually running again."

"Why not do both? You've got two sons who need work."

"I don't know about Dustin. Or James." Mandy looks into the water. "I used to promise him things would get better. Like I thought I had a better plan for him. But that didn't really work out. It was always for me."

"There's always JR," Miss Becka says. "He was my employee."

"And look how that ended."

"He saved your husband's ass."

"And we've been paying for it ever since," Mandy says.

Something tells Miss Becka to look up and an eagle's cruising high overhead. "There he is," she says. "My father."

"Wish I had my phone," Mandy says.

Passing the flask back and forth, they decide today's round of fishing might be done. Their legs are already tired and relaxing on the porch sounds pretty good, fish or no fish. They agree that the eagle sighting was the real catch.

But Miss Becka gets the feeling that something's going on below the surface. "Let's trade rods for a sec."

The cork handle's warm from Mandy's grip. Miss Becka casts out, and on the second drift past the downed tree across the deeper run, the indicator bops once beneath the glassy surface. She lifts the rod, pulls in line and brings in a silver shad. "These are the real survivors," she tells Mandy. "They were here before the locks and dams got built. Before the trout got stocked. And they'll be here long after, too. I love these guys."

"Good enough for me." Mandy shakes the flask. "I should probably get going soon."

Miss Becka tosses the little fish back. "One more cast," she says, and drifts the same stretch, lets her line run out, arc back, and on the rise something hits it fast and starts fighting. "That time of day," she says. She brings it in slow, careful not to snap the 5X tippet. A brook trout. Dark and spotted with little ringed planetary dots. She rinses her hand in the water, grabs the fish up and turns the hook out the corner of its mouth. "Young and feisty," she says, "which means it was born in this water. Parents were probably from my breeding pool."

"No way." Mandy looks closer.

Miss Becka holds the trout up so Mandy can witness its brilliance. "Almost native, but not quite. It is wild, though. You want to let it go?"

"Okay." She takes the fish in both hands, cradles it, then lowers it into the water. "It's so beautiful."

"Isn't it?" Miss Becka says. "Now let go."

The fish darts out of Mandy's hands, races across the soft pebbled floor striped with golden ripples and disappears.

TWENTY-SEVEN

Out off I-40 on an empty concrete lot where there was once a gas station, a man's sitting in his work truck wearing his American Pest Control uniform. He's taking his lunch break with no lunch, just waiting for his next appointment and watching freightliners barrel past east and west.

He clicks on the AM and it's 650 WSM playing the usuals, so he scans for the local talk-radio guy. That old codger's crazy as shit but sure is fun to listen to. Especially if you're stuck working a shit job.

When he finds the signal, Wins-a-ton's still running for office and he sounds more pissed off about it than ever: *They're trying to take our statue, and I'm the only one willing to put an end to it and—* He turns the volume down and figures he'll vote for him. What are his other options, somebody who isn't even from here?

He hears a strange tapping sound on the roof of the cab. The sky's clear, no rain. Then he hears the sound of flapping and sees a strange-looking bird come down into the bed.

He opens up his back cab window, calls it with a clicking noise like you'd do with a dog and it flaps right into the cab with him. It's a parrot.

He doesn't know what else to do, so he lets it hop around pecking at crumbs. Then it angles its head and looks directly at him. "Morning," it says. "Who's there?"

TWENTY-EIGHT

Growing up she always wanted horses but only got chickens. Her favorite hen was a big dominicker named Maud and she had her a husband, a little banty rooster named Colonel. He was always pecking and scratching and yelling at Maud about where to go and what to do. Maud just went along with it, taking her dust baths and waiting for him to turn around, and when he did she'd jump up and snatch everything he'd gathered without him even knowing it. Take it right out from under him. Smart lady, Mandy thought.

Back when Winston was on the pain meds with his arm healing, she'd tell him that story and laugh to herself because he couldn't even see the truth in it. Well, that was his problem. If he was half as smart as he claimed to be, he would've double-checked that paperwork. But he didn't, he trusted her just enough not to. So she went and got what was hers, took it without him even knowing it. Hell, didn't take it, just *claimed* it as she'd planned it out with her lawyer. Now she's got the deed stuck to the fridge under a smiley magnet and a locked money-box of auction cash hid up in the attic, and Winston understands only as much as he's able to these days.

Poor old mister Banty, spinning back around and saying "Who?" but she's already long gone.

She hears a little outboard humming, then some voices down on the river, so she comes outside and sees James and Shelly pulling the canoe up onto the bank. It's been a little bit since she saw him and doesn't know what to say now. Good luck to those two. They're a cute couple, and that'll last only about as long as anything does, which isn't long at all. She can see a little of herself in Shelly, which is why she doesn't like or trust her very much. Mandy told James to come on back home when Shelly does to him what she did to his brother. And here he is, with her in tow. Even from here he looks distressed. So Mandy goes on down like a good mommy to see what's wrong.

"We came by earlier looking for you," he says. "Where were you at?"

"I was out with Miss Becka." Mandy says, "working on my better plan. Like I used to tell you about. And what's wrong with you? Where y'all been?"

"Looking for Dustin," James says.

"Again? He was here, then he left."

"Always," Shelly says. "We think he's out on the river somewhere because we heard him on Winston's station yesterday."

"After he shot himself," James says.

"What?" Mandy says. "What'd he do?"

"Shot himself in the face right in front of our house," Shelly says. "Then JR and Willy loaded him into the truck bed. Meanwhile James ran off down the road."

"But then I came back," he says, "because I had to see Dustin one more time. For myself, you know? And he was gone."

"So then I asked James if he saw where they took him. But he didn't, so we went driving. Couldn't find them anywhere. Ended up at a boat ramp, and that's when James gets the idea to try the radio."

"I just hit the volume and here comes Dustin's voice coming through the speakers. I was like, what the fuck? Right there on Winston's station. Dustin's sayin' lightning brought him back to life, claimin' everything Winston claims, sayin' he could see the past now and it was here. Said God had a purpose for them and this country, and that they'd hold an auction soon, old made new. Then Winston takes over, talking about how Dustin's blind but now can see even better and everybody better vote for him. He went on like that."

"Meanwhile," Shelly says, "I'd also called the cops, and now they're calling me and saying they're at my house but they don't see anything. And I'm all like, no shit, you guys are a little late."

"And I'm sitting there realizing my brother's alive again. Sitting there putting one and one together. The pistol had little shells in it that he'd made. I'd shot it before and should've known. Cartridge things. Dustin isn't dead, but he's hurt. We need to find him. We need to help him."

"*I* need to go back up to my house," Mandy says. "That's all I need. I can't do this anymore. I cannot." She breaks eye contact with her youngest, turns away and walks off feeling lightheaded.

When JR comes back with Willy, she decides, she'll let them stay. That's her only better plan now and it'll have to do. Like Miss Becka said, maybe they can help raise her horses and get the mill going again. JR can do that. Even if he's a shit-weasel, he's always looking for work. He'll be back. You can bet on it.

Inside, Mandy takes a little pop from the flask. She waits a while until she hears Winston returning, his voice booming through the speakers as he floats around looking for his lost fortune, screaming about the past and the future. From the rear window, she sees his stern-wheeler anchoring in the middle of the river. But she doesn't see JR or Willy on deck. So who's out there with him with a shirt tied around his face? Dear God, it's her oldest. Dustin.

That's when Winston gets on the bullhorn, announcing, "Biddy biddy one, biddy biddy two. Tricky dicky, tricky dicky, how-dee-do!"

For years now there's always been an unfortunate mother-tug inside her when she sees her boys—but never as gut-wrenching as this. Still, it's just too bad she can't give in to it. She'll only make space for whoever makes space for her. It feels bad to do so, but that's it.

What ever attracted her to Winston in the first place? That's the basic question we all run into, and hers is best explained like this.

Right after they moved into this house, he took her to the Wilson County Fair's Ferris wheel, and when their seat stopped right at the top he started shaking it, scaring her to death. And the only way to get him to quit scaring her was to move closer to him and hold him. So that's what she did. And she refuses to ever let that happen to her again.

TWENTY-NINE

Backstory's everywhere around here, scattered like loose change across the hills and into the hollows. Miss Becka and her childhood friends used to call these petrified coins Indian money, some cylindrical stacks leaning in staircase formation, others aligned perfectly flush as if counted and then organized by some ancient banker. But if she'd known better, and she didn't, not yet, she'd have understood the deeper truth, the elemental reality: three hundred and twenty million years ago all of this was a shallow ocean, and down below it—attached to the substrate that's now limestone bedrock—were what looked like lilies in the sea whose columnal stalks attached and rooted them into a deeper floor of clay, sand and boulder. These organisms were called crinoids and once they'd lived long enough to move from their anchored juvenile state into independent free-floating adulthood, they dropped their stems and floated into the currents above like stars made of feathers, discarding their fragments and leaving behind countless columned stems to fossilize across the land and eventually emerge in creeks or up along the highland rim, the edge of the basin in which Nashville sits today, there for kids to find and be told stories about and believe in those stories long after they themselves should've broken free and ascended up into the beautiful facts.

She learned about all this in college in an intro course called History of Life. Here's where she was taught that if you want to move past what you were born into, you've got to accept the knowledge of others and let them help lead you out. When she was told what the familiar fossils of her childhood actually were, it changed her perspective on everything: *That's who I come from*, she told herself sitting there in the classroom. *Those ancient animals disguised as flowers, that's who I am*. She no longer wanted membership into any religion or political party, gave up the myths and lore within her own family history and desired only to be a small participant in this global cosmic flow. She wanted to help others during her short visit here on earth, to live her life on this lush old seabed, and finally to go back into it herself.

Easy enough, right?

This morning she's out on the porch reading the *Lebanon Herald*, with another article on the General Hatton monument debate. *CAUSE TO COME DOWN?* the headline reads.

"What more cause do you need," she says, "when it's a lost one."

Lately she's been talking aloud to the paper. When she catches herself doing it, she flinches and then looks around to see if anybody's noticed, but she's always alone.

She leans back in the chair, crosses her ankles and wiggles her toes. The coffee mug's perched at the end of the palm-smooth armrest, releasing wispy white breath into the early-hour air. Last night was a struggle not to drink, but she held off, and this morning now has the saccharine shimmer of hope and possibility.

She reads about the progress the youngsters have been making, pretty damn impressive, and it sounds like the town's finally going to remove the damn statue, just trying to do it without pissing off the racists and getting Winston elected. The question they're chewing on is what they'd do with it. Move it? and where to? Who'll get to keep it? That's mostly what the article's asking about. Then right in the middle of it's a little photo of what might be an answer. It's of the folks standing around the statue, and Miss Becka recognizes two of them: Winston, with his crazy silver chops, pointing up at the general with his bullhorn, his eyes wild as if he's charging into battle, and Dustin, standing there stone-faced in a pair of mirrored aviators, hollow and enigmatic as a contemporary river-rat Lazarus. The caption beneath the photo reads, LOCAL ENTERTAINER WINSATON ALCORN OF REBEL RIVER AUCTIONS OFFERS TO BUY HISTORIC MONUMENT, SEEKS NOMINATION FOR REPRESENTATIVE OF TENNESSEE'S 46TH DISTRICT.

"God*damn*," Miss Becka says. "Will we *ever* be done with you?"

She puts the paper down and blows into her mug. She picks it back up, checks the date and sees it's more than a week old. Double-goddamn. The coffee's getting cold, but she continues blowing over it while gazing out at the river. Fucking hell, he just won't quit.

Under her bed she keeps a Marlin single-shot bolt-action twenty-two, her squirrel-slaying father's first rifle. So old it doesn't have a serial number. Great for small game, the woodchuck in your garden, the rabid racoon at your door on a rainy night. But for protection against deranged lunatics? You'll need something bigger with more stopping power. But she knows where to find that. Every Sunday he's selling them, just gotta listen to his station to find out where. It's a new location every week, depending on where the ferry runs out of gas. Lately, though, he's been doing a lot of business at the Lebanon boat ramp, right there on the river.

She's never been a gun person, hardly even a self-defense person, always figured that kind of living brought on far more trouble than it's worth. But after a certain point, this shit needs to stop. And sometimes all it takes is one person to start it and one person to shut it down.

"Okay, Dad," she says. "What should I do?"

I already told you, he says.

"Did you?"

But he goes silent.

"What did you tell me?" she says. "Remind me again."

Please, Daddy, return just one more time for guidance. She closes her eyes and clenches her fists. This is taking her back to the nursing home, the last time she saw him alive. He pointed with his finger at one eye then the other. What was that about? She rewinds the memory, and he does it again. What does it mean? Open your eyes? So she opens them and looks around for a sign. Still nothing.

"Let's go for a walk then," she says. "C'mon, Dad."

Regally and stiffly with a twisting limp of gout, she walks along the forest trail stabilizing herself with a hickory walking stick and goes up the ridge to a clearing where you can see the river sparkling and turning below. She keeps heading up until she gets to the ancient white oak, many arm-widths wide. There she hears the call, a high-pitched piping. She looks around but doesn't see it, can only hear it. She hums one of their tunes, imagines the blood harmony vibrating like two tightly wound wires. Out of breath, ankle throbbing, she rests under the oak's branches, which are even thicker than most of the trunks on this hillside. You can tell from how they're splayed out that this was once the only tree up here. Everything else had been logged, so it grew taller and wider. A field oak. About fifteen feet up, the trunk splits into a curving V, which is maybe why it never got felled and logged. Too crooked for their machines. Plus nobody could make a straight board out of it. Sheep and cattle and even farmers used it for shade, and then soldiers. This oak saw Winston's cherished war.

A little round stone with a star-shaped center is pressed into the mud at her feet. She prods it with her stick and it comes up with a short stack attached to its underside. Where there's one there's a billion more. She scrapes away the leaves with her foot to study the crinoid fossils. Among these pre-human relics, she can search for answers, for simple directions.

She kneels and brushes away more leaves and dirt. Circular crinoids are pressed tightly together, like eyes watching her. She senses the approach of some kind of meaning. Her right hand twists and curls along her right leg, as her father's did after the stroke. She runs her left hand over the crinoids, then brings those fingers up to her cheek. She touches her left eye, as her father touched his. And then her right, just as her father did.

And finally she understands. That's what you were trying to say. She can almost hear his voice: eye for an eye.

THIRTY

Remember the paint cans? Yeah, but he'd like not to. These days, with him getting older, his far-memory's been kicking in and bringing up all the old stories he thought he'd forgotten for good. Though maybe they're not done with him yet. Like when he was a kid and they used to crap in those old paint cans, then go toss them in the creek. All while his father was up in the house complaining that they were running out of cans because he'd already used up all the paint they had on their barns.

Winston tells this story to Dustin now and reminds him that he should be thankful for what they've got here. The river life. The good life. Doesn't get any better, really. "My old man? He didn't like to work."

"I really don't either," Dustin says.

"Huh, must skip a generation. Like father, like son? Nah. More like, like grandfather, like son. Some folks just *can't* work. They just can't."

"Maybe that's me," Dustin says.

"That ain't you. You just can't see is all."

"I'm getting hungry, though." Dustin points into his mouth. "Real hungry."

"You already said that."

"What're we gonna do?"

"About what?"

"Me getting hungry."

"You just keep that line in the water," Winston tells him. "You're bound to catch somethin' at some point. Law of averages."

"We can't just live off nothin'."

"That's true," Winston says, "and that's why you're gonna catch us somethin'."

"We been parked here since sundown and I ain't had a single bite."

"Vittles bittles," Winston says. "Victory victuals. Fishy fishy here, fishy fishy there, swimming by this boat you best beware."

"I dunno."

"Just keep an eye on that bobber."

Dustin's sitting on the edge of the ferry's concrete deck, resting his chin on the lower bar of the railing and staring blindly through his shades into the dark evening water. The bobber floats vaguely out there with some leftover chewed-up chicken wing run through the hook.

They're taking a break from business down on Old Hickory Lake, which has been more than lucrative, and running back east up into Lebanon to retrieve the Hatton monument. Though the statue was on public land there in the town square, it was owned by the Sons of Confederate Veterans, Winston's best allies, many of whom have also been big supporters of Rebel River Auctions. When the city finally decided to take the General down, the Sons agreed to remove it from the premises with the understanding that Winston would put him on the prow of the ferry and make his righteous sacrifice even more visible to the public. A traveling confrontation meant to spark loud, incoherent debates about this fragment of exploded history. What he didn't tell the Sons was that he considered this an attraction for the Wins-a-ton business, not just some homage to another old dead officer. This would really draw in the crowds and, at the same time, increase his local status as hero and savior while he tried to lock in his spot in the General Assembly. He's been talking about his rescue mission constantly on the radio.

So Winston came up with a plan for how to transport the statue and get it on his ferry. He'd cruise in on the river and dock at the access area near the Lebanon filtration system, and then the Sons would be responsible for hauling the General over to him and hoisting it on board—with hundreds of local folks watching every minute. New channels would be there with cameras, and Winston would take the opportunity to give them a little face-time. He knew he'd already made it into the car stereos of various work trucks and repair garages around the county. But this was his chance to step into the living rooms of every household in the district and let everyone see what he was all about.

And what *is* he about? Well, Winston'll figure that out tomorrow when all the mics are right in his face.

He and Dustin spent today getting ready for it, cleaning up the boat and clearing plenty of space for the deposit. Winston measured the prow, taped a square on the deck where the statue would land, even drilled some pilot holes into the concrete for its base to get bolted down—all while raging about how JR and Willy had abandoned them at such a crucial stage. Then he shaved his jowls carefully, still mumbling vile complaints, to prepare for some amplified talking and to look good for the TV. He even made Dustin take a bath in the river.

The one thing they forgot to do was pack provisions. So en route, he stopped at a marina, filled up on diesel and bought a box of chicken wings. They ate that up for lunch while chugging along to where they are now, but the current was so strong after recent storms that it took a lot longer to get to where they were going. Even Winston's getting hungry again.

But he doesn't want to admit that to Dustin, so he goes into the cabin where both of their cots are laid out. He sits at the radio-station soundboard and makes some notes for tomorrow. When the TV stations start asking him about what he's doing, he plans to go political by saying he's saving history from crazed commies. Maybe mentioning that this county needs a new voice, a better representative, just as Tennessee needs leaders who aren't afraid to stand up for their history and their heritage. Something like that. Since he speaks like the people, he can speak *for* them. That sounds good, and he can feel it out when the mics come on. He performs better on the spot, shoots straighter from the hip. But right now he can't concentrate because his belly's growling.

He lights an oil lantern and goes back out onto the deck. Dustin's sitting there with the line reeled in, delicately inspecting the bare hook with his fingers. "They robbed us clean," he says.

"That's cause you didn't set the hook when they started munchin'."

"I hear something back up behind us," Dustin says. "Listen."

"On the bank?"

"Yeah."

"I hear it too. That snappin' sound?"

"Somebody's electric fence gone haywire." Dustin tests the air with his nose. Ever since he lost his sight, his hearing's sharpened and his sense of smell's nearly like a hound's. "Maybe somethin's caught in it."

"You think so?" Winston says. "I'll go check."

"And I'll stay here."

Winston lowers the ramp with the hydraulic motor and descends into the dusky, dewy bank of kudzu and rocks and mud. There he crawls up the incline, holding the flickering, smoking lamp in front of him like some forsaken pioneer and follows the sound until he comes up to an alligator snapper that's wider around than a trashcan's lid. Just as Dustin predicted, it's caught on a lower line of electric fencing, wet and fully grounded, taking the entire wattage with every pulsing zap.

The turtle looks freshly dead, its limbs hanging loosely from its pyramid-patterned shell. Winston roots around in the brush and finds a stick, then slips it up under the turtle and rolls it off the wire. With gigantic spiked legs and a wrinkled distended neck, the animal's the size of a small hog. He grabs hold of the shell and drags it down to the boat. But when they get to the ramp, the snapper comes to life and begins hissing and clawing at the mud. When Winston dangles his rubber hand in front of its face, it considers the offering with its little beady eyes and pinprick nostrils, then strikes and latches with its curved dinosaur beak. Winston steps on the shell, pulls his rubber hand away to extend the neck, then unsheathes his knife from his belt and stabs right through the top of its armored, prehistoric skull.

Maybe a hundred years old, but dead now.

Then he comes up the ramp, dragging the turtle between his legs.

Dustin turns to listen. "What was it?"

Winston sets it down next to him, holds the head steady and pulls out his knife. "Stay still," he says.

"Okay."

Winston holds the blade under Dustin's nose. "You smell that?" he says. "What is it?"

Dustin shows his teeth with a ravenous smile. "That's snapper."

"It sure is. You work on shellin' him and I'll get the grill goin'."

Sitting cross-legged and carefully feeling every inch with his fingers, Dustin begins cleaning the animal with Winston's knife. He cuts off the head, slides the body over to the edge and lets it bleed out into the water. When that's done, he flips the body over, traces the knife tip around the bottom shell and saws through the joint separating the front half from the back piece, which he then pops open like a can lid. He scoops out the entrails with his hands. From the underside of the top shell he slices the legs loose and puts them in a pile by his side.

"Grill's hot," Winston says. "How's it looking over here?"

"You tell me."

"Not bad, not bad." Winston takes the knife from Dustin and works the skin off the legs. Pounds of meat each. He carries them over to the grill and lays them on the smoking grate in a sizzling hiss. Then he pours salt all over everything, shuts the lid and turns the heat down. "We'll smoke 'em out, then feast. How's that sound to you?"

"Pretty good." Dustin puts some of the guts on the fishing hook and is about to cast out again. "We're gonna have more to eat than we know what to do with."

"Told you not to worry," Winston says. "We've been provided for."

. . . .

After supper, stuffed with turtle meat, they lie in their cots with the cabin windows popped open to release the swampy fumes.

"So tell me," Winston says. "Man to man. You didn't really go to the army, did you."

"Not really." Dustin's on his side in the dark with his glasses off, the shadowy sunken sockets of his eyes facing Winston. "Not like you did."

"So what happened to your first eye?"

"Stumpin'."

"Stumpin'?" Winston says.

"That's right."

"You lost your eye in a game of stumpin'."

"That's how. I'd been workin' with a framin' crew in Georgia. Mix of spics and hicks. After a job one day, we went drinkin' beer in a park. Got into a game of stumpin', sharin' a hammer and drivin' nails into a stump, you know."

"I know how stumpin' works," Winston says defensively.

"And this new kid who was winning, he flipped the hammer in the air, caught it, hit his nail hard as he could and sent it flyin' right into my face."

"And what'd you do?"

"Wrote it off as a workplace injury and collected paychecks long as I could. That's where I was. That's what I was doin'."

"Are you lyin' to me?"

"Yeah," Dustin says.

"That's my boy."

"And how about you?" Dustin says. "Were you really in the infantry? You never talk about it. Never told us a thing about it."

"Course I was. But we got bigger battles to fight." He runs his fingers through his bushy chops. "And a big day ahead of us tomorrow. Now get some shut-eye."

"Yessir," Dustin says. "That I can do."

. . . .

The slight rocking from the wake of a passing boat. The sun shining and warming up the cabin. Dustin's cot is empty.

He's sitting out on the deck beside the turtle shell, and the bones from last night's cookout are stacked neatly inside the bowl with the large-beaked head on top. Dustin holds the fishing rod in his lap, the bobber cast out into the water.

"How long you been up?" Winston says.

"Daybreak."

"Any luck?"

"Not that I know about."

"You savin' that shell for something?"

"Yeah."

"What for?"

"Sell it."

"Good." Winston unzips at the railing and pisses into the river. "We gotta get going soon."

"Okay." Dusin reels in the line through his father's foam.

Winston looks out across the water, staring off at an idea. "Time to go get our cargo. Give refuge to the retreating general. I been waitin' for this day."

"Who's gonna be there?"

"News crews. Auction regulars. Fans and supporters. Probably waiting for us already. Don't worry, we'll be among family."

"Really?"

"We're celebrities, ain't we? They love us, don't they?"

Dustin reels the bobber up onto the tip of the pole. The hook's hanging right in front of him, no trace of bait on it. He feels for it in the air, then secures it to the handle. "Ready," he says.

. . . .

The ferry chugs laboriously up the turgid river, its paddle board churning cylindrically through the discolored water as the vertical pipe streams dark clouds of exhaust into the air. At a roaring combustible crawl, they approach the Hunter's Point Bridge where 231 stretches across the Cumberland in a long gradual arc of pillared concrete and steel. Winston spots some action in the parking lot of the access area: a few TV vans with cameramen and anchors, a small crowd of townies divided by some cops. Signs and flags and a whole lot of red.

"Looks like Christmas come early," Winston says.

"What is it?"

"You'll see."

"What if I can't?"

"No more ifs, you hear?"

"Yessir."

Winston turns the boat into the mouth of the inlet, gears down and stops alongside the floating dock. He comes out of the pilot's cabin and drops anchor from the stern, then goes back and drops another from the bow. He slings his bullhorn over his shoulder, looks around and finds Dustin standing at the front railing, around where the monument will go, and facing the crowd. Folks are cheering and others booing. Dustin stands there in front of them, expressionless, his sunglasses reflecting all of them in each lens.

"Sounds like the auctions, don't it?" Winston says.

"Yessir, it does."

Winston opens his arms wide. "Home-game advantage."

There's a crew of middle-aged guys carrying signs that read *Heritage Not Hate* and *Make the South Rise Again.* The other group's mostly younger people, with some hippies thrown in, probably from the college and local communes, holding up signs like *Your Heritage Is Hate* and *Burn It Down.* At the edge of the lot, a couple raised pickups are flying flags of the Confederate and Don't-Tread-On-Me variety. Winston gives a vague salute to those boys back there. Keep it crazy, that's how you wins a ton.

"What's going on?" Dustin says.

"Just a few little disagreements is all," Winston says.

"And that's a good thing for us."

"Why?"

"Divide and conquer."

"How you mean?"

"You just sit back and watch," Winston says. "Follow me close now."

Dustin keeps a hand on his father's shoulder as the old man opens the gate, steps onto the dock and walks down into the parking lot. Cops are standing in the crowd, trying to keep the teams separated.

A man in a suit points a mic at Winston and says, "How do you feel, sir, about the removal of the Confederate monument?"

"Feel?" Winston says. "I feel fine. How about you? How're your feelings feelin'?"

"Do you support its removal?"

"I ain't the one removin' it. I'm just givin' it a home. How you feel about that? Your feelings like that, don't they?"

"Some people are calling it disrespectful," the man says, "to give prominence to such a symbol. As you're doing."

"What about the Sons?" he says. "Havin' to move a nice piece like that around and not gettin' no thanks for it. I'm just here to help."

"And where do you plan to go now? And what do you plan to do with it? Aren't you worried about vandalism? This statue is quite a target right now."

"Call me the bull's eye." Winston taps his chest with his rubber hand. "Y'all want somethin', you come at me to get it."

"Okay..." The man glances at the camera, and the cameraman gives him a thumbs-up.

Winston isn't as tall as the reporter, yet he stands squared up, not quite looking at him but through him, hard and rough and impossible to read, either ready to fight or tell a joke. He brings the bullhorn up to his mouth. "This here guy's feelings," he announces, "are about as useful to me as the mud I scrape off my boots at night before I walk into my house."

Cheering and yelling. More cars and trucks pulling in, honking and revving. Somebody's handing out red flyers with a blue X and white lettering across the front: ALCORN FOR 46TH DISTRICT. LET'S WINS-A-TON.

"And is it true," the reporter says, "that you don't have a home? That you lost your house and are living on this boat?"

"This boat *is* our home."

"And do you broadcast your radio show from here?"

"Nice try," Winston says. "No comment."

"We know you've been getting involved in politics. Many say you're probably going to be the district's next representative. Do you feel prepared for such an endeavor?"

"I don't feel nothin'," he says, "but I know what I know. And I'm sure prepared to do whatever these good folks want me to."

"Is that why you're taking the monument?" the man says. "For the needs of others? Or is it for attention and power?"

"Just glad we could give it a home," Winston says. "It ain't right that honorable men gotta be on the run these days."

"You're well known for your auctions, and your radio show has quite a following. Some people now regard politics as your primary interest. What's the first thing you would do—"

"The first thing I'd do is happenin' right here, right now," Winston says into his bullhorn. "I just wanna make this place proud again. Proud of who we are."

Some guys in the crowd start clapping and chanting, *Wins-a-ton, Wins-a-ton*.

"But if nobody's brave enough to stick up for the stuff that matters, like old General Hatton here, well, I guess somebody's gotta step in and I'm the man to win because I wins a *ton*."

"Make us proud again!" one man shouts, then his side of the crowd starts chanting, *Proud again, proud again! Rise again, rise again.*

Winston puts his arm around Dustin and brings him into the picture. "This is my son, wounded visibly while serving our country bravely. Just like his daddy here, when I was in the armed services. Ain't that right, Dusty?"

Dustin stands there unresponsive.

Phones are out and recording the whole scene. "You live on that boat with your son to avoid taxes?" someone says. "When's your next radio show?" another asks.

"This here's the historic escape ferry," Winston says, "and we can live on it how we wanna live. It's a place where we can talk how we wanna talk. And that's what I want everybody to have. A county, a state and a *country* where you can be who you wanna be, who you really are, without them tearin' down your statues and takin' your history from you."

The crowd's yelling and pushing and getting wild.

"But what about the real history of slavery?" the

reporter says. "And if this is your home, why are you putting a highly controversial monument on it? Are you a sympathizer? Do you believe in the myth of the lost cause?"

"I don't believe in losin'," Winston says, "cause I only win. That's who I am. I'm Winsaton. I don't believe in no lost nothin'."

More TV anchors push forward, pointing mics and asking questions. "Are you going to auction it off? We've heard rumors that this might be a political stunt. Is that true, or is it more personal for you and doesn't have anything to do with you running for office?"

"I ain't into offices," Winston says. "But I'll do what I gotta do to get done what I gotta get done." Winston turns to the first reporter. "You feel me, Mr. Feely?"

"Yessir," Dustin says, and the reporter shakes his head.

"This Rome Ferry," Winston says, "by birth-nature gives refuge to men on the run. That's what it done for me, for the soldiers past, and that's what it's gonna do for General Hatton today. Look there!" He points to the road with his rubber hand. "Here she comes now."

The old statue looks small on the back of the flatbed boom truck turning into the parking lot. Heavy-duty ratchet straps are lashed across the bust with a chain running up from it to a retracted crane. Stuff gets tossed at it from the crowd and a fight breaks out. Cops hold their arms open to clear a path as the truck pulls in along the boat ramp next to the dock. The driver gets out, unmoors the statue and begins operating the crane from the control panel behind the cab. The chain tightens, the straps creak and the concrete figure lifts off the bed an inch and stops. The truck driver climbs down to inspect the chain and the straps one last time. "Where's Winston Alcorn?" he shouts.

Winston triggers the siren on the bullhorn. "Present!" He salutes the man. "Put it up at the front facing forward. I got the area taped off."

The driver nods and goes back to the panel. The statue rises above everyone's heads on that side and swings out over the water, where a rippling reflection shows the stone figure. When it's finally hovering above the deck, the driver walks up the ramp to check on the placement and see if it's unobstructed.

"We're comin'," Winston says. "You get back to the lift and I'll guide him in."

Reporters start yelling more questions as Winston walks away from them with Dustin close behind. As the monument lowers, Winston holds it steady and pushes it into the correct place over the prow. It eases down precisely where he wants it, and he stands there gazing up at the stone general, who's not quite as tall as Winston had imagined. The chiseled face, far from regal, simply looks dead.

When the driver begins removing the straps and chains, Dustin carries an impact driver and four large-diameter concrete anchors up to the prow, feels around the base of the monument and then starts fastening it to the deck.

Once the job's finished, the new figurehead stands there looking stoically and immutably confused. Winston turns to the crowd and makes a final announcement through the bullhorn: "If this is what the world's comin' to, then maybe y'all need somebody who ain't afraid to take a stand and do what's right for the common man." He hits the siren a couple times. "I'm takin' this here piece of history, our story, down the river and up the river so everybody can see it. Even traitors'll have to look at it. So y'all come visit us wherever we land, it's gonna be a real good time. Biddy biddy here, biddy biddy there, gave it a home after the square!"

Dustin follows the side railings along the deck and brings up the anchors. Winston goes into the cabin and turns on the engine. The crowd's now pressing right up to the water's edge, cheering and holding up their phones while the boat backs out into the river. The farther current carries them away, the crowd grows smaller and smaller, less significant, contained by that little concrete patch of parking lot. So easily controlled.

THIRTY-ONE

She lets her phone ring and buzz longer than usual, just sits here on the couch watching it light up and freak out on the cluttered coffee table. It's been days since she talked to anybody, so she can hardly remember what a person in her position is supposed to say right now. *Hello?* Such a strange word, a weird shape that's hard to hold in the mouth. The breathy *H* in the back of the throat, the liquid *L* at the tip of the tongue, the puckered *O* of the lips. This feels too sensual to offer an unknown caller.

The phone stops ringing, goes to voicemail, then starts again. Okay, fine. She snatches it up in ornery haste. "What?"

"Good day to you too, Miss Becka."

Only one voice could make her smile right now. "Charlie," she says.

He laughs. "It is I."

"How're you doing, honey?"

"You haven't heard?"

"What?" she says. "Won't we be seeing each other this weekend?"

"I'm calling about Madison."

"What about her?"

"I hate being the bad-news paper-boy..." he says.

Hello, she wants to tell him. *Hello, hello, hello.*

"... but I found her behind the bar the other night."

"I thought she quit. Was she working?"

"It was around four in the morning when my phone gave an alarm notification. I figured the rats had set it off or something."

"That'll happen."

"So I went over, found the door unlocked and heard something down behind the bar. It was her. Laid out on her back. Bottles everywhere."

"What was she doing?"

"Pukin' and moanin'. I got down in it with her, sprayed some water on her face with the soda gun and then called Bobby."

"That's her brother?"

"Right, and he came down and got her in about five minutes. Called me the next day and said he was taking her to Cumberland Heights for detox. No more bars for Madison."

"Good God. She really went to town, huh?"

"Wouldn't be the first time."

"When was this?"

"Few days ago," he says. "I'm surprised you haven't heard."

"I've been out of the loop."

"The loop's over-fucking-rated. I'm sick of it."

"I hear you," she says. "But goddamn. What's this mean for the Bomb Shelter?"

"I talked with her family about that and they asked me to step in. Said if I turn it around, I can keep it."

"*Hello*, Charlie! C'mon now, that's great."

"I think I can do it."

"I know you can. If you need the help of a pissy, post-menopausal bartender, I'm happy to put in my application."

"Honestly," he says, "I'm sorry, but I don't."

"You know there are laws against ageism, right?" She's trying to be funny but can tell he isn't in the mood. The room feels too stifling so she steps out onto the porch. "Is there anything you *do* want help with?"

"The tavern needs to start from scratch," he says. "New energy."

"New energy." Miss Becka eases down into her chair. "My middle name."

"I'm sorry."

"Don't apologize. I get it. You're asking me to retire, just like the PO did."

"Please don't do this," he says.

"I'm not."

"Look," he says, "I might be able to start my own business, after decades of getting screwed around. And I don't want any more crazy shit to happen. No more drinking while working."

"None?"

"Zero."

"How're you gonna enforce that?"

"Rules," he says. "I'm going to enforce it with rules."

Miss Becka takes the phone away from her ear, puts it down, then picks it back up. "I hear you," she says. "and I don't blame you."

"So are you cool with me doing this? Taking over and changing things?"

"What say do I have?"

"None, but I'd like your blessing."

She stares down at the river. "I can do that," she says. "Go forth and prosper, all that stuff."

"Seriously though."

"I am serious. I'm happy for you. You're the right man for the job."

"Then what's the matter?"

"I just don't know what I'm gonna do with myself."

"You'll figure something out," he says. "World's your oyster."

"That's what I'm scared of," she says. "Idle hands..."

"I wouldn't know anything about that."

. . . .

You can't just retire if you don't have a plan. You knew that all along. And you still threw things away that might've given you some kind of future. What did you expect? That the universe would magically work for you? It already did that, and you trashed it.

She walks up the trail to her car, turns the ignition and chants to the hum of the engine: "Better a witch than a bitch. Eye for an eye, you go bye bye."

She dials her radio to Winston's crackling AM station and drives for hours along roads tracing the river. The windows are down and her hair's blowing all across her face. She keeps driving, listening deeply into the static, waiting for a voice.

She should be getting hungry or thirsty, but she's so hyped on adrenaline that nothing matters except for finding his broadcast. She's getting close to Hartsville and about to give up when the station breaks wide open and she hears him talking. On the bridge over the Cumberland, she slows down and looks in both directions. No ferry in sight, but the signal's clear, so on the other side she pulls over onto the shoulder and listens.

...sunny day is money day, y'all know what to do, come on down to Hunter's Point for a little milky-moo, we'll be sitting on the river, at the end of the road, with a new statue on board and deals you can't not afford... with the election coming up, they're more pissed at me, cause they can't stop the flood of what the people want to be...

"Can't not afford," Miss Becka says.

...come and meet General Hatton, donate to the cause, take a picture with him, bring the kids and all four paws, I been convinced, ladies and gents, that this country needs me like a landlord needs rent, and that's why I'm runnin' for office, only cause you want me to, not for fame or fortune, only for you, everything must go in order to support the race, and the only papers I need are green ones showin' face...

A truck rocks Miss Becka's car when it passes and from its bed flies a single flag showing the American design fading into the Confederate's. And at this moment she finally understands how serious he is, that this isn't a joke, and that though he's lost his home and the old mill, he could very well win the district with one successful rally. A shiny chrome W was bolted across the tailgate of the monster-truck that just roared by her.

He's already given sanctuary to Wilson County's racist monument. He gave it a home after stealing hers. She studies herself in the rearview, her wild silver hair tangled into a nest. "He's got the statue and he's running for office," she says. "He could actually pull this off."

A vehicle turns in behind her. Probably the cops, or somebody checking if she needs help. Two people come up to the passenger-side window, a guy and a girl, though she's not really looking at them, just trying to act normal. "I'm fine," she says. "Just sitting here for a break."

"Miss Becka," the woman says.

She looks up and it's Shelly standing there. And James right beside her.

"How'd y'all find me?"

"You're parked on the highway," Shelly says, "and we live right back there."

"I knew it was your car," James says. "Shelly didn't believe me, but we turned around and boom!"

Miss Becka turns down the radio. "Boom, boom, boom."

"Are you okay?" Shelly says.

"Just said I was, didn't I?"

"I couldn't hear what you were telling us," James says.

"Y'all still living together?" Miss Becka asks.

"We're still working on some stuff," Shelly says. "But mostly we're worried about what Winston's doing with Dustin. Using him as a mascot as he runs for office? It's crazy. But from getting shot at to his son blinded in the line of duty, he's definitely gonna win."

"That can't happen," Miss Becka says. "I'll stop him before it ever does."

"And how're you gonna do that?" James says.

"Maybe you can help me. Maybe *you* can do it."

"Do what?" James says

"What's going on?" Shelly asks. "What's wrong with you?"

"The auction." Miss Becka puts the car in gear. "I need to go."

Shelly drops her hand from the door and steps back into the ditch as Miss Becka hits the gas, kicks up some gravel and drives off.

THIRTY-TWO

For Winston, death has always seemed acceptable, even worthwhile, as long as you're delivering it to somebody else.

And even if he was the one dying, he could come to terms with that too, but only if he knew his own death would continue providing grief or at least some financial inconvenience for the folks he was leaving behind. That's his philosophy: immortality by becoming an everlasting burden.

He's drinking Mapco coffee, making plans for the auction and what to do if the protestors show up. What if somebody starts shootin' at him again? And was that really little James, like everybody's saying? He'd rather not believe that. After rescuing the monument last week, the radio's been getting a lot of texts for Winston, plus a few calling for his assassination, which sure has helped the campaign.

He isn't surprised, but it's got him thinking.

Today's the first Sunday since the statue-rescue, and he's been pushing the auction hard. He and Dustin are set up on the bank near the Hunter's Point boat launch. He made a fake vendor permit that he's glad to show to anybody who wants to see it. But so far it's been fine. When the cops come by, they just check to see if anybody's harassing *him*. He thanks them for their service and they go on their way. That's how this works.

And that's how today should go too, so why's he thinking about all this other stuff? Don't let them distract you. Keep your eyes on the prize, old son.

"Dustin," he says.

"Yessir?"

"I want you to tell your story to the crowd tonight. They need to know you're a patriot and I want 'em to hear it from you."

"Okay," Dustin says. "That'll be fine."

"And I want you to keep tellin' that story long after I go down."

"Go down?" Dustin says.

"Everybody's got a bucket to kick at some point, and I'm getting old. I just wanna make sure you'll tell folks about who I was. And I want you to keep it goin'."

"Course I will. But you ain't goin' anywhere. I know that much."

"Oh, I know I'm not," Winston says. "But if I do."

"C'mon," Dustin says. "Let's get ready for the auction. It's almost four already."

Winston watches his blind son sitting there on a folding lawn chair on the ferry's deck. The enormous turtle shell's cleaned up and right next to him, ready for selling. "How do you know what time it is?" Winston says. "How you do that?"

"The sun." Dustin holds his hand in the air. "I can feel it."

THIRTY-THREE

They'll blame it on her living alone. They'll blame it on her drinking too much. They'll blame it on her never getting married. They'll blame it on her losing her job. And they'll blame it on a thousand other things, when the honest reason behind all her decisions for the past couple weeks is her father. She can still hear him. She knows what he's saying. He knows what she's doing. He sanctioned it.

To confuse them when they finally come looking for her, she's been sleeping in her car. Right now she's parked in the top lot of the old mill. She drove over last night with a vague plan in mind, something about showing them what it feels like, but she can't quite remember how right now. The lot's much bigger than it used to be, expanded from all Winston's auctions.

But there are still things Miss Becka recognizes, like the old line of hackberries here at the edge. She's reclined in the driver's seat, looking up at the old trees, imagining how the scene will play out. They'll hike down the trail to her cabin, come up on her porch and realize she's gone. "Wait a second," she says in mock detective-speak. "Miss Becka isn't here. Check out the cobwebs, she hasn't been home in a while. Where'd she go? We can't find her!" The thought sends her into a coughing fit of laughter. "You crack me up," she tells herself.

When the mill was going strong, they mostly sawed eastern red cedar. Sold all kinds of cuts in eight-foot lengths, from two-bys to fence posts and beams. She can still smell the mountains of sawdust and woodchips. The shavings made good mulch. And they sold the outer strips in bulk bundles by the ton. When a board was left out in the light too long, it turned from red to silver. Kind of like her. But after a little linseed oil, all the brilliant colors came right back.

"That's what you need," she says. "A little touching up."

Those were the days, but nothing's gained from living in the past. She raises her seat up, pulls the tarnished cigarette case from her breast pocket and lights a nice little rollie. It's early still, not even eight o'clock, and she was hoping Mandy would come out and check on her, like Miss Becka did for their family so long ago. But forget all that. You can't expect good deeds getting returned anymore. Nobody cares about old Miss Becka and her unrequited favors. She pouts a little until she hears footsteps coming up the gravel.

"Becka," Mandy says.

"Dandy Mandy, how-dee-do? You been fishin' like I taught you to?"

"You okay?" she says. "Did you sleep out here last night?"

"Like you haven't done it before."

"Not in a while."

"I saw James." Miss Becka inspects her cigarette.

"He was with Shelly."

"He called to tell me you were stopped in the road and acting crazy."

"Crazy?" she says. "Me?"

Somebody shouts to Mandy from down at the mill. It's JR, wanting to know where something's at.

"We're putting up some stables," Mandy says.

"Oh, those horses."

"That's the plan."

"Listen." Miss Becka extends her arm out the window with the little ciggie between her fingers. "I'm wondering if you can do something for me. If you can help me."

JR comes walking up the hill, leaning forward with his thumbs hooked in his pockets and his sidekick right behind him. "What's going on?" he says. "I be damned, is that Miss Becka? She ain't lookin' for work is she? You know me and Willy got this covered." He glances over his shoulder. "Don't we?"

Willy lingers cautiously, nodding in vague agreement. A hound limps at his side, then points its head at the sky and bays. Like it knows something.

"That dog," Miss Becka says.

"What about it?" Mandy says.

"Don't let them see me," Miss Becka says. "Please don't let them."

"What're you talking about?" Mandy says.

"I don't have any more time," Miss Becka says. "It's my time now. So please don't."

"What the hell are you *talking* about?"

And just like that Miss Becka's out of there and on the highway, rolling toward Lebanon. She goes into town and circles the old square a few times, admiring how it looks without the Confederate horse and rider, and then drives on toward the river. From the road, she spots a large white tent on the bank, making this look almost like a revival. The ferry's anchored beyond it, with the relocated monument standing in the bow stupidly indomitable. Scattered throughout the area are political yard signs for Winston, some handmade, others printed on plastic, all with red-and-white lettering: WINS-A-TON 46, WINS-TN, VOICE OF THE PEOPLE BY THE HAND OF GOD.

She parks behind a new pickup, turns the car off and sits there smoking. The evening's cooling down fast. Eventually she hears Winston testing his bullhorn: "Check, check, check, right here on deck, starting in a hour, spend a little money to get some power. Come buy a trinket, a little bitty dinket, send me straight to the top so I can help sink it..."

Folks are starting to arrive, carrying lawn chairs and wearing red hats and t-shirts, many printed with an image of Winston's megaphone. "Okay," Miss Becka says. "Okay." She wipes her face with her hands, pulls on her fishing cap and wraps a winter scarf around her neck. "Who we got here?" she says, then gets out of the car and walks down to the edge of the crowd. It's everywhere—the noise of people milling around and discussing why they know Winsaton's the best man for the job. "He ain't part of any establishment," one says. "He *says* what I *think*," goes another.

The deck of the ferry's set up like an outdoor pawnshop, with tabletop displays of power tools, jewelry, guitars and guns. Finally, when the crowd's large enough to suit his expectations, Winston comes out from the pilot's cabin with Dustin following behind. He raises the bullhorn into the air, triggers the siren and the crowd erupts with deafening volume.

"They tried to take our statue," he says. "But guess what? I took it back! And that's what we're doing for our country. We gotta get it back."

"Take it back!" a man shouts, providing the spectators with a new refrain.

"Yessir!" Winston points at him. "That's what I plan to do. They tried to kill me, but guess what? They couldn't! So we're gonna need your support. We gotta raise the funds, and it starts right here, right now. Y'all ready to do some biddin'? Cause I ain't kiddin'."

"Let's do this!" a woman yells, waving her purse in the air.

"On demand at your command," Winston says. "If ya wanna take a stand just raise that hand."

At his galloping, furiously steady pace, he begins selling his junk, starting with the smaller stuff and saving the bigger items for the end. When the guns come up, the prices go higher right away. Miss Becka's waiting for something she knows how to use, and isn't any pistol or .22.

"Next up here," Winston says, "now we got a twelve-gauge pump action. Talk about poppin' power, this baby's got traction. Startin' at two Bens with a one biddy one, biddy two biddy two, biddy three biddy three..."

A couple men in the front, despite looking like buddies, are betting against each other and bid the shotgun up to five-hundred and fifty.

"Tell me who's bold or is it sold," Winston says. "Going once, going twice..."

"Here!" Miss Becka raises her hand as high as she can. Her palms are damp with sweat, and she can feel the cool evening breeze of fall. "Seven hundred."

"We got seven made in heaven. Seven, seven, seven, let's get eight or nine."

"Ammo come with it?" Miss Becka calls.

"Come on up to the stage and we'll pair you with the right gauge. For a little up-charge step right on the barge. We got shells factory-made and killing-grade."

"Seven-fifty."

"Come on down here, ma'am, let's see that pretty face. The biddin's done ended, so let's settle up and show these good folks what a real supporter looks like."

Miss Becka walks through the crowd and up the ramp onto the deck of her family's old ferry. She can feel it rocking a little under all the weight and movement on board. Winston hands her the gun and taps the box of shells on the table. Miss Becka opens the box and pulls one out.

"Whoa there," Winston says, and many in his audience chuckle or laugh.

Miss Becka looks at him closely, intensely. In his eyes there's a deranged flatness, a depthless quality created by a lifetime of bad deals. He's in character and can't get out of it. "Whoa *what*?" she says.

"You gotta pay for it first, darlin'."

"Seven-fifty cash." Dustin's sitting there on a stool next to the table.

"What if I can't?" She takes out her wallet and opens it, showing Winston that it's empty.

"How you gonna buy it without no money?"

"I was hoping you'd give it to me."

"She wants somethin' for free!" Winston yells at the crowd through his bullhorn. "Is that how this piss-poor old world works?"

"Hell no!" is their answer, and they start booing and hissing and chanting "Wins-a-ton! Wins-a-ton! Wins-a-ton!"

He lowers the bullhorn and speaks directly to Miss Becka. "What're you doin'? We had a deal, lady. Who the fuck do you think you are?"

When she was a girl, her father took her to the floodplains to shoot clay pigeons. They'd sing together while walking out and coming back. In between he taught her how to operate her little twenty-gauge. Told her that while shooting you should always keep both eyes open, it helps with the periphery. He'd hold up a finger on each hand and slowly move them farther apart. "Both eyes open," he'd say.

She brings the action back, squints into the chamber and sees it's empty. She closes the action, turns the gun upside-down, slides the shell into the magazine tube, turns the gun back upright, opens the safety with her trigger finger and pumps it again so she can feel the bolt drive the shell into the chamber. "Before I buy it," she says, "I want to make sure it works."

"Oh, she works just fine," he tells her. "But you can't buy it. Not with nothin' you can't."

"I won't need to buy it after this."

"Dustin?" Winston says.

Miss Becka points the shotgun at him and pulls the trigger. Winston turns away, but not in time. The blast's so loud that it silences everything. Winston's shirt opens up in the chest and a dark circle expands outward. He steps backward while grabbing forward, butts into the railing, tumbles over it and splashes into the water. Miss Becka can feel warm little drops on her face. They feel like tears, almost.

The shotgun's at her feet, she must've dropped it. People are staring at her. Next to the gun is the bullhorn and she picks it up. "We're done here," she tells everybody. "The show's over."

Nobody moves. She looks past the railing at the river and sees Winston's rubber hand floating on the surface, bobbing downstream on the rolling Cumberland, moving westward.

"What'd you do?" Dustin says. "He was just havin' fun."

Panamerica is a home for the American voice in the genres of literary fiction and reportage. We publish books that highlight what is most distinctive about American writing, including the mix of high and low subject matter and voices; deadpan and absurdist humor; the tragedies and triumphs of ordinary people living alongside their neighbors; and the ability to invent and inhabit new worlds.